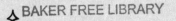
Marry
in
Haste

ANNE GRACIE

BERKLEY SENSATION
New York

BERKLEY SENSATION
Published by Berkley
An imprint of Penguin Random House LLC
375 Hudson Street, New York, New York 10014

Copyright © 2017 by Anne Gracie
Penguin Random House supports copyright. Copyright fuels creativity, encourages
diverse voices, promotes free speech, and creates a vibrant culture. Thank you for buying
an authorized edition of this book and for complying with copyright laws by not
reproducing, scanning, or distributing any part of it in any form without permission.
You are supporting writers and allowing Penguin Random House to continue to
publish books for every reader.

BERKLEY and BERKLEY SENSATION are registered trademarks and the B colophon
is a trademark of Penguin Random House LLC.

ISBN: 9780425283813

First Edition: May 2017

Printed in the United States of America
1 3 5 7 9 10 8 6 4 2

Cover art by Judy York
Cover design by Sarah Oberrender
Book design by Kristin del Rosario

For Libby Barker and Rita Al-Mourani—
friends, colleagues and enthusiastic readers.

Prologue

No, 'tis slander, whose edge is sharper than the sword.
—WILLIAM SHAKESPEARE, *CYMBELINE*

Berkshire, England, 1811

"I'M SORRY, MY DEAR, BUT YOU REALLY HAVE NO CHOICE!" Sir Humphrey Westwood's voice was quiet. Sad. Somehow it made his words cut deeper, shaking her fragile composure more than if he'd shouted and threatened to beat her.

She grasped his sleeve. "Papa, who told you these things—these terrible lies! Who?"

He shook off her hand, dismissing her with a flick of his arm. "It's common knowledge. Irwin says everyone—the whole parish, even the vicar—*the vicar!*—has known for weeks but were too embarrassed to tell me." His face crumpled in weary anguish. "They say the father is always the last to know."

He picked up his hat. "I'm going to church. No, my dear, you're not coming. You've made enough of a spectacle of yourself. I can barely hold up my head in public as it is."

"But, Papa, it isn't true. None of it!" Shaking, sick with bewilderment—and betrayal—she watched him shrug on his coat and wrap his scarf around his neck. She went to help him tuck it in, as she always did, but he shook her off as if he couldn't bear her to touch him.

"Don't try to cozen me, Emmaline! It won't work this time."

Her hands dropped. She stepped back, unbearably hurt.

"Despite everything, Irwin is willing to marry you—for

my sake and yours. Be grateful for that, and do as you're told." The expression on his face near broke her heart. Her father was as hurt, as devastated by this thing as she was.

But she wouldn't, couldn't—would rather die than marry her father's friend, their neighbor, Mr. Irwin.

"Papa, I *promise* you I didn't do what they say I did."

But her father's mind was blocked, blinded—shamed— by the lies he'd been told. And because of the mistake she'd made once before.

He shook his head in sorrow. "To be so utterly without shame . . . I have failed you as a father." He opened the front door. "I am going to church now and will make arrangements with the vicar to have the banns called. Irwin has invited me to dinner afterward. When I return you will agree to marry him, or I will wash my hands of you forever."

The cold implacability of his words scalded her to the bone.

She said in a low voice, "I won't agree, Papa. I wish to marry for love—like you and Mama—"

"Don't speak to me of your mother!" His voice shook. "For the first time in my life I'm glad—yes, glad!—she's not alive to hear what has become of her daughter."

"I'm sorry, Papa," she half whispered, her eyes filling with tears. "But I have done nothing wrong, not this time. And I won't be forced to marry a man I don't care for."

Her father said bleakly, "Then you are no daughter of mine." And he closed the door.

Chapter One

We know what we are, but know not what we may be.
—WILLIAM SHAKESPEARE, *HAMLET*

London 1818

"*WHAT* DID YOU CALL ME?" MAJOR CALBOURNE RUTHERFORD stopped dead, two steps into the Honorable Gil Radcliffe's discreet government office in the heart of Whitehall.

Radcliffe's brows rose. "You didn't know?"

Cal shook his head. "Are you telling me something's happened to my brother Henry? And that I'm now *Lord Ashendon*?" Cal's father had died a year ago, and his older brother Henry had inherited the title and estates.

"I assumed that's why you'd returned to London, after what is it—ten years?" Radcliffe waved Cal to a seat and ordered his clerk to bring tea and biscuits.

"Damn!" Cal sat down heavily. It wasn't grief he felt—he and Henry had never been close. "Henry wasn't even forty. What happened? How did he die?"

"Tried to ride his horse full pelt across a fast-running, rocky stream. The horse stumbled, your brother fell and broke his neck—he was drunk at the time, of course." There was a short silence, then he added, "The horse had to be put down. Damned shame—it was a fine beast."

Cal snorted. What an irony. Henry had lived almost the whole of his life leading a sybaritic life in the fleshpots of London, while Cal had been sent off to fight for his country at the tender age of seventeen. If anyone had been expected to die young . . .

Radcliffe leaned back in his chair, his expression thoughtful. "So if you're not here to resign your commission, why did you come?"

Just then the clerk came in with the tea and ginger biscuits. Cal waited until the man had left. "Well?" Radcliffe prompted.

Cal sipped his tea. Hot, strong and sweet, just as he liked it. He took a biscuit and crunched through it, enjoying Radcliffe's tension. "I'm pretty sure *El Escorpion* is English."

"The Scorpion is *English*?" Radcliffe stiffened. "No! He can't be! Are you certain?"

Cal grimaced. "Not certain. Just a feeling I have."

"A *feeling*." Radcliffe snorted, and sat back. "Really."

Cal wasn't annoyed by Radcliffe's skepticism. He'd be impatient too if one of his officers, after hunting a notorious assassin for two years without success, came to him with nothing more than a feeling in his bones. But vague and insubstantial as it was, Cal felt that he was finally onto something. "This last killing, as he raised his rifle to shoot, I saw him silhouetted against the night sky and—"

Radcliffe leaned forward. "You recognized him?"

"No, he was too far away. But later, when I was mulling it over, I realized there was something familiar about his action."

"His *action*?"

Cal nodded. "I fought alongside men of the Rifle Brigade a number of times during the war, and something about his stance and the way he brought his rifle up to shoot reminded me of one of those fellows. I know I've seen him before. I can't tell you his name, I probably wouldn't recognize his face, but I'm as sure as I can be that he's English and was a sharpshooter during the war. I think he's using a Baker rifle too; if he can shoot a man in the head from more than two hundred yards away—well, not many weapons have that capability."

Radcliffe nodded thoughtfully. "It's possible, I suppose. And you think he's returned to England?"

Cal shook his head. "I don't know. He's gone to ground, as usual—could be in any one of a dozen countries. But I thought I'd go to Rifle Brigade headquarters, get a list of sharpshooters who've left the regiment and see what they're up to now. It's not much to go on, but it's—"

"More than we've had so far," Radcliffe said with satisfaction. He drew a pen and paper toward him. "I'll draw up your leave papers."

Cal blinked. "*Leave* papers? But I'll be working."

"You have personal matters to sort out—a title and inheritance to deal with, papers to sign, matters to arrange. Personal matters."

There was no point pushing him. Radcliffe enjoyed being enigmatic. At school he'd had been brilliant, but devious, and even then he had a reputation for collecting information— all kinds of information, political and personal. It made him perfectly suited for his current position, sitting at the center of a web of intrigue that stretched from London halfway around the world, directing things from behind a desk.

Radcliffe completed the document with a flamboyant signature and dusted it with sand. He reached for his official seal, without which the papers would be invalid, pressed it into a blob of hot scarlet wax then handed it to Cal.

Cal glanced at it. "Four weeks' leave? I hope it won't take that long."

Radcliffe gave a faint smile. "I recommend you call on your lawyer first."

CAL HEADED STRAIGHT FOR THE OFFICE OF PHIPPS, PHIPPS and Yarwood, his late father's lawyers. The news that he was now Lord Ashendon had rocked him. But he was determined it would not make any significant difference to his life.

Grand estates and great wealth brought responsibilities with them, and with the title came other duties of the kind Cal, as younger son, had never been prepared for. And absolutely didn't want.

He'd always done his duty, been a good soldier, even though he'd hated the waste and destruction of war. Now, in peacetime, he'd discovered that working through tangled European affairs on behalf of his country suited him. Napoleon's activities had erased borders and smashed alliances. A new Europe was forming and the intrigue was endless. And fascinating.

Cal went where he was ordered and did the jobs that Whitehall, in the guise of Gil Radcliffe, sent him to do. His current task was to track down and capture or kill the assassin known as the Scorpion.

And after the Scorpion had killed Cal's friend Bentley, the hunt had become personal.

He didn't need—or want—any distraction from that.

"WHAT DO YOU MEAN YOU DON'T HAVE A COPY OF HENRY'S will? You're the family lawyer. You should have it on file."

The lawyer, Phipps, shifted uncomfortably in his seat. "Your brother parted company with this firm more than eight years ago, after a . . . a difference of opinion with your father."

"I see." Cal was well able to read between the lines. Henry had ever been the quarrelsome sort, and his father had had the same hasty, choleric temper. And both of them had a tendency to nurse a grudge. "I suppose they never made it up."

The lawyer inclined his head. "That is my understanding, my lord. And from what little I can gather, your brother was . . . not a worthy successor to your late father's position. The family affairs are in . . . somewhat of a tangle. Until we find his will and apply for probate, nothing else can proceed."

Cal swore under his breath. Trust Henry to leave things in a blasted mess.

"Of course you'll resign your commission, my lord."

Cal shook his head. The whole thing was a wretched nuisance, but he was damned if he'd resign. "I'll extend my leave if necessary, but once the business is done, I intend to return to Europe. I have responsibilities abroad."

Phipps gave him a shocked look. "But now you have responsibilities *in England*, my lord." His tone implied that no foreign responsibilities could compare with English ones.

Cal shrugged. "Agents can be appointed to see to the day-to-day running of the estate."

Phipps pursed his lips. "At the very least, my lord, you must make immediate arrangements for your dependents."

"Dependents?" Cal frowned. "I have no— Oh, you mean my half sisters." Of course. He hadn't seen the girls for years, but he remembered them as sweet little things who used to follow him around like puppies. "Where are they at the moment?"

"Bath, my lord."

"Still in school, then." Some exclusive seminary for girls, as he recalled.

"No, my lord, they are currently in the care of Lady Dorothea Rutherford."

"They're in good hands, then," he said indifferently. Aunt Dottie would have taken the bereaved little girls under her wing, and after a suitable period of mourning they could return to their school. "Now, is there anything I need to sign?"

The lawyer's lips thinned. "I feel obliged to remind you, my lord, that under your father's will, your half sisters were left a substantial sum in trust for when they marry or turn five-and-twenty. They are considerable heiresses, in fact, and, as such, need to be protected from fortune hunters." He paused. "Whether your aunt is up to that task, I could not say." His tone made it clear he had grave doubts, but discretion held him back.

Cal said nothing. Phipps was clearly something of a fusspot.

"Your aunt is also your dependent. Unlike your sisters, your father made her no allowance—yes, my lord, I also thought it quite irregular—his only unmarried sister, and with no fortune of her own—but against all my advice, he left her welfare to your brother's care."

"Good God! Left to Henry's tender care? It's a wonder Aunt Dottie isn't starving in the streets. What possessed the old man?"

"My sentiments exactly, my lord."

"Make her an immediate allowance out of my personal income, then," Cal said. "A generous one. When probate comes through we can make a more permanent arrangement through the estate."

He had a soft spot for Aunt Dottie. She'd knitted him endless pairs of warm red woolen socks ever since he'd gone off to war—red because she thought they ought to match his scarlet regimentals. She'd kept sending them as fast as she could knit them—enough to supply Cal and half his friends.

His friends, at first inclined to laugh at the color, had accepted them gratefully during hard winters in the mountains. Aunt Dottie's scarlet socks had saved many a toe from frostbite.

They'd also turned many a washtub of white underclothes pink, but as neither the socks nor the underclothes were visible, nobody much minded.

He didn't need them now, working in more civilized conditions, and no longer wearing a uniform, but parcels of thick scarlet socks still followed him through Europe, even though he'd told her several times he had no more need of them.

"Of course, my lord." Phipps made a note. "And what of the girls?"

"They should be safe enough in Bath with Aunt Dottie for the moment."

"I strongly advise you visit them, my lord."

Cal stood up. "Is that all?"

Phipps's mouth tightened. "Where will you be residing, my lord, should I need to contact you?"

"I take it Ashendon House is closed."

"Indeed it is, and has been since your father died—your brother preferred his own house." He paused diffidently, then added, "He dismissed all your father's servants."

Cal's brows drew together. Some of those servants had served his father for decades. "I assume he pensioned the older ones off, and gave the others character references?" He read the answer on Phipps's face.

Damn Henry for a selfish louse. To dismiss a servant without "a character" was to condemn them to future unemployment. A poor return for years of loyal service.

Phipps cleared his throat diffidently. "I, er, took the liberty of penning character references for those few who came to see me. As for the others—I gather most of the upper servants found suitable positions quite quickly. Your late father was known among the ton to be an exacting employer, so people assumed—quite rightly—that any servant who'd worked for him and kept a position with him longer than six months would be well trained and reliable."

Cal nodded. "Make inquiries of the remainder. Any of an age to retire, arrange a suitable pension, depending on their length of service. The others, discover their situation and let me know. I would not have my brother sully my father's reputation for fair dealing."

Smiling, Phipps made a note. "Do you intend to reopen Ashendon House, my lord? If you wish, I could make arrangements—"

"No, leave it as it is. I'll stay at my club—the Apocalypse." Ashendon House was his father's London home, and too big and formal for Cal's taste. A waste to open it and employ a dozen or more servants for the handful of nights Cal intended to stay in London. And he didn't want to raise expectations.

"Your father was a member of Whites." A hint, if ever Cal had heard one.

"The Apocalypse suits me well enough." The Apocalypse Club had been started some years before for officers and former officers who'd been to war. It had a relaxed, slightly raffish ambience that perfectly suited Cal's mood.

Besides, there might be men who'd served with the Rifle Brigade there who could help him in his quest for information.

THE APOCALYPSE CLUB PROVIDED JUST THE HAVEN CAL had hoped for. He'd run into a few old acquaintances on the first night and spent a convivial evening catching up on news and gossip before making an early night of it.

The next morning he'd made a hearty English breakfast—a nostalgic pleasure after the continental breakfasts he'd become used to—then set off to Rifle Brigade headquarters to inquire about men who'd been dismissed after the war.

Rifle Brigade sharpshooters had proved so useful in the late war that the Rifles hadn't been as drastically reduced in size as most of other regiments. Most of them were still in the army, which meant their every move was easily accounted for. It made the list of men he planned to investigate that much shorter.

By the end of the day, Cal had compiled a very useful list of names—men who were reputed to be able to take out a man's eye from more than two hundred yards away but who were no longer in the army.

It was too long a list, however, for one man to investigate—the men were scattered across southern England. Reluctantly—because he wanted to catch this bastard himself—he took the problem back to Gil Radcliffe.

They divided the list into five geographical regions. Cal took southwestern England, which took in Bath, as well as Cal's family seat, Ashendon Court in Oxfordshire—he ought to at least check on the place, now that he was responsible for it. And while he was at it, he could call in on Aunt Dottie and the girls.

Radcliffe assigned some of his best men to the other four regions.

With Radcliffe's facilities at his disposal, Cal was quickly able to cross a number of names off the list. Four men had died by accident or disease. Another two had been killed in drunken brawls.

Three of the men on the list had been transported for poaching. Cal shook his head at that. Teach a man to shoot straight, then punish him for hunting to feed his family. The world didn't make sense.

That night Radcliffe took him for a meal at his own club, Whites, and Cal ran into more old acquaintances there; a few fellows he knew from the army, and some from his long-distant schooldays. The first of the schoolfellows seemed remarkably pleased to see him, and insisted Cal dine with him the following night.

"No need for formal dress, old fellow, just a casual affair, *en famille*."

Cal was a little taken aback at the man's delight in seeing

him. He'd had very little to do with Frampton at school. Still, it wasn't as if he had any other engagements, so he accepted.

To his surprise within the next hour or two he was invited to several more casual, intimate family dinners from men he barely remembered. Bemused, but seeing no reason why he should refuse, he accepted them all. He supposed it was their way of welcoming a returning soldier, even if the war was well in the past. They had no idea he was still on active service, and he had no intention of telling them.

The next day he continued working through the list of names, starting with the ones in London. He found two more former sharpshooters, one of whom had been a hero of Badajoz but was now a drunk, a skeletal wreck of a man whose hand shook so much he could barely hold the murky bottle he clutched to his chest like a baby.

The other he found, after some trouble, begging in the street. He'd lost three fingers of his right hand and couldn't get a job. Former soldiers were everywhere, surplus to requirements. His wife and children had left him. They wouldn't stay with a man who couldn't feed them.

Cal gave the man a guinea and walked away, disturbed by what he'd found.

England had not done well by her brave soldiers.

THAT EVENING CAL FOUND HIMSELF SEATED CLOSELY between Frampton's two very friendly sisters. They gave him their undivided, enthusiastic, slightly competitive—and slightly unnerving—attention. Frampton and his mother smiled benevolently.

It had been years since Cal had sat down to a simple family meal—though there was nothing simple about this one. The table groaned with extravagant dishes. The sisters Frampton paid the food little attention. They lavished Cal with questions and compliments. Endlessly. His every utterance was treated as a gem of infinite wisdom, or an example of exquisite wit, provoking gales of feminine laughter.

It was very odd. Did all returned officers get this kind of welcome? While the common soldiers starved in the streets?

It was only when the servants placed a veritable feast of mouthwatering cream-filled puddings and jellies on the table, and the young Misses Frampton didn't so much as lift their avid gazes from Cal, that he finally twigged.

He thought about the other invitations he'd received. Each one of the exceptionally friendly and hospitable fellows he'd met just happened to have unmarried sisters. The hair on his scalp lifted softly.

It wasn't Major Cal Rutherford they'd invited to dine, it was the new Lord Ashendon—the rich, unmarried, damnably eligible Lord Ashendon.

Cal was well used to the attentions of women, but every one of his flirts and lovers had been women of the world, sophisticated and experienced—and uninterested in anything permanent. They wanted his body, not his name and fortune, and that suited him well.

Innocent-but-eager young ladies on the hunt for a rich and titled husband were a totally new experience. He didn't have time for this sort of nonsense. He was here to do a job.

The elder Miss Frampton ran her hand along his thigh. Cal jumped and almost spilled his claret.

The younger Miss Frampton snuggled closer and stroked his arm.

At the end of the dinner when the ladies retired, leaving the gentlemen to their port, Frampton said, "Lovely girls, my sisters. Best sisters in the world. Wouldn't want them to marry just anyone, y'know."

Cal nodded and gulped his port. As Frampton continued to wax lyrical about his sisters and their many virtues and fine qualities, Cal made a decision. It was time to investigate the men on the rural part of his list.

The minute the dinner was over, he returned to his club, called for a stiff brandy, and penned a series of apologetic notes, canceling all future engagements, claiming he'd been called away on urgent family business.

He sent a note to Radcliffe and also to Phipps, the lawyer, informing them of his intention to leave for Bath first thing in the morning. One of the men on his list lived near the village of Three Mile Cross, which was on the way, more or less.

The lawyer was efficient, Cal had to give him that, for as he was finishing his breakfast the next morning a servant arrived to inform him his carriage awaited him.

It was a traveling chaise, very smart, with the wheels picked out in yellow and the Ashendon coat of arms emblazoned on the gleaming black side panels. A team of four matched bays fretted and fidgeted impatiently. The driver grinned down at Cal and gave him a sketchy salute.

"Mornin', Master Cal—m'lord, I should say. Delighted to see you back in England safe and sound." It was his father's old coachman.

Cal nodded, trying desperately to recall the man's name. Hawkins, that was it.

Hawkins's grin widened as Cal greeted him by name. "Grand day for a run to Bath, m'lord. Horses are mighty fresh—needin' a good run, they are."

Cal glanced at the horses. "A fine-looking team."

Hawkins nodded. "Your brother's 'orses. Kept an eye on 'em, and when I got the message from your pa's lawyer, well, I knew where to get 'em."

Cal frowned. Had Hawkins been kicking his heels all these months since his father's death?

Hawkins laughed at Cal's question. "Oh, bless you, no, m'lord. I been driving them London hackney carriages." He paused and spat. "Rubbish they are. Very happy I was to hear you were home and needing a coachman again."

"You mean you quit your job to take me to Bath?"

"A'course," Hawkins said indignantly, as if no other choice were possible. "Served the Rutherford family all me life, I 'ave."

Cal climbed into the carriage. Hawkins's rash decision disturbed him. From the little he'd seen so far, jobs in London were in short supply.

The forces of family and societal expectation were closing in around him, but Cal was determined to fight free of them. He wasn't one to shirk his duty, but he was determined, nevertheless, to live his life the way he chose to.

He liked the adventure and uncertainty—even the danger—of his current life. Elevation to the peerage was the last thing he wanted. But he'd do what he had to—once he'd caught the Scorpion.

He would get that bastard or die trying. He owed it to Bentley.

Cal had met Bentley at school. Several years older than Bentley, Cal hadn't come across him until he'd turned a corner one day and found a scrawny young boy doing his best to fight off three larger boys. He obviously had no idea how to fight, but that didn't stop him from trying. His fists were flying, but not connecting, and though he was being thrashed, he wouldn't give up.

Admiring the lad's courage, if not his skills, Cal had waded in, sent the bullies packing then turned to inspect the damage. Bentley was a sight—probably the most unprepossessing youngster Cal had ever seen, with a too-big head balanced on a long skinny neck, and ears that stuck out like bat's wings. Dripping blood, he had a black eye and a swollen nose and was covered in scrapes and bruises, but he was grinning from ear to ear as he thanked Cal profusely for his help. And asked would Cal give him boxing lessons.

That kind of courage had to be rewarded. Cal and his friends had befriended and protected the boy, and they'd remained in sporadic contact ever since.

Beneath the unpromising looks, Bentley turned out to have a brilliant mind. He'd taken a first at Oxford and joined the diplomatic corps. He'd made his mark in the negotiations at the Congress of Vienna, and the last time Cal had seen him, he'd just been given a responsible diplomatic position in Portugal.

Bentley's widowed mother had also kept in touch. She'd written to Cal when Bentley was first posted abroad and asked Cal to look out for her son. He'd promised he would.

And then the Scorpion had shot Bentley down, right in front of Cal.

Cal still had nightmares sometimes, seeing Bentley's head explode, seeing the lanky young body crumple like an old rag, his blood spilling out on the pale Portuguese tiles. That fine brain, the dauntless spirit snuffed out like a candle—all the lad's hopes and dreams and plans for the future, shattered by a bullet.

And Cal's promise to Mrs. Bentley, broken.

Bentley's death haunted him. Catching the murdering bastard was Cal's first priority. After that? Who knew?

He couldn't imagine living a settled, domestic life in a quiet corner of England, having dull meetings with estate managers, going over account books, talking to tenants about repairs and leaking roofs. And drainage. And sheep.

Or the even duller duty of sitting in Parliament listening to long and dreary speeches. And worse—having to make them.

Cal shuddered.

And then, because he owed it to the title to beget an heir—and the whole blasted world knew it—he would be hunted endlessly by the likes of the Misses Frampton. And their mothers. And brothers.

And finally he would give in, and make a dutiful marriage to some highborn lady. Even then it wouldn't stop—there would be the obligatory social rounds, the meaningless, endless politenesses. Morning calls. Balls. Soirées. Almack's. Ratafia.

Conversation over breakfast.

He shuddered again. He was only twenty-eight, dammit. He had years before he needed to provide the estate with an heir. He had neither the time nor the inclination for petty family matters.

The carriage swept smoothly along, the hooves of the horses beating a rhythmic tattoo on the hard, even surface of the toll road—English roads were better than those on the Continent.

Cal watched the scenery slip by. England was so green; he'd forgotten that. Green and peaceful. And dull. He stretched out his legs, leaned back against the padded leather squabs and dozed.

IT WAS DARK AS THEY DROVE INTO BATH, THE MOON HIDDEN behind a thick blanket of cloud. Three Mile Cross had proved to be a wild-goose chase. Cal had found a former sharpshooter, but he wasn't the Scorpion. This man was employed as gamekeeper on a local estate, and his movements over the last few years were fully accounted for. He hadn't left the village, let alone the country.

Still, he'd shared some suggestions with Cal and brought him up to date on the whereabouts of some of the men on Cal's list, so the visit hadn't been a waste of time. And at just after seven o'clock, Cal was knocking on his aunt's door.

It was opened by an elderly, white-haired man with a familiar-looking face that Cal couldn't for a moment place. Then it struck him. "Logan, isn't it? I didn't expect to find you here. How are you?"

Logan had been a groom at his father's estate when Cal was a boy. Unusual to find a groom acting as a butler, but hard physical work would be beyond the man now—he must be sixty-five or more. Aunt Dottie always did have a soft heart.

Logan grinned. "I'm very well, thank you, sir—my condolences on your loss. Losses." He took Cal's coat and hat. "We were expecting you, of course, only not quite so soon." He must have seen the surprise on Cal's face, for he added, "Mr. Phipps sent word you'd be coming, though he didn't say when. Miss Dottie was that thrilled when she got his letter this evening. You always were her favorite."

It wasn't quite the thing for a butler to be so confiding, especially of his employer's feelings, nor yet to refer to her familiarly as Miss Dottie, but Cal supposed an ancient retainer groom-turned-butler couldn't be expected to know the finer points of servant-mistress etiquette.

"You'll find her in the back parlor—that being the warmest room in the house—she does feel the cold these days. It's second on your right, down the hall, sir—my lord, I should say." He gave Cal a rueful grin. "Hard to get used to it."

Cal couldn't agree with him more. "Lord Ashendon" still sounded to his ears like his father.

When Cal opened the parlor door he felt a sudden pang. Aunt Dottie was as small and plump as ever, but her famed peaches-and-cream complexion was now like softly crumpled silk, and her hair, once a charming, unruly froth of amber curls, was now the purest silvery white.

"Aunt Dottie?"

She jumped up with a small squeak of excitement, sending balls of scarlet wool and knitting flying, and embraced him fervently. "Dearest boy, let me look at you—so tall you've grown—and so handsome! And will you look at those shoulders!" She tilted her head critically, scanning him from head to foot, then gave a small decisive nod. "By far the best looking of all the Rutherford men! I shall be the envy of every lady between the ages of fifteen and a hundred when you escort me to the Pump Room in the morning."

Cal laughed and bent to collect her scattered needles and wool. "A hundred, Aunt Dottie?"

She settled herself back in the armchair and said earnestly, "Dear boy, some of them are even older than that! You have no idea. I feel like a spring chicken when I go there— such a delightful feeling. But even though some of them are ancient—positively antediluvian, I do assure you—they still ogle any passably good-looking man without the least shred of shame." She gave him a mischievous smile. "Quite heartening, really."

"Heartening?" He finished winding up a stray ball of wool that had rolled under the settee and handed it to her.

She nodded. "To think that sort of thing lasts. Aging is so much less to be dreaded when you see that even ancient crones can still flirt, and think about . . . *you know*. And possibly even *do* it, as well."

Cal blinked. *You know? Do it?* No—he wouldn't ask. It wasn't the sort of conversation he expected—or wanted— from his elderly spinster aunt. In a blatant bid to change the subject, he asked, "Where are the girls?"

There was a short silence. Seeming not to have heard his question, Aunt Dottie frowned over her knitting. The door opened and he looked up, half expecting his sisters, but it was only Logan, carrying a tray.

"Ah, there you are, Logan," Aunt Dottie exclaimed in what almost sounded like relief. "Food for my nephew, is it? Excellent! You must be famished, Cal dear."

Logan set the tray down on a small table close to Cal. The tray contained a plate of hearty-looking sandwiches, a wedge of pie and a tankard of ale.

"Eat up, eat up, dear boy," Aunt Dottie urged.

Cal took a mouthful of ale and picked up a sandwich. "Where are Rose and Lily, Aunt Dottie?"

Again there was a short silence. He took a bite from his sandwich, glanced up and caught his aunt exchanging a silent, panicked glance with Logan.

Something was up. Cal finished the sandwich and waited.

"They're asleep," Logan said after a moment.

"Yes, that's it! Asleep," Aunt Dottie agreed, adding quickly, "Upstairs. In their bedchambers. Fast asleep. We won't disturb them. You'll see them at breakfast in the morning. Thank you, Logan dear. That will be all." Logan left.

Cal looked at his aunt. "Logan *dear*?" he queried. "Aunt Dottie, you really shouldn't call your butler *dear*."

"Oh, pooh, why not?"

"Because he's your butler."

"Nonsense! Logan has been my friend since I was fifteen years old. My father is dead, and now your father is dead as well, so there is nobody left to make a fuss—you won't be stuffy about it, will you, Cal? Because if I want to call him *dear*, I will."

Cal blinked. Aunt Dottie had always been an original. Now it seemed she was becoming a little eccentric. She sat there placidly knitting, a little smile on her face. Was his supposedly guileless little aunt trying to distract him from the issue at hand?

"So," he said. "My sisters are fast asleep at"—he glanced pointedly at the clock on the overmantel—"half past seven?"

"Oh, bother, I've dropped a stitch."

He waited while she fiddled with her knitting, her cheeks suddenly rosy.

"Well?" he prompted after a minute.

"If we'd known you were going to arrive tonight, of course they would have waited up," Aunt Dottie said, avoiding his gaze. "But the poor dears were yawning, and barely able to stay awake, so of course I sent them off to bed immediately after we'd finished eating. They were so *very* tired. Poor Lily almost fell asleep in her soup! And yawning, oh, my goodness, such yawning."

She set aside her knitting. "In fact, I'm feeling rather tired myself." She stretched artistically and gave an unconvincing yawn. "Oh, dear me, yes, I'm afraid I'm quite ready for my bed. In fact I think, if you don't mind, Cal dearest, I'll go up to bed myself because"—she essayed another fake yawn—"I'm suddenly very, *very* tired. Old age, you know."

She had to be the worst liar he'd ever met.

Cal set down his tankard of ale. "Now, Aunt Dottie, why don't you tell me what's really going on? Where are my sisters?"

Chapter Two

What hath night to do with sleep?
—JOHN MILTON, *COMUS*

WITH A GUILTY LOOK, AUNT DOTTIE SAT BACK IN HER CHAIR and waited, her hands folded in her lap like a child expecting a scolding. "I'm not precisely sure," she admitted.

Any amusement he'd felt at his aunt's antics drained away. "What do you mean you're not sure? Are you telling me they've run away? Or worse?" His sisters were heiresses, after all. Minors. Swift thoughts of ransom, kidnapping or worse ran through his mind.

"Oh, no, no, *no*," his aunt said quickly. "Nothing like that. As I said, they'll be down for breakfast in the morning." She gave him a reassuring smile. "They always are."

"They always are?" Cal's eyes narrowed. "Are you telling me they *often* go missing?"

Aunt Dottie wrinkled her nose thoughtfully. "I wouldn't say *often*."

"Good God!" He stared down at his aunt. "So they're out there somewhere, alone and unchaperoned? Unprotected? Good God, they're only"—he did a quick calculation and came up with a figure that surprised him—"eighteen and nineteen."

"Yes, dear, I know."

"How the hell could you let them go out like that?"

"Well, of course I don't *let* them," she said indignantly. "How could you think such a thing?"

"What? But—"

"No, they do it all on their own. I have tried remonstrating with them, but"—she gave a helpless shrug—"they go anyway. Well, it is hard on them, you must admit, being so young and pretty and full of life, and not being able to attend parties or balls. If we'd *known* you were coming, I'm sure they would have stayed in, but the letter arrived after they went to bed."

Cal focused on the most relevant point. "Why can't they go to parties and balls?"

She gave him a shocked look. "Because they're *in mourning*, of course." She gestured to her own outfit of unrelieved black. "Which is why they've taken it so hard, your brother dying just eleven months after your poor papa's sad passing."

Cal frowned. "I didn't know Henry and the girls were close."

"Oh, they weren't. Henry never came near them. I doubt he would even have recognized them if he bumped into them in the street. Which is why the girls were so upset at his passing."

Cal thought about it, then shook his head. "I don't follow you."

Aunt Dottie gave him the kind of look one might give to a simpleton. "Another year of mourning, you see, and this time for someone they only cared for in a . . . a *dutiful* way. Or not at all, if we are to be honest." She added meditatively, "It wouldn't have been so bad if Henry had died soon after your papa, instead of just before their mourning period was up." She shook her head. "But then, he always was an inconsiderate boy."

Cal ignored that little leap of logic. "And another year of mourning means another year of no parties or balls for you and the girls?"

Aunt Dottie nodded. "Henry was their half brother, and my nephew—and the head of our family, after all. Not to honor him with full mourning would be scandalous."

His brows rose. "And letting two young girls roam the streets at night is not?"

She made a cross little sound. "I keep telling you, Cal, I don't *let* them do anything. I have pointed out the error of their ways; I have remonstrated with them and explained possible consequences. All to no avail."

"You could lock them in at night, send them to bed with no supper—any one of a dozen things that would teach them to mind you."

"I will *not* act the jailer toward my beloved nieces!" she exclaimed, outraged, and then added, "Besides, it doesn't work. I had Logan lock them in their bedchamber once, and they climbed out the window instead—which you must admit is *far* more dangerous than . . . whatever it is they do when they're out. I still shudder to think of them lying smashed on the cobbles outside." She produced a lace handkerchief, which he took as an ominous warning of waterworks to come. "And what if there was a fire?" she finished distressfully. "Would you have them burned in their beds?"

"Aunt Dottie—"

"Don't look at me like that—I don't *know* how they get out—Logan says by the kitchen door, so he leaves it unlocked for them to return—well, we can hardly lock them out at night, can we? Anything could happen to them then! Besides they always come down for breakfast perfectly well and happy."

"I just bet they do," Cal muttered. Good God, no wonder Phipps had urged him to come to Bath. His aunt obviously had no control over the girls whatsoever.

"There's no harm in them," she insisted. "They're just young and lively and . . . a little impatient."

Cal disagreed. Lack of discipline was clearly the problem, but there was no point in arguing. It was obviously pointless to expect his softhearted little aunt to administer any kind of control over his sisters. As for enlightening an innocent maiden aunt of the kind of thing that could befall unprotected young girls—if she didn't realize it by now, Cal wasn't going to try. It would only distress her further—and to no purpose.

Besides, after tonight the girls' misbehavior would come to an end. Cal would see to that. Assuming they returned home unharmed.

* * *

AFTER HIS AUNT HAD GONE TO BED—GENUINELY TIRED this time—Cal stationed himself at the kitchen table with a recent newspaper and a glass of cognac and settled down to await the return of his recalcitrant sisters.

He tried to read but found that the news of England was distracting in the wrong sort of way. The country was in a mess, with riots, poverty and crime. He didn't understand. The war hadn't reached England at all. How could everything have changed so much?

He tossed the newspaper aside, got up and paced around the stone-flagged floor. Inaction didn't suit his mood at all. Which was ridiculous—in his work abroad, he'd often had to wait patiently and quietly, for days, sometimes weeks at a time.

But it was a different matter when he was waiting for his young half sisters.

Where were the little minxes, and what the devil were they up to?

It didn't matter. Once they returned home—he wasn't even going to consider *if*—he'd damned well ensure they wouldn't go a-wandering again.

Henry should never have left them in the hands of Aunt Dottie. It was clear she couldn't control a fly.

The clock over the fireplace chimed midnight. Dammit. He was going to wring their necks.

Forty minutes later he heard a sound outside. He rose to his feet, folded his arms grimly and waited.

The kitchen door opened, framing two young women wearing hooded cloaks and black velvet masks. They entered, talking and giggling in low voices.

"Where the devil have you been?" Cal snapped.

They jumped, and turned shocked faces toward him. The taller one recovered first and retorted, mimicking Cal's tone exactly, "Who the devil are you, and what are you doing in my aunt's house?"

Not one of the men under Cal's command had ever had

the temerity to answer him back in such a way. He narrowed his eyes. "I asked you a question, young lady."

She put up her chin. "None of your business."

In a cold voice that would have sent shivers down the spines of his soldiers, Cal said, "It is very much my business, so out with it, now. And take off those ridiculous masks."

The smaller one glanced at her sister, then pushed back her hood and untied her mask. She hugged her cloak around her, watching him with, Cal was glad to see, wide-eyed trepidation. She was a sweet-faced girl, with a dimpled chin, wavy light brown hair and big gray eyes. His father's gray eyes. Cal's too.

The taller girl threw back the hood of her cloak, pulled off her mask and tossed it carelessly on the kitchen table. Obviously the ringleader of the pair. She was the image of his late stepmother—a beauty, with perfect features, blue eyes framed with long, dark lashes, and rippling golden hair, pulled up in a fashionable knot.

She stood, regarding him defiantly. "I have no idea who you are, so why the devil should I explain anything to you? We answer to our aunt, not you!"

A small part of him—a very small part—registered disappointment that his sisters didn't immediately recognize him. On the other hand, would he have recognized them? He doubted it. It was ten years since they'd seen each other. Still, the fact that he was in their aunt's house should have been a clue. Even if they hadn't known he was back in England.

Her attitude annoyed him and instead of explaining who he was, Cal found himself echoing his old nurse. "Young ladies who use that kind of language are asking to have their mouths washed out with soap and water." Only in his case it had been "young gentlemen."

She folded her arms and arched a mocking eyebrow. "Who swore first? *You* placed the conversation in the gutter from your opening utterance. I merely followed you there."

Cal opened his mouth to deliver a blistering reprimand, when the shorter girl—Lily?—said, "Nurse used to say that all the time, and in *just* that tone." She placed a tentative hand on his sleeve. "You're *Cal*, aren't you? Our big brother Cal, who went away to war and never came home again."

"Yes, I— Ooooff!" He broke off as she hurled herself at him in an enthusiastic embrace that nearly knocked him off his feet.

She hugged and kissed him excitedly, pelting him with questions he had no time to answer.

"When did you get here? Are you back for good? Which one am I? Lily, of course, don't you remember? You used to carry me around on your shoulders. I remember you being so tall. I should have recognized you sooner—you look a lot like Papa, doesn't he, Rose? But more like that portrait of Grandpapa Rutherford. Why didn't you tell us you were coming, Cal—does Aunt Dottie know?—oh, but what a lovely surprise. Have you eaten?"

Cal was taken aback by the exuberant torrent of affection. Laughing, he did his best to answer her questions, but there was only one she seemed really to care about.

"No, I won't be staying. I'm only here to—to settle my affairs. Henry's death has complicated matters, but as soon as I've sorted things out, I'll be returning to Europe." Young girls didn't need to hear about assassins and murder.

"Oh." Her excitement faded. "Oh, well, it's still lovely to see you, even for just a short while. Isn't it, Rose?"

Rose looked rather less thrilled to see him. She stepped forward, gave him a polite hug and kissed his cheek lightly. "Welcome home, brother."

Lily slipped out of her cloak and slung it over a chair. "Are you hungry?" She glanced at his empty glass. "Would you like me to get you another drink? Why are you sitting in the kitchen so late, anyway?"

"It's warmer here," Rose said quickly, with a warning look at her sister.

Lily missed it. "Yes, but it's much more comfortable in the parlor. Why don't we take Cal in there and—"

"I'm sitting in the kitchen after midnight," Cal said in a stern voice, "because my hoydenish little sisters sneaked out on their own at night, endangering their lives and their reputations and worrying their aunt sick."

"Rubbish," Rose interrupted. "Aunt Dottie knows perfectly well—" She broke off.

"—where you were?" Cal finished.

"No." She flushed slightly but continued with that air of cool defiance he was coming to know. "But she knows that we always come home safe and sound."

"She knows *nothing* of the sort!" Cal slammed his fist on the table, making both girls and his glass jump. "For all she knew, anything could have happened to you. You could have been robbed! People in London—and other cities, and don't think Bath is exempt from crime—have been knocked unconscious, stripped of their clothing—fine clothing like you are wearing under your very fine cloaks, right down to your lace-trimmed fine lawn underwear. It would all fetch a pretty penny in the underworld—and like those other victims, you'd be left naked in the gutter." He paused to let his message sink in. "You can imagine what might happen to a naked girl left unconscious in the gutter, can't you?"

Rose gave a little shrug. "Nothing happened to us."

"Because you were *lucky*." Cal decided to be brutal. "You might have been raped—yes, raped. Or beaten. Or kidnapped and sold into slavery. White slavery—do you know what that means? Sold into a Turkish harem, or a brothel in the seamiest foreign cities. And never seen again."

Lily stared at him with wide, horrified eyes, Rose with flat, disbelieving insolence.

"Or you could have been murdered. But as far as I'm concerned, your worst sin is upsetting your aunt. She was in *tears* this evening," he lied. "Telling me she had no idea where you were—yes, your gentle, sweet, elderly aunt was in tears, because she's been made responsible for the care and welfare of two inconsiderate, disobedient, headstrong, insubordinate, uncaring hoydens."

"If Aunt Dottie was in tears, it was because you were nasty and bossy and yelled at her. You upset her, just like you're upsetting Lily," Rose said. She put her arm around her sister's shoulders and squeezed. "See, you've made Lily cry."

Under Cal's horrified gaze, Lily's wide gray eyes filled, and fat tears slid slowly down her cheeks. She wept silently, making no sound, no sobs or wails or sniffles, just standing there, gazing at him through misery-drenched eyes.

Cal hated to see women weep at any time, but this . . . Somehow the very silence of it was more unnerving than ever.

"Lily, stop, I didn't mean—" Cal put out a helpless hand. Both girls shrank away from him. Dammit, he'd meant to frighten them into obedience, not make them frightened of him. "Now, now, no need to cry. I'm sure you're sorry. The main thing is, you're all right now, and tomorrow we'll sort out what to do."

With a protective arm around Lily's woebegone figure, Rose gave him a look of deep reproach. "I think you've done enough. I'm going to take Lily upstairs now." She turned her sister toward the door. "She probably won't get any sleep tonight. Your threats and horrid stories will probably give her nightmares. She's very prone to nightmares."

At the door Rose added, "You certainly know how to make a homecoming memorable, Brother Dear. Lily was so happy to see you—and now look at her. I hope you're proud of yourself." She shut the door quietly, leaving Cal alone with his guilt and his frustration.

He hated it when females cried. Nothing made him feel so helpless. He felt like a complete brute, bringing Lily to tears. Lily was a little sweetheart, warmhearted and inno-cent. She obviously wasn't the problem—Rose was.

Rose hadn't turned a hair. By God, she was a tough little nut. She'd defied him all the way, cool as you please, mak-ing it quite clear that, brother or not, she had no intention of knuckling down under his control.

She'd soon learn. He wasn't going to put up with her disobedience. Or her insolence.

Part of him was secretly almost proud of her refusal to be intimidated. If only she'd been born a boy, what a soldier she would have made. He'd given the girls the kind of rak-ing down he'd give a careless young officer under his com-mand, but had she cared? Had she buckled? Not a whit.

But Rose wasn't a boy. She was a damned nuisance. And for the moment at least, she was his damned nuisance.

And he still didn't know where they'd been or what they'd been doing.

THE MOMENT THE KITCHEN DOOR CLOSED, ROSE RELEASED Lily from her comforting grip and the two girls hurried up the stairs. They entered their shared bedroom and closed the door behind them.

"You can stop now," Rose said, tossing Lily a handkerchief. "He won't come in here."

"It takes a moment," Lily said, carefully wiping her cheeks. "I'm not a tap, you know."

"You're as good as one—better! I so wish I could do it. It's such an excellent weapon."

"Not a weapon, a defense," Lily corrected her. "Or a distraction. But I felt a bit mean tonight, doing it to Cal on his first night home."

"Pooh! He deserved it. He was being perfectly horrid. All that talk about white slavery and Turkish brothels and being stripped and left naked in the gutter. He was trying to make us feel bad, and so we—well, you, made him feel bad in return. It worked a treat, I must say. Did you see his face?"

Lily nodded. "I still feel mean."

"Nonsense, it was excellent strategy. He doesn't care about us, Lily. He's just like Papa and Henry—he doesn't give the snap of his fingers about us, or how we feel, as long as we're no trouble to him. He's not even staying in England."

"Perhaps, but—"

"Ten years he's been gone, with barely a word, and what's the first thing he does when he comes home? Stays up late to trap us and yell at us."

"He didn't actually yell," Lily pointed out. "He was scary, but very quiet."

Rose grinned. "Like your tears."

"I wish you hadn't told him I get nightmares."

"You do sometimes."

"Yes, but not often." Lily hung up her dress, a leaf-green

hail-spot muslin with dark pink piping. "I remembered him as such a kind big brother."

"The few times we ever saw him."

"Yes, but that wasn't his fault. He was away at school most of the time, and then he went to war."

"And the war's been over for several years now, but did he come home? Did he show any interest in us? Or did he leave us here to . . . to *stultify*!" Rose hung up her own dress, a cerulean-blue polished cotton, and smoothed it with a longing hand. "Last year's fashions and I still love this dress. I am so *sick* of wearing black! I'll be more than *twenty* by the time we're out of our blacks next year, Lily. I want to start my life *now*, not next year!"

Lily sighed again and tucked her socks, one inside the other. "I know." She pulled her nightgown over her head. "Do you think Aunt Dottie really did cry about us being out?"

"If she did, it was his fault. She might not like us going out from time to time, but she doesn't *fuss*, not since that time we climbed out the window. And she knows we can look after ourselves. She, at least, cares about us and doesn't see us as inconvenient nuisances."

Lily nodded. "Aunt Dottie is a darling."

Rose glanced at her. "You're a lot like her, you know."

Lily sighed and pressed her hands over her rounded stomach. "I know. I try not to eat so much, but I'm still fat."

"Silly, I meant that you're kind and loving and sweet-natured. And how often do I have to tell you, you're not fat, you're curvy."

"I'd rather be beautiful, like you."

"Hah! I'd rather be free to do what I want."

THE FOLLOWING MORNING, CAL SAT DOWN BEFORE breakfast to pen some letters, the most important of which was to Aunt Agatha in London. He should have paid a call on her when he first arrived in England—she was a high stickler for correct form—but it was too late for that.

Aunt Dottie was famously softhearted; her older sister was frankly feared. He couldn't see the girls getting the better of her.

He also sent a note to Phipps, informing him he was in Bath for the next three or four days, and to forward any mail here. There were several more men on his list he could check on from Bath.

He found some wax to seal the letters, signed the outside with an army free frank and realized that he could frank them as Lord Ashendon now. He added a brief note to the outside of the lawyer's letter requesting he find the Ashendon seal and send it on to Cal.

The clock in the hall chimed ten as he placed the letters on the hall table, ready for the post. At that moment his aunt and the two girls came down the stairs.

It was like a parade of crows. Each of them was dressed in unrelieved black. Cal blinked. It hadn't occurred to him until now, but the girls had not been wearing black the previous night.

Black quite suited Rose, setting off her bright coloring, but it sapped any color from Lily's cheeks. Or perhaps her pallor was the result of nightmares, courtesy of her long-lost brother.

He stifled the pang. Better a few nightmares than the kind of thing that could happen to young girls out at night alone.

"Good morning, Aunt Dottie, Rose, Lily."

Beaming, Aunt Dottie turned to her nieces. "See, girls, this is the delightful surprise I promised you—it's your brother Cal, returned at last from the wars."

Clearly the girls hadn't told Aunt Dottie of the previous night's meeting. They didn't move. Aunt Dottie laughed and gave them a little shove. "Don't be shy, girls, he's your brother. He's the same dear boy he always was, just taller and broader in the shoulders. Go and give him a welcome-home kiss. Remember how much you missed him when he first went away?"

"Good morning, Cal," Lily murmured, and came forward and planted a light, polite kiss on his cheek. It was a far cry from the warm and enthusiastic embrace of the previous night.

"Good morning, Brother Dearest," Rose said, kissing the air next to his cheek. "A delightful surprise indeed." She bared her teeth at him in a parody of a smile.

It was war, then.

Aunt Dottie didn't seem to notice the tension. Cal stood back to let the ladies precede him into the breakfast room, Aunt Dottie first, and Lily bringing up in the rear.

"How did you sleep, Lily?" he murmured as they entered. She gave him an odd, almost guilty look. "Very well, thank you."

"I'm glad," he said quietly.

Breakfast was a fairly stilted affair. Aunt Dottie chattered happily, throwing questions at Cal and encouraging the girls to do likewise. They sat there like oysters. She seemed to think they were shy in his presence.

Cal knew better. He wasn't forgiven yet. Not that he needed their forgiveness; he'd done the right thing, he knew. Lily was reserved, not yet trusting the man who'd made her cry at their first meeting as adults. And Rose—well, Rose turned every opportunity for conversation into an indirect snipe at him. It was almost amusing. She was very sharp and quick witted.

"And what are your plans for today, Aunt Dottie?" he asked as he buttered a piece of toast.

"Well, of course we always start the day with a visit to the Pump Room, don't we, girls?" The girls gave an unenthusiastic murmur of agreement.

"Don't look like that, girls—the waters are nasty tasting, but they're very good for you. Lily's spots cleared right up, remember?"

Lily flushed and looked down.

Her complexion was smooth and unmarked, as perfect as her sister's. Cal remembered the agony of his own spotty period. "But Lily's complexion is perfect," he said. "I can't believe she ever had a spot in her life." He grimaced. "I, on the other hand, suffered with them terribly as a youth."

She looked up and gave him a shy smile. Rose shot him a hard-eyed stare. Suspicious little cat, she was. He winked at her and she bridled.

"What are your plans today, Cal?" Lily asked.

"He's coming with us to the Pump Room, of course," Aunt Dottie declared.

At Cal's ill-concealed look of dismay, Lily giggled and Rose's scowl turned to a grin of pure pleasure. "Won't that be delightful, Brother Dearest?" she purred.

Aunt Dottie continued, "Well, you don't imagine I'm going to let Almeria Bracegirdle think she's the only one who can enter the room on the arm of a dashing young gentleman, do you? Her grandson, Albert, looks well enough on his own, but beside Cal he will look like a . . . like a . . ."

"Like a poodle," Rose said.

"A *poodle*?" Aunt Dottie laughed. "You have a wicked tongue, Rose dear, but you're quite right. He *is* a poodle. Oh, dear, I shan't be able to keep a straight face when I meet him now. A poodle!"

"And how long does this Pump Room visit usually last, Aunt Dottie?" He was hoping for a quick visit: make their entrance, eclipse the poodle, drink the nasty waters and leave. "Half an hour? Forty minutes? It's just that I have some business to transact today."

"Forty minutes? Oh, no, it will take *much* longer than that," Rose said with spiteful relish. "We're usually there for *hours*."

She was teasing, of course. He glanced at his aunt, who nodded complacently. "Rose is quite right. An hour at the very least, but more usually two. We have so many friends and acquaintances there, you see, it's quite the social occasion."

"It's our only social occasion," Rose muttered.

"Oh, no, dear, you know that's not quite right," her aunt said reprovingly. She turned to Cal and explained, "After the Pump Room, we usually visit some of the shops on Milsom Street and elsewhere. Bath has some delightfully modish shops, you know, for all that people say it's not as fashionable a place as it used to be."

"And we go to the library," Rose said. "Lily *loves* the library."

Cal frowned. There was some undercurrent there he didn't understand.

"It's a very good library," Aunt Dottie agreed. "And we frequently stop for a bun and a cup of tea at one of the tea rooms—there are several elegant establishments we like to patronize, don't we, girls? And we quite often attend a concert—what was the one we attended last month?"

"The string quartet," Lily murmured.

"That was it, and a very superior performance it was too."

"And we can even go for a walk in the Sydney gardens— that's quite acceptable for people in mourning," Rose said in a bright tone that was almost savage.

"Yes, on a sunny afternoon, it's very pleasant," Aunt Dottie agreed placidly. "But if you have business, Cal dear, this afternoon is quite free. I usually take a nap around three while the girls read and embroider."

And there, in a nutshell was the cause of his sisters' restlessness: They were bored. Restricted from the livelier social events by their state of mourning, and spending most of their time in the company of an old lady and her friends. And from the sounds of things, with no friends of their own age.

He'd likely be kicking over the traces too, if he were forced into such a dull routine at that age. Anything would be better than that.

"Whereabouts is the school you girls attended?" he asked. "It's in Bath, I know, but what's the address?"

"Why would you want to know that?" flashed Rose. "You never wrote to us when we were there, after all, so why now?"

"Rose dear, that's no way to talk to your brother," Aunt Dottie said gently. "He's head of the family now and must be treated with respect." She gave him directions to the school, finishing with, "But I confess, I'm curious too, as to why you'd want to know."

"Business," he said. "Would you pass the marmalade, please, Rose?"

She passed it, watching him through slitted cat eyes.

Chapter Three

One half of the world cannot understand
the pleasures of the other.
—JANE AUSTEN, *EMMA*

THE PUMP ROOM EXPERIENCE WAS AS GRUESOME AS CAL
expected. Aunt Dottie paused outside the building, ran a
critical eye over him, straightened the black armband she'd
produced for him after breakfast and then stood on tiptoe
to smooth back his hair, as she had when he was a small
boy. Then she placed her hand on his arm, took a deep breath
and moved forward.

Clearly they were to make An Entrance.

All kinds of people patronized the Pump Room and came
to drink the waters or bathe in them, people from all levels
of society, but the worst invalids and the poorest folk usually
came—and went—first thing in the morning.

This was the fashionable time, and the place was crowded
with elegantly dressed ladies and gentlemen, mostly elderly
or middle aged, some in bath chairs or resting on sticks,
most with an attendant, a servant, a poor relation or a companion.

Aunt Dottie stepped inside and paused—or perhaps the
right word was *posed*—her hand resting possessively on
Cal's arm. They stood framed in the doorway, while Aunt
Dottie surveyed the room with all the triumph of a hunter
returning to a starving village, having bagged a nice fat
buck.

The buck concerned swallowed, reminded himself of all those red woolen socks and allowed himself to be displayed.

A snort from behind him indicated that one at least of his sisters found the spectacle vastly amusing. He didn't need to turn his head to know which sister.

There was a short hush, then a buzz of speculation rose.

"See? They're all dying to know who my tall, handsome escort is!" Aunt Dottie said gleefully from the side of her mouth.

She then led him forward in a slow triumphal circuit of the room, greeting everyone and introducing him as "My nephew, the new Earl of Ashendon. The dear boy has been away at the wars for the last ten years, defeating the Corsican Monster."

"Single-handedly," Rose interjected from time to time in a low voice that only she, Lily and Cal could hear.

"And the minute he arrived in England, he came straight here to see me and the girls," Aunt Dottie would conclude proudly. Cal tried not to squirm.

What followed was invariably a brief, polite exchange, touching a little on Cal's experience abroad before venturing delicately (or otherwise) toward the only subject most of the ladies there were interested in: whether Cal was married or betrothed.

The moment he admitted he wasn't, the invitations came gushing forth. Unmarried and widowed daughters, nieces, granddaughters, great-nieces and a few more distant relations were produced and introduced to Cal—no, to Lord Ashendon.

Presented for his inspection, they blushed prettily (or otherwise) while their relations extolled their various virtues, skills and aristocratic connections. In one case, a very blunt grandmotherly type pointed out of an excellent pair of child-bearing hips. The poor girl turned beet red and looked as though she would happily sink into the floor, but she rallied when Cal gave her a sympathetic smile, and fluttered her eyelashes at him hopefully.

They invited him to tea, dinner, picnics, intimate family

parties and musical afternoons, all designed to further his acquaintance with the female of the moment.

Cal did his best to parry the flood of invitations politely but firmly, claiming that he had no time for courting, that he wasn't at the moment looking for a wife, that this was a brief visit only and that he would be returning abroad shortly on important government business.

It didn't seem to matter to the ladies. Their girls were not so fussy or demanding as to need extensive courting. Would it not be better for Lord Ashendon to marry now and leave his wife to look after his estates, a wife who even as she tearfully waved him good-bye might be bearing his heir, thus securing the Ashendon succession?

To think he'd fled London because of the Frampton sisters. Out of the frying pan . . .

He was very aware of his sisters' amusement, and as he progressed through the room his apologies became firmer and less regretful, and his government business more immediate and urgent.

And, dammit, it was.

He was almost grateful to be presented with "the poodle," a ridiculous young dandy with elaborately curled, fluffed and pomaded yellow locks. He wore tight breeches in a shade he told Cal was called primrose—"the latest mode, I do assure you"—a lavender coat so nattily cut that it no doubt took all his valet's strength to squeeze him into it and a profusion of fobs and chains that reminded Cal of the Christmas trees he'd seen in Vienna the year before.

But as the fellow had no unmarried sisters or cousins, offered Cal no invitations to tea, dinner or any other social occasion and showed no interest whatsoever in Cal's marital prospects, Cal decided the poodle was a fine fellow.

After nearly two hours, Cal finally escaped, citing urgent (and possibly dangerous, added Rose) business to attend to. He left Aunt Dottie and the girls to enjoy Aunt Dottie's triumph with her particular cronies over crumpets and sweet buns at their favorite tea room.

Cal strode up the hill as fast as his dignity would allow him. Fleeing the battlefield was becoming a habit.

* * *

CAL'S AUNT HAD GIVEN HIM A STREET NAME, BUT NOT A
number, but when he saw a line of schoolgirls filing into an
imposing building under the supervision of a tall female
dressed in dark blue, he knew he'd found the school.

It was set on a corner, with an excellent view over the
city of Bath and surrounds, and was enclosed on three sides
by a high stone wall, set with shards of broken glass along
the top. He grinned. Nobody would be getting in or out of
that place except by the front door.

A discreetly lettered brass plate beside the entrance said
Miss Mallard's Seminary for the Daughters of Gentlemen.
Cal rang the doorbell and waited.

A grim-looking female in black opened it and peered at
him suspiciously. "Yes?"

"I'd like to speak with Miss Mallard."

She looked him up and down. "Whom shall I say is
calling?"

"Major Ca—" He broke off. "I mean Lord Ashendon."

She scrutinized him with hostile pale blue pebble eyes.
"Please come in. I'll see if Miss Mallard is available." She
let him into a spacious, black-and-white-tiled vestibule, to
the right of which rose a handsome staircase. She indicated
some chairs set in a line along the wall. "Wait there." And
then added grudgingly, "Please."

Amused at the woman's barely repressed hostility—did
she think he'd come here to ravage her precious girls?—Cal
sat down to wait.

A wave of whispering and murmuring above him caused
him to turn his head and look up. On the landing of the stairs
a huddle of young girls had gathered and were eyeing him
with speculative interest.

There was a burst of muffled exclamations of "Lavinia,
no!" "Lavvie, don't!" and "You'll get into trouble, you know
you're not allowed to . . ." and a pretty young girl of about
fourteen or fifteen ran down the stairs and confidently
plopped herself on the chair beside him.

She turned to him with a coquettish smile. "How do you

do? Are you waiting for the Duck, because I'll keep you company if you like, my name's Lavinia, Miss Lavinia Fortescue-Brown of the Surrey Fortescue-Browns, you're new here, aren't you, are you thinking of sending someone here? Your sister, perhaps, you're too young and handsome to have a daughter of school age, so go ahead, ask me anything, I've been here for years, but I'll be leaving soon and I can tell you anything you want to know about—"

"Lavinia Fortescue-Brown." The voice came from above, calm, quiet, but somehow commanding. It cut off the torrent of words coming from Miss Lavinia Fortescue-Brown of the Surrey Fortescue-Browns in midstream.

Cal looked up to see who had produced this minor miracle. A tallish female dressed in drab dark blue came gracefully down the stairs. It was the woman he'd seen earlier, ushering a column of girls into the school.

She was handsome rather than pretty, with high cheekbones and a short, straight nose. Her hair seemed to be brown and curly, though most of it was pulled tightly back and hidden under an ugly spinster's cap.

Lavinia jumped to her feet. "Yes, Miss Westwood?"

Cal rose to his feet. The tall lady didn't so much as glance at him. Another man-hater, perhaps? What a waste.

She wasn't a beauty, but she had a look of elegant distinction. Her complexion was good, her nose small and straight, her chin firm, and her mouth . . . soft ripe raspberries in a dish of pure cream.

"You're supposed to be upstairs preparing your French poetry recital, Lavinia, not bothering strange gentlemen."

The strange gentleman was busy looking at the lush, feminine mouth and wondering what it would take to break that smooth nun-like composure.

"Oh, but Miss Westwood, I wasn't *bothering*—"

"Upstairs. Now." She said it in a pleasant, almost conversational tone of voice, but there was no denying the steel beneath. Lavinia cast a wistful look at Cal but took a few reluctant steps toward the staircase.

The tall lady turned her gaze on Cal. She had the most amazing eyes, an arresting gray-green, like sage, or frosted grass, framed with thick dark lashes. She said crisply, "You are being attended to, I presume, sir?"

"Yes, but perhaps—"

A soft scream cut him off in midsentence. They turned to find Lavinia Fortescue-Brown of the Surrey Fortescue-Browns sprawled dramatically at the foot of the stairs. She gazed helplessly up at Cal, whimpering and fluttering her eyelashes.

The tall lady frowned and bent over the girl. "What have you done, Lavinia?"

The girl's gaze didn't shift from Cal, who stood beside the teacher. "I tripped, Miss Westwood. I've twisted my ankle. It's *frightfully* painful."

The teacher was a coolheaded one, no doubt about it. She seemed entirely unconcerned. She twitched the girl's hem aside and made a cursory examination of the ankle. "Hmmm. Can you stand?"

The girl made an attempt to get up, gave a loud moan and fell back helplessly. "Oh, it hurts, it hurts! I can't walk at all." She gave Cal a piteous look. "Perhaps the gentleman could carry me upstairs."

Before Cal could offer to help, the teacher said, "Oh, there's no need to bother the gentleman. He's much too busy to carry injured schoolgirls around."

"I don't mind—" Cal began.

She gave him a swift quelling look. "No, no, the school porter will carry Lavinia."

"Not Grimes!" Lavinia exclaimed in disgust.

"Of course Grimes," the teacher affirmed. "You will recall from your lessons, Lavinia, that the word *porter* comes from the French 'to carry.' Carrying things and people is Grimes's *job*. He will be delighted to carry you upstairs."

There was a short silence, then the teacher said dryly, "Or perhaps the pain is not so bad now and you can manage by yourself."

The girl sighed, and with a moan or two—much less dramatic now—managed to stand. Under her teacher's eye, she bid Cal good-bye and, clutching at the banister, began to hobble pathetically up the stairs, wincing at each painful step. Limping, he noticed, on the wrong foot.

The teacher watched her go, then turned to Cal, her eyes dancing with humor. "She is somewhat of a minx, our Lavinia." As Lavinia turned at the landing, cast Cal one last tragic glance and limped bravely out of sight, the teacher added, "Grimes is in his sixties and has hair growing—quite vigorously—out of his nose and ears."

Cal chuckled. He was impressed with her handling of the girl. Firm, but with humor and a light touch.

She glanced past him. "Ah, here is Theale. I'll leave you, then. Thank you for your tolerance." She turned away and hurried back up the stairs in the wake of her pupil.

The grim female in black gave Cal a gimlet look. "Miss Mallard will see you now."

Cal followed her, well pleased with what he'd learned. Miss Mallard's Seminary for the Daughters of Gentlemen might be the very answer. There was discipline here—good discipline and high walls topped with broken glass.

All he needed, really.

EMMALINE WESTWOOD FOLLOWED HER CHARGE UP THE stairs, trying not to be aware of the hard gray gaze of the tall, spare man standing below. Who was he? She'd noticed him in the street earlier.

Her first impression, as he'd come striding up the hill, was of a hunter: lean, dark and somehow . . . predatory. The last place she'd imagined he would head for was Miss Mallard's Seminary.

Talk about fox in the henhouse. Even if it was the chickens that were doing the hunting.

"Hurry along there, Lavinia," she said. The girl was casting languishing glances back down the stairs.

"Oh, but—"

"You're limping on the wrong foot," Emm observed.

"Oh." Lavinia started to limp on the other foot, then realized. She cast Emm a worried glance. "I'm not in trouble, am I? I was only trying to help the gentleman."

"Most praiseworthy of you," Emm said dryly. "He seeming so helpless and lost. And apparently in need of people to carry."

Lavinia giggled. "Wasn't he delicious, miss? So stern and handsome and tall, and those eyes . . ."

"You, miss, are a minx," Emm told her. "Now be off with you. Get on with your French poetry exercise. And I'll give you an extra poem to translate and learn as punishment for your mischief."

Lavinia sighed, but she was getting off lightly and she knew it.

Emm paused, then added, "Lavinia, before you go, I want you to think about this: Which young lady do you think a gentleman would find most interesting—the girl who thrusts herself eagerly into his company, unasked, or the young lady who remains ever-so-slightly aloof—a prize to be won?"

Lavinia looked perplexed. "You think he thought me too eager?"

Emm fought a smile. The girl had been flirting outrageously in the way of the very young and innocent. "I have no idea what that particular gentleman thought. All I ask is that you think about the impression you wish to give."

"But if I am too cool and aloof, gentlemen might not even approach me."

"There is no danger of that," Emm assured her. "You're a very pretty girl with a lively and affectionate nature. You will have your pick of gentlemen, I'm sure. A little reserve will not frighten men away—it will only make you a prize more worth the winning."

Lavinia gave her a doubtful look.

Emm said lightly, "Men—most people, in fact—value the hard-won prize over that which comes to them easily, don't you think?"

"I never thought of that."

Emm smiled. "I'm not suggesting you change your personality, just that you try to consider the impression your words and actions might give. A girl's reputation is a delicate thing, and it rests almost wholly in the hands of others. People who don't know you can misinterpret your actions and make false judgments about you, and once that's happened, there's very little you can do to change things."

If only someone had told her that when she was Lavinia's age.

Lavinia thought that over and nodded. "I see." She took a few steps, then paused and turned back. "You are so wise, Miss Westwood. Why did you never—?" She broke off, blushing. "Sorry," she muttered, and hurried away.

Emm knew what she had been going to ask. Why had Emm never married? The girls speculated constantly about that, she knew. She'd never explained, and never would.

The girls had come up with a range of stories, she knew, the most widely accepted being that she'd been in love with a soldier who'd been killed in the war.

Emm never discussed it. The truth was uglier than anything the girls, in their innocence, could come up with. Emm still didn't quite understand how it had happened.

Just that it had. And her life had been ruined.

No, not ruined, she told herself firmly. She was happy here. She loved teaching, she really did. And the girls were wonderful.

But it wasn't how she'd dreamed her life would be.

She hurried to her room to prepare for her next class. Geography. A frustrating subject; not only had the borders of so many countries been changed by Napoleon's conquests, they kept changing after his defeat. It was almost impossible for a teacher to keep up.

She set out the globes and tried not to think of the tall, hard-eyed man waiting below. What would bring such a man to Miss Mallard's Seminary?

"THE RUTHERFORD GIRLS?" THE ELEGANT SILVER-HAIRED headmistress stared at Cal in horror over her *pince-nez*. "You want me to take Rose and Lily Rutherford back? No and no and no!"

Cal said soothingly. "Not permanently, just for a few weeks or a month, until I can—"

"No!" She removed the *pince-nez*, placed them in a case

and closed it with a snap. Business completed. "Not for a week, not for a month, not even for a minute!"

"Why not?"

"Your half sisters are too old for this establishment. Too old and too . . . restless. They would lead the younger girls astray."

"What if I paid double the usual fees?" She didn't respond, so he said, "Triple?"

She thinned her lips. "Did you not understand me when I said no, Lord Ashendon?"

He sighed and sat back in his chair. "No, I'm just desperate. Can't you help me just a little, Miss Mallard? You had them here for five years, after all."

She snorted. "And between them, they turned my hair white."

"I know Rose can be a handful, but Lily—"

She threw up her hands. "Lily! That girl drove my poor teachers to distraction."

"*Lily* did?"

"She is unteachable, quite unteachable."

Cal frowned. "Are we talking about the same Lily? Sweet-natured and biddable—"

"Oh, yes, she's very sweet-natured, but nobody can *teach* her. It's not that we haven't tried everything we can think of, but it's very bad for the reputation of my school to turn out a pupil who after five long years still cannot spell and can barely read."

There was a short pause, then Cal said, "Are you telling me that Lily cannot read and write?"

She nodded. "Didn't you know?"

He shook his head slowly. He didn't quite believe it. Lily didn't seem at all stupid to him.

But dammit, there was no solution for him here after all. "So nothing I can say or do will convince you to take them back?"

"My advice to you is to get them married off as quickly as you can. They are of age. Rose is almost twenty and Lily is eighteen. Make them some other man's problem." She rose in implacable dismissal. "Good day to you, Lord Ashendon. And good luck."

* * *

CAL SPENT THE REST OF THE AFTERNOON VISITING OTHER seminaries for young ladies—Bath was full of them—but without success. Either the girls really were too old or their reputations had traveled before them. He suspected the latter.

Walking back to his aunt's house, he was surprised to see an old friend striding grimly along on the other side of the street, deep in a brown study. Ned Galbraith, a few years behind Cal at school, had gone to war at the same time. He'd resigned his commission in 1814, rejoined for Waterloo, then sold out again.

Cal hadn't seen him since Waterloo. "Galbraith," he called.

Galbraith glanced up and the frown cleared from his face. He crossed the street and the two men shook hands.

"Can't stay to chat," Galbraith said after the initial greetings were over. "Got an engagement in"—he pulled out a fob watch and consulted it—"quarter of an hour. I'm staying at York House. Join me for dinner? We can blow a cloud and catch up."

"Can't, I'm afraid," Cal said regretfully. "I've only just arrived in Bath and I need to look after my young half sisters."

Galbraith's brows rose. "Don't they have nursemaids for that sort of thing?"

Cal grimaced. "They're not children. They don't require a nursemaid, more like . . . a watchdog."

"Like that, is it? Well, if you change your mind, you know where I'm staying. I'm here for a week or two."

"Weeks? Not here for the waters, are you?" Galbraith looked as fit and healthy as ever.

"Lord, no—filthy stuff. If you haven't already tasted it, don't. Might as well drain water through your old socks and drink that. No, I'm"—a peculiar expression crossed his face—"I'm courting."

"Courting? You? Good lord! I always thought you were as marriage-shy as me."

"I know. I was. I am. But"—he gave a wry grimace—"needs must when the devil drives."

"Your grandfather?"

Galbraith nodded. "Got it in one. Since my father died, the old man hasn't stopped fretting. Says before the angels call him, he wants me firmly buckled to a respectable, levelheaded gel, and with a lustily squalling heir in the nursery."

Cal couldn't help but snort. "The angels?" From all accounts Galbraith's grandfather, old Lord Galbraith, had been a notorious rake in his youth.

"Turned religious," Galbraith said, faintly amused. "Respectable as a vicar now."

"Damn."

"Damn indeed." He added in a dry voice, "He's even picked out the girl."

Cal was shocked. "What, you don't get a choice?"

"Of course I do, but . . ." He shrugged. "The old man is failing, and I—I've given him nothing but trouble all my life. I've decided to marry quickly, so he can die in peace. And since it makes no difference to me who I marry . . ."

"No difference? You don't believe that, surely?"

"Why not?" Galbraith said indifferently. "All cats are gray in the dark. And you know as well as I that with a title comes the obligation to procreate." He gave Cal a twisted smile. "Marriage, it comes to us all in the end."

"Not me," Cal said emphatically. And then he remembered his own title and the need for an heir. "At least not for a good long while yet. But who is this girl he's picked out for you?"

"Tell you all about it when you come to dinner. Make it Thursday. Give you a couple of days to find a watchdog for the girls." Galbraith consulted his watch again. "Must go. The blushing bride awaits."

Cal continued on his way, a little disturbed by what he'd learned. Gossip at the Apocalypse Club had Galbraith down as a cold bastard and, since returning to England, he'd apparently developed a reputation in the ton as cynical rake and a care-for-nobody. Whatever he was now, most agreed that Galbraith had been a damn good officer—a man to rely on.

But Cal had known Ned Galbraith since school, and back then he'd been quite a different boy. War changed men; some more than others.

And now the rake was to be married. A convenient marriage to a levelheaded female. Cal gave an inward shudder. He couldn't think of anything worse.

Why did people always think marriage was the answer to everything?

The headmistress's words came back to him. *Get them married off as quickly as you can . . . Make them some other man's problem.*

A tempting prospect, but such things weren't so easily arranged. Not quickly, as any rate.

Still, with any luck Aunt Agatha would step in as he'd asked her to. She was his godmother, after all, as well as his aunt. Unlike Aunt Dottie, who was as soft and sweet as flummery, Aunt Agatha was not an aunt to be sneezed at. As a boy he'd been terrified of her—as had his father and every other adult he knew. Except, strangely, Aunt Dottie, but then Aunt Dottie had always been a law unto herself. She saw the world differently than most people, and Cal was beginning to see just how differently.

Aunt Agatha would soon sort the girls out.

EMM LAY IN BED THAT NIGHT, MULLING OVER THE EVENTS of the day. In the forefront was the tall man she'd met at the bottom of the stairs.

She met so few men—young men—these days.

Apart from the attentions of a couple of elderly widowers who attended the same church as she did, men even older than her father and suffering from a variety of ailments—there was a reason they lived in Bath, after all—with the life she lived, there was very little chance of meeting anyone her own age.

Let alone someone her own age who was so very attractive.

Those cold-seeming gray eyes had lit with humor when he realized Lavinia's little ploy. A small exchange, a little humorous understanding—oh, she was making too much of it.

Wasn't he delicious, miss? So stern and handsome and tall, and those eyes . . .

He was all that, and more. But Emm would never have

been brave enough to comment on a man's attractions, not aloud like that, and certainly not with such frank enjoyment.

Was it her age? Or a legacy of the way she'd left home? *A girl's reputation is a delicate thing . . .*

Emm pressed a hand to her stomach. In a few years she'd be thirty.

Year after year girls returned to the school, proudly displaying their husbands, and as often as not, with a babe in arms to show off and be cooed over. Emm did her share of cooing—she loved babies—but afterward . . .

Oh, it was shameful to envy the girls their happiness, their babies.

She'd lost all chance of that, and she had no one but herself to blame.

On the other side of the thin wall, she could hear the low buzz of Miss Johnstone and Miss Thwaites talking anxiously. Theale, Miss Mallard's assistant, had let slip— accidentally on purpose—that Miss Mallard was thinking about retiring, causing a mild panic among the staff members. Would the school be closed? Or sold? And if so, what would happen to them?

Emm refused to worry at this stage. It might be just a malicious rumor started by Theale—it wouldn't be the first time. The woman positively enjoyed upsetting people.

If the rumor was true, Emm was fairly confident she could get another job. Miss Mallard would give her a good reference, she was sure. Bath was full of girls' schools, and Miss Mallard's was one of the more select.

But Miss Thwaites and Miss Johnstone were elderly, poor and without family. They'd told Emm that if the school did close, they would pool their meager savings and rent rooms in a cottage by the sea, there to live out the rest of their days, perhaps eking out their income by giving lessons in music, deportment and French.

It was a depressing prospect. Even more depressing was the thought that her own future would, in all probability, be much the same. She too was poor and wholly dependent on whatever she could earn. And she had no family to turn to. There had only ever been Papa, and now he was gone.

As always at the thought of her father, guilt and grief surged up within her. If only she had seen Papa, spoken to him before he died. Explained, apologized. Made peace with him. Told him how much she loved him.

She'd thought—hoped—he'd come after her, but instead, in a rage that must have lasted much longer than his usual fits of temper, he'd disowned her—changed his will, leaving her nothing, not a penny. And then he'd died.

Of a broken heart, Mr. Irwin had told her. He'd bumped into her in the street, just outside the Pump Room—he was in Bath on his honeymoon—and had broken it to her, right in front of everyone—that her father was dead, had been dead, in fact, for almost a year.

You caused your father's death. You broke his heart and killed him, he'd told her with spiteful relish.

Why would anyone need to inform you? he'd sneered in answer to her shocked, stammered questions. *You disgraced yourself, refused his bidding and ran off, never to be heard of again. Your father wrote you out of his will—left you nothing, not a penny. When he died, there was no reason for anyone to contact you.*

He'd added gleefully, *You've lost everything—you have no family, no home, no fortune. Serves you right for being such a stubborn little bitch!*

She'd always known Irwin would never forgive her for refusing him, but the vitriol in his voice and manner had shocked her.

Emm thought of what she'd told Lavinia that morning. *A girl's reputation is a delicate thing, and it rests almost wholly in the hands of others.*

She was the living embodiment of the truth of that.

Chapter Four

*It was his object to see as much as he could,
with as little apparent observation.*
—JANE AUSTEN, *EMMA*

IN THE DAYS THAT FOLLOWED, CAL DID HIS BEST TO simultaneously watch over his sisters, get to know them and keep them entertained. His efforts weren't appreciated.

He'd decided to check whether the headmistress's comments about Lily were true, so he'd asked her to read—and that had ended in tears on Lily's part and fury on Rose's when she'd learned what he'd done.

For the next few days he was given the silent treatment—not by Lily, who simply avoided his gaze and whispered every response as if he'd whipped her—but from Rose. And from somebody delivering the silent treatment, she did it in the noisiest way possible, with long-suffering huffs and world-weary sighs.

But Cal wasn't going to give in to that kind of nonsense, and when Aunt Dottie asked him what he'd done to upset the girls now, he snapped that he'd done nothing wrong, merely asked Lily—in the most reasonable way possible—to read a few lines of a letter to him.

Aunt Dottie looked at him as if he'd just admitted to strangling a kitten. "She's very sensitive about it, you know."

"I think I've worked that out, Aunt Dottie," he said, but she was oblivious of sarcasm. She patted his hand. "They'll come around, you'll see."

Keeping them entertained in the evening was also a trial. He'd suggested cards, which got Rose's hackles raised because apparently Lily got cards confused—though how the hell he was supposed to know that, he couldn't imagine.

Luckily he hit on the idea of spillikins, which Lily enjoyed and was good at. The evening finished on a much more pleasant note, but as Rose said before they retired for the night, "You can't expect to keep us entertained with endless nursery games, you know."

He cared about his sisters, he really did, but he was also chafing at the bit to be rid of these petty domestic problems and be back on the trail of an assassin.

He hoped Aunt Agatha would get here soon. He was fed up with sitting up late every night, simply to make sure the girls weren't able to sneak out. And he was very fed up with having to watch what he said. Conversations with the girls was like picking his way through a treacherous swamp; you never knew where the dangers lurked.

"I don't know why you make such a fuss of having to wear black, Rose," Cal said after one particularly trying meal where Rose hadn't missed a single opportunity to snipe at him. "Mourning colors suit you perfectly."

She sent him a suspicion-laden look.

"It's the combination of the black with your guinea-gold hair," he said and, after a pause, added, "Wasp colors."

She laughed, tried to turn it into a cough, failed and gave up. So his sharp-tongued little sister had a sense of humor after all. He liked her the better for it.

"We don't always have to be at dagger drawn, you know," he said quietly.

Her smile died. "Don't we?"

By the time Thursday evening arrived, Cal found himself looking forward to dinner with his friend Galbraith with a ridiculous degree of anticipation. York House was the finest hotel in Bath, and the food would be excellent, but even more than a good dinner with fine wines, Cal was looking forward to an evening of straightforward, uncomplicated, blessedly logical masculine company.

* * *

"I TELL YOU, NED, DEALING WITH FEMALES IS THE VERY devil!" Cal said after a fine meal, washed down with some excellent wine. They were now settled in comfortable over-stuffed armchairs in front of a cozy fire, and on their second cognac, and both men were feeling delightfully mellow.

"Thought you liked women."

"I said females, not women."

Galbraith considered that. "Not sure I see your point. Females *are* women."

"No! That's where you're wrong. All women are females, but not all females are women."

There was a short silence. "You mean some of them are those what-d'you-call-'em—man milliners?"

"No, of course not. I mean there is an age when a young female is not yet a woman—and, Ned, at that age they might look sweet and innocent and as if butter wouldn't melt in their mouth, but take it from me, they're devils in disguise. A man cannot put a single foot right. One wrong move and they snap it right off!"

His friend snorted. "Too soft a heart with females, that's your trouble. Keep cool, stand firm, and never compromise. Always worked for me."

Cal shook his head. "All very well for you to say. You don't have sisters. Believe me, being responsible for young females of that age—particularly young female *relatives*—well, it's worse than . . . worse than . . ." He tried to think of an example that Galbraith would appreciate. "Remember that time when I was still wet behind the ears and was given that troop to command—most of them from the stews of London and only in the army as an alternative to being locked up in prison for God knows how long?"

"Lord, yes. Thugs and villains to a man. Scum of the earth."

Cal nodded. "Trying to control my young sisters is harder than that."

"Harder than commanding that riffraff?" Galbraith gave

a snort of amusement. "Pull the other one. I've seen grown men—hard nuts they were too—shaking in their boots when called up before you for some infraction or other."

"Yes, but *they* knew I could have them flogged."

Galbraith gave Cal a sideways glance. "Don't remember when you ever resorted to flogging."

"I did once or twice—extreme circumstances." Cal stared into his brandy glass. "But you can't flog girls or even threaten it."

"Suppose not."

"And soldiers don't burst into tears at a—very mild— reprimand, or flounce from the room, or sulk, or look at you with big wounded eyes! Or ignore my—very reasonable— orders and go their own merry way!"

There was a muffled sound from the chair opposite. Cal narrowed his eyes. "Are you laughing at me, Galbraith?"

"Wouldn't dream of it." He met Cal's gaze for a pregnant pause, then burst into laughter. "Lord, yes, I'm laughing. It's priceless! Major Calbourne Rutherford, bested by a couple of schoolgirls."

"Not schoolgirls," Cal said gloomily. "The school wouldn't take them back."

"Don't tell me you asked the school to take them back."

Cal nodded. "Damned headmistress refused."

There was another shout of laughter from his unsympathetic friend. "So, what are you going to do?"

"I've written to Aunt Agatha."

Galbraith's brows rose. "You mean Lady Salter? That old tartar? Good move. She'll knock the nonsense out of them. Knocks the nonsense out of everyone, your aunt Agatha."

Cal swirled his cognac, gazing balefully into the firelight reflected in its smooth golden depths. "I don't know. Rose will give her a pretty good run for her money, I'll wager."

"And the other one? What's her name? Lucy?"

"Lily. Yes, she'll probably eat Lily alive." He frowned, imagining little Lily faced with Aunt Agatha. Then he shook his head. "But I can't help that. I can't lock them in their bedchambers, and I can't and won't let them wander the streets at night. Good God, Ned, anything could happen to them."

"What about a governess?" Galbraith suggested after a moment. "Sort of governess-companion-chaperone type of female. With a bit of watchdog thrown in."

"You mean a wardress," Cal said gloomily. "But it's too late. I've already sent for Aunt Agatha."

Galbraith snorted. "Same thing, isn't it?"

The two men sipped their brandy and stared into the flames. The fire crackled and hissed.

Cal drained his glass and stood. "It's late. I'd better get going."

IT WAS COLD AS CAL WALKED BACK TO HIS AUNT'S HOUSE, the chill from the surrounding hills sliding down to pool and gather in the town. The scent of coal and wood fires thickened the faint mist. His footsteps echoed in the night silence. The streets were deserted.

Galbraith's reaction had made Cal thoughtful. Had he been a little premature in sending for Aunt Agatha? She wasn't a monster, just strict and a little intimidating. It was mostly men who were terrified of her. Particularly men related to her.

Aunt Dottie, her younger sister, wasn't the least bit intimidated by her, and as far as he could tell from the letters that Aunt Dottie sent with the socks, Aunt Agatha led a very social life and had plenty of friends.

It had always puzzled him: Aunt Dottie, sweet-natured, gentle and affectionate, had never married, and yet her sister, sharp-tongued and formidable, had married three times.

To men who had died not long afterward, he reminded himself.

Had he overreacted in writing to her? The last couple of days with the girls hadn't been too bad—if he didn't count Rose's occasional snipes. They hadn't sneaked out or misbehaved in any serious way. As he'd thought on first acquaintance, they just needed a firm hand.

But he had no intention of hanging around indefinitely to provide it. He had a job to do that was a damn sight more important than playing watchdog to a pair of young hoydens.

Maybe Aunt Agatha had mellowed.

He turned the corner into Aunt Dottie's street and squinted against the darkness. Three cloaked female figures were approaching the house from the other direction. Two walked with arms around each other, subdued and downcast. The third figure, a taller female, looked as though she was shepherding them along.

A trickle of foreboding slid down his spine. He strode forward.

A lamp outside his aunt's house gave faint illumination to the scene. "What the devil are you two doing outside? I gave strict orders—" He broke off, looking closer. "What the hell happened to you?" he said in quite a different voice.

Rose had a burgeoning black eye, and Lily—the side of Lily's face was red and swelling. Even in the poor light he could see it was going to be a nasty bruise. A cold rage filled him. "Who did this to you?"

The tall female with them reached past him and rang the doorbell. It jangled in the dark house. "There was some trouble at the talk."

He swung around and saw it was that teacher, Miss Something-or-other. With the mouth. And the eyes. "What talk?"

"By members of the Female Reform Society."

The Female Reform Society? *Politics?* Rose and Lily? He didn't believe it. "*You* took them there? Without so much as a—"

"She didn't know we were there," Rose said swiftly. "We went by ourselves."

The door behind him opened and Logan stood there, blinking. Golden light spilled out from inside, illuminating the girls' injuries more clearly. Rose's eye was swollen almost shut and darkening by the second, and her smooth, soft complexion was abraded in places. The side of Lily's face was dark and swelling and her soft, vulnerable mouth had blood on it from a split lip.

The girls flinched at Cal's expression. "A man was bothering Lily—" Rose began.

Lily flushed. "I tried to push him away but—"

"He hit her, hit my little sister!" Rose's voice was throbbing with rage.

"So Rose went for him and then I tried to—"

Cal cut them off with a furious gesture. Political rallies were notorious for erupting in violence. The thought of his little sisters having to fight off some filthy thug filled him with horror. And ice-cold fury. "Why the *devil* were you attending a political rally in the first place! No—don't bother—I don't want to know. The point is, you were supposed to be safely *in bed*. How often have I warned you how *dangerous* it is to venture out on your own at night and—"

Rose burst out. "You don't want us to have *any* fun! What's wrong with showing an interest—"

"Rose," the teacher said quietly.

Rose glanced at her. "Sorry, Miss Westwood." And said not another word. Not so much as a peep.

Cal blinked.

The teacher turned to Cal and said in a pleasant manner that barely disguised the acid beneath, "Shall we continue to stand in the street hurling accusations and counteraccusations, or should the girls be taken in out of the cold and have their injuries tended to?"

"Of course." Annoyed because she was right, dammit— and because he'd almost lost his temper and he *never* lost it—Cal gently pushed the girls inside and stood back to let their teacher enter before him.

She gave him a brisk nod and turned to leave.

Cal frowned. "You're not coming in?"

"Thank you, but no."

Cal turned to the butler. "See to the girls, Logan. Wake one of the maids to attend them. A slice of steak will help Miss Rose's eye. Unguent and some ice for Miss Lily's bruises—but apply some leeches first if you have any. They'll stop the worst of the bruising."

"Ugh! Not leeches!" Lily exclaimed.

Cal ignored her. "A hot bath for each of them, a cup of hot milk with honey and a little brandy, and then bed." He looked at the girls. "I'll speak to you two tomorrow." Logan looked at him with a question in his eyes, and Cal added, "I will escort Miss Westwind home."

"Westwood. But there is no need—" she began.

He said tersely. "Shall we stand in the street discussing it, or . . . ?"

She gave him a look he couldn't read, then shrugged. "If you insist, but there's really no—"

"I insist." He offered his arm.

To Cal's surprise he didn't have to adjust his pace to hers as he did with most ladies. She walked with a long-limbed elegance, an easy graceful stride. Their steps matched perfectly. She was tall for a lady; the top of her head was, under the ugly gray hat she wore, level with his eyes.

"Do you often attend political rallies?" he asked her.

She gave him a sidelong glance. "When they interest me." She added after a pause, "Why? Are you the kind of man who thinks that it's unfeminine for women—excuse me, *ladies*—to show an interest in politics?" It was a challenge.

"Not at all," Cal said. "I don't care what you're interested in. I was just making conversation."

They walked in silence for the next few minutes.

"I want to thank you for bringing my sisters home."

"You're welcome."

"I was surprised that they thought a political talk worth sneaking out for."

She glanced briefly at him. "I suspect it was less the subject of the talk as the adventure of being out on their own at night." Her voice reminded him of a white wine he'd drunk in Alsace once; crisp, dry and a little astringent. But with unexpected depths and a fine, smooth aftertaste.

"They shouldn't be out at night at all, let alone unescorted," said Cal with feeling. "I have utterly forbidden it."

"Which adds to the appeal of the adventure."

Her calm acceptance of their misbehavior infuriated him. "You shouldn't be out alone and unescorted at night, either," he snapped. "Especially at a political rally." There were riots everywhere in England these days. People got hurt.

"Lord Ashendon, I am a spinster of six-and-twenty and am quite my own mistress. I am not accountable to you or anyone else for my behavior."

"I know that," he growled. "But your foolishness encourages others to imitate you." It was unfair and he knew it.

And of course, she wasn't the kind of female to let it pass. She snatched her hand off his arm. "Do not try to put the blame on me! Your sisters had no idea I was planning to attend. I don't believe they had any plan to attend the rally, either—they just saw the crowd and followed out of curiosity."

She marched on a few steps in silence, but she was clearly building up a head of steam. "Their adventurousness has *nothing* to do with me, and everything to do with the way they've been . . . oh, *'cabin'd, cribb'd, confin'd'* for the last year—and for most of their lives!"

He might have known a teacher would resort to flinging Shakespeare around, as if it were the clincher to every argument.

She continued, "And it's especially difficult for them to accept when *they* must dress entirely in black and are not allowed out because they're in mourning for their father and their brother, and yet *you* can go out carousing, wearing whatever you like and—"

"Carousing?" he interrupted wrathfully. "I'll give them carousing! I was dining quietly with a fellow officer, a friend I haven't seen in y—" He broke off, noticing, in the light of the lamp overhead, a stain on her otherwise pale face. "Stand still," he ordered, and when she glanced at him in surprise he caught her by the shoulders and turned her toward the light.

A bruise was forming on her cheekbone, and dried blood made a dark crust around one of her nostrils. And, now that he looked, drops of blood stained the front of her clothing.

"Dammit, you were injured too. Why didn't you say something?"

Flustered, she tried to move away. "I'm perfectly all ri—"

"Don't move, I said." He cupped her face gently in his hands, the better to examine her injuries.

Or so he told himself.

He'd left his gloves at Galbraith's hotel. His hands were

bare but warm. Her skin was cool from the cold night air, silky and damp from the mist. Pale and soft as moonlight.

The darkening bruise on her cheekbone woke an anger in him that surprised him. He gently smoothed his thumb along her jawline. She stiffened.

He cradled her face in the lightest of holds and studied her. She stood motionless, expressionless: a trapped doe braced to flee.

She had only to pull away or say something and he would release her. He could feel the tension vibrating through her, but she said nothing.

Her eyes watched, wide and dark, twin pools of mystery, colorless in the night.

She made not a sound. He could feel her breath, soft and warm.

Her cool, silky skin was warming under his fingers.

Her mouth—God help him—her mouth was dark and luscious and damp and enticing. Without thinking he bent to taste it, a light, swift kiss that somehow . . . lingered.

She stiffened a moment, then made a soft little sound and her mouth softened under his. She tasted of . . . oh, lord . . . rose petals and moonlight and innocence. And beneath it all lay heat, luscious womanly heat.

Ravenous hunger went spiraling through him. He drew her closer to deepen the kiss, but she resisted, pushing back at him with a little sound of anger. Or distress. He released her instantly.

She stumbled back a few unsteady paces. He put out a hand to support her, but she jerked away. One burning glance at him through wide, unreadable eyes and she turned her back on him, taking deep unsteady breaths that gradually calmed.

He watched her, pulling her composure back together like a suit of armor.

His own pulse was still pounding. His brain made no sense of what had just happened. He hadn't intended to kiss her. He barely knew her. She was a respectable woman, a teacher in a girls' school. Practically a nun.

Though that mouth didn't belong on any nun. And now the taste of her was in his blood . . .

He should probably apologize, but he was damned if he would. He didn't regret a thing, only that it hadn't lasted nearly long enough. And that he'd been raised a gentleman.

The uncivilized part of him wanted nothing less than to possess her, to plunder her sweetness, to ravish that lithe, slender body until they were both sated and—

She turned back to face him, her expression smooth and calm as a pail of milk. "Shall we move on?"

—And to shatter that damnable ever-present composure. There was a passionate woman beneath it, he was sure; he'd tasted it in her. His blood had leapt in recognition.

But if that was how she wanted to play it, pretending the kiss had never happened, he would cooperate. He was, after all, a civilized man.

And dallying with innocents was playing with fire.

He offered his arm and, after the faintest of hesitations, she took it. They walked on in silence.

Around them the city slept. In the distance a vixen screamed.

Overhead the clouds thickened, and the darkness intensified. They passed a house where lights still burned, and she glanced in as they passed. A woman bent over a writing desk, writing busily.

"She's working late," he commented, seeking an innocuous comment to break the tense silence.

"I shouldn't look, I know. It feels as if I'm invading their privacy, but if people don't draw their curtains . . ." After a moment she added, "I'm always curious about how other people live."

As she would be, he reflected, seeing she had no home of her own. Or so he assumed. "Have you lived at the school long?"

"It feels like most of my life," she said wryly. "I was a pupil there as a girl."

"And you returned there to become a teacher?" There was a story there, he was sure, and he wanted to hear it.

But all she said was, "Yes."

They walked on. "You should be proud of your sisters, you know," she began, and seeing he was about to snap her nose off for that piece of impertinence, hurried on, "Oh, not because they sneaked out without permission—yes, they admitted that to me when I asked who was supposed to be escorting them. And that was very wrong of them. But the trouble wasn't really their fault—"

"Political rallies are invariably violent," he growled.

"Not necessarily, but be that as it may, when Lily was in trouble, Rose flew to her sister's defense like a little wildcat. And then Lily tried to defend Rose. Of course, it's not the most ladylike—"

"Ladylike!" he exploded. "No, it was not damned well ladylike! It was insane! What the devil kind of teacher are you anyway, praising them for brawling in public?"

She withdrew her hand and gave him a long cool look. "The kind of teacher who thinks for herself—and does not like to be cursed at," she said calmly, and walked on. "As for brawling in public, the girls were defending themselves—and each other. Would you prefer that one of your sisters abandoned the other to preserve her own safety?"

She glanced at him and gave a little nod when she saw his expression. "Of course not. Should they have simply fainted, then, as society suggests is the proper ladylike response to upsets of various sorts?" Again she glanced at his face. "I agree. Had they been so foolish, they would have been trampled by the crowd milling around."

"But if they hadn't been so disobedient in the first place—"

"Of course, but having done so, what were they to do when faced with trouble? They acted with courage, and did their best with the limited skills and knowledge at their disposal," she finished crisply. "Here we are at the school—no, no need to ring the bell. I have my own key." She took it from her reticule and let herself in. "Thank you for your escort, Lord Ashendon. Good night."

And before Cal could say a word, she shut the door gently in his face.

He stared at the door a moment, cursing under his breath. Blasted woman had an answer for everything.

Except a kiss. That she simply dismissed as if it had never happened. But he could still taste her.

As he made his way back home through the deserted streets, rain started, a light patter of drops at first, but turning swiftly into a downpour. Cal broke into a run, but even so, by the time he reached Aunt Dottie's house he was drenched.

Of course. A perfect end to a perfect dratted night.

Chapter Five

**Many women long for what eludes them,
and like not what is offered them.**
—OVID

EMMALINE WESTWOOD SHUT THE DOOR ON LORD ASHENDON,
took three steps toward the staircase, sank onto the steps and
leaned against the carved wooden baluster.

That kiss . . .

She was still trembling inside from it, could still savor
the dark, masculine taste of him. The heat that had streaked
through her at the touch of his mouth, like rich, liquid
lightning . . .

And oh, afterward, the effort of holding her composure,
of making rational conversation in the wake of . . . *that*.

Somehow, thank goodness, she had. It was as if there
were two Emmaline Westwoods; the rational commonsensical Emm who was somehow able to walk and talk and
sound perfectly composed, like a talking doll or one of those
automatons she'd seen at a scientific exhibition once.

The other—the foolish, romantical, *credulous* Emm—was
still reeling, dazed at her reaction to what she *knew* was just
a simple kiss. The heat from it still echoed deep inside her.

What had made him do it? For a few magical; entrancing
moments she'd felt . . . well, *imagined* . . . But no. It was a
ridiculously foolish Cinderella imagining, and she'd do well
to put that nonsense right out of her mind.

Rich handsome earls didn't suddenly fall in love with

plain spinster schoolteachers. Especially ones they'd met twice. And knew nothing about.

So why had he done it?

Did he imagine she was open to such attentions? Was her respectability not obvious to him? Had she given him some kind of unwitting encouragement?

Did he think because she went out at night by herself, attending political talks, getting involved in—

The brawl. Was that it? Did he think because she'd let herself get involved in such an unladylike contretemps that she was somehow fair game for casual masculine attentions of the improper sort?

And if so, then what did that make his sisters? Was it one rule for daughters of the aristocracy and another for poor unregarded schoolteachers?

Of course it was.

She ought to be insulted, ought to be angry.

Instead, she'd been . . . entranced. And a small, a very small, rebellious, *un*commonsensical, *foolish* part of her wanted to stay that way.

She sat at the foot of the stairs for several minutes, hugging the smooth wood of the baluster, reliving and reexamining the kiss, asking herself questions she couldn't answer—but answering them anyway. Eventually the icy drafts coming from under the door cooled her heated thoughts and returned her to rationality.

And the awareness that she had far more important things to worry about. If Miss Mallard was thinking about retiring—and it seemed as though the rumor was true after all—she'd probably hand the school over to her horrid nephew. Who no doubt would sack them all and sell the school.

That was something *real* to worry about.

The other was just a kiss. Lord Ashendon probably hadn't given it another thought. Emm was overreacting, like an affection-deprived, overimaginative spinster. Which was exactly what she was.

She rose and walked quietly up the stairs, looked in on her students as she did each night to check that they were all in bed and sleeping soundly and then climbed the last narrow flight of stairs to her own small room.

If you didn't count the basement, Miss Mallard's Seminary was arranged in order of ascending . . . austerity, she supposed was the nicest way to put it.

The ground floor of the seminary set the tone of distinction Miss Mallard wanted the school to project. Her office, the parlor where prospective parents were wooed and given tea and biscuits and sometimes a glass of sherry, and the spacious and elegant saloon used mainly for concerts and musical performances—were all on the ground floor, and furnished in the first style of elegance.

The higher you went, however—the classrooms on the next floor up, the boarders' bedchambers and sitting room above that—the plainer and more functional the surroundings until you reached, by increasingly narrow and steep stairs, the attic where Emm, and the two other teachers who had the misfortune to be without any other income, lodged, along with the servants.

Emm's room was the smallest. It was cramped, freezing in winter and hot in summer, but she considered herself blessed, partly because it was too small to share, and she prized her privacy, but also because it was one of only two attic rooms with a window. The window was small and square and got grimy very quickly with the smoke from the town below, but it looked out over her own private kingdom— the world beyond Bath.

She loved that window, her own little eyrie, loved looking across the rooftops of Bath to the green rolling hills beyond. Gazing out that small window never failed to lift her spirits, no matter what the weather.

Right now there was no view, in the dark, with rain beating furiously down. She stripped off her gloves, watching the rain form silver rivulets across the glass and hearing it gurgle loudly down the drainpipes.

Lord Ashendon would have walked home in that rain. Good. Serve him right.

No, she didn't mean that. It was good of him to walk her home. She folded her gloves one inside the other and remembered how he'd taken her hand and tucked it firmly into the crook of his arm.

Men didn't usually notice her at all. Too old, too tall, too plain, too poor. Practically invisible.

And yet those piercing, dark-rimmed silvery eyes had noticed her, had scanned her face so intently, the breath had simply disappeared from her body. Warm, strong, bare hands had cupped her face as if she were some delicate creature.

Her heart had started galloping in her chest . . .

She'd told herself to be sensible, that it was nothing; simple good manners to show concern.

They'd stood so close she could see the fine-grained pores of his skin, the shadow of masculine bristles that darkened his jaw and a pale, almost invisible scar along the bottom of his chin—a saber cut? Or a bayonet injury from the war?

And then . . . when he'd slowly lowered his mouth to hers, gently, so lightly at first, and then . . . all thoughts had been driven from her brain. There was only his mouth, moving over hers, searching, tasting . . .

Oh, for heaven's sake, stop dwelling on it, foolish woman. It was a whim, an impulse of the moment. He was probably a rake.

She hung up her cloak, laid out her nightgown across the bed and started to strip off her clothes, as fast as she could because the room was cold and getting colder.

Rose and Lily used to talk about their uncle, the soldier-hero, seeming both proud and fond of him. A shame they seemed so hostile to each other now. But then people who had a family often took it for granted.

She slipped into bed and breathed a thankful sigh as her frozen toes encountered a solid patch of warmth. One of the maids—probably Milly—had slipped a hot brick into her bed. Oh, blessed, blessed heat. *Thank you, Milly.* She pressed her feet against the cloth-wrapped brick and waited for them to defrost.

She'd had a little adventure, that was all. Something to recall with pleasure. Without regret.

She'd lied when she'd claimed she was her own mistress. Usually when Emm went anywhere in public she was accompanied by the other teachers who lived in: Miss Thwaites and Miss Johnstone, both of whom moved at a snail's pace. Neither of them had been interested in attending a talk by the Female Reform Society, so she'd slipped out alone. And not for the first time.

Miss Thwaites and Miss Johnstone had spent most of their adult lives at the Mallard Seminary. Sometimes, when Emm lay in her bed, hearing the murmur of the two older ladies talking, the thought that she was going to end up just like them made her almost desperate.

But what else could she do?

Tonight she'd had a small adventure, she reminded herself. She'd attended a political talk, gotten caught up in a fight, walked alone after midnight through the deserted streets of Bath on the arm of a tall, handsome gentleman—and been thoroughly, magically kissed.

All of the delights of scandalous behavior and none of the consequences.

If anyone had seen her walking alone with Lord Ashendon at that hour, the repercussions would be unpleasant at the very least. Miss Mallard would be far from pleased; the teachers at Miss Mallard's Seminary had to be like the wife of Caesar—beyond reproach. On pain of instant dismissal.

But nobody had seen them. Emm grinned to herself as she snuggled down in the bedclothes and waited for the heat to spread. She was as rebellious at heart as Rose and Lily. Just older and wiser and more discreet.

Her sheets smelled faintly of lavender and roses. Emm collected the flowers in season, dried them and filled little muslin bags of the mix to keep her linen smelling sweet. On chilly nights like tonight, it was a pleasant reminder of summer. And gave out echoes of her childhood. The smell of happiness.

Pity she couldn't bag or bottle the smell of Lord Ashendon to remember him by. She closed her eyes, remembering his cologne, sharp and spicy, and a little exotic, and the faint scent of wood smoke and tobacco in his clothing.

And the underlying scent of man, dark and virile and enticing—not like any kind of man she was familiar with.

Grimes, the school porter, the only man allowed in the building, smelled of coal dust and snuff and beer and unwashed old man. Miss Mallard's nephew reeked of sweat and cheap pomade. The vicar smelled of starch and soap and peppermint drops, and after church, when he stood too close, there was usually a whiff of sweet, dark communion wine.

Lord Ashendon had smelled a little of brandy—not reeking or anything, just a hint on his breath and in his mouth. She wouldn't have recognized it, except that Papa had drunk brandy and the scent had called him to mind.

Her eyes flew open. *Brandy!* Of course.

Lord Ashendon had been drinking. He'd been out with his friend, he'd said so.

So he was drunk—not so drunk you'd notice; he held his liquor well—but it explained everything. He'd no doubt kissed her because he was drunk, and she was female, and there, under his nose. And because he'd decided she was the kind of female who attended political events and got into brawls. And who thought nothing of walking alone after midnight.

Mystery solved.

Emm pulled the bedclothes tighter around her, but despite the warm brick, despite the blankets and her warm flannel nightgown, the cold crept through her.

"MISS WESTWOOD, MISS WESTWOOD." SOMEONE WAS knocking on Emm's door. She blinked blearily awake. It seemed only a few minutes since she'd gone to bed, but it was light outside. "Miss Westwood!"

"Come in." The door opened and a maid entered carrying a jug of warm water covered with a cloth. "Oh, Milly, thank you for that hot brick last—"

"Never mind that, I mean, you're very welcome, miss, but the Du—er, Miss Mallard—wants to see you right away. Before breakfast, she said."

Emm flung back the bedclothes. "Any idea why?"

"No, miss. Just that it was important. I brung you some hot water to wash in. So hurry."

"Hot water! Bless you, Milly. May you be swept off your feet by a rich and handsome man who will adore you and indulge your every wish!" Which was Milly's dream. She'd confided in Emm when she first came to Bath. She was certainly pretty enough.

Emm washed and dressed with all haste. What could Miss Mallard want with her at this hour? It was most unusual.

A thought struck her as she was fastening her garters. Had Miss Mallard or one of her cronies spotted Emm at the event last night? Or walking unchaperoned with Lord Ashendon?

She checked her appearance in a small looking glass. There was a darkening patch on her left cheekbone. Her nose was a bit red and one side was very slightly swollen, but it wasn't very noticeable. She hoped.

She dusted her face with a little rice powder. It was forbidden for the staff at Miss Mallard's to use cosmetic products of any sort, but Miss Mallard's eyesight was fading, and Emm hoped she wouldn't notice. And if she did, well, she would blame the wardrobe door.

She hurried downstairs. Miss Theale, Miss Mallard's sour-faced assistant, met her at the foot of the stairs. She jerked her head at Emm. "In the office."

Emm knocked and was admitted. She sat, preserving an air of calm, and waited.

Miss Mallard was in the process of writing what looked like a letter. She blotted it, set her pen aside, and said, "Good morning, Miss Westwood. I'll come straight to the point."

Emm braced herself.

"As you know," the headmistress continued, "I am planning to retire at the end of the term."

Emm nodded, her throat suddenly dry. It wasn't about her outing last night. From the expression on Miss Mallard's face, it was something much more serious.

Miss Mallard admitted to sixty years on this earth, but most who knew her privately agreed she was closer to seventy. Her desire to retire was no secret. It had all of the staff worried. What if the school closed? Where would they go?

Emm had nothing to fall back on. No home, no family—nothing. She folded her hands in her lap and waited for the axe to fall.

"I have given much thought to the future of this establishment." Miss Mallard removed her *pince-nez* and polished them meditatively with a soft cloth. "I've given my life to the education of young ladies and I fancy I have achieved a wonderful record—three duchesses, two marchionesses, five countesses, six viscountesses . . ."

Emm wanted to scream. She'd heard this litany before. All the staff and most of the pupils probably knew it by heart.

Emm always wanted to end it with *And a partridge in a pear tree*.

"—which is a record I think no other establishment for young ladies can better."

"No indeed," Emm murmured.

"And so I am reluctant to let the school simply close."

Emm held her breath.

"And although my nephew, Mr. Edgar Mallard, will inherit the school on my death, he could not, of course, run it. A gentleman running a seminary for young ladies—the very idea!" She gave a girlish giggle.

Emm forced a smile. When would she get to the point? Was she going to sell the school? And if so, to whom? And when?

And what would happen to the staff? New brooms often wanted to sweep clean. They could all be out on the street in a matter of weeks.

Miss Mallard replaced her glasses. "I have given much thought to who would run it. Of the permanent staff, Miss Thwaites and Miss Johnstone are too old—they will no doubt retire themselves shortly. Miss Clegg is too young and flighty and besides"—she leaned forward and said in a lowered voice—"she is hoping to be *married*! Well, we can't have *that* sort of thing, can we?"

"No indeed."

"So the choice is obvious. You shall become the headmistress after me."

Emm blinked. *"Me?"* She'd expected to hear that some outsider was going to be appointed. "You want *me* to become the new headmistress?"

Miss Mallard gave a brisk nod, clearly pleased by Emm's amazement. "I cannot think of anyone better. You have the finest education any woman can have—a Mallard education—you have the girls under excellent control and as the daughter of a baronet, you have the birth and background that will reassure our aristocratic parents that their daughters are in excellent hands."

"Miss Mallard, I don't know what to say." Excitement filled her. Oh, what she could make of this place.

"You don't need to say anything. I am writing to my nephew this morning to inform him. He has been pressing me for a decision for some time." She indicated the writing materials in front of her. "Of course, he will continue to oversee the accounts and so on, but that kind of thing is best left to gentlemen anyway, I find. They have the head for such things, while we ladies have our minds on more elegant matters."

Emm smiled and nodded, her mind spinning with plans. First on the agenda, once she became headmistress, would be a battle with Edgar Mallard over expenditure. He was the most parsimonious creature and begrudged any expenditure that was not directly related to the needs of the pupils or impressing their parents. For a school that prided itself on its elegance and quality, it paid its staff disgracefully and pinched pennies appallingly. Edgar Mallard's motto seemed to be, if it wasn't visible to the parents or pupils, it didn't matter.

Emm had battled with him before over such things as the servants' and teachers' quarters, the quality of the food, the provision of heating, wages and other matters he considered unworthy of his attention—or his money.

When Miss Mallard retired, Emm vowed, things would change.

And *her* school would not be judged by whom her pupils married, but by what they learned. And what they did with their lives—marriage or not. Her girls would have choices.

They'd be taught to think, not merely obey and be decorative. Oh, yes, she had plans. . . .

The bell rang for breakfast, and Miss Mallard returned to her papers and waved vaguely toward the door, indicating that the interview was over. Emm rose. "Thank you, Miss Mallard. I'm very honored by your trust in me. I promise you, I will do my very best to ensure that Miss Mallard's Seminary for the Daughters of Gentlemen will continue to flourish long into the future."

She stepped into the hallway in a daze—headmistress!—but was brought back to reality by a thundering on the stairs as thirty-five hungry schoolgirls headed for breakfast. "Girls, girls! Walk, don't run. You are *not* a herd of elephants, all evidence to the contrary."

Giggling, they moderated their speed and walked down the stairs as they were supposed to, two by two at a ladylike pace. Emm supervised, smiling. She loved these girls, so young and lively, full of hopes and dreams and with such a zest for life. She wanted to embrace them all.

She had a future to look forward to now.

CAL FOUND THE BREAKFAST ROOM DESERTED WHEN HE came down next morning. Logan brought his coffee in. "The girls settle in all right last night?"

"Indeed they did, m'lord. We carried out your instructions and the steak helped with Miss Rose's eye. There, er, there were no leeches available for Miss Lily's bruises."

Cal snorted. "In other words, she begged you not to put those nasty slimy creatures on her."

Logan gave him a rueful smile. "It's those big gray eyes of hers . . ."

"I know. We males have no defense against them, do we?" He took a sip of his coffee. "It's a pity. Leeches might be disgusting, but there's nothing like them for limiting bruising. Still, too late now. Are the girls up yet?"

Logan shook his head. "Still abed, m'lord. They were very tired."

Hiding from him, more like, Cal thought.

"I hope we didn't disturb Aunt Dottie last night, with all the coming and goings."

"Not at all, m'lord. She slept like a baby the whole night through. Sleeps very well, does Miss Dottie."

"Now how could you possibly kn—" But Logan had already left the room, leaving Cal to brood over his excellent coffee. The situation with the girls could not go on. Bad enough they kept sneaking out at night, but now they'd been injured. And it could have been much worse.

Logan returned in a few minutes, bearing a covered silver dish, which he placed before Cal.

"Why didn't you stop them, Logan? I trusted you to keep an eye on them. Dammit, can I not even leave this house for a minute?"

Logan removed the lid, revealing an appetizing-looking plate of ham, fried eggs and mushrooms. "I am a *servant* in this house, Lord Ashendon," he said pointedly. "It is my job to *obey* the wishes of the inhabitants, not control them— even if I could. That, my lord, is *your* job." And he sailed from the room.

He was right, damn him. Cal moodily addressed his breakfast. It was excellent, as was the coffee, but it didn't cheer him up any.

Logan returned a few minutes later bearing a silver salver. "The post, my lord."

Cal leafed through the letters and spotted one addressed in a sprawling, stylish hand. "Aunt Agatha!" He seized it eagerly and broke the seal.

It was short and pithy.

My dear Ashendon,

I received your letter—and what a piece of impertinence it was! Do you imagine I have nothing better to do than to rush down to Bath—of all dreary and unfashionable places—to relieve you of your responsibilities? Do you think I have no life of my own? They are your half sisters—

*deal with them. I said no good would come of your father's
second marriage—no fool like an old fool—and now, see
how right I was.*

> *Your loving aunt,
> Agatha, Lady Salter*

His loving aunt. Hah! He crushed the letter and hurled it
into the fire. Damn, damn and double damn. He'd been
counting on Aunt Agatha. What the hell was he going to do
now? Aunt Dottie couldn't control a flea, he couldn't lock
the girls up—much as he'd like to—and for some reason he
couldn't understand, they seemed to have no fear of dis-
obeying him.

But he couldn't stay here indefinitely, watching them—he
had an assassin to track down. The bastard had killed eight
people so far—that they knew of. Including Bentley.

The last time Cal had seen Bentley alive, he was full of
idealistic notions about building a fairer, better world, so
proud of being appointed to such a responsible position,
determined to bring honor to his country.

If only Cal had spotted the assassin on the roof earlier . . .
One minute sooner, and he could have shouted a warning . . .

After the funeral, he'd written to Bentley's widowed
mother. One of the hardest letters he'd ever written.

He called for another pot of coffee and sipped it slowly.
What had Galbraith suggested last night? *A sort of governess-
companion-chaperone type of female. With a bit of watchdog thrown in.*

Cal sat up. He knew one of that sort of female. He'd
walked one home that very night.

He'd kissed her. But that was an aberration. The brandy
after all that wine had been a mistake. He didn't think he'd
drunk that much, but obviously he had and it had gone to
his head.

She had gone to his head. Those eyes, that mouth . . .

Nonsense. He'd been too long without female . . . companionship, that was all. He had a better use for her than that.

He remembered how at the school she'd effortlessly quelled the gushings of that girl, Lavender Thingy-Whatsit of the Somerset Thingy-Whatsits.

More to the point, he recalled how last night with one word—one word!—she'd stopped Rose in mid-tirade. Rose!

He was a fool not to have seen it at once. Miss Windwhatever! She was the obvious solution. He could go off and do what he had to, leaving the girls with her, knowing she could control their wilder starts. And that they liked her.

She had some odd ideas, of course, but as her employer, he'd soon set her straight on those. As long as she kept her opinions to herself, she was welcome to think whatever she wanted.

Best of all, he'd be off doing the job he was supposed to do, and he wouldn't be there to be tempted by her mouth. Not that he couldn't control himself. The brandy had been the problem last night, and he rarely overindulged.

Who needed Aunt Agatha? The solution had been right under his very nose all this time! Miss Windrush! He rang the bell and called for his coat, hat and gloves. He was going out.

Chapter Six

*If one scheme of happiness fails, human nature turns
to another; if the first calculation is wrong, we make
a second better.*
—JANE AUSTEN, *MANSFIELD PARK*

"I WISH TO SPEAK TO MISS WINDRUSH," CAL TOLD THE gorgon who answered the door.

"There is no Miss Windrush here." She made to push the door shut.

Cal stuck his boot in it. "I might have mistaken her name. Tall, thin female, brown hair, about so high." He indicated with his hand. "One of your teachers."

"You mean Miss Westwood?"

"That's the one."

The gorgon sniffed. "Teachers are not allowed to have gentleman callers."

"I'm not a gentleman caller," Cal snapped, shoving the remembrance of a certain kiss from his mind. "I'm here on business. School business."

The woman considered him a moment. "Very well, I'll have to ask Miss Mallard. Wait here." She pointed to the chairs in the hallway.

He told Miss Mallard, when she condescended to see him, that he merely wished to ask Miss Westwood for advice about his sisters. "I noticed her on my last visit and liked the way she handled the girls in her charge. And my sisters speak well of her, so I thought she might be able to offer me some advice on how to handle them," he lied. He wasn't going to admit he was going to try to poach one of her teachers.

Miss Mallard gave her gracious assent, and the gorgon headed upstairs to fetch Miss Westwood. She came down the stairs, looking puzzled and a little wary. "Lord Ashendon? Is everything all right?"

A delicate flush suffused her creamy complexion, and he had an immediate rush of recollection of how she'd felt in his arms. And how she'd tasted.

It wasn't important, he reminded himself. All that counted was that she could silence Rose with a single word.

"You can talk in there," the gorgon told Cal, and pointed to an elegant sitting room. "And leave the door open. I'll be out here."

"Ghastly woman," Cal muttered. He closed the door and pulled out a chair for Miss Westwood. She sat gracefully, her hands folded in her lap, her eyes meeting his steadily.

He scanned her face for signs of injury. He could see a faint sign of the bruised cheekbone, but she'd covered it with some kind of cosmetic. Her nose was slightly swollen, but otherwise she looked as he'd remembered. Elegant. Composed. Intriguing.

Silence filled the room. Her flush deepened, and Cal realized he'd been staring at her mouth. Again.

"You are recovered from your mishap?" He realized she might take that to mean his kiss, so added hastily, "The altercation at the political meeting, I mean."

"Quite recovered, thank you." She moistened her lips, and he found his gaze riveted to her damp, rosy mouth again. Damn!

He rose, walked to the fireplace, cleared his throat and addressed himself to her left eyebrow. "Before I explain the purpose of my visit today, I must apologize for my behavior last night. It seems I had a little too much to drink and my actions crossed the bounds of, of gentlemanly behavior."

Her eyes met his for a long moment. They seemed to see into his very soul. She gave a little nod. "I thought it must be that. Apology accepted." She glanced down and smoothed her skirt with long, slender fingers. The delicate rose flush faded.

Cal stiffened. Was she implying he'd been clumsy? "It was an unusual circumstance," he began.

"Are the girls all right?" she asked in a brisk, teacherly voice.

Clearly the subject of the kiss was closed. He didn't know whether he was relieved or annoyed. "Yes, yes, of course. At least, I haven't seen them yet—they're still abed, but they'll be all right."

She frowned slightly. "Still in bed at this hour?"

"Avoiding me," Cal said. "Putting off the moment where they'll have to face the music."

"You mean you're going to punish them? Tell me, I'm curious as to what you plan to do."

"Well, that's just it," he said, grateful for the opening. "I don't know how the devil—excuse me—how the deuce I *can* punish them. Nothing I say or do seems to have the slightest effect. Lily cries at the slightest criticism—"

"Crocodile tears or the real thing?"

"What?"

"Lily has the ability to cry at will. If she's crying big crystal tears with no other sign of distress, they're crocodile tears. If she's weeping noisily, red-faced and gulping, her distress is real. So which is it?"

He looked at her in amazement. "I *knew* you were the person to ask. What do they pay you here?"

She stiffened. "I beg your pardon. What business is it of yours?"

"Whatever it is, I'll double it if you'll come and work for me."

Her brows, fine and elegantly winged, rose. "Work for you? As what? Governess? Companion? Duenna?"

He nodded, relieved she hadn't added *mistress*.

"All of those. My aunt is utterly unable to control the girls, and I need someone responsible to take charge."

"Not you, I presume."

"No, I have commitments elsewhere to which I must return. So what do you say? Will you take them on?"

"No, thank you." She said it without the slightest hesitation, as if she didn't even need to think it over.

"What? But I offered to double your wage." It was a handsome offer.

"Yes, but you want me to give up a permanent position here in exchange for a short-term position. Moreover, from what you tell me, I'd need to watch over your sisters twenty-four hours a day, seven days a week, whereas now I get a half day off a week and two evenings free to do whatever I want."

He frowned. He couldn't afford to give her time off. Who knew what the girls would get up to if she was off somewhere having a free evening? "I'd pay you extra not to take those free times."

She appeared to consider it, then shook her head. "Your sisters will marry in a year or two and then where would I be? Out of a job and unemployed." She folded her hands. "So thank you for the very generous offer, but I must decline it."

"Blast!" He stood and took a few impatient strides around the room. "I can't change your mind?"

"No." She rose. "Will that be all?"

"Sit down!" She stiffened and he said, "Sorry—I forget myself. I have the habit of barking out orders sometimes. I mean, stay a little while longer. Please."

"I shan't change my mind."

"I understand. I won't press you, I promise."

She hesitated, then resumed her seat.

He sat down opposite her, ran his fingers through his hair and thought about what to say. "Look, you know my sisters better than I do. I truly want what's best for them, but I freely admit, I've been a soldier most of my adult life, and I'm out of my depth with young girls. I would welcome some advice from an expert."

Her brows rose. There was a short silence. "You've surprised me, Lord Ashendon. I don't know many men—no, make that any men—who would seek advice from a woman."

He shrugged. "Ten years in the army teaches a man to take advantage of local, expert knowledge, no matter what the source."

She gave him a long, level look, then gave that brisk little nod he was coming to recognize. "Very well. Your sisters are bright, they're young and they're bored."

"I know that, but their behavior is— Look at the way they sneaked out last night. And it's not the first time."

"What did you expect? That they'd be happy to spend a year—and now another year—wearing unrelieved black, with limited society, attending repetitious and dull social events with mostly elderly and infirm companionship—oh, yes, they told me all about how their lives had become since leaving the seminary. What sort of society is that for lively young ladies? From what I understand, a visit to the Pump Room, chatting with octogenarians or a walk in the park is the highlight of their day! Is it any wonder they're rebelling?" She rolled her eyes, those very fine sage-green eyes. Her pale complexion was now a delicate pink. Indignation rather than . . . embarrassment? Whatever it was, it suited her.

"You could change that if you accepted my offer of employment."

"I told you, it's out of the question. And please don't try to shift your responsibility onto me."

She had claws, this teacher. "So what do you advise?"

"Give them something *real* to occupy them, something challenging and interesting. Something useful, that's worthwhile doing. Something fun."

He tried to imagine what that might be. "My aunt knits—"

She made a scornful sound. "Would you be happy to sit indoors and knit and sew all day and most evenings?"

"No, of course not. But men are different."

She curled her lip. "They certainly are—they get to choose what they do!"

"Not always," he said. Interesting. The passion with which she was arguing suggested he'd hit a nerve. "Most of the decisions that materially affected my life were made by my father, without any consultation as to my preferences. I didn't choose to be sent away to school at the age of seven, and I was told at the age of about ten that I would be joining the army when I grew up. As a younger son it was that or the church, and my father had no time for priests."

She opened her mouth and he added, "And then I was sent abroad to fight at the age of seventeen, and if you think *any* soldier gets to choose anything, you've got rats in your attic."

It also wasn't his choice to inherit the title and the responsibilities that went with it, but he doubted she'd have any sympathy for that. Most people expected him to be thrilled by the acquisition of a title and a fortune. Most people had no idea.

"I suppose you're right," she said after a moment. "But it seems to me you must have enjoyed your army life. Is that not what you're so anxious to return to? Or am I mistaken?"

"You're not mistaken, but it's not for my own pleasure. I have work to do—important work. Government work."

"Yes, of course," she agreed with deceptive smoothness. "And compared with 'important government work,' what does the welfare and happiness of your sisters matter? Forgive me, I meant your *half* sisters."

The implication that they mattered less to him because they were only half sisters was infuriating. Vixen. She had the ability to deliver the sharpest of insults in the subtlest of ways. It reminded him of—

"You taught my sister Rose quite a bit, didn't you?" He put a slight emphasis on the word *sister*.

She frowned at the abrupt change of subject but responded coolly, "I taught both your sisters."

"Did you indeed? Then why can't Lily read? You seem competent enough." It was deliberate provocation. He was interested to see how she'd respond.

She met his gaze squarely. "I don't know."

"Don't know or don't care?" Her eyes flashed. Ah, that touched a nerve.

Her mouth tightened. "Lily is a dear, sweet girl who has tried harder to learn than any pupil I have ever known. I have tried every method of instruction I know, and some unorthodox methods as well. It is a mystery to me—and a tragedy—that she can still barely read or write."

"You're telling me my sister is stupid?"

"She is not *at all* stupid," she said fiercely. "But for some reason known only to God, she cannot learn to read or write."

"Can she count?" There was that flash again.

"She can count," she said evenly. "She cannot, however, do simple sums—not on paper."

"Anything else she cannot do?"

"She gets her left and right mixed up."

"Is that all?"

She glared at him. "Isn't that enough for the poor child to deal with?"

He shrugged and got up to leave. "It need not be a huge disadvantage in the long run. Most men don't look for brains in a wife, and as you say, Lily is very sweet-natured."

Miss Westwood clenched her fists. "Lord Ashendon."

He waited, one brow raised.

"Lily is affectionate, intelligent, loyal and hardworking! Only a bully punishes a person for what she cannot help."

He gave her a flinty look. "I don't bully my sisters, Miss Westwood. I'm trying to help them."

She looked him straight in the eye. "No, you're trying to get them off your hands with the least amount of trouble to yourself."

It was just close enough to the bone to have Cal's own fists clenching. Damned impertinent schoolmistress. He gave her a curt nod. "Good day to you, madam."

WELL! EMM SAT FOR A MOMENT AFTER LORD ASHENDON had left. Double her current wage! It was a very generous offer.

Had Miss Mallard not decided this morning to offer her the headmistress position, she might have accepted his job.

His job.

When the message had come to her this morning that Lord Ashendon was downstairs asking to speak to her, all kinds of thoughts had rushed through her mind. Foolish thoughts. Scandalous thoughts.

And when he'd stood there at the beginning, staring at her mouth, her heart started thumping in her chest when she thought . . . wondered if he was going to ask her to become . . . But of course, she was foolish even thinking it.

Luckily she hadn't said a thing, because he'd apologized for the kiss—it was the brandy, after all—and made her a job offer. Governess. Companion. Duenna to his sisters.

Which was so much more reasonable and practical—and respectable—than anything Emm was thinking of. Really, she was as bad as the girls, reading more into any gentleman's attentions than existed.

Thank goodness Miss Mallard had chosen this morning, of all mornings, to make her plans for the school clear. Because if she hadn't, Emm might have accepted Lord Ashendon's job. And with all these foolish yearnings she was subject to lately, anything could have happened.

If he was a rake, and if he thought to combine the role of governess/chaperone with the extra position of mistress . . . well, if she was honest with herself, Emm might be tempted.

And that would never do.

ROSE AND LILY CAME DOWNSTAIRS SHORTLY AFTER NOON, subdued but eyeing him warily. Rose's eye was badly swollen, a mere slit of red-rimmed silver-blue in a sea of nasty-looking dark purple. Several other abrasions marked her face. The whole side of Lily's face was swollen and bruised and her mouth was lopsided. She could barely talk.

Cal was appalled. He'd intended to read them the riot act, but at the sight of their poor battered faces—his little sisters—he was filled with a mix of helpless anger, belated protectiveness and shame. Because he was supposed to be looking after them.

Aunt Dottie came with them, clucking distressfully and fussing over the girls. She gave Logan a dozen contradictory orders, sending for various remedies, demanding something *be done!* and ordering the girls' favorite dishes for luncheon. Treating them like little heroines.

Which they damn well weren't! They'd sneaked out against his specific orders and now they'd reaped the rewards of their disobedience and recklessness.

Maybe they'd learned their lesson at last. He ought to be pleased.

But looking at the dreadful mess some unknown swine had made of his sisters' faces, Cal couldn't bring himself to be pleased at all. He wanted to murder the bastard who'd dared to lay hands on them.

"If you'd told me you wanted to go out last night I would have—"

"What? Taken us?" Rose snorted. "To a political meeting? About working women?"

"I might. You never mentioned you had any interest in politics."

Rose shrugged. "We don't. It was the first meeting we've been to and it was boring, wasn't it, Lily? We were all ready to leave, but then—things livened up." Rose tried for an airy grin but winced in pain.

"But what happened?" Aunt Dottie exclaimed. "Tell me! How did this dreadful thing happen?"

"This man tried to touch me . . . personally. And when I objected, he got nasty," Lily said, her words muffled because of her swollen mouth.

"Nasty? He *hit* Lily! Gave her a backhander across the face and did that to her." Rose indicated Lily's swollen face. "So then I punched him!"

"Rose! You *punched* someone?" Aunt Dottie exclaimed in horror.

Rose said in a hard little voice, "He deserved it, Aunt Dottie! Nobody hurts my sister and gets away with it." She flexed her hand gingerly and added with satisfaction, "I bet I'm not the only one with a black eye this morning. But I wish I'd broken his nose."

Both girls had swollen, scraped and badly bruised knuckles on their right hands. Cal rounded the table, picked up Rose's hand and gently examined it. Rose watched him with an odd expression.

"You're lucky you didn't break your hand," he told her as he released it.

Aunt Dottie moaned. "Whatever has happened to my sweet young nieces? Punching people. A vulgar public brawl!"

He examined Lily's hand next. Luckily neither girl seemed to have broken any bones. "You're lucky too."

"*Lily!* Do you mean—don't tell me you hit a perfect stranger too!" Aunt Dottie said in failing accents.

"No, she punched Miss Westwood," Rose said, her good eye brimming with amusement.

What? Cal stiffened. That was how the teacher had been hurt? Lily had punched her?

Aunt Dottie's eyes almost popped. "That nice young teacher? Lily—*why* on earth would you punch dear Miss Westwood? I thought you liked her."

"I do. It was an accident." Lily awkwardly removed her hand from Cal's light grip. "I was trying to stop the man from hurting Rose."

"But Lily, a lady should never . . ." Aunt Dottie shook her head, lost for words.

The teacher's words came back to him. *Should they have simply fainted, then, as society suggests is the proper lady-like response?*

The teacher had never breathed a word of this last night. Protecting Lily from his disapproval.

Was he such an ogre?

No one could blame Lily for resisting molestation. Of course Rose would rush to her sister's defense. He'd seen how protective she was of her younger sister.

And Rutherfords naturally fought back.

Rose glared at Cal as if it were his fault. "Don't look at me like that, Cal. Nobody hurts my sister and gets away with it! I'm glad I did it! I showed him!"

"Rose, you cannot be *boasting* about this dreadful thing, surely," Aunt Dottie said, appalled.

"That's enough, Rose. You're upsetting your aunt," Cal said curtly. He resumed his seat. "I think we've heard quite enough about this contretemps, girls. Now drink your soup before it gets cold."

They finished the meal in silence, more or less. Aunt Dottie began to expostulate once or twice, but Cal silenced her with a look.

"There is an excellent play starting at the theater tomorrow night," Aunt Dottie began when they had finished their meal. "Perhaps—"

"No!" Cal slammed his fist on the table, making them and the cutlery jump. "They broke the rules and they must be punished for it."

"Oh, but—"

"No, Aunt Dottie. They're not showing nearly enough regret or repentance for my liking. Rose is almost proud of her disgraceful behavior." The fact that he was also proud of her was beside the point. She had to learn.

"If I'd been a boy, you would have been proud of me for defending my sister," Rose muttered.

"But you aren't a boy," Cal snapped. "You're not even a lady!" Aunt Dottie gasped, but Cal went on, "You girls know very well you were in the wrong, sneaking out at night against my express orders. You probably think you have been punished enough, but—"

"Oh, Cal—"

"I must insist, Aunt Dottie. They need to learn their lesson. For the next two weeks they're not to attend any function—public or private. They're not to have any outings at all, not even a walk in the park. They shall remain inside the house, and"—he tried to think of what they should do—"and ponder the wages of disobedience. And reckless behavior."

Rose snorted.

"What?" Goaded, he turned on her.

"You mean we cannot even go to the Pump Room?" She put her hands to her face in mock distress. "Oh, dear, that *will* be a hardship."

"Rose," her aunt began.

"Well, as if we even *want* to go out anywhere, looking like this," she said scornfully. "You couldn't make me leave the house if you tried, Brother Dear. Come along, Lily, let's read the next chapter of our book."

Cal gritted his teeth. It was a miracle someone hadn't already strangled Rose.

"You shouldn't provoke him, Rose." Lily climbed up onto her bed.

Rose made an impatient gesture. "I can't help it. He rubs me up the wrong way. He hasn't been near us for years, didn't even write to us while he was away, and now he comes back throwing his weight around and ordering us about as if—as if we're soldiers in his horrid command!"

"He is head of the family," Lily pointed out.

Rose snorted.

"Henry never came near us either and he wasn't away at war, being shot at all the time."

"Henry was a lazy selfish pig."

"And Cal?"

"He's selfish and mean and thoughtless."

"He was lovely when we were little," Lily said. "I remember him taking us for piggyback rides on his back, over and over, as often as we wanted."

"Yes, well he's changed, then, hasn't he?"

"There might be reasons for that," Lily said quietly. "We cannot know what he endured. War is a terrible thing."

Rose hunched a careless shoulder. "He wasn't wounded."

"That we know of. Not all wounds show."

Rose turned on her. "If it was so terrible for him over there, why is he so eager to go back? He doesn't care about *us*, Lily—he just wants to stick us in a safe place and get back to his life. He doesn't care how we feel or what we want." She paced to the window and gazed out into the gray afternoon. "Two weeks stuck in here, Lil—I'm going to go mad!"

"But you said—"

"I know. But I won't give him the satisfaction."

"He's trying, Rose," Lily said quietly.

"He certainly is—extremely trying."

FOR THE NEXT WEEK OR SO, WHILE THE GIRLS WERE recovering from their injuries—and because there was no danger of them sneaking out and showing their bruised and battered faces in public—Cal took the opportunity to check another four names on his list. He traveled to Frome and Midsomer, down to Bruton and then to the other side of Glastonbury. All to no avail.

The longest any of the men had been absent from home in the last five years was a week, and that was to attend a fair. It was disappointing, but at least he was narrowing the field.

He returned to Bath to find a letter from his lawyer that threatened to turn everything upside down.

A disturbing rumor has come to my ears. I hesitate to repeat gossip—and would stress that I have not yet been able to verify it—but there is talk that your brother Henry left a child—a living child.

Cal wasn't surprised. It would be a bastard, of course. Given Henry's proclivities, he wouldn't be surprised if there were more. But a bastard child was easily dealt with—settle an allowance on the mother and make provision for the child's future. All very straightforward. Nothing for a lawyer to get his drawers in a knot about.

He turned the letter around to read the cross-writing.

In the course of my inquiries, I met a fellow who, on finding I represented the new Lord Ashendon, spoke with some heat of Henry's son, George, who I gather is something of a wild child. According to this fellow—who I must say seems quite respectable—your brother begot this lad by an earlier marriage.

I stress that I have no actual evidence of such a marriage and can only conclude that if it did take place, your brother for some reason kept it secret. Of course I have set inquiries in motion, but if this fellow is correct and your brother Henry did leave a son, a legitimate son—well, you will perceive the implications for yourself.

Cal did indeed. But why would Henry have made a secret marriage? There was no reason for it to be secret. Unless it was bigamous—that was a possibility.

Henry had married Mariah just over sixteen years ago, when Cal was twelve and Henry was just two-and-twenty. Mariah had died not quite two years ago and the babe with

her. If this boy was being talked of as a wild child—he
would have to be at least fourteen or fifteen.

It didn't make sense. Cal returned to deciphering the
letter.

> *My informant is from Alderton, a village some fifteen*
> *miles north of Cheltenham, and I understand the child*
> *resides nearby at a place called Willowbank Farm. The*
> *legitimacy or otherwise of this boy needs to be estab-*
> *lished as quickly as possible. Rumors are dangerous*
> *things and estate affairs could be held up for months if*
> *not for years if there is a dispute. I hesitate to ask your*
> *lordship to go in person, but I am off to Canterbury—*
> *finding your brother's will is of the first urgency—and*
> *the fewer who know about this boy, the better. In the*
> *meantime, should you require a legal opinion when you*
> *get there, may I recommend an old acquaintance of my*
> *father's, Mr. Samuel Chiswick, a lawyer, semiretired,*
> *who lives in Alderton. He is both reliable and discreet*
> *and should be able to advise you.*

Cal refolded the letter. Odds on the child would be a
bastard. Phipps was going on hearsay and rumor, which was
ridiculous for a man of the law.

But if the boy did turn out to be legitimate, *he* would be
the new Lord Ashendon, which would free Cal from the rest
of the nonsense. He could make the necessary arrangements
and get back to his life.

Besides, he had another two names to check near Cheltenham. Two birds with one stone.

He sent for Hawkins and instructed him to have the carriage ready first thing in the morning. They were going to
Alderton, a small village north of Cheltenham.

He spoke to the girls before he left and extracted a promise from them that while he was away, they wouldn't venture
out at night unescorted. They weren't happy about it, but
when he promised to take them out somewhere exciting
when he returned, they reluctantly agreed. "Word of a Rutherford."

* * *

"ARE YOU RESPONSIBLE FOR THAT HELL-BORN BRAT?"

"I beg your pardon," Cal said in freezing accents. He'd just stepped down from the carriage, which had pulled up in the main street of Alderton, outside the lawyer's office. And this fellow had taken one look and rushed up to him.

The man looked from Cal to the crest on the carriage and back again. "You've got the look of a Rutherford, all right, and that's the Ashendon crest. You're the new Lord Ashendon, ain't you?"

Cal gave him a cold stare. He had no intention of explaining himself to this mannerless oaf.

"Sorry, should have introduce m'self. Gresham," the man said, unfazed. "Local squire. Master of the Hunt, for all the good it does me." His small blue eyes gleamed angrily in his meaty red face. He turned and beckoned to a tall fellow in baggy breeches and muddy top boots. "The new Lord Ashendon," he told his friend, and jerked his chin toward the crest on the carriage.

The tall man gave his friend a startled look, glanced at the crest and turned to Cal with a warm smile. "Welcome to Gloucestershire, my lord. We are delighted to see you here at last. Simply delighted." And before Cal knew it the fellow was pumping his hand with enthusiasm.

"Planning to remove the little wretch from the district, I hope," the squire interrupted. "Haven't had a proper hunt in years. Much longer and someone's going to shoot the brat."

Cal stiffened.

"Not your fault, we know that," Muddy-boots said hastily. "Blame your brother. Never showed any interest in the child. Not young George's fault, not really. A child needs a firm hand on the bridle—"

The squire snorted. "Firm hand? Needs a damned good thrashing if you ask me. Interfering in *the hunt*, dammit— it's not, not *English*!"

"I will deal with the matter," Cal said crisply. "In the meantime, I'm looking for the lawyer, Chiswick." He indicated the doorway with the brass plate attached.

"Out, I'm afraid," Muddy-boots said. "Saw him heading out of town an hour ago."

"I see. Could you direct me to Willowbank Farm?"

Muddy-boots gave him the directions. Cal glanced up at Hawkins, who nodded to indicate he'd heard them.

Muddy-boots gave a satisfied nod. "Can we count on you removing that—er, removing young George from the district, Lord Ashendon?"

"I'll make my decision when I've gathered all the relevant information. Good day, gentlemen." He climbed into the carriage and rapped on the roof, and in minutes the village was behind them.

Henry had obviously acknowledged the boy—at least locally, if not to his family. He sounded like a youth, rather than a child—a wild and uncontrollable one, at that.

The army was the perfect place for wild, uncontrollable youths. A disciplined environment and a worthy job to do, a little responsibility and the wildest lad could be tamed. A cavalry regiment, perhaps, for young George. It was the obvious solution.

Chapter Seven

WILLOWBANK FARM LOOKED SHABBY AND NEGLECTED.
Weeds studded the rutted lane that led to the house, and the
garden was overgrown and straggly. The paint on the frames
surrounding the windows was peeling, as was the front door.

As they drove up, a large gray wolfhound loped toward
them, barking. The front door opened and a lanky youth
appeared. "Finn. Come here!" The dog gave the carriage
wheels a longing look, then trotted obediently back to his
master.

Dressed in worn buff riding breeches, a shabby green
jacket and high leather riding boots splattered with mud,
the youth made no move to come and greet the visitor. One
hand on the dog's collar, he eyed the carriage and its occu-
pant with suspicion.

He looked to be about sixteen or seventeen, with an an-
gular face, pointed chin and closely cropped curly dark hair.
There was a faint, barely discernible resemblance to Henry.

Cal leapt lightly down from the carriage. "Would you be
George?" he asked, realizing he didn't know the boy's surname.

The boy scowled and raised his chin. "Who's asking?"
And there, suddenly, was the resemblance Cal had been
looking for: the famous Rutherford scowl, evident in half
the ancestral portraits that graced the family portrait gallery
at Ashendon.

"I'm your uncle, Cal Rutherford." Cal held out his hand.

The boy made no move to take it. He scanned Cal suspiciously for a good minute, his hand tight on the dog's collar. Then he released the dog with a muttered order to stay, and moved reluctantly forward. "George Rutherford."

Cal watched the way the lad strode toward him. "No, you're not," he said slowly. "Georgina, or Georgette, maybe, but not George."

His niece's gray eyes flashed. "I prefer George."

"I'm sure you do, but what does it say on the parish register?"

She met his question with a mulish expression and a chin lifted in silent challenge. There was a streak of dried mud across her forehead. He waited. After a moment she said sulkily, "Georgiana. But I don't answer to that."

"We'll discuss it later. In the meantime, I presume there is someone to help see to the horses?" Usually a stableboy would have come out at the first sign of a coach arriving, but there was no sign of anyone.

"I'll see to them."

Cal's brows rose. "Thank you. I'll meet you in the house in, shall we say ten minutes?"

"You're very free with my home," she snapped.

"A habit of uncles," Cal answered with mock sympathy. He was pleased to have her distracted. It would give him a chance to get the lay of the land.

HE FOUND THE SITTING ROOM, A SHABBY BUT COMFORTABLE-looking room with overstuffed armchairs and lined with bookshelves. A small fire glowed sullenly in a large stone fireplace. Darker patches on the faded paint showed where paintings had once hung. Where were they now?

Cal noticed a small pile of papers—legal documents?—on a table next to the window. He picked up the top one.

It was a letter from Chiswick, the lawyer in Alderton, advising Miss Georgiana to find her mother's marriage lines and other documentation so he could contest her father's will.

Marriage lines? Then Miss Georgiana was no bastard after all.

He glanced through the lawyer's letter again, then read through the fair copy of Henry's will that lay beneath it. He felt a spurt of anger on the girl's behalf.

The will made no mention of Georgiana. He'd left her nothing. Not a penny. Dammit, she was his daughter. Henry had no business leaving her without any visible means of support.

How did she live? Who was looking after her? There was no sign of any other adult in evidence. Cal sifted through the documents to see what else he could learn.

A cold draft from the door alerted him to his niece's return. "How dare you! Those papers are private!" She stormed forward and snatched them out of his hand, her gray eyes sparking with anger. Eyes the exact same color as Cal's. "Who do you think you are, walking into my home and looking through my private—"

"I told you, I'm your uncle, Calbourne Rutherford, Lord Ashendon since your father died, and currently head of your family."

She put her chin up. "I've only got your word for it that you're my uncle."

"That and the evidence of your looking glass—if you use one," he added, noticing a fresh smear of mud on her cheek. Did she always greet her guests with a dirty face and smelling of the stables?

She scowled, and the family resemblance was even more pronounced. Oh, lord, everyone was going to take this touchy ragamuffin for his daughter.

"How old are you?"

She stiffened. "None of your b—"

"You look about sixteen."

"I'm eighteen. I turned eighteen last month."

"And who is looking after you?"

She snorted. "I'm not a child. I don't need to be looked after. I can take care of myself!"

"Let me rephrase the question; whom do you live with?"

"Finn." She put a hand on the dog's collar. "And Martha."

"Where is this Martha?" Her companion or chaperone, presumably.

"In the kitchen—where else?"

"Be so good as to fetch her."

"Fetch her yourself. You can't just march in here and start throwing orders around!"

"I think you'll find I can. I'm your closest relative, which, until you're twenty-one, makes me your guardian. You'll do as I tell you."

"I won't!"

"If you've read and understood these documents, you know the law will support me. Now run along and fetch this Martha, will you?"

As much as anyone could flounce in breeches and boots, his niece Georgiana flounced from the room, making her point by slamming the door resoundingly behind her.

He stood, warming himself by the fire, contemplating his rash statement. But he could see no way around it. He had to take her under his control. This place was a disgrace and as for her behavior, well, it seemed she was running true to form with Rutherford females.

"You wanted to speak to me, sir?" An elderly woman stood in the doorway, smoothing her apron with anxious hands.

"Martha?"

"Aye, sir, Martha Scarrat, cook and housekeeper, and before that, nursemaid when Miss George were a wee babe."

Cook and housekeeper? He frowned. "Is there anyone else to help you? Any other servants?"

She shook her head. "No, sir. Not since—well, not for a few years now. Mr. Henry stopped sending the money some years ago. But we manage." She hesitated, then said, "You have a slight look of Mr. Henry, sir, would you be a relative of Miss George's?"

"I am her uncle, Lord Ashendon."

Martha bobbed an awkward curtsey. "Sorry, m'lord. She said someone wanted to speak to me and stormed outside. Got a bit of a temper, Miss George has, but she's a good-hearted lass."

Cal nodded. A good-hearted lass? An undisciplined brat,

more like. "You said you'd cared for Miss Georgiana since she was a babe. Where is her mother?"

"Miss Mary—I mean Mrs. Rutherford—died not long after giving birth to Miss George. Mr. Henry had left her by then. Fair shattered her heart, he did."

"My brother married her? You're sure of that?"

"Oh, yes sir, old Mr. Foster—Miss Mary's father—made sure it was all legal like. He wasn't going to have some London rake seduce his precious only daughter and not do right by her. They were married right and tight in the church here—the banns called and all—and he made Mr. Henry buy her this house and make her an allowance. Documents were signed, they were. The lawyer in the village, Mr. Chiswick, has copies."

"I see." Documented and legal, he had no doubt. So why hadn't Henry informed his family?

The old woman added, "Miss George and me have been on our own since her grandparents died. Jem, the stableboy, stayed for a while, but a body can't live without wages, so he left last summer."

"And what about your own wages?"

The old woman gave him an indignant look. "I don't need paying to look after Miss George, sir—I love that child like my own. Were you wanting something to eat, sir, because I've some soup on the hob and a nice bit of bread and cheese, if you'd like your dinner early."

Hooves clattered on the cobbles outside, causing Cal to turn and look out the window. There was a blur of movement and then all he could see was a lithe figure astride a black stallion disappearing into the distance, a gray wolfhound loping along beside it.

Cal swore. "Was that—?"

"Miss George, yes. She does that from time to time—goes off on her lonesome with nothing but her horse and that hound—high spirited, she is—but never you mind, sir, she'll be back in a day or so."

"A *day* or so?" And where the hell did she stay while she was on these . . . outings?

The old woman nodded comfortably, not seeming to notice

his outrage. "Aye. Never more than three days. But there's no need to worry, sir, she always comes back, safe and sound. Now, will you be wanting—"

"A brandy, if there is such a thing in this benighted house."

"No brandy, I'm afraid, sir, but there's some parsnip wine if you fancy that." She smiled at him in a motherly fashion. "Now don't you fret about Miss George. It does no good, sir, no good at all. She goes her own ways, that lass. Always has and always will." And she shuffled off.

"Not if I have anything to do with it," Cal muttered as his niece disappeared over the horizon.

Damn Henry for a neglectful parent. Why the hell hadn't he told Papa about the girl? Papa might have been a cold man, but he had a strong sense of family—and duty—and would gladly have taken a legitimate granddaughter in to raise with his own daughters.

Instead Henry had treated his only living child like a dirty little secret and left her to sink or swim on her own. Well, that would change.

This was no way for a young woman of good birth to live, in an isolated, run-down old farmhouse with no company but an old woman, a dog and a horse—and no income. And with half the hunting fraternity of the district apparently baying for her blood.

He sighed. Georgiana was even more undisciplined than his sisters. Putting them together would be like trying to put a fire out by adding oil to it. But he had no choice.

He swore under his breath. Dealing with two spirited young Rutherford females had nearly driven him to drink. What the hell was he going to do with three?

He had to take Georgiana back to Bath with him and prepare her—somehow—to enter her proper milieu. Or rather, pay someone to prepare her. He thought of the long-legged teacher again. She'd know how to do it. He'd have to increase his offer, make it worth her while.

HE WROTE A NOTE TO AUNT DOTTIE AND TOLD HER TO expect him back in a few days, along with a previously unknown niece. He wrote another letter to Phipps, explaining the situation, and a note to the lawyer Chiswick, asking him to call at Willowbank Farm at his earliest convenience.

He rang for Martha and Hawkins and gave them instructions to go into the village, post the letters, deliver the note and purchase whatever was needed for them all to be comfortable for the next few days—food, household goods, stable supplies, whatever.

He handed Martha a sum that made her eyes bulge. "And of course, anything you might require for yourself, Mrs. Scarrat. I will be making arrangements to have your back wages paid to you, but in the meantime, purchase whatever you want."

As they turned to leave, he thought of something else. "Mrs. Scarrat, am I to understand that the clothing my niece wore today is her usual attire?"

"You mean breeches and boots? Yes, sir, I mean, my lord."

"Then be so good as to purchase her a couple of dresses. And whatever else goes with and under them." He handed her an extra few banknotes.

The old woman's eyes widened. "Dresses, sir? But Miss George won't wear dresses. She won't wear nothing except breeches and boots."

Cal gave her a steely smile. "We'll see about that."

CHISWICK THE LAWYER CAME FIRST THING THE NEXT morning. At first he was inclined to be stiff and formal and clearly prepared for battle, but once Cal had made it clear that he was disgusted by his brother's neglect of his daughter and wanted to do right by her and her servants, the silver-haired old gentleman rapidly unbent.

"I don't understand why Henry kept the marriage so secret."

"She wasn't of his station," Chiswick told him. "Perfectly respectable family—good yeomen farmers—but not the right kind of wife for the heir to the Earl of Ashendon."

"Do you think she tried to entrap Henry into marriage?"

Chiswick shook his head. "Nobody around here knew

who he really was until long after the wedding. He came among us as plain Mr. Rutherford—rusticating, I believe the young bloods used to call it. Well, he took one look at pretty young Mary Foster and made a beeline for her. Sought her out at every opportunity."

He sighed regretfully. "A lovely girl she was, just seventeen. Pretty as a picture, sweet-tempered and innocent as a spring lamb." He shot Cal a glance from under gray beetling brows. "Your brother seduced her, the blackguard."

Cal nodded. "But he must have cared for her enough to marry her."

Chiswick snorted. "No choice in the matter. Mary's father, George Foster, was a formidable fellow, for all that he was a farmer. Once he realized what had happened, he marched Henry up to the church, instructed the vicar to call the banns and kept Henry locked in the cellar until his wedding day." He chuckled. "Henry was beside himself with rage at first— I went along as legal counsel to draw up the settlements—but the moment Foster demanded to know who Henry's father was and threatened to go and fetch him, Henry quietened down and went through the service like a lamb."

"My father was also a formidable man," Cal said. "He would have made Henry pay." If not for seducing an innocent, for getting caught. "At the very least he would have cut off Henry's very generous allowance. Henry would have hated that."

"We found out who he really was after Mary had died giving birth to young George." Chiswick set his cup down and sighed. "I'd written to let him know, of course—" He saw Cal's surprised look and added, "Oh, yes, he left her a few weeks after the wedding."

Cal swore beneath his breath. A brother to be proud of indeed. Abandoning his pregnant seventeen-year-old wife.

"I went up to London to notify him in person—and to point out his duty to the babe. That's when I found out who he really was, that he was the heir to the Earl of Ashendon," the old man said in a level voice. "The notice of his betrothal to Lady Mariah Eglinton appeared in the *Morning Post* exactly one month later."

There was a long silence, broken only by the crackling of the fire and the wind outside in the trees.

The old lawyer added, "Young George doesn't take after her mother much—she's all Rutherford for the most part. But when she smiles, ah, when she smiles, you can see her mother in her then. Sweetest smile in the world."

Cal was yet to see George smile. He was most familiar with her version of the Rutherford scowl.

"The family had no idea of any of this," Cal told the old gentleman. "If my father had known, he would have taken the baby in and had her raised at Ashendon Court, as was her right. She wouldn't have been"—he gestured—"running wild."

Chiswick gave a wry grin. "And there would be a dashed sight fewer foxes in the district."

"Has she really managed to disrupt the hunt? I met a few fellows in the village yesterday who expressed themselves in the strongest terms."

Chiswick nodded. "Have you seen her ride?"

"I have," Cal said grimly.

"With that black stallion of hers and a bag of smoked herring heads, she's managed to bring the local hunt pretty much to its knees for the last three seasons. Got a soft spot for wild creatures, has young George."

"Well, the hunters can relax. I'll be removing her from the district."

The old man shot him a searching look. "To what purpose?"

"I have two half sisters the same age as she is. It will be easier to look after them all together." He saw the man's hesitation. "What? You don't imagine I'd leave her here, running wild and trying to hold things together on her own, do you?"

"It's not that," Chiswick said. "Have you told George yet? I can't imagine she'll agree. Very attached to her home, she is."

"Georgiana is eighteen," Cal reminded him. "It's time she was thinking about marriage. I'll launch all three of them together in London next season."

As he uttered the words he realized it was the very solution. *Get them married off as quickly as you can. Make them some other man's problem.*

"Won't she be in mourning for her father?" Chiswick asked. "And your sisters for their uncle?"

Damn. That was right. They were supposed to spend a year in mourning because of Henry. Another year of mourning for his sisters.

People took these conventions so seriously. Why make such a display of death? As if draping yourself in black made any difference to how much you grieved. Or didn't.

During the war, Cal had lived with death all around him, an everyday occurrence, a constant presence. He'd lost friends, good friends and comrades. He still missed some of them. But he'd learned not to wallow in the pain or dwell on the loss—not that there was any time for wallowing in wartime.

He thought of the outbreak of public mourning for the death of Princess Charlotte the previous year. It wasn't just about grieving, though the nation did sincerely grieve her loss. It was also a show of respect.

But as far as Cal was concerned, death was a reminder to mankind to get on with the business of living. His preferred response to death was to celebrate life, not shroud yourself in black and retreat from it.

A year of mourning for Henry? Henry didn't deserve it. And neither did the girls.

No, Cal would launch all three girls together in London this coming season.

And then he remembered. He'd be on the Continent in a couple of weeks, God willing.

Well, someone would launch the girls. His aunt or someone. He'd work out who later.

GEORGIANA STAYED AWAY FOR ANOTHER TWO NIGHTS AND two days. Cal used the time to check on the men on his list. Without success.

He would have wagered she'd have stayed longer had the weather not turned nasty, with a bitter wind and driving sleet coming down in sheets.

As it was, she simply appeared shortly before dinner on the third day, soaking wet, her boots and breeches covered in mud, but otherwise as cool and unconcerned as if she'd just stepped out for a moment. And without a word of acknowledgment—or apology—for her outrageous disappearance.

"Don't fuss, Martha dear. I'm perfectly all right. It's just a bit of mud and water. Is there any hot water? I'll take a bath if there is."

"And so you should, Miss George—catch your death one day, out like a savage in this weather, you mark my words! Now, get along upstairs. I'll fetch the hot water to you at once."

"And when you've had your bath," Cal said as the girl turned to go, "you will change into one of the two new dresses you'll find in your bedchamber."

"Dresses! I'm not wearing any dresses!"

"Suit yourself, but no dress, no dinner," Cal said indifferently. "I'll see you before dinner in the sitting room."

She gave him a mulish look. From the kitchen wafted the scent of roasting beef and Yorkshire pudding. Apple pie and clotted cream to follow. He'd wager she was ravenous. From the look of her she'd been living rough, sleeping in some old shed or haystack. There was straw in her hair. He wanted to throttle the stubborn little wretch for her foolishness.

The thought occurred to him, not for the first time, that she would have made a superb soldier. He squashed it.

She'd learn.

Georgiana entered the sitting room half an hour later, wearing one of the dresses. Her skin looked fresh and clean; her short, dark hair, still damp, curled attractively around her face. A little attention to grooming and deportment and she'd be a beauty.

"I hope you're satisfied. I look ridiculous!" she snapped as soon as she saw him.

Cal stood as she entered. He shook his head. "You don't, you know. You look very pretty. You look better as a girl than as a boy." It was true. As a boy she looked skinny and lanky, but somehow the dress transformed that into a slender, deceptively delicate femininity.

She scowled horribly at him and flung herself into one of the overstuffed chairs in front of the fireplace. She went to cross her legs, as she usually did in her breeches, and discovered that dresses didn't allow for such freedom of movement. She swore.

Cal was hard put not to laugh out loud. He controlled the impulse. Treating her with the dignity of a grown-up lady was the only way to reconcile her to her new state.

"Would you care for a sherry?" he asked.

She didn't answer, so he poured her one anyway. When he turned to give it to her he found her standing behind him, still scowling. She took it, tossed it down in one gulp, then coughed.

"It's meant to be sipped," Cal told her, and refilled the little glass.

"It's horrid," she said. "I notice you're not drinking it."

"No, but ladies don't drink cognac. You wouldn't like it, either."

She gave him a filthy look, drank her sherry down—again in one gulp—coughed, put the glass down and prowled around the room. She noticed that the documents on the window table had been rearranged and whirled around. "Snooping again, were you?"

"Familiarizing myself with my ward's situation, yes," he said. "And writing letters."

She picked up the ink pot. "Oops!" She didn't sound the least bit upset. Quite the reverse. "Oh, dear. What a calamity. And my new dress too."

He looked up. She'd spilled an entire pot of black ink down the front of her new gown. It was ruined. He gritted his teeth.

"You mustn't have stoppered the ink pot properly," she said, innocent as a kitten. "I'll just go up and change, shall I?"

"No, wear this shawl over it," he told her. "It will cover the stain." He tossed her an old woolen shawl that had been draped across one of the chairs. He had no doubt that if he allowed her to change, the second dress would go the way of the first.

"That's Martha's shawl."

He shrugged. "I'm sure she won't mind. Now, shall we

go in to dinner, or is there something else you need to destroy first?" He offered her his arm.

They ate Martha's magnificent dinner in silence.

"I'll see you in the other dress for breakfast," he told Georgiana at the end of the meal. From the look of her, she'd sleep like a log all night. "And if anything untoward happens to the other dress, you will get no breakfast."

She gave an indifferent shrug, but he could tell by her expression that the fate of the second dress would now be delayed until after breakfast. Which exactly suited his plans.

Chapter Eight

GEORGIANA CAME DOWN TO BREAKFAST WEARING A BLACK scowl and a blue flowered dress—his threat had worked. Thank God for young women with healthy appetites. Her footsteps on the wooden floor suggested that beneath the dress she was wearing her boy's riding boots, but Cal was prepared to accept that in the spirit of compromise.

Having spent up big in the village, Martha served a slap-up breakfast—eggs, ham, fresh-baked sweet rolls, hot chocolate for Georgiana, coffee for Cal. It was something in the way of a last supper, though his niece didn't know that. She was too busy resenting Cal to notice Martha's uncharacteristic silence.

He'd made his plans during his niece's three-day absence. He'd made arrangements with Chiswick and sworn Martha and Hawkins to secrecy.

As they finished off the last of the magnificent breakfast, he heard Hawkins bringing the carriage around. Georgiana looked up. "Are you going somewhere?"

"Yes, I'm leaving for Bath this morning."

"Excellent!" She grinned at him then, and though it was a grin of triumph, not to say glee, he glimpsed a trace of the sweetness Chiswick had mentioned.

"Have you finished your breakfast?"

"Yes."

"Then say good-bye to Martha."

"Oh, my precious girl!" Martha burst into tears and hugged her.

"What's going on? Why are you upset?" Georgiana hugged her back, glaring at Cal over Martha's shoulder. "Are you sending Martha away? Because if you are—"

"No, no, my darling girl," Martha sobbed, smoothing Georgiana's hair back from her face. "Don't worry about me, his lordship's been everything that's kind and generous. He's even sent for my sister and her boys to come and live here. It's just . . . I'll miss you."

"Miss me? But why? If you're staying here—" She broke off, whirled around and faced Cal with a belligerent expression. "What are you up to? I'm not going anywh—"

"You're going to Bath with me." Cal bent and tossed her over his shoulder. "Good-bye, Martha," he said, quite as if he didn't have an infuriated niece kicking and wriggling and spitting fury like a wildcat. "I'll keep you up to date with arrangements. Thank you for your assistance."

The struggling stopped for a moment. "Martha, did you *know* about this?" The betrayal in her voice was heartbreaking. Cal hardened his heart against it. If he'd simply told her, there would be more drama and argument and no doubt she'd gallop away on her black stallion for another three days or more. He didn't have that much time to waste.

Martha sobbed, "I'm that sorry, lovie, truly I am, but it's for the best. I can't be living in the city, you know that. You're upset now, but in the long run, you'll know it was the right thing."

"I *won't*! I'll never forgive you—no, not you, Martha—*him*!" She pummeled his back with hard little fists. "I know who's to blame for this, this *kidnapping*! He's even *worse* than my pig of a father!"

Cal strode toward the front door. His ribs were regretting the riding boots now. He should have made her change into the soft little slippers ladies usually wore.

Hawkins waited outside with the carriage door open. "All secure?" Cal asked him.

"Yes, m'lord."

Cal deposited his niece in the carriage and climbed in after her. Hawkins shut the door after him and climbed swiftly up to take up the reins.

Inside the carriage, Georgiana made a dive for the opposite door. She struggled with the handle for a moment, then turned to glare at Cal.

"It's locked," he told her. "There's no point in fighting. You're outnumbered." He rapped on the roof of the carriage and, with a lurch, it moved off.

She stuck two fingers in her mouth and let out a long shrill whistle.

He sighed and continued, "If you've quite finished deafening me—"

"I'm taking Finn." She let out another earsplitting whistle.

"No, the dog stays here," he said, firmly shutting his mind against the memory of his own desolation at having to leave his own dog behind when he was sent off to school. "He's far too big and ungainly for my aunt's town house. And he would be miserable shut up in her small backyard." More to the point, Cal had no intention of traveling in a closed carriage with a damp, muddy, smelly beast the size of a pony.

"So I am to have nobody and nothing of my own, then?" She'd tried for toughness, but there was an underlying pathos to her words.

"I know it's all very strange and unsettling, Georgiana, but bear with me. I cannot descend on Aunt Dottie with a collection of large animals and an old retainer, as well as a great-niece she knew nothing about. Her house isn't big enough, for a start."

"Then leave me here!"

"At times, we all have to do things we don't want to do. Your grandfather was the Earl of Ashendon. His life was laid out for him because of who he was. Your late father was, for the last year of his life, also the Earl of Ashendon, as I am now. None of us had any choice in it—we were simply born to that position, and fate did the rest. And the same goes for you."

She gave him a startled look. "Me?"

He nodded. "Your father was an earl, so you are now Lady Georgiana Rutherford—has nobody ever told you that?"

She shook her head.

"Well, you are, and it is not fitting for Lady Georgiana Rutherford to continue living the life you've been living here."

"But I'm happy here."

"You can be happy anywhere if you put your mind to it. Now don't worry—Martha is perfectly content with the arrangement. As soon as it's convenient I'll send for the dog— and yes, the horse as well. It's obvious you love to ride and he's a fine animal."

She sniffed. "How do I know you'll keep your promise?"

"I am not in the habit of breaking my word," he said stiffly.

She rolled her eyes. "Heard that before. Apparently my father was fond of saying, 'My word is my bond,' and we all knew what that meant."

"I am *nothing* like your father."

She shrugged. "Who will take care of Sultan? He can be difficult. He hates strangers—"

"Chiswick said he thought Jem Stubbins, your former stableboy, would be willing. He is currently working for a butcher, a job that is not to his taste. I trust you approve?"

She scrunched herself into the corner seat farthest away from Cal. "Thought of everything, haven't you?" It wasn't a compliment.

After about ten minutes on the main road, the carriage slowed. Hawkins opened the communication hatch.

"What is it, Hawkins?"

"It's Miss George's dawg, m'lord. It's following us."

Georgiana's face lit up. "See, Finn goes everywhere with me. He always has. Let him in, oh, please let him in."

"Keep going, Hawkins. The dog will give up soon and return home."

"I hate you!" Georgiana curled up in her corner, a hostile ball of misery.

The carriage picked up speed again. Fifteen minutes later, Hawkins slowed again. "It's still following, m'lord."

Georgiana leaned forward and put a hand on Cal's knee. Tears glimmered on her long lashes. "Please. Finn won't give up. He'll follow us until he drops. His paws will be bleeding . . ."

Cal sighed. "Let the blasted animal in." The carriage came to a halt and he opened the door. Georgiana whistled again, and a moment later the dog clambered awkwardly into the carriage, his ribs heaving with exhaustion, a panting red tongue lolling halfway down his chest.

Georgiana gave the great beast a rapturous welcome, cooing over him as if he were a lapdog. "Finn, oh, Finn darling. What a good, clever dog you are! Yes, you are!"

Cal watched gloomily. The dog was huge. He was wet, he was muddy, he had probably never been bathed in his life. Now that he was reunited with his mistress, his long scraggy tail lashed ecstatically back and forth, sending joyous splatters of mud and filth in all directions—mainly over Cal's pristine coat and breeches.

And the smell—dear God!

Georgiana gave him an apologetic glance. "He must have found a dead bird to roll in. He's very fond of rolling in dead things."

Of course he was. Cal tried not to breathe.

The roads were clear, the weather good, the ostlers at the coach houses fast and efficient, and they made good time to Bath. Hawkins secured the horses and let down the carriage steps. Cal, his hand gripping the dog's collar, waited to let his niece descend first.

"Bring our luggage in, then see to the horses," he told Hawkins.

"*Our* luggage? I don't have any luggage," Georgiana said.

"Martha packed you a bag."

"*Et tu*, Martha," she muttered. So, she'd had some sort of education after all.

Cal eased himself past the enormous hound, descended the steps and, before the dog could push past him and jump down, he quickly closed the door, shutting the dog inside the carriage.

"But, Finn—" Georgiana began.

"Will go with Hawkins, who will have him thoroughly washed and dried before springing the beast on Aunt Dottie."

"You're the beast," she muttered.

"How am I goin' to wash a dawg that size?" Hawkins grumbled. "More to the point, *where* am I goin' to do it?"

Cal flipped him a guinea piece. "How you manage it is your business. This is Bath—there will be somewhere. I want him back clean and fresh and free of fleas. And then you will clean the carriage from top to bottom—and particularly the inside, which now has a distinct stench of *eau de dog*."

Hawkins peered in at the dog, who immediately woofed at him, a big deep sound. "He won't bite me, will he, Miss George?"

"Not if he likes you." Then she laughed. "No, he doesn't usually bite people. Although . . . he's never had a bath before. Perhaps I'd better go with—"

Cal caught her by the sleeve. "You're coming inside with me. Hawkins will manage. You need to meet Great-Aunt Dottie and your aunts."

"WELCOME, DEAR GIRL, WELCOME TO THE FAMILY! I'M YOUR aunt—oh, that would be great-aunt, but just call me Aunt Dottie like the others do." She embraced Georgiana with all the affection and enthusiasm in her soul, as if the girl were a child she'd loved all her life and had dearly missed.

And in a way, she was, Cal thought. Aunt Dottie was such a dear.

Georgiana stood awkwardly in her embrace, uncertain of how to respond. Rose and Lily—whom he was pleased to find at home—stood quietly by, watching curiously.

"Oh, my, but you're a Rutherford through and through, aren't you?" Aunt Dottie exclaimed. "It was *wicked* of Henry not to tell us about you, positively wicked! Not that you look a lot like your father—Henry took after his mother more— but Cal, now!"

All eyes turned to Cal.

"You're the living image of Cal before he was sent away to be a soldier. Oh, now, now, don't pull that face, my dear, I don't mean you're not pretty—of course you are, very pretty

indeed—just as Cal was at sixteen. He was such a pretty boy
back then, quite ravishing, I do assure you."

Cal rolled his eyes.

"Oh, heavens, where are my manners? You haven't even
met your aunts yet, have you, Georgiana, and here am I
babbling on like the veriest brook! This is your aunt Rose
and her younger sister, Lily. Rose and Lily, come and greet
your new niece, Georgiana."

"George."

Aunt Dottie blinked. Her gaze dropped to the girl's neckline, where there was faint but undeniable evidence of femininity. "I beg your pardon."

"My name. I prefer to be called George."

"Really?"

"I've been called George for as long as I remember." She
shot a defiant glance at Cal. "He's the only one who calls
me Georgiana. I don't answer to it."

"You'll learn to," Cal growled.

"Of course, my dear, if you wish to be called George—"
Aunt Dottie began.

"No," Cal said. "It's not appropriate." Especially given
her predilection for wearing boots and breeches. He didn't
want his niece getting a name for eccentricity—deserved
or not. Not before he had her off his hands, at any rate.

"Nonsense," said Aunt Dottie briskly. "If that's what the
child prefers—"

"It's not fitting."

"Why not?" Rose interjected. "You prefer being called
Cal instead of Calbourne."

Her new niece gave her a cautious smile.

"Yes, but Cal is not a girl's name. George is—"

Rose slipped her arm through Georgiana's. "What about
Calpurnia, the wife of Julius Caesar? I bet Caesar called her
Cal for short."

Cal gritted his teeth. "Her proper name is George*iana*."

"You call her that then, dear," Aunt Dottie said happily.
"We'll stick to George—a perfect compromise. I think
George, especially for such a pretty girl, is rather charming.

It would be different if she were plain and mannish, of course, but she's not. In fact, I think the name will underline her femininity delightfully. Besides, she'll be called Lady George by most people, which has a certain cachet, don't you think? Now, shall we all go in to supper? Cal dear, your arm."

Cal gave up. He took his aunt in to supper.

The girls seemed to be getting on well, he observed gloomily. Of course they were. Divide and conquer? No such luck.

At the end of supper, Lily said, "Let us take George up to our bedchamber—she'll be sharing with Rose and me—Logan moved another bed in yesterday. We'll help her unpack."

"I don't have much to unpack," Georgiana said, looking at Cal. "But what about my d—"

Cal cut her off. "When Hawkins has completed the task I set him, then we shall see. Go along upstairs; I will prepare Aunt Dottie for what is to come." He narrowed his eyes at her in a silent order.

She eyed him doubtfully, gave a halfhearted shrug and allowed herself to be led away.

"That sounds exciting," Aunt Dottie said. "What is 'to come'?"

Cal sighed. "Let us go into the sitting room and I'll explain."

GEORGE'S NEWFOUND AUNTS LED HER TO A LARGE, elegant bedchamber with a wide bay window that overlooked the street. It was as large as the big sitting room at home, and even with three beds in the room, it still didn't feel cramped. The walls were covered with pale green paper in an elegant Chinese design, and two of the bedcoverings had obviously been made to match.

A shabby valise was sitting on the third bed. "Shall we send for a maid to unpack that for you?" Rose asked.

"No!" She moderated her tone. "I mean, no, thank you. I prefer to do it myself."

"Logan found that for you to use." Lily pointed to a small

chest of drawers beside the bed. "I hope there's enough room for all your things. And you can share our wardrobe, of course."

Rose and Lily sat on their own beds and waited expectantly. George swallowed. Everything here was so fancy and fine, she was embarrassed to open her case and expose the paucity of her possessions. What had Martha packed for her?

She opened it and, as expected, on the top lay her new petticoats and chemises and other female bits and pieces, separated from whatever lay beneath by a layer of paper. They were plain and the fabric was a bit coarse—Alderton village didn't run to fancy clothing. She shoved them quickly into the drawers, feeling angry with herself. She didn't care about clothes anyway. It was just . . . she wanted her new relatives to think well of her.

She reached for the layer of paper, dreading what she might find underneath. The hideous pink, ink-stained dress? More dresses from the village? She lifted the paper and blinked. As she quickly flipped through the neatly packed layers her grin grew. She did a little dance. "Thank you, Martha!"

"What is it?" Rose and Lily leaned forward curiously.

"I thought I'd never see these again." She lifted up a pair of her breeches. Martha had packed all three pairs of breeches, several coats, four good shirts and two waistcoats, as well as her two best pairs of boots.

"Breeches?" Rose exclaimed. "*Men's* breeches?"

"These are mine," George said gleefully. "Until your brother started interfering in my life, that's all I ever wore." She plucked distastefully at her blue dress. "He forced me to wear this thing."

"How dare he!" Rose said indignantly. "That fashion is years out of date, and the fabric is cheap and a bit garish." She bit her lip. "Sorry, I hope I didn't offend you."

George laughed. "Not at all. I hate it too."

"It's also too loose," Lily observed sympathetically. "Or have you lost weight recently?"

"No, he made Martha buy it for me in the village while my back was turned. I expect there wasn't much choice. But I couldn't care less about fashion. I don't want to wear dresses at all. They're not at all comfortable, and they're so . . . so flimsy and fragile. I feel naked wearing them."

The two sisters exchanged glances. "Naked? I've never noticed that," Lily said.

"Well, you probably haven't worn breeches. When I put this dress on this morning—only because he threatened to starve me—I felt so . . . exposed."

Rose nodded. "The neckline?"

"Yes, but mainly around the legs. There are *drafts*," she said darkly.

"But your legs are completely covered," Lily said, puzzled.

George grinned. "They are now." She pulled up her skirts and revealed the breeches and boots she wore underneath.

Rose and Lily exclaimed—they were clearly a bit shocked—but they begged George to put her boy's clothes on so they could see how she looked.

George was happy to oblige and when she was fully dressed, they made her walk up and down in front of them. "You really do look like a boy," Lily said in wonder.

George shrugged. "I don't care about that—I don't mind being a girl, but breeches are warmer and more comfortable and much better for riding. Why should we freeze in flimsy bits of nothing, while men are warm and comfortable?"

"Can I try them on?" Rose asked. "We're about the same size."

George handed her a pair of breeches. Rose stripped off her dress and in minutes was standing in front of the looking glass, staring at her reflection. Then she swaggered around the room in the boots.

George grinned. "More comfortable, aren't they?"

Rose grimaced. "I'm not sure. They feel a little strange."

"You get used to them."

"Lily, why don't you try them on?" her sister suggested.

"They won't fit me," Lily said. "I'm too fat."

"No, you're not," George and Rose said at the same time. "You're curvy and feminine," George added, and Rose gave her a little nod of approval.

"Here, try these ones on." George handed her the loosest pair of breeches, and Lily squeezed into them.

"What do you think?"

"They suit you," George told her. "How do you feel? Comfortable, aren't they?"

"A bit tight, but otherwise . . ." Lily pranced and wriggled, and pulled some he-man poses that made them all laugh. "They feel delightfully naughty."

Rose frowned. "Yes, but nobody would ever mistake you for a boy."

George turned to her in surprise. "What does that matter?"

Rose smiled. "It doesn't. Now we'd better get changed back into our dresses. If Cal discovers your breeches he'll probably confiscate them."

They slipped back into their dresses. "Why are you both wearing black?" George asked. "Your aunt too."

"We're in mourning for our father, Aunt Dottie's brother," Lily explained.

"And after that we'll be in mourning for our uncle Henry. Another whole *year*," Rose said savagely. She paused. "But Uncle Henry was your father, wasn't he? So why aren't *you* wearing black?"

"I wouldn't wear mourning for him if you paid me," George declared. "He was a lazy, selfish pig who broke my mother's heart. He left me to rot—didn't tell a soul about me, pretended I didn't exist and never came near me, not ever in my life that I remember. He didn't care if I lived or died, so why should I wear mourning for him?"

The two girls exchanged glances. "We didn't like him, either," Rose said.

"But you *have* to wear black for such a close relative," Lily said. "Society expects it. People think you're heartless and disrespectful if you don't."

George shrugged. "I don't care. It would be hypocritical of me to wear black for a man I despise, and I'm not doing it. What do I care about society anyway? I never asked to come here—he forced me—your brother, I mean. Besides, I look terrible in black. Like a crow."

Rose and Lily looked at each other. "Do you think we look like crows?" Lily asked.

George gave them each a thoughtful glance. "Not her."

She jerked her chin at Rose. "Black is a good foil for her coloring, that golden hair and that peaches-and-cream complexion and those blue, blue eyes. But you and me, Lily, with our dark hair and pale skin and gray eyes, we need a bit of color to liven us up."

"I know." Lily gave a dejected sigh. "I'm so fed up with looking like a crow. I don't even like crows. They're so, so . . ."

"Mournful," Rose supplied, and they all laughed.

George went to the door, opened it and looked out.

"Why do you keep doing that?" Rose asked. "It's the third time you've looked out into the hallway. Are you expecting something? The rest of your luggage, perhaps?"

"I don't have any more," George told her absently. "No, I'm waiting for my dog."

"Your dog! You have a dog? What sort is it? Where is it? Does Aunt Dottie know?"

"His name is Finn, he's an Irish wolfhound, and a complete darling. Your brother refused to let me bring him, but Finn followed me for miles and miles until he—your brother—had to give in and let him into the coach. As to whether Aunt Dottie knows, I think he was going to tell her about Finn after we went upstairs. Does she like dogs?"

"I don't know," Rose said. "As far as we know, she's never had one."

"If I can't have Finn," George said, "I'm not staying here."

"Don't worry," Rose told her. "Aunt Dottie is an absolute love. I'm sure she'll let you keep your dog. Where is he, George?"

"Hawkins, your brother's coachman, took him somewhere— I don't know where—to be given a bath. He's to bring him to me when he's clean and dry. But that was hours ago, and I'm getting worried." She looked out into the corridor again.

"But Hawkins won't bring him up here," Rose said. "A coachman doesn't come upstairs. He'll have put your dog in the backyard or the—"

But George was gone, running down the stairs. The others followed. "Through the kitchen," Rose said. "This way."

They burst into the kitchen and came to a dead stop.

"Is this here your animal, miss?" Cook demanded. She gestured angrily. Finn sat over near a big square table in the center of the room, looking ridiculously clean and unbelievably innocent. "I don't 'old with beasts in my kitchen. Nobody told me we was getting a dog. What am I supposed to do with it—look at 'im, the miserable great lummox."

"I'm so sorry," George began. "I didn't know that Hawkins—"

Rose took her arm and squeezed it meaningfully. "Don't say a word," she murmured.

"Are you sure it's even a dog?" Cook continued. "Looks more like a ruddy great 'orse to me. And who's going to feed it, I ask you? A great big thing like that, well, it'll eat us out of house and home, I reckon."

Finn laid his muzzle on the table and heaved a huge, tragic sigh.

"Well, will you look at that," Cook exclaimed crossly. "He's sittin' down and his head is higher than the table. And will you just look at them eyes."

They all looked at his eyes.

"Have you ever seen such a miserable-looking creature," Cook stormed. "He might smell like a nosegay, but why anyone would want to bring a great whiskery, clumsy creature—"

"He's not clumsy—" George began indignantly.

"Shhh," Rose and Lily hissed from either side of her.

"—like that into a decent God-fearing gentlewoman's house, I don't know," Cook continued. "And as for who's going to feed him, I know full well who *that's* going to fall on, oh, yes I do."

"I'll feed—"

"Oh, I know you young ladies are always full of good intentions, but it's poor old Cook who has to make sure everyone is fed—and this poor creature is half starved, I'll be bound."

"He's not, he's—"

"I've already given him the gravy beef that was for tomorrow's pie, and a marrow bone that was to go for soup, and he's eaten all the leftover sausage rolls—and just look at him!"

George looked. Finn looked disgustingly well satisfied to her. He turned his mournful never-been-fed-orphan look back on Cook.

"All right, then, just one little piece of the venison we're havin' on Friday, but that's the last you're getting from me!" Cook bustled off to cut a slice of venison from the haunch hanging in the larder.

George turned an amazed look on the other two, who were convulsed with muffled giggles. "She likes him?"

They nodded. "Whenever Cook starts scolding like that, it means she cares and is trying to hide it," Lily whispered.

Rose nodded. "She was exactly like that with the butcher, and they got married last year. That's why she doesn't live in anymore—she lives with the butcher, just down the street."

"A butcher? She lives with a butcher." George couldn't believe her luck.

Lily nodded. "There'll be no shortage of meat and bones for Finn, that's for certain."

They waited until Finn had devoured the venison and been scolded for his manners. "Two gulps? What do you call that, my lad! Disgraceful!" Cook told him. "Now be off with you and don't you come begging around my kitchen anymore. I'll bring you a nice meaty bone for breakfast."

They took Finn upstairs. George couldn't believe how clean he looked. His rough gray coat even looked soft, though of course it wasn't. Remembering Cook's nosegay comment, she bent down and sniffed him, then burst out laughing. "He smells of lavender. Oh, dear, good thing we're in the city, eh, Finn—those country dogs would make such fun of you. Now, come and meet the girls."

Finn, like the gentleman he was, sat and shook their hands politely, then, formalities over, he heaved a satisfied sigh and sprawled bonelessly out in front of the fire.

Chapter Nine

Gather ye rosebuds while ye may, old Time is still a-flying.
And this same flower that smiles today,
tomorrow will be dying.
—ROBERT HERRICK, *TO THE VIRGINS,*
TO MAKE MUCH OF TIME

THE NEXT MORNING WHEN THE GIRLS CAME DOWN TO
breakfast, Aunt Dottie looked at Georgiana's blue dress and
pursed her lips. "Is that all you have to wear, my dear?"

She nodded. "More or less."

"Then first thing after breakfast the girls and I will take
you shopping! Not only is that dress sadly outmoded, it's
far too bright a color, given your state of mourning."

"I won't wear black!" Georgiana declared. "Not for a
man who—"

"Eat your egg, niece," Cal snapped.

"But—"

He shot her a hard, silencing look and turned to his aunt.
"Georgiana is correct, Aunt Dottie—she won't be wearing
black for Henry."

"What?" All three girls gasped.

"But she *must*," Aunt Dottie exclaimed. "It would be
quite outrageous of her to wear colors with her father so
recently dead."

"Henry's will makes it quite clear that nobody should
mourn him."

Georgiana looked at him sharply but said nothing.

"Henry's will?" Aunt Dottie said.

"The will makes it quite clear that nobody should wear
black for Henry. And as his brother and his heir—and as

head of the Rutherford family—I must insist that you respect it, difficult though you may find it to put off your blacks before time."

Cal buttered a piece of toast while the news sank in. Aunt Dottie might not like it, but she would respect the orders of the head of the family. She always had. And she'd make it clear to everyone in society that their lack of mourning was by Henry's will and Cal's orders.

Nobody would blame Aunt Dottie or the girls. They would blame the autocratic Earl of Ashendon. Who, with any luck, would be somewhere on the Continent.

Cal was very aware of Georgiana's intense gaze boring silently into him, but he ignored her. She'd read Henry's will. She knew there was nothing in it about not wearing black.

But there was nothing at all in the will about *her*, either— and that was what had decided Cal.

He hadn't said that Henry's will had forbidden them to wear mourning; he'd said nobody *should* mourn him. A small but vital difference.

If his niece questioned it, he would mention a later will. But judging by her silence, she wasn't going to question him at all. And why would she? She got what she wanted.

"Does that mean we get to put off our blacks too?" Lily asked, her eyes sparkling.

Cal nodded. "In a week, it will be a year since Papa died and after that, yes, you may return to dressing as you used to, in white and colors and whatever."

The two sisters exchanged glances. "And go to parties?" Rose asked.

"Of course."

"And balls?"

"Yes, yes, whatever is suitable. You shall make your come-out next season."

There was a short, shocked silence. "You mean *this* spring? The season that starts in three months' time?" Rose almost whispered it.

Cal nodded. "Yes. Pass the marmalade, if you please."

"Which one of us will come out first?" Lily asked worriedly. As the youngest, she would expect to go last.

"All of you together," Cal said.

At that there was a babble of exclamations and excited speculation. Shopping would have to be done: morning dresses, walking dresses, ball dresses ordered, and from a London modiste—nobody in Bath was sufficiently fashionable—and pelisses, slippers, hats, gloves, fans. The lists grew.

Cal ate his toast and drank his coffee, well pleased with the result. The prospect of a London season would distract the girls from further mischief for the foreseeable future. Now all he had to do was find someone to launch them. Aunt Dottie would come, of course, but she'd be the first to admit she wasn't up to the rigors of a London season.

Aunt Agatha might not be willing to come to Bath to help him, but introducing three pretty nieces to the ton in their first London season was exactly the kind of thing she'd enjoy—though she'd be sure to extract her pound of flesh from Cal.

It would be worth it.

Between Aunt Agatha and Aunt Dottie they would manage, as long as Cal provided them with a suitable chaperone who would keep the girls in check and escort them to the more everyday events. And he knew exactly who that would be.

And once he had all that organized, he could leave.

"We will still need to purchase suitable clothing for George while we are here in Bath, and until the mourning period for your father—her grandfather—is up," Aunt Dottie pointed out when the first excitement had died down.

"Do I have to—?"

Cal cut his niece off. "Purchase a wardrobe of black gowns for only a bare week's wear?" Aunt Dottie hated waste.

Aunt Dottie pondered that. "I suppose she could wear some of Rose's dresses. They're much the same height."

"A perfect compromise," Cal said quickly, with a hard look at Georgiana to shut her up. "Quite unexceptional to wear black for the next week or so as a mark of respect for her grandfather. And perhaps you could buy something in half mourning—shades of lilac and lavender. You always looked lovely in purple."

"It's very irregular." Aunt Dottie still wasn't happy about it.

"Of course you will explain that it's on my instructions, as head of the family, out of respect for Henry." Lack of respect.

She gave him a thoughtful look, then nodded. "Respect for Henry—yes. That would be acceptable. Well, then, come along, girls, fetch your coats and hats. And Rose dear, find George something more suitable to wear. We're going shopping."

A MOUND OF CORRESPONDENCE HAD ACCUMULATED IN THE short time Cal had been away. He took it into the library and sorted it into estate business—a towering heap—and personal—a single scrawled, hand-delivered note. Nothing from Radcliffe, dammit, but a letter from Phipps had confirmed he'd obtained Henry's will and found it substantially unchanged from the copy Cal had already seen. There was no mention of Georgiana.

Cal had just broken the seal on the note when a soft knock on the door made him look up. It was Georgiana, a slender waif dressed all in black with a black hat and black gloves.

"What is it?" he asked warily.

"That wasn't in my father's will. About no mourning."

He shrugged. "Different will. Your copy was an old one. I have a copy of the latest one here." The fewer people who knew the truth, the better.

She studied his face, unconvinced, but before she could ask him anything else—like had her wretched father remembered her in any way at all, poor child—Rose poked her head in the door. "Come on, George, we're going shopping—for *colors*. Bye, Cal."

"Shopping." George grimaced good-naturedly, then gave Cal a smile and a friendly nod of good-bye. It was the first time they'd been in any kind of accord, and he found himself smiling as he returned to his correspondence.

The note was from his friend Galbraith, inviting Cal— actually begging Cal—to join him at York House that night, for dinner and commiseration. He didn't say what the com- miseration concerned, but Cal could join the dots.

He penned a swift acceptance and rang for Logan to deliver it to Galbraith at York House. Then he turned to the documents concerning the Ashendon estate and grimly began to work his way through the pile, making notes as he went.

His mood grew blacker. There was a huge backlog of estate matters to be attended to. Their father had been meticulous, a hard taskmaster who'd left a huge and complicated estate in apple-pie order. Henry had simply let things grind to a halt.

But it would be no hardship to go to Ashendon and see to things personally. Three names on his list were from Oxfordshire.

Some time in the afternoon he heard the girls and Aunt Dottie return home. From the sounds of laughter and excited girlish conversation, he gathered they'd a good day.

Cal kept working.

An hour later Rose entered, carrying a tray containing a pot of coffee and a plate of sandwiches. "Cook thought you'd be hungry, but Logan said you wouldn't want to be disturbed, so I said I'd bring it in."

Cal thanked her, picked up a sandwich in his left hand and kept working.

She loitered, twirling a golden curl around her finger. "Thanks, Cal, for telling Aunt Dottie to get us something in lilac. Even though it's still a mourning color, lilac suits all of us, you know—me, Lily and George. We've ordered the prettiest dresses. And bought some divine hats."

"I'm glad." He had no idea about colors and what would suit whom, but he was pleased the girls were happy for a change. He picked up the next document.

"Cal," she said in a soft, coaxing voice. "You said we weren't to go out in the evening without an escort."

He gave her a narrow look. "Yes?"

"And we haven't—don't worry—we've been ever so good, I promise. But there's a night fair down on the common tonight. Could we—I mean, would you take us? There are jugglers and fire-eaters and tightrope walkers, and—"

Lily poked her head around the door to add, "And a puppet show and coconut shies and toffee apples and a menagerie and stalls selling—"

Cal held up his hands to stop the flow of enticements. "Sorry, not tonight, girls. I have an engagement. Another time, perhaps."

Their faces fell. "Oh, but it's only on for one night."

"There will be other fairs."

"But—"

"Girls, you've just been shopping with your aunt and purchased the first colors you've worn—legitimately worn, I mean—in a year. And you have a new niece to get to know. Isn't that enough to keep you happy for the evening?"

"But we haven't been out for ages!" Rose said. "Not to anything. Not even the Pump Room."

"All we've done for the last two weeks is knit and sew and talk and do puzzles and fold paper firelighters. Aunt Dottie hasn't let us go anywhere," Lily added.

He was not unmoved by their plight—two weeks inside would make anyone restless. But he'd already made arrangements to go out. Galbraith clearly wanted a break from his courtship, and after weeks of girls and aunts and drama, Cal was in desperate need of some uncomplicated male companionship himself.

"Another time," he told them firmly. "No, no arguments. Thank you for bringing me the sandwiches and coffee, Rose. Good-bye."

YORK HOUSE HAD PROVIDED ANOTHER FINE DINNER, LIVING up to its reputation as the finest hotel in Bath. The wines served with dinner had been excellent and now, in the same private parlor as before, the two men were making inroads into a very fine bottle of cognac—Galbraith's inroads being rather heavier than Cal's.

A fire crackled merrily in the grate. Cal had recounted the tale of the debacle of his nephew George, and now talk had turned to Galbraith's prospective bride.

"Quiet girl—doesn't say much. Doesn't smile much, either, and when she does, she doesn't show her teeth. Odd that. Thought for a while there she mightn't have teeth, or that they were rotten or something but no, she bit into a biscuit and they're white and even enough." He sipped his cognac and added thoughtfully, "Haven't actually heard her laugh, yet. Very serious girl."

"You're really going to marry her?" Cal asked, a little disturbed by the dispassionate description.

"Grandfather's coming to Bath. Head of family, needs his signature on the settlements. Been making the journey in easy stages—did I mention he's not been well?"

Cal nodded. "He's not actually on his deathbed, then? So you don't have to marry this girl if you don't fancy her."

"No reason not to marry her," Galbraith said. "She's pleasant enough and pretty enough, agrees with everything I say—"

"Yes, but it doesn't sound as if you like her much, so why go ahead with it? Your grandfather dotes on you, so—"

"Can't let the old man breathe his last thinking I've let him down. Again."

"What do you mean? You distinguished yourself—"

Galbraith cut him off with a curt gesture. "I just need to give him this one thing."

"Does it have to be this girl? Don't you know anyone else?"

"I run with a pretty rackety crowd these days—don't know any respectable females. This girl is the daughter of one of his oldest friends." He drained his glass and refilled it. "She's very virtuous. Practically a saint. Itching to straighten me out and lead me down the path of righteousness," he said with a cynical grin.

"Good God."

Galbraith gave a careless shrug. "If it lets the old man die happy . . ."

"But will she make you happy?"

"All marriage is a gamble," Galbraith said indifferently and set down his glass. "Now, real reason I asked you here tonight, want you to be my best man at the wedding."

Cal shook his head. "I'd be honored to, but I'll be back on the Continent in a couple of weeks."

"What about next week? Still here then?"

"Probably, but—next week? You're not going to get married—?"

"No date set yet, but it'll be soon. Need to get the knot tied while the old man's still alive and kicking. Do my best to get an heir on the way before he gives up the ghost." He patted his pocket. "Got a special license."

"Good God."

"Don't look so appalled. Marriage. Comes to us all in the end." Galbraith lifted his glass. "So a toast, old friend, to my finally becoming a tenant for life."

It was as dismal a wedding toast as Cal had ever heard. "A tenant for life," he echoed.

CAL LEFT GALBRAITH STARING INTO THE FIRE. IT WAS A cool, clear night and he walked home from York House in a thoughtful state of mind. He didn't envy his friend one little bit.

Marriage. Comes to us all in the end.

True enough. Cal would have to marry and beget an heir too, one day.

But not yet. Not for a long time yet. When he was at least thirty-five or more.

He let himself into Aunt Dottie's house with the front door key and found a small candle lantern burning softly, waiting for him to light his way upstairs. As he passed the girls' bedchamber he heard a whine and a scratch at the door. The dog, wanting to relieve itself, no doubt.

Cal opened the door, holding it wide to let the dog pass. He glanced inside and stiffened. The bed nearest the door was unoccupied. He leaned inside the room and held the lantern higher.

Every bed empty, damn them.

He took the dog outside for the call of nature, returned him to the bedchamber, then settled down in the kitchen to wait.

He was angry and disappointed—with himself as much as anyone. He'd imagined he'd been making progress with the girls, but clearly they were determined to go their own way, no matter what. So they were disappointed with his refusal to escort them to the night fair. Life was full of disappointments.

An hour later, he heard the sound of soft laughter and the key turning in the kitchen door. The door opened and two young men swaggered in, complete to a shade: coat, hat, breeches, boots and each carrying a cane. They were followed by Lily, wrapped warmly in a cloak.

Cal rose from his seat at the table. "Make sure you bolt the blasted door, or I'll have a reason to sack that butler my aunt is so fond of."

The two "young men" jumped, then turned to face him with expressions of varying defiance. Georgiana looked wary, Rose was trying to appear unconcerned but looked a little shamefaced and Lily looked frankly upset. "It's not Logan's fault—" she began, but Cal cut her off with a sharp gesture.

"I know damned well whose fault it is." He turned the lantern up, the better to see their faces. "Well? What do you have to say for yourselves?" He waited. "*Word of a Rutherford*, you said when you promised me not to go out unescorted at night."

"Promises made under duress don't count," Rose said. "Besides, *you* promised to take us somewhere exciting when you returned, and you didn't. In any case, we did have an escort. George escorted us—and we both dressed like men, so nobody could tell—"

He smashed his fist on the table, making them all jump. "George is not *any* kind of escort and you know it, and if you think you look like a man you're very much mistaken." He glanced at George. "I should have burned those damned breeches."

"You can't, they belong to me!" she flashed.

"I'm the head of your family and your legal guardian. I can do whatever the hell I want!"

"There's no need to swear at us," Rose muttered. "I don't

know why you're making such a fuss. There were no consequences. Nobody noticed us and nothing happened, so don't say such things. You're frightening Lily." Rose put her arm around her sister's shoulders and squeezed, but Cal was wise to her tricks this time.

"Don't you dare try those crocodile tears on me again," he snapped.

Lily stopped on a hiccup, her big gray eyes still swimming with unshed tears. He looked away. Even though he knew she could produce them at will, her tears still had the power to stir him up inside.

"I'm sorry, Cal," she said, sounding truly penitent. She added in a hesitant tone, "I brought you something from the fair." From her reticule she pulled a toffee apple on a stick and held it out to him.

Cal made no move to take it. Lily put it on the table in front of him.

There was a long silence. "I ought to beat you all!" he said eventually.

"You wouldn't dare." George braced herself, pale but defiant.

"I've had men in the army flogged insensible," he informed her coldly. "A good beating might wake you little hellions up to the consequences of your actions."

"You just try it and I—I'll run away," George said. "You know I can."

"Don't worry, George," Lily said softly. "Of course Cal won't beat us."

"How do you know I won't?" Cal growled. Did she think a toffee apple could change his mind?

Lily gave him a tremulous smile. "Because you gave me piggyback rides when I was seven."

"*What?*" The logic of that escaped him completely.

"Yes, and because the first time he caught us coming in at night, he was absolutely furious, but the minute Lily started crying, he fell completely apart, didn't he, Lil?" Rose said. "He went from being all cold and mean and nasty to being all worried and gruff. It was really rather sweet."

Cal stared at her, dumbfounded. *Sweet? Rather sweet?*

Ye gods! "Oh, just go." He shoved the lantern—still burning,
but not for much longer—across the table toward them. "Get
up to bed—and don't wake your aunt. I'll speak to you tomorrow. Not another word, Rose," he said as she opened her
mouth to argue. "One word out of *any* of you and you'll *all*
be on bread and water for a week. Stale bread and no butter!
Now go!"

They went.

But he heard Lily say, "He doesn't mean that, either,
George."

"He does. He's threatened to starve me, twice." George
sounded aggrieved.

"Yes, but did he actually *do* it?" Lily asked. "No, of course
not. Cal's our big brother and even though he tries to hide it,
he loves us and takes care of us. All of us."

THE GIRLS TOOK THE LANTERN WITH THEM, LEAVING CAL
in the kitchen, in the dark. In more ways than one.

He loves us and takes care of us. All of us.

Where would she get such an idea? He'd never even mentioned the word *love* to any of the girls, so it didn't make
sense.

Nor did that nonsense about giving them piggyback rides
when they were little. It was just a piggyback ride, not a
declaration of love. A lot of piggyback rides, now that he
came to think of it. The girls had always demanded it, on
the few occasions he was home. It was just something he did.

Was that why they disobeyed him so easily? Because
they imagined he loved them and so would forgive them
anything? Aunt Dottie too?

Females. Imagining everything revolved around love.

It was his duty, as a brother, an uncle and now head of
the family, to look after the girls. If there was one thing Cal
understood, it was responsibility. He'd had it drummed into
him all his life.

But love? He was a stranger to the emotion. He couldn't
even remember his mother; she'd died when he was a toddler. As a young boy he'd spent hours staring at her portrait,

trying to remember her, wondering what she'd thought of him, what she'd been like, but all he had were servants' tales. He'd never talked about her to Henry or his father. It wasn't that his father had forbidden it, as such; it was just . . . not done.

As for his father, he'd felt a deep regard for him, but he'd been a distant, exacting and cold-natured parent, more concerned with obedience than love.

Had Cal loved him? He didn't know.

He thought of his friend Galbraith, who openly admitted he loved his grandfather—enough to marry a woman he didn't particularly care for, just to ease the old man's passing from this world.

Would Cal sacrifice himself for his father that way? He considered the possibility and decided he might. But it would be duty, rather than love.

Would he sacrifice himself for the girls and Aunt Dottie? He'd lay down his life for them if they were in any kind of danger, of course, but then he was used to risking his life for others. It was a soldier's life. King and country, or his family—it wasn't much different. One did what one had to.

But love? He'd had liaisons with women over the years, but the strongest he'd ever felt was fondness. They'd been practical arrangements from the start, and he'd always taken good care of them. None of them had loved him. If they had, they'd never mentioned it.

He'd always been glad of that. He wouldn't know what to do with a lovelorn mistress. Several of his friends had been entangled in affairs of the heart—unrequited love on one side or the other. It was messy. Undignified.

Cal probably took after his father and Henry. Naturally coldhearted and not particularly lovable.

The only person who'd ever loved him was Aunt Dottie, and Aunt Dottie loved everyone. He was fond of the women of his family—though possibly not Aunt Agatha. Could one be fond of a dragon?

But he had to do something about the girls. It was clear they would continue on their own merry way, flouting his rules whenever it suited them, secure in the illusion of his love and forgiveness. His father would have had them beaten for such disobedience, but Cal couldn't bring himself to do that.

He needed someone who they would *know* didn't love them, someone they respected who could control them.

Someone like that long-legged, cool-voiced teacher.

Chapter Ten

Whether they give or refuse, it delights women
just the same to have been asked.
—OVID, *AMORES*

"I'LL TRIPLE YOUR SALARY."

One of Miss Emmaline Westwood's finely arched brows
rose in a look of mild interest. "Triple?" She smoothed the
lace gloves enclosing her long, slender fingers, cool as new-
made butter.

Dammit, she should be more impressed than that. It was
an extremely generous offer. He'd come first thing in the
morning, hoping to have it all organized before he spoke to
the girls. They hadn't come down to breakfast. No surprise
there.

But the teacher wasn't responding as he'd planned. She'd
appeared today without that ugly cap, her brown hair drawn
back into a smooth coil at the back. Tiny curls escaped her
discipline, clustering around her nape and ears, but did she
fiddle with her hair, like most women of his experience? Not
a bit.

She sat facing him, her countenance as bland as milk,
receiving his offer as if barely interested. Of course, that
could be a bargaining tactic.

"Yes, triple. Because there are now three girls—my or-
phaned niece, who is roughly the same age as my sisters."
Which made for three times the trouble, though he wasn't
going to admit that.

"And for triple my current salary—whatever that is; you

haven't even asked what I earn yet—you want me to take them to London—"

"Along with my aunt, Lady Dorothea Rutherford."

She inclined her head. "Along with your elderly aunt. And you want me to chaperone the girls—"

"Guide and control them."

"Help prepare them for their come-out, take them shopping, supervise their wardrobe, organize a ball at your London home, accompany them to various ton occasions—"

He made an impatient gesture. "Yes, yes, all of that. The usual nonsense."

She gave him a level, teacherly look that made him aware he was interrupting. Her gaze remained steady as she finished, "So that you can leave them and return to your 'important government business.'"

He frowned at the hint of skepticism in her voice. "It *is* important government business."

She gave a perfunctory half smile. "Of course it is. And you want to be able to leave the girls behind with a clear conscience."

"Ye— No, I'm thinking of what is best for the girls."

Her brow rose again, an arch linking skepticism and inquiry. "To hire a stranger to look after them?"

"You're not a stranger to them. Only to Georgiana."

"I'm a stranger to you. You know nothing about me."

That headmistress had indicated she'd been educated here as a girl, which meant she must be well enough born, though obviously her family had fallen on hard times since then.

"Your position here vouches for your character. As for the rest, you seem well enough educated and quite ladylike."

"Merci du compliment." Irony frosted her voice. Or maybe she was just demonstrating the range of her education.

That luscious mouth had thinned to a firm line. She seemed to be waiting for him to explain further, so he obliged. "I know you're good at handling girls of that age, that you've held a responsible position in this seminary for some years and that my half sisters respect you. That seems to me sufficient for such a position. As to the requirements of the job, naturally as well as your wage, I'll pay all your additional expenses: clothes, shoes, shawls, fans"—he gestured vaguely—"whatever is required."

"I see."

"*And* there will be a bonus each time one of the girls marries." Dammit, he was starting to sound desperate.

A faint pucker marred her smooth forehead. "A *bonus*? To see them *married*?"

He nodded. "And an extra bonus if you get them all fired off in one year."

The fine green-gray eyes glittered. The lace-clad fingers curled into fists and for a moment Cal though she was going to—what?—hit him? Nonsense. She blinked and the flash was gone, as if he'd imagined it.

"But once this desirable outcome is achieved, I'd be unemployed."

"Yes, but in the meantime you'll have earned yourself a handsome sum. As well, you'll have made a lot of useful connections in the ton. I'm sure you'd have no trouble finding another position."

"As a chaperone or governess?"

He shrugged. "Who knows what opportunities you'd find?" She could even land herself a husband. Once she was properly dressed, with those eyes and that mouth . . .

There was a short silence, then she folded her hands and said, "Thank you for your offer, Lord Ashendon. However, Miss Mallard has informed me that she intends to retire at the end of term. She has offered me the position of headmistress in her place. It is not as well paid as your offer, but . . ."

He said incredulously, "You're turning down the experience of a London season and all it has to offer, in favor of a dreary job keeping schoolgirls in order?"

"Isn't that what you want me to do with your sisters?" She gave him a swift half smile as if to take the sting out, but he wasn't fooled.

She smoothed the lace gloves again. "Your offer is very tempting, I admit. But that's part of the problem. After a year or two of living the high life in London, it would be very hard to adjust to this life . . . again." She said the last word on a breath, so softly he almost didn't catch it.

"So you're choosing to hide away here in a drab little girls' school, instead of taking a risk?"

She gave him a startled glance. "Nonsense. There's no question of my hiding." She lifted her chin and said with crisp authority, "I *like* teaching, Lord Ashendon, and I enjoy working with schoolgirls. Moreover, as headmistress, I will be able to make some innovations to the curriculum and operation of the school. I find the prospect quite stimulating. And challenging."

He snorted. "If you say so. I don't believe I mentioned the size of the bonuses." He named a sum that made her blink.

"It is indeed substantial," she admitted.

He frowned. "But you're still refusing me."

She nodded. "A woman like me"—he assumed she meant poor and single—"must look to her future. The position of headmistress here is, more or less, a position for life, and I would be foolish to risk long-term security for short-term gain. So yes, my mind is made up. But thank you for considering me. Good-bye."

He rose to his feet, severely put out, and made his good-byes brusquely. He collected his hat, gloves and coat from the dragon at the door, flung on his coat, jammed his hat on his head and strode off down the street.

Dammit, where was he going to find another female so suitable? He thrust his hands into his leather gloves. How could she—how could anyone—turn down the opportunity for a glamorous year or two in favor of—what did she call it? A position for life.

Galbraith's words from the previous night echoed in his head. *A tenant for life.*

He stopped, stock-still in the street, staring at nothing. People stepped around him, giving him curious looks and muttering about the inconsideration of some people. He ignored them. His mind had seized on an idea.

He turned and marched back toward Miss Mallard's Seminary for the Daughters of Gentlemen.

*   *   *

EMM MADE NO MOVE TO LEAVE THE ROOM. SHE HAD TWENTY minutes before her next lesson. He'd closed the door behind him when he left, and she knew the moment she opened it and stepped outside, Theale would be waiting, wanting to know why Lord Ashendon had come to speak to her, instead of Miss Mallard, again. Theale was as inquisitive as she was mean-spirited.

Emm wanted a few minutes to herself, to consider what had just happened in peace. Solitude was a rare and precious thing at Miss Mallard's. As was privacy.

So you're choosing to hide away here in a drab little girls' school, instead of taking a risk?

His careless accusation had shocked her. From a stranger who didn't know her at all, it had cut very close to the bone. Was she hiding?

She *had* been hiding when she first came here. Hiding from the world, the gossip and horrid speculation, but mostly from the pain of Papa's betrayal. His lack of faith in her, his belief in the words of others—false words, false accusations.

His demand that because of malicious gossip she marry a man she did not love. His ultimatum. His last living words to her, as it turned out.

She'd refused, fled like a wounded creature and, somehow, ended up at the school. She hadn't known where else to go. There were no relatives to turn to. Her friends in the district had either shunned her or been horridly awkward and distressed, not knowing what to believe. Such was the gossip, her presence would taint them.

One mistake, one heartfelt foolish girlish mistake that had come back to haunt her. Because at one time, years before, she *had* been foolish, had acted recklessly and rashly placed her trust in a man.

And after that, after the heartbreak, she'd been grateful for the forgiveness of her father. A forgiveness that didn't even last five years.

She hadn't ever traveled much outside the local area, except to go away to school. So in her blind distress, she'd fled to the only other place she knew: her old school.

Miss Mallard had taken her in, heard her story, tut-tutted a bit and given Emm a job and a place to live.

Was she still hiding? No. Lord Ashendon was wrong. It was loyalty that kept Emm here, not cowardice. She owed Miss Mallard a debt of gratitude.

She picked at a hole in her crocheted glove. She'd been here seven years. That was a lot of gratitude. Did she owe Miss Mallard a lifetime? A week ago, when the future of the school and her position was in doubt, she'd felt quite desperately insecure, wondering what on earth she would do if the school closed.

Now she had the promise of the headmistress-ship, and Emm's future and that of the school was assured—and the plans she had for it would make it the best young ladies' seminary in Bath.

And yet his accusation that she was hiding away from the world had rattled her.

Because there was an element of truth in it? Perhaps more than just an element.

Or was it Lord Ashendon himself who'd rattled her?

She appeared to be foolishly susceptible to his good looks. And the gentlemanly way he'd escorted her home the other night. And that far-from-gentlemanly kiss.

She'd thought of it, and him, more than once—oh, who was she fooling? She thought of him every night, alone in her small attic bedroom.

As pathetic spinsters were rumored to do—spinning un-likely fantasies about men they hardly knew.

The moment Theale had told her he was waiting down-stairs and had requested private conversation with her, Emm had felt the most ridiculous fluttering. She'd even removed her spinster's cap—just to tidy her hair, she'd told herself—but she hadn't put the cap back on. Theale had noticed and given her a scornful sniff and a knowing look.

He'd smiled when she arrived, and it had taken Emm a few seconds to gather her wits. He was tall and broad-shouldered and so assured that somehow he seemed to fill the room. She'd found a hole in her gloves and occupied herself in keeping it hidden. She really ought to make herself another pair.

He'd outlined his plan, and Emm had forced herself to look past the handsome face, those intriguing gray eyes and the knowing, clever mouth, and concentrate on his words. His very damning words.

Like many of the parents of the girls here, he was careless of the real needs of his half sisters and niece, more interested in his own convenience than anything else. The other day she'd thought—or imagined—that he seemed sincerely worried about them.

Today she'd seen him in his true colors.

A bonus for *firing them off*. Like cannons. Pushed into marriage whether they were ready or not. And would he care whom they married? Would he even give them a choice?

No, just a bonus to whoever got them off his hands within the year.

But no girl should be pushed into marriage, and Emm would never be a party to such a scheme, no matter how large or tempting the bribe. For call it what you like, that bonus was nothing more than a bribe.

He might be selfish, superficial and self-centered, but he wasn't stupid. That accusation he'd made about her hiding away was quite . . . perceptive.

Now with time to reflect a little more calmly—and without his presence to distract and, and *beflutter* her—she could admit that there was some truth, a very small amount, in what he'd said.

Nevertheless, she didn't regret her decision at all. Not one little bit. She would make a good and useful life for herself here in the school. It might not be glamorous or exciting, but it would be a worthwhile life.

And if that thought didn't precisely cheer her up, well, she hadn't slept well last night, that was all. A good and useful life would be quite sufficient. And very safe.

THE SOUND OF VOICES IN THE HALL CAUGHT HER ATTENTION. It sounded like an argument. Theale and . . . a man?

Before she could go to see what the problem was, the door flew open and Lord Ashendon stood there again, taking up all the space. And the air. "See, she *is* still here," he said. He turned to Emm. "Tell this dra— female that you are willing to speak to me. She seems to imagine I'm going to attack you or something."

"He just pushed his way in—" Theale began.

"It's quite all right, Miss Theale, I will speak to Lord Ashendon," Emm told her. She shut the door and waved him to a seat. "Did you forget something? I have a class in five minutes."

"I won't take long."

She waited.

He was still carrying his hat. He fiddled with it a moment, smoothing the brim between his gloved thumb and fingers. He set the hat down on the small table at his elbow and crossed his legs. He cleared his throat.

She waited.

He uncrossed his legs and tugged off his fine leather gloves, setting them down beside his hat.

"My class starts in three minutes, Lord Ashendon," she prompted. "Is there something else you wanted to say to me?"

"Yes, dammit, I'm getting to it," he snapped. He swallowed, then fixed her with those hard gray eyes, like a butterfly on a pin. "You want a position for life. Very well, I'll marry you."

There was a short stunned silence while Emm tried to gather her wits. Then, "*What* did you say?"

"You heard me." He seemed to realize his rudeness, and said in a hard voice, "I just asked you to marry me."

"Oh, it was a question, was it?" she said dryly. She was pleased to hear her words come out quite calmly. It wasn't at all how she felt. Her insides were madly churning.

He was talking *marriage*? To a woman he barely knew, whom he'd met *four times*?

And kissed once.

His jaw tightened. He straightened his shoulders, as if about to face a firing squad. "Would you do me the honor of marrying me, Miss Westwood?"

Emm swallowed. They were words she'd never dreamed of hearing again, although the delivery left something to be desired. But the question itself made as much sense as some of her wilder fantasies. She forced herself to ask in as steady a voice as she could manage, "*Why?* Why would you want to marry me?"

He frowned as if the answer was obvious. "You said security for a lifetime was what mattered most to you. Marriage will give you that. And as my wife, you will be in a much better position to introduce the girls to the ton. You'll have the authority and influence that a mere chaperone or governess would not."

Emm couldn't believe her ears. He was still conducting the job interview. Only this time the offer on the table was marriage.

Like the job description he'd made earlier, she was to supervise and arrange the launch in society of his half sisters and niece, accompany them, be responsible for them, and so on. But instead of a wage and bonuses, she would receive a generous annual allowance for as long as she lived; the use of any and all of his properties, as she wished; a carriage and team. To sum up, she would perform all the usual duties of a wife.

As Emm listened, doubts trickled coldly down her spine, dousing the flush of unwary warmth that had flowed through her. It was too good to be true. It was—it must be a joke at her expense.

Rich, handsome and wildly eligible earls did not make offers of marriage to women they barely knew. Especially not to women of no particular beauty, no fortune and no standing in the world. Who'd been on the shelf for years.

If he truly wanted a wife to launch his sisters, he had only to lift his finger and dozens of the pretty, well-connected young ladies currently on the London marriage mart would flock to accept his hand. He'd find almost as many in Bath— she'd heard about the stir his appearance in the Pump Room had caused.

No, he was angry with her for refusing his generous job offer, and now he was making this proposal as some kind of twisted revenge. He and his friends would probably laugh about it later in their horrid clubs.

About the foolish susceptible spinster.

Ridiculous how it hurt, nevertheless.

"You cannot be serious," she said crisply, rising from her seat. "I must go, I have a class to teach."

He stood, frowning. "You don't believe me." He said it as if he couldn't quite believe it.

She searched his face. He looked almost convincing. But she didn't, couldn't believe him. Mustering all the dignity she could, she said quietly, "Good-bye, Lord Ashendon," and held out her hand.

He took it in both hands. "I make the offer in all sincerity, but I understand you might need some time to consider it."

She said nothing. She couldn't. His hands were warm, cupping hers, so much smaller and icy cold by contrast.

He scanned her face and gave a brisk nod. "Think it over. I'll call on you tomorrow at nine to hear your response. Good day, Miss Westwood. I'll show myself out." He picked up his hat and gloves, bowed to her and left.

Emm stared at the closing door, distantly registering the click as it shut, and then her legs started trembling. She collapsed bonelessly onto her chair, her mind awhirl with possibilities and counterpossibilities. *Marriage?* To *Lord Ashendon*?

A moment later the door opened again. She tensed, but it was only Theale. "You're going to be late for your lesson." Theale loved to catch people in the wrong.

"I know. I'm coming," Emm managed, and rose shakily to her feet.

Theale's eyes gleamed with suspicion. "You look rattled. What did he want?"

Emm shook her head. "Nothing. Nothing at all."

EMM BEGAN HER LESSON IN SOMEWHAT OF A DAZE. LORD Ashendon's proposal kept buzzing around her brain like a swarm of contradictory bees, flinging out questions, impossible-to-answer questions.

He'd claimed the offer was sincere. He'd sounded as if he meant it!

But he couldn't *possibly* be serious! Who would choose an obscure country teacher to launch his high-spirited, high-bred sisters into society? The cream of society, at that.

And why Emm, of all people, a woman he'd met on a bare handful of occasions? Because she was here, under his nose? Because she'd given him no encouragement? Because he didn't like to be crossed? Because he had to win?

She had no answers. Luckily a class of lively girls soon pulled her back to reality.

She didn't stop for a minute all day, which helped put things at a distance. Finally, well after dinner, when the girls were all in bed, Emm finally got the chance to slip up to her room and think. She sat on her bed, pulling the thin, worn counterpane around her for warmth.

Whether it made sense to her or not, he *had* asked her to marry him. The more she thought about it, the less he seemed like the kind of man who would joke about such a thing. *Marriage.*

She walked to her window and stared blindly out into the dark night.

All the usual duties of a wife.

She pressed cold, shaking hands to her cheeks. He was Lord Ashendon. Of course he would want an heir.

She hardly knew him. She would be placing her life—and body—in the hands of a man she'd met four times. And didn't much like.

But whose face and body haunted her dreams.

His plan hadn't changed, just the payment. He would probably want to marry Emm in quick order, place the girls in her hands and return to whatever drew him on the Continent.

Presumably he planned to impregnate her before he left. She wasn't even going to think about that—oh, who was she fooling? She could think of very little else.

But he didn't want Emm herself—how could he? He didn't even know her, had shown no interest in who she was, where she'd come from or how she'd come to be working in the school she'd once attended as a pupil.

He didn't care who she was. He just wanted someone on whom he could dump his problems and then leave. Someone who wouldn't have any choice in the matter. A wife.

Oh, lord.

But oh, she would have security for life. And, God willing, a baby of her very own . . .

Rose and Lily would be her sisters-in-law, and Georgiana, the girl she hadn't yet met, her niece by marriage. They'd have a London season together, a first for all four of them. She could ensure that the girls weren't forced into marriage. She'd let them choose for themselves, and Emm would make sure the men they picked were worthy of her girls.

Her girls. Sisters, a niece and a child of her own. After all this time, a family.

She undressed swiftly and slipped into bed. The hot brick was waiting for her, thawing her frozen toes. *Thank you, Milly.*

She lay in bed, shivering with a combination of cold, excitement and apprehension. And prayed that he meant it.

Chapter Eleven

I ... chose my wife as she did her wedding gown, not for a
fine glossy surface, but such qualities as would wear well.
—OLIVER GOLDSMITH, *THE VICAR OF WAKEFIELD*

"I'VE COME FOR MY ANSWER." LORD ASHENDON STOOD IN
front of the fireplace, booted feet apart, hands linked behind
his back, dominating the room. "Will you marry me?"

Emm's throat was dry. "Yes, Lord Ashendon, I will marry
you."

"Excellent. I've instructed my lawyer to draw up the
marriage settlements. I will want the business conducted as
soon as possible . . ."

Emm stood there, shaking. She'd just agreed to marry
Lord Ashendon. With one short sentence she'd changed her
life, wholly and dramatically. She felt hollow inside, strangely
bereft.

He kept talking, listing the things needing to be done.

She wasn't quite sure what she'd expected his response
to her acceptance of his proposal to be, but it wasn't this, as
if he'd ticked off an item on a list and was moving on to the
next.

He appeared quite unmoved, as if her agreement were a
foregone conclusion.

Which she supposed it was. And didn't that make her
feel beggar maid to King Cophetua?

Tall, ridiculously handsome, the very figure of a romantic
hero, he delivered his plans for their marriage as if he were
briefing a troop of soldiers. "You are welcome, of course, to

have a member of your family examine the settlements document and negotiate any alterations before it is finalized."

"I have no family," Emm said. She wanted to hit him. An agreement to marry should not be taken so . . . so *practically.*

Surely, at least there should be a kiss.

Which was ridiculous, she berated herself silently. Did she imagine Lord Ashendon had fallen in love with her after four brief meetings?

"Oh." He considered that a moment, then continued, "I will go up to London tomorrow and obtain a special license. We shall be married in a week's time."

"A week's time?" It came out almost as a squeak.

"Yes?" He looked at her as if she'd made some irrelevant interruption.

"I cannot possibly marry you in a week."

He frowned. "Why not?"

Because it was too much of a rush, because she wasn't ready to be married to a virtual stranger at the end of a week, because her head was still in a whirl of tangled thoughts and emotions. Because, because, because.

She was feeling more than a little agitated, so she walked to the window and looked out for a moment. The view was nothing like the one from her little attic room, but somehow it calmed her. "I will need a new dress."

He looked at the dress she was wearing, grimaced slightly and nodded. "Very well. Buy one. Buy a dozen. Buy whatever you need. Have the bills sent to me at my aunt's address. It won't take a week, will it?"

"Probably not," she conceded. If she was going to be his wife—Lady Ashendon! A countess!—she'd need more than one new dress, but she supposed she and the girls would have to buy all they needed in London. Bath had some good dressmakers, but they wouldn't match up to the finest London could offer. And he would expect the finest.

"But I must also give Miss Mallard more notice than a week; she will have to find a replacement for me."

"I will deal with Miss Mallard."

"That you will not," she said immediately, and when he

gave her that look she was starting to become accustomed to, the one that suggested she was stepping out of line, she added, "Miss Mallard is entirely my business. You have no idea what I owe her, and I will not have you ordering her around." And riding roughshod over her sensibilities.

"Ordering her around?" he echoed. "I do *not* order ladies around."

He seemed so genuinely insulted that she had to stifle a laugh. "No, of course you don't," she agreed. He had no idea of how he appeared to others. "Nevertheless, I will be the one who speaks to Miss Mallard."

He clearly didn't like it, but after a moment he gave a brusque nod. "Very well, but whatever she says, the wedding will take place at the end of the week. And if she cuts up stiff about your leaving, you may refer her to me." It sounded like a threat.

"Why, what would you do?"

"Make financial compensation for the loss of your services, of course." The gray eyes narrowed. "What did you think I'd do?"

She shook her head. "It doesn't matter." It wasn't so much how she feared he might treat Miss Mallard, it was that she didn't want him completely taking over her life. He was like the tide, sweeping everything and everyone before him. She needed to be a rock and hang on to the small piece of independence she had left.

She glanced out of the window again and took several deep, calming breaths. "Why must the wedding take place so quickly? You realize it will cause a great deal of talk."

"What does that matter? It's nobody else's business," he said impatiently. "As to why it must be soon, I believe I informed you that I have urgent business to attend to."

She sighed. "Yes, your 'important government business.'"

"Precisely. So the sooner everything is arranged, the sooner I can leave. Now, have we covered everything? Make whatever arrangements you want for the wedding—order whatever you want and have the bills sent to me. I've booked the abbey for next—"

"You booked the abbey? Already? You must have been

very sure of my answer." And Bath Abbey, instead of St. Swithins, where the Mallard community normally attended! It would be very grand. She supposed an earl would expect to be married in the grandest place possible.

He looked a little self-conscious but said gruffly, "I like to be organized."

"And if I'd refused you?"

His brows rose at that, but he merely shrugged. "I would have canceled the booking."

Or would he have gone off to find another hasty convenient bride? No doubt Bath was full of them—he'd only have to step into the Pump Room and lift his finger. But there was no point in pursuing that line of thought. She'd agreed to marry this man, and in so many respects it was everything she'd dreamed of as a girl. Almost.

If only the man himself were a little more . . .

Oh, he was as handsome a man as ever she'd dreamed of—handsome, and strong and powerful. But he was so . . . businesslike.

There wasn't a romantic bone in the man's body.

Though why she should dream of romance when she was six-and-twenty and should be beyond all that . . . They were schoolgirls' dreams. Or spinsters'. Romantic and unrealistic. Pure fantasy.

He'd made it plain—more than plain—that this was a purely practical marriage. A job, no more, no less. And she had accepted the job.

She would no longer be a poor, unregarded schoolteacher, wholly dependent on the goodwill of her employer. She was going to be a titled lady—a countess!—with a home of her own and a family to care for. And since her husband would be somewhere on the Continent, Emm would be her own mistress. It was foolish to long for romance, pointless to dream of love. Security and independence were far more important.

She glanced up at him and caught him staring at her mouth, a dark intense stare that was almost like a touch. Warmth flooded her. Nervously she moistened her lips.

He looked up and met her gaze. His eyes were hard and gray and unreadable.

All the usual duties of a wife.

She shivered. In barely a week she would be married to this man. Her body would be his, to do with as he pleased.

Without a word, he held out his hand to her. Nervelessly she offered hers. As he had the previous day he enclosed her gloved hand in both of his, his grip sure and warm and firm. "It will be all right, I promise."

Emm had no idea why that reassurance should rattle her more than anything, but it did.

"You ARE *WHAT*?" MISS MALLARD STARED AT EMM FROM over her *pince-nez*. She fumbled in her desk drawer, pulled out a vial of smelling salts and set it in front of her in an ominous warning. "Is this some frightful jest, Emmaline? Married? You? At your age?"

"I'm afraid it's true, ma'am."

Miss Mallard picked up the smelling salts and took a deep sniff. Her head jerked; she gasped, then blew violently into a lace-edged handkerchief. Emm, well versed in this ritual, passed her a glass of water.

The headmistress drank, then glared at her through streaming eyes. "How could you, Emmaline? After all I've done for you. You were to become headmistress after me!" Her head sank into her hands, and she moaned brokenly, "How sharper than a serpent's tooth . . . Oh, asp that pierces the bosom that has nurtured you all these years."

"I'm sorry, ma'am," Emm murmured. Miss Mallard always did get her quotations mixed.

Miss Mallard took a deep breath, picked up her *pince-nez*, jammed them back on her nose and fixed Emm with a piercing glare. "And who, might I ask, is the blackguard who thinks to steal you away from me? Don't tell me, it's that dreadful old widower from church—the one who sent you flowers that time—I forget his name."

"Mr. Bell, you mean? No, it's not—"

"No, no, the other one. Short, fat and entirely bald. He has no fortune, you know. And a wandering eye."

"No, it's not Mr. Atkins, either." Miss Mallard would hate the truth even more, Emm thought.

"Then who is it?"

Emm took a deep breath. "Lord Ashendon."

There was a sudden shocked silence broken only by the sound of a pair of silver-rimmed *pince-nez* hitting the desk. Miss Mallard's eyes almost popped from their sockets. She lifted the smelling salts, looked at them vaguely, as if unsure what they were, and put them down again. "Lord Ashendon?" she repeated in a failing voice.

"Yes, ma'am."

There was a long silence. "Lord Ashendon, brother to the Rutherford girls?"

"Yes, ma'am."

"The man who was here the other day? I spoke to him. Tall, handsome, rich—*that* Lord Ashendon? He's asked you to marry him?"

Emm nodded. "Yes, ma'am, and he wants the wedding to be next Tuesday. I'm afraid it's very short notice, but Lord Ashendon is adamant."

There was another long silence. Then, "For *next Tuesday*?" She gave Emm a sharp look. "You're not in the family wa— No, of course not. There hasn't been time. I take it you knew him from before."

"No, ma'am. I never set eyes on him before last week."

Miss Mallard blinked. "Good heavens!" She considered it for a moment, then said in a bracing voice, "Well, whatever his lordship's reason for such a rush, he shall not find us wanting! Short notice indeed, but we shall prevail, I am determined. We'll fire you off in style, my dear. I'll speak to the vicar about the ceremony—"

"It's not to be at St. Swithins. His lordship has booked the abbey."

"The abbey?" Miss Mallard's eyes gleamed. "Oh, excellent." She pulled out a pad of paper and started to make a list. "New dresses for both of us, of course. Cancel your classes for today—for the rest of the week, in fact. Thwaites, John-

stone and Clegg can fill in for you. You and I will go at once
to Madame Floria's and order new dresses for the occasion.
You cannot possibly marry Lord Ashendon in that old rag!"

Emm blinked. She hadn't thought it was quite that shabby.

Miss Mallard scribbled on her notepad, muttering furiously. "Invitations must be sent out! Heavens! Tuesday next!
We shall never get everything done. And flowers—at this
time of the year they will have to be heavy on the greenery."

She made another note. "The menu for the wedding
breakfast—something elegant and delicious. Is it the right
season for quails? I must consult Cook."

Bemused, Emm said, "Ma'am? Are you perhaps, thinking
of organizing the wedding? Because there's really no need—"

Miss Mallard glanced up. "No *need*? What a foolish question, child. Of course there is."

"But it's to be a small, quiet wedding only."

"Nonsense! You don't think I'm going to let an opportunity like this pass, do you? Not only do the *pupils* of the
Mallard Seminary marry well—we have three duchesses,
two marchionesses, five countesses, six viscountesses and
the rest"—she dismissed the lower titles with a wave—"even
our *teachers* can marry earls!"

THE DAYS THAT FOLLOWED DISAPPEARED IN A WHIRL OF
activity. First came the visit to Madame Floria the dressmaker,
who, once she heard whom Emm was to marry—and at the
abbey, where no doubt the bishop would wed them—gladly
and ruthlessly set aside her current orders and vowed she
would have a most beautiful dress ready in time.

Emm then proceeded to disgust both Miss Mallard and
Madame Floria by preferring a simple dress in sage green
wool to their choice of silver tissue and lace.

"I don't want anything fussy. It's to be a quiet, practical
wedding," she told them. "Besides, I would rather be warm."

"Nonsense, Emmaline. You're to be a *countess*. His lordship might be impetuous in his haste to marry you, but you
have a position to think of. You would not wish his lordship
to be embarrassed by a drab bride, now would you? Of course

not, so begin as you mean to go on." Miss Mallard was determined Emm would make a splash, the dressmaker too.

In the end, they settled on a dress of cream silk, trimmed with lace and pearls simply cut, with puffed sleeves and topped—in a sop to what Miss Mallard called Emm's ridiculous insistence on warmth; brides who were to become countesses apparently didn't *need* to be warm—with a long-sleeved spencer in cream silk velvet, delicately ruched, with a high collar, and buttoned down the front with pearl buttons. And when Madame Floria produced a lovely cream shawl of silk and cashmere, it was pronounced to be perfect.

It was the most expensive clothing Emm had ever owned, and the most beautiful, and since all her other clothes were extremely plain, not to mention rather worn in places, Emm decided to take Lord Ashendon at his word and ordered a dress in the sage green wool as well and a warm pelisse in claret velvet. She had no idea where they were going after the wedding—to London, or to his family seat, wherever that was, or somewhere else, but green wool was far more practical for traveling than cream velvet.

And there was some wisdom in beginning as she meant to go on. She might feel like the beggar maid to his King Cophetua, but she'd be damned if she would dress like it.

On that thought she ordered another two dresses, and a pelisse in dark green with silver braiding *à la hussar.*

To the order she added chemises, petticoats and various other undergarments, as well as stockings and four nightgowns, two in cotton lawn and two in thick flannel. Her own nightgowns were well worn, mended and patched in places and not something she wished anyone to see, not even a maid, let alone her husband.

These she insisted on paying for herself. It was bad enough expecting Lord Ashendon to pay for her wedding dress, but just the thought of him perusing a bill for her undergarments caused her cheeks to heat.

Then there were shoes to purchase—and here Emm fell for a pair of cream kid slippers, not in the slightest bit practical but so sweet and pretty, and a dashing pair of red leather ankle boots.

After years of hoarding every penny, it was frighteningly easy to fall into a frenzy of shopping, but Emm did her best to control herself. When you were marrying a man for reasons unrelated to love, you didn't want to begin the marriage by going on a spending spree with his money.

The days flew past. There were invitations to write, fittings at Madame Floria's, consultations with Cook and local suppliers over the wedding breakfast menu and most nerve-racking of all, a visit to Lady Dorothea and the girls who would become her sisters-in-law and niece by marriage.

She'd assumed Lord Ashendon would be there to introduce her as his affianced bride, but he hadn't yet returned from London.

Emm had had some idea that they might resent her marrying him—she knew perfectly well the world would judge it a most unequal match, and while she'd always gotten on well with Lady Dorothea and the girls, having a pleasant acquaintanceship with a schoolteacher was one thing; welcoming that same schoolteacher into your family was quite another. And having a nobody suddenly outranking you . . . well, she couldn't blame them for resenting her.

But as it happened, the Rutherford ladies welcomed Emm warmly, only the girl called George hanging back, which was not surprising, since they'd never met. It didn't take long for Emm to realize that a good part of Rose and Lily's delight was rooted in their determination to be bridesmaids, and she immediately invited all three girls to attend her at her wedding.

Rose and Lily accepted with joy. George demurred, but her youthful aunts insisted that she would soon get used to dresses and of course she would be a bridesmaid. Emm blinked at the references to not being used to dresses but supposed it would become clearer as she became better acquainted with the girl.

The girls immediately fell to discussing what they would wear and in what colors—apparently their late brother had forbidden the wearing of mourning black: the best thing he'd ever done for them, according to Lily. The *only* thing he'd ever done for them, Rose said.

Lady Dorothea smiled benignly on the girls and helped Emm compose a list of people on the groom's side who needed to be invited. There weren't many relatives, she assured Emm, and the short notice as well as the distance would ensure that few guests would attend.

"But don't worry, Ashendon will give a ball to introduce you to everyone when you go to London," she assured Emm.

Emm had her doubts. It seemed Lord Ashendon hadn't informed his aunt of his plans to marry Emm and head off to the Continent post-haste. But if he hadn't told Lady Dorothea, she wasn't going to do it for him.

Back at Miss Mallard's, the news had spread through the school like wildfire, and the girls' excitement became almost a frenzy when Miss Mallard announced that the entire school would attend the wedding.

Everywhere Emm went she saw clusters of girls, whispering and giggling with, as often as not, Lavinia Fortescue-Brown at the center of each group. On further inquiry she learned that Lavinia was claiming she'd introduced the happy couple. Heaven knew what other tales she was telling—the girl had a very fertile imagination.

But when she summoned Lavinia and demanded to know what she had been telling the others, Lavinia's answer floored her. "Your advice about not encouraging men, that they want what they can't have, and being cool to them will only make them more eager—well, I didn't really believe you at the time, but it was *so* right, wasn't it, Miss Westwood? And you're the proof!"

Emm blinked. "I am?"

Lavinia nodded vigorously. "You were so cold that day toward Lord Ashendon—almost rude, really—and now you're going to marry him!"

WHEN CAL TOLD GALBRAITH, HIS FRIEND LET OUT A HARSH crack of laughter. "Both of us donning the shackles of respectability! How the mighty have fallen. And of course I'll be your best man."

Cal had returned to Bath the previous day. It was a little

late to be asking someone to play best man, but he knew Galbraith would be here and available. "So it's all going ahead?"

Galbraith nodded. "Grandfather is in high gig—he and the girl's father have been wrangling happily over the settlements all week. Soon as they're settled, the deed will be done. And at Bath Abbey, no less." He grimaced. "You inspired that idea, you swine. I was hoping for something small and private, but no, they're thrilled at the idea of a wedding conducted by a bishop"

"Sorry. The bishop was a friend of my aunt's." As Aunt Agatha had pointed out in a scathing response to his letter informing her of his intended marriage, *If you must marry a nobody in a hasty skimble-skamble wedding, doing the deed in the abbey might—and I say only might—limit the gossip.*

"Can't you tell them you'd prefer a small, quiet wedding?"

Galbraith shrugged. "In truth, I don't much care. Weddings are women's business."

True enough, Cal thought. Between them, Miss Westwood, Aunt Dottie, Miss Mallard and the girls had managed the whole thing. Cal was very grateful to be spared the bother. All he had to do was turn up.

THE MORNING OF EMM'S WEDDING DAY DAWNED CLEAR, with the promise of sunshine.

All morning—all week, really—the school had been a hive of excitement with the entire school preparing to attend. The girls, all dressed in their best white dresses, had just left, walking down the hill to the abbey in an orderly but excited crocodile, escorted by Miss Johnstone, Miss Thwaites, Miss Clegg and Miss Theale.

Miss Mallard was having a last-minute consultation with Cook and the servants, putting the finishing touches to the wedding breakfast.

Emm waited in the hall. She'd assumed that she would walk to the abbey with the rest of the school, but Lord Ashendon had sent a note the previous day to say his carriage would collect her. The ceremony was set for eleven. It was quarter to eleven, so any minute now.

Emm paced back and forth. She would rather have walked with the girls. At least it was something to do.

Her footsteps echoed. The school had never been so quiet. For the hundredth time, she glanced at her reflection in the looking glass. She didn't look like herself at all. She looked younger. Prettier. Her skin, framed in cream silk velvet, seemed to glow. And her hair . . . Who'd have thought hair could make such a difference?

Earlier in the week, Miss Mallard had arranged for the most fashionable hairstylist in Bath to attend Emm—all things were possible for a future countess, it seemed. Monsieur Phillipe was an elegantly dressed, flamboyant "Frenchman" whose accent came and went, revealing a hint of Liverpool between the Gallic exclamations.

He'd spent some time draping Emm's hair in various ways, examining her from all angles, all the time muttering to himself. Then he'd seized his scissors and shocked Emm by snipping off several locks at the front.

"Tst!" he exclaimed when she objected. "You have all zis beautiful 'air and you scrape all of it back in one ugly knot. It does nothing for you. Tst!" And he snipped on regardless.

Only when he'd finished did he allow Emm to look in the mirror.

Emm had examined her reflection, turning her head this way and that. Her hair was naturally curly—Papa had called it "perpetually untidy"—and she'd always kept it long so she could keep it in a neat bun. Monsieur Phillipe had left it long at the back, but all around her face tiny soft curls clustered.

Papa would have hated it, but Emm was almost breathless. Who knew she could look so . . . ? She was almost pretty.

Seeing her reaction, the hairdresser clucked with satisfaction. "See, Monsieur Phillipe *always* know what will suit a lady—better than the lady, *n'est-ce pas*? I soften ze face and emphasize ze vairy fine cheekbones for you, mademoiselle. And with no need of ze curling irons."

"Thank you, Monsieur," Emm murmured.

"Now I suggest you have your maid gather it up like so, perhaps with two leetle braids, like so, and then—"

"I don't have a maid," Emm told him. "I will be doing my hair myself."

Monsieur Phillipe staggered back in theatrical Gallic shock. "Oh, *non non non*! It cannot be! I do not expend my artistry on a lady, only to have her do it *herself*!"

"But I'm perfectly capable. I've been doing my own hair all my life."

He dismissed that argument with a "Tsst!" and a scornful wave. He sent for Miss Mallard and after she'd been directed to admire his genius, he declared, "But ze lady has no maid of her own, and It Will Not Do!"

"Good heavens, you are quite right, Monsieur. I should have thought of it earlier. I will contact the employment agency at once. They will send some up lady's maids for interview—"

"That's not necessary," Emm said.

"But you must have your own personal maid," Miss Mallard insisted. "You have a position to maintain." Monsieur Phillipe nodded vigorously. "If you enter Lord Ashendon's home without your own maid," Miss Mallard continued, "all the servants will look down on you."

Emm lifted her chin. "I don't care." She wouldn't allow anyone to look down on her, servants or not.

"Perhaps not, but Lord Ashendon will."

It was Miss Mallard's second favorite saying, a clincher to every argument—*Lord Ashendon will expect*—and the devil of it was, Emm had no basis to argue back. She barely knew Lord Ashendon, let alone what he expected or wanted. As far as she knew, "no trouble" best summed up what she knew of his wants. Would arriving without a maid be classed as trouble or not? What did she know of what earls expected?

"Very well, if I must have a maid, I will take Milly with me."

Miss Mallard snorted. "Milly? My housemaid? Nonsense, that girl isn't trained to be a lady's maid."

"Vairy true." Monsieur Phillipe nodded wisely. "You must have a girl who knows how to care for ze hair and clothes."

"Then she will learn. Will you be so kind as to show her how to do my hair, Monsieur?" Emm asked. "Because I will take Milly or no one."

Milly was kind and clever and at Miss Mallard's she scrubbed and cleaned from dawn to midnight—and still thought to put a hot brick—unasked—into Emm's bed. The counterarguments flew around the room, but Emm stayed firm. It would be Milly or no one—as long as Milly agreed. Emm thought she'd jump at the chance.

Milly, summoned, had arrived at the door, pale and worried-looking and smoothing her dress with nervous hands. It took her a moment to comprehend what Emm was saying, and when she did, her whole face lit up. "Oh, miss, you mean I'm to come with you and be your lady's maid? In London? Truly?"

Smiling, Emm nodded. "If you'd like to."

"Would I like to? I'll say I would!" Milly glanced at Miss Mallard's pinched expression and added tactfully, "Of course I'll be sad to leave Miss Mallard's, but if you think I could be of help, Miss Westwood, I'd be glad to work for you." Her eyes were shining.

"Then that's settled," Emm said. She was spending more of Lord Ashendon's money, but if a maid was something he'd expect her to have, she had no option.

Monsieur Phillipe pursed his lips and then snapped his fingers. "Come here then, girl, and let me see what you can do." Under his critical supervision Milly arranged Emm's hair.

Eventually he sniffed and said, "It will do. Now, remember what I said, start simple and practice at every opportunity. I will, of course, style Miss Westwood's 'air for ze wedding, but after that you will be on your own. There are schoolgirls here—practice on them." He arched a brow at Miss Mallard, who gave a grudging nod. "Come to my par-

lor and I will provide you with all the implements you will
need for ze lady's hair. I will also give you some cream for
your hands. Your skin is rough, like a scrubbing girl's. A
lady's maid must have hands like silk, understand me, girl?"

"Yes, sir." Milly curtseyed.

"Send the bill to Lord Ashendon," Miss Mallard said
crisply. Which was, Emm knew, Miss Mallard's new favorite saying.

And now the wedding day had arrived, cold, but bright
with sunshine.

Milly, after helping Emm to dress, had gone ahead to the
church with the girls. Miss Mallard had wanted her to help
Cook, but since she'd already engaged extra staff for the
event, Emm had insisted. Milly worked for her now, and she
wanted her at the wedding.

Oh, where was that carriage? The waiting was unbear-
able. She wanted this wedding over and done with.

The ancient medieval abbey was chilly. The interior
smelled of beeswax, incense, ancient stone and Christmas,
Cal thought as he entered, though Christmas was long past.
He soon saw the reason: Clusters of pine and other evergreens
bound with long white ribbons were attached to the end of
every pew, with some kind of white and pink flower at the
center of each cluster. On closer examination he saw that the
flowers were made of wax and varied greatly in form and
elegance. Odd, but he supposed flowers were hard to come
by at this season.

Though someone had managed: Huge sprays of larkspur
and lilies and Queen Anne's lace graced carved oak pedes-
tals on either side of the nave.

Cal ran a finger around his collar. It felt unaccountably
tight.

Ned Galbraith eyed him. "Uniform don't fit anymore?"

"It fits." He might be on temporary leave, but he was still
a soldier on His Majesty's service, and dress uniform was
the appropriate garb for his wedding.

"Nerves, then."

"Not particularly," Cal lied. He was, in fact, ridiculously nervous. Galbraith, on the other hand, seemed unaccountably hearty. "What's put the smile back on your face?" he asked his friend. "Dutch courage?"

"Haven't touched a drop. No need," Galbraith said. "The wedding's off."

"Off?" Cal's blood froze for a minute. "Oh, you mean your wedding. What happened?"

"Grandfather and the girl's father had a falling-out. No, what am I saying? It was the Falling-Out of the Century. Couldn't agree over the settlements. Then they started to shred each other's characters, dredging up incidents from the dim dark ages—did I mention they'd known each other practically their whole lives?—so there was plenty to dredge. And then the girl clinched the matter by saying she thought I'd make a terrible husband, that I was a rake and a libertine, cold-hearted, irreligious, unprincipled and irredeemable!"

Cal frowned. "That's a bit strong."

"Lord, no, it's all perfectly true. I don't give a damn what she thinks of me—I was only doing it for the old man."

"And how has he taken it?"

Galbraith gave wry grin. "The canny old bastard's gone home in high dudgeon—no sign of him being at death's door anymore, in fact he left here wonderfully refreshed—by the fight, in my opinion, though he claims it's those disgusting Bath waters. At any rate, whatever the cause, for the moment at least, I'm free as a bird." People started filing into the church. "Here they come, it's starting. Last chance to cut and run, Rutherford."

"No chance of that." Cal straightened his shoulders. His stomach hollowed a little more. It was a straightforward practical arrangement, he reminded himself. A marriage of convenience.

A susurration of excited murmurs drew his attention, and he turned to see an apparently endless line of young girls, all dressed in white, filing into the church. Under the supervision of a couple of elderly ladies they seated themselves on the bride's side, whispering and giggling.

One of the young girls caught Cal's eye and waved enthusiastically. Lavinia Thingummy-Whatsit of the Shropshire Thingummy-Whatsits. He lifted a hand in acknowledgment, which caused a surge in the giggles and excited exchanges, followed by a flurry of teacherly shushes.

It looked as though the whole school had come to see Miss Westwood married. Good. He was glad she had someone.

The organ started playing, and his pulse leapt—was the ceremony about to start?—but it was only some bland piece, no doubt intended to reinforce an atmosphere of holy contemplation—and drown the schoolgirls' steadily rising chatter and their teachers' hushing.

The pews continued filling, and it was soon seen that the bride's side was very respectably occupied, while the groom's was lamentably sparse. It seemed Miss Westwood had a great many friends and acquaintances come to wish her well on her wedding day.

On Cal's side, it seemed mostly made up of the curious—Aunt Dottie's friends and acquaintances and those who'd tried to snare him for their granddaughters. He spotted "the poodle" and his grandmother, looking quite . . . poodle-y.

The organ stopped. Silence hung for a moment in the ancient abbey, then the music swelled. Purcell. Cal straightened. This was it, then. He turned to face his convenient bride, and his mouth dried.

She paused a moment at the head of the aisle, straight and slender and . . . exquisite, in cream silk and lace, dark hair clustering in tiny curls around her face, a lace veil pinned over her hair, spilling down over her shoulders, framing her alabaster countenance in mystery without quite covering it.

"You didn't tell me she was a beauty," Galbraith murmured in Cal's ear.

Cal didn't reply. He didn't know. He hadn't realized.

Her face was pale and set, as if prepared for an ordeal. She glanced at him and her gaze passed on, as if she were looking for someone else. Then she frowned slightly. Her gaze returned to him and her eyes widened.

For a long moment she didn't move. They stood there

staring at each other while the music surged and swelled all around them, and the congregation watched.

He wondered for a second if she was about to turn and run but then, with a little jerk, she moved forward and began to walk toward him.

Chapter Twelve

HAIL sun-beams in the east are spread;
Leave, leave, fair bride, your solitary bed;
No more shall you return to it alone.
—JOHN DONNE, "EPITHALAMION AT LINCOLN'S INN"

IF IT HADN'T BEEN FOR ROSE, EMM MIGHT HAVE FORGOTTEN
to move at all. She almost hadn't recognized him.

She'd always thought him a handsome man, but now, seeing him waiting at the altar—waiting for her—stern and
severe-looking in his uniform, with its tight-fitting, heavily
braided scarlet coat, white breeches and gleaming high boots,
he was . . . magnificent.

The sight of him quite took her breath away. And for a
few moments had robbed her of all intelligent thought.

Thank goodness Rose still had her wits about her. She'd
given Emm a discreet shove in the small of her back and
hissed, "Go *on*, Miss Westwood."

And Emm had recollected herself and started the long
walk down the aisle. To marry this magnificent man, this
stranger that she hardly knew.

The church smelled of pine and when she noticed the
little posies with the white wax flowers tied to the end of
each pew, she realized the reason for the flurry of wax flower
making that had occupied the girls at the school in the last
week. Each flower made with love for her wedding.

And there they were, all her girls, smiling, nodding, a
few waving, all misty eyed. Some already weeping.

Her eyes blurred. She blinked hard to chase the tears

away and tried to smile. She would not cry, she would not. This was not the romantic wedding they were all dreaming of. It was a convenient arrangement, nothing more.

She reached the altar and placed her hand, cold and nerveless, in his.

"Dearly beloved . . ."

The ceremony passed in a blur.

". . . ordained for the procreation of children . . ."

Yes, children. She fastened on the thought. She ached for a child of her own.

". . . if any man can show any just cause . . ."

She waited, tense, as if somehow, ridiculously, there would be a line of people ready to come forward shouting, "Stop the wedding." But of course, nobody made a sound.

"Who giveth this woman to be married to this man?"

There was a small stir of surprise in the congregation when Miss Mallard stepped forward to give Emm away. It was unconventional but not illegal. Emm glanced at Lord Ashendon, but he made no sign of either approval or the opposite. He looked straight ahead, his face stern and unchanging.

"Wilt thou have this man to thy wedded husband . . ."

She heard her voice repeating the vows, sounding admirably calm and collected, as if someone else were making the responses for her. She didn't feel at all calm. Serpents writhed in the pit of her stomach.

"With this ring I thee wed . . ."

She felt the gold ring slide onto her finger, and it was warm, not cold, from being held in someone's hand. His hand.

". . . with my body I thee worship . . ."

She tried to swallow, and couldn't.

". . . I pronounce that they be man and wife . . ."

Man and wife. It was done.

There followed prayers and a sermon and psalms and communion and the signing of the register, and she went through them all in a daze, making all the right responses but all the time one thought ringing in her brain: *I am married. I am Lord Ashendon's wife.*

* * *

THE WEDDING BREAKFAST WAS, EMM SUPPOSED, A ROUSING success as far as Miss Mallard was concerned. As well as Lord Ashendon's family and a few friends, mostly of his aunt, Emm had a bare handful of her own friends attending, and some acquaintances from church.

The rest had been invited by Miss Mallard, apparently with a view to highlighting what she'd come to regard as her own personal triumph. *". . . three duchesses, two marchionesses, five countesses, six viscountesses. . . . and now our beloved Miss Westwood has become the Countess of Ashendon!"* If Emm heard her say it once, she heard it a dozen times. And guess who was the partridge in the pear tree?

Emm talked to everyone, acting much as if this were one of the usual school events involving prospective parents. Lord Ashendon introduced her to his best man, Mr. Galbraith, and a couple of distant cousins who had traveled from adjacent counties to attend the wedding.

Her bridal attendants, Rose and Lily and Georgiana, who'd muttered that she only answered to George, looked fresh and young and lovely in varying shades of pink to palest lilac—the first time in forever, Rose told her, that they'd been allowed to wear colors.

Lady Dorothea, dressed in deep purple, was busy explaining to everyone that it was her late nephew's desire, expressed in the Strongest Possible Terms in his will, that nobody should wear mourning for him. And that Ashendon, as the Head of the Family, had made it An Order.

"You'll meet most of my relations when we go to London," Lord Ashendon murmured in her ear, so close she could feel his breath on her skin. She jumped.

"And when shall that be?" Emm asked, realizing she had no idea where she was going next—not even where she would spend the night tonight. Her wedding night.

She was wholly in her husband's control now.

"Soon," he told her. "I need to attend to a few matters at Ashendon Court, my principal estate, first."

"And where is Ashendon Court, my lord?"

He said, as if he expected her to know, "In Oxfordshire." And when she continued to regard him with a faintly quizzical air, he added, "Not far from Stanford-in-the-Vale. You'll see it tomorrow."

"Tomorrow?"

"Yes, it will be too dark to see anything by the time we arrive tonight."

"Tonight?"

"Yes." He glanced at a clock on the overmantel. "We leave in half an hour."

"Half an hour?" she echoed, feeling somewhat like a parrot. "But I haven't . . ."

"Haven't what? Packed?" His brows drew together. "Surely you anticipated a bridal trip."

"I did, of course," she told him. "Foolish of me, no doubt, but I assumed I would be consulted on the matter. And at least asked whether I would wish to undertake a long journey by carriage on my wedding day." She gave him a cool smile and went to begin saying her good-byes, a little knot of irritation stiffening her spine.

She supposed an earl would be naturally autocratic, especially one who'd been an officer for most of his adult life. But she didn't have to like being ordered about like one of his soldiers.

She'd assumed he would have engaged a suite at York House or one of the other premier hotels in Bath. Or that they would spend a few days at some grand home belonging to one of his friends or relations. It had even occurred to her that they might sleep the night at Lady Dorothea's—though that was not ideal.

She would rather have as much privacy as possible for her wedding night.

Because that was a hurdle yet to come.

THE CARRIAGE PULLED AWAY TO A CHORUS OF GOOD-BYES and well-wishes, some of them surprisingly tearful. Emm waved through the carriage window until the school was out of sight. Battling with unexpected emotion herself, she sat back against the well-padded leather seats and found Lord Ashendon's hard gray eyes observing her closely.

Without a word, he handed her a large white handkerchief.

She took it and wiped away the few tears that dampened her cheeks.

"You are sad to leave?"

She thought about it. "Not really, but I've lived there for most of my life—pupil and teacher, and . . . I have friends there."

She'd been content enough at the Mallard Seminary, but never really happy. She'd been granted refuge there seven years ago and was grateful. She'd loved working with the girls, but they passed through the school and went on to make new lives for themselves, no doubt never giving Emm or any of the teachers another thought.

Emm's future prospects had been depressingly predictable. Now, married to Lord Ashendon, she had no idea what the future would bring. It was exciting . . . and a little daunting.

"You will be able to visit your friends when you visit my aunt."

"I know." But it wouldn't be the same. What friendships she'd made had developed through proximity and habit, mostly.

He glanced at her maid, sitting quiet as a mouse beside her. "You will too . . . er—"

"Milly," Emm told him.

Miss Mallard had told Emm that Milly should wear her thickest coat and take a rug, as she'd be riding at the back of the carriage, but Lord Ashendon had handed Emm up, then turned to Milly and indicated she was to ride inside as well.

The conversation for the next few miles was general and a little stilted, consisting mainly of comments on the passing scenery. Milly's presence prevented anything intimate or personal from being discussed, for which Emm was grateful.

Was that why he'd seated the girl inside, or was it kindness on his part? It was a cold day, and his coachman was wrapped and muffled to the eyebrows.

She hoped it was kindness.

At the first stop to change horses, Lord Ashendon produced pillows and rugs from a compartment inside the carriage, saying, "Get some sleep, if you can. It's a long journey and we won't arrive until long after nightfall."

Emm and Milly wrapped themselves warmly and snuggled down. The carriage was comfortable and beautifully sprung. Milly dropped off quickly, but Emm found herself feigning sleep. She was too aware of Lord Ashendon. At first he simply watched the scenery slip by, then his gaze came to rest silently on her. She could feel the weight of it, even though her eyes were shut.

Was he also thinking of the wedding night to come?

She was wound tense as a spring.

A blast of sound woke Emm from a fitful doze.

"Hawkins, requesting the gates be opened," Lord Ashendon explained.

"We're here, then?" She tried to peer out but could see only the carriage lights and shadowy darkness beyond.

She heard the coachman grumbling, "Who? Who? Lord Ashendon and his lady, of course, who did you think! And you knew we was coming so why the 'ell didn't you 'ave the gates open and waiting?" The gatekeeper mumbled something she couldn't make out, and the gates opened.

The carriage passed between two large brick pillars and continued along an avenue of twisty old trees so ancient their branches met overhead. It was like passing through a tunnel.

"Yews," Lord Ashendon commented. "Planted by some long-dead ancestor."

Ashendon Court came into view. Lights were blazing from a dozen windows. "It was originally built in the sixteenth century, a manor house, but my great-grandfather had it extended and modernized last century. He added the wings. But you'll see it all in the morning."

The carriage halted and half a dozen servants came running down the front steps to greet them. Lord Ashendon introduced them all to Emm, then said, "Mrs. Moffat, the housekeeper, will show you to your room. Wash, refresh yourself, and when you're comfortable, come down to the dining room. You must be famished."

Emm wasn't in the least bit hungry. Quite the opposite.

Entering the house, she followed the housekeeper and caught a glimpse of what must have been a medieval hall. A great, gloomy cavern of a room, it was paneled in dark wood with an arched, smoke-darkened ceiling crisscrossed with heavy wooden beams. The walls bristled with weapons—swords, blunderbusses, pikes, shields—and antlers. Knights, or rather their suits of armor, stood sentry at each corner of the room, watched over by the dull, reproachful eyes of a dozen or more mounted and stuffed animal heads and half a dozen portraits of dour and disapproving gentlemen—presumably her husband's ancestors. A roaring fire blazed in a huge old stone fireplace, the light thrown by its flames causing the knights and weapons to glitter and the dead eyes of the dead beasts to gleam.

"This way, my lady."

Emm followed the elderly woman upstairs.

Twenty minutes later she was seated at one end of a long, highly polished table. Lord Ashendon sat at the other end. Servants flowed back and forth between them, serving what the housekeeper called a simple meal: soup, roast chicken, a dish of vegetables and a custard tart. And wine, several different kinds, one with soup, one with chicken and so on.

Emm ate very little and drank even less, though she knew that wine might help relax her. It might also cause her to throw up. There was little talk exchanged—they were seated too far apart for it to feel in the slightest bit conversational, and she wasn't about to shout commonplace pleasantries at him.

After what seemed like an age, Lord Ashendon made a gesture and the servants silently withdrew. He set his napkin aside. "You're not eating."

"I'm not hungry." The serpents were back, writhing in her stomach.

There was a short silence, then he said quietly, "Would you prefer to delay the wedding night? Wait until you are less tired. And we are better acquainted."

"No."

He gave her a searching look. "You're sure?"

"I'm sure." She wanted to get it over with.

"Very well, then. I'll join you in your bedchamber in half an hour."

CAL SIPPED HIS COGNAC SLOWLY. HE'D NEVER LAIN WITH a virgin before. He'd have to take it slow and careful. Gently does it.

He closed his eyes. Like restraining wild horses. He'd wanted her, dreamed of taking her ever since he'd kissed her that one time. One taste and . . . fire in the blood.

But he would control himself. Tonight, at least.

He finished his cognac and went upstairs.

His valet was still abroad, but his father's elderly valet, Higgins, had unpacked and put all his things away and was waiting with hot water. Higgins seemed to have been kicking his heels here for the last year. Had Henry done nothing at all to organize the estate?

Cal had no need for a valet, but Higgins waited hopefully, so he allowed the man to help him remove his coat, waistcoat and boots, then dismissed him for the night. Higgins left, carrying Cal's boots.

He stripped to the waist, washed, cleaned his teeth and then, as an afterthought, shaved himself carefully. Her skin would be tender. He dried his face, splashed on a little cologne water and combed his hair.

He turned and saw that Higgins had laid out a nightshirt and dressing gown on his bed. A nightshirt? He never wore the things.

But she was a virgin. Maybe he should wear it so she was not too shocked by the sight of a naked man. A naked, erect man. His body was already thrumming with anticipation.

Start as you mean to go on. He stripped off the rest of his clothes and shrugged into the dressing gown.

Would she even know what to do? What he was going to do to her?

He'd heard stories of ladies who had no idea of what

passed between men and women, who'd screamed and fought on their wedding night, who'd been horrified and disgusted by the whole process.

Of course the first time was supposed to be a little painful, but he'd always heard that if you took care with a virgin, took things slowly, made sure she was well warmed up, her passions ignited and her juices flowing, the pain would be negligible.

Trouble was he'd never taken a virgin before. His previous lovers had all been experienced women who knew what they liked and demanded he give it to them.

Cal prided himself on his ability to ensure a woman's satisfaction as well as his own. This was his wife. First time or not, he would do his best to make it good for her.

He knocked softly on the connecting door.

EMM LAY IN BED, WAITING, TENSE AS A VIOLIN STRING, straining her ears. She could hear him moving about in the dressing room that connected their two bedrooms, the low hum of male voices—talking to a servant?—a few splashing noises. A lot of silence.

She'd washed quickly, using the French rose-vanilla soap that was a gift from one of the girls, and cleaned her teeth. She slipped on her bridal nightgown, a gift from a favorite former pupil, Sally Destry, now married and a countess in London. Arriving in a box from something called the House of Chance, it was unlike any nightgown she'd ever seen: peach silk, almost transparent, with soft, loose ruffles that almost—but not quite—preserved her modesty.

If ever she needed a nightgown like this, it was tonight.

Then a knock, and before she could say a word, the door was open and there he stood, a dark silhouette against the light in the room behind. "You haven't fallen asleep, then," he murmured.

Her laugh was a little forced. He was wearing a silk brocade dressing gown in dark reds and golds. There was a deep vee of bare skin at his throat and a slight dusting of chest hair.

She'd left just one candle burning beside the bed.

"I suppose you would prefer darkness," he said.

She made a noncommittal sound. She'd prefer some light. She wanted to see him. But that wasn't very bridal, she supposed.

He snuffed the candle out. The room was dim, lit only by the light from the fire, dancing and ephemeral. Just enough for her to see him. She was glad of it. He was worth looking at.

He sat on the edge of the bed and leaned over her, his arms braced on either side of her body. He smelled clean and warm and his cologne was light, bracing, enticingly masculine.

"It will be all right, you know."

Emm hoped so. She was trembling a little. She shouldn't be, but she couldn't help it. She ran her tongue over her dry lips.

He made a low sound deep in his throat, bent and touched his mouth to hers. The lightest of caresses, a bare brush of skin against skin. Masculine aromas teased her senses. Heat, spice, a beguiling hint of tooth powder and brandy. He teased, tantalized, aroused. She wanted more, heard a soft murmur and realized it came from her.

His fingers were in her hair, cupping her head, angling her mouth to him as he eased her lips apart. The taste of him flowed into her, potent, dark heat of man. His mouth sought, demanded a response she hadn't expected, hadn't known was in her.

His mouth enslaved her. Ripples of sensation washed through her. She melted, mindless, clutching onto him as if she were falling, not pressed beneath his hard heated body.

He cupped her breast, brushed fingers across her nipple, and a jolt of pleasure-pain-heat speared through her. She arched herself against him, moving restlessly, not knowing what she craved, except more.

He sat back, a sudden withdrawal that abruptly chilled her. Her eyes flew open. He rose and pulled off his dressing gown. His eyes locked with hers, he stood naked before her, a Greek god sculpted in alabaster, his member proud, erect.

She'd never seen a man wholly naked. She devoured him

with her eyes, knowing she ought to be more modest, more bridal. More virginal. But she couldn't help herself. He was magnificent.

He bent and flipped the sheets back, cooling her heated body. He stood looking down at her for a long moment. She couldn't read his expression. His face was in shadow. "Pretty nightgown," he murmured. "But we don't need it tonight."

He lifted her nightgown up, over her legs. "Lift your bottom." She lifted. Then it was over her belly and breasts. "Raise your arms."

She was naked before him. Exposed.

She wanted to hide, to cover herself, and not out of modesty. She was too tall, too thin, not endowed with the kind of curves that women should have. But she was what he'd married, for whatever reason, and she braced herself for his examination.

"You're beautiful," he murmured, and lay down beside her, his body half covering her, skin to skin, from thigh to breast, all hard masculine heat.

She supposed all men said that to their brides on their wedding night. She appreciated his kindness. She slipped her arms around his neck and pulled him to her. She wanted more of his kisses. Heated, drugging, luscious kisses.

He explored her then, thoroughly, with hands and lips. He ravished her with his mouth, nibbling, licking, finding places on her body that she had no idea were so sensitive. Or arousing.

His hand slipped between her thighs, and he lavished attention on her breasts, while all the time his cunning fingers drove her mindless, teasing, soothing, drawing ripples, waves, shudders from her body.

Her body vibrated to his every touch. Absorbing him, enraptured by the relentless, seductive ravishment of his mouth and hands, she slowly lost all sense of herself. She was nothing, a being consisting of nothing but sensation. And aching, desperate need.

He moved over her, and without conscious volition her legs parted, trembling with anticipation.

She felt him, hot and heavy and blunt at her entrance,

and her body clenched with longing. He hesitated, and without thought she pushed herself against him.

He entered her with a long, hard thrust and a loud moan. She took him with something between a whimper and a gasp. He paused, lodged deep within her, then began to pull back.

She locked her legs around him, hauling him closer, taking him deeper.

And then with a heavy, guttural sound he was moving inside her, plunging . . . thrusting . . . driving her . . . to frantic need. Desperation. And ecstasy.

Lost to everything, she shuddered and thrashed around him. A final, husky groan, a gush of warmth within her. She trembled on the pinnacle of . . . something . . . and then . . .

The room was dim when she finally opened her eyes. The candle in the dressing room had burned to a stub; the fire was down to coals.

She must have fainted. Or something. But only for a few minutes, she was sure. He lay beside her, breathing heavily, as if he'd just run a mile.

She was panting too, but she felt loose, floaty, totally relaxed. Euphoric.

Why had nobody ever told her that lying with a man could be like . . . like *that*?

The chill of the night was creeping over her bare skin. She reached for the covers to pull over them.

"Awake, are you?" He sat up and turned to look down at her. She could just see his profile, limned by the dying firelight.

"When were you going to tell me?" His voice was hard. Accusing.

Oh, God. "Tell you?" she managed in a voice that shook only a little.

"That you weren't a virgin."

There was a long silence. A thousand possibilities raced through Emm's mind. But only one was the truth. "I hoped you wouldn't notice."

Chapter Thirteen

A girl, no virgin either, I should guess—a baggage
Thrust on me like a cargo on a ship
To wreck my peace of mind.
—SOPHOCLES, *WOMEN OF TRACHIS*
(TRANS. E. F. WATLING)

CAL COULDN'T BELIEVE HIS EARS. "YOU HOPED I *WOULDN'T notice?*"

She swallowed and nodded.

He waited for an explanation. She pulled the bedclothes up to cover her nakedness, then sat there silent and unmoving, making no attempt to explain or justify herself.

Anger licked at him. He'd striven so hard to ensure that her first time was the best he could make it—and it wasn't her first time at all. It didn't help to know that, far from exerting total control over himself, he'd utterly lost it.

But that was her fault, responding like . . . like . . .

He grabbed his dressing gown and flung it on, shoving his arms into the sleeves so violently he heard something tear. He didn't care. He seized the candle, marched to the dressing room and lit it from the stub that was about to gutter.

He lit two more candles—this wasn't a conversation you could have in the dark—and placed them where they would light her face best. He stood over her, arms folded. "Who was it?"

For a long moment he thought she wasn't going to answer him. Her eyes were wide and dark; her skin glowed, honey and silk in the soft candlelight. Her expression was unreadable.

The scent of their lovemaking filled his nostrils. Rose and vanilla, aroused woman, and musky, salty, raw unbridled sex. His body stirred in response. He wanted her again. Already.

His patience snapped. "Dammit, I asked you a question. And don't bother giving me a pack of lies. Who the hell was it?"

She seemed to be considering what to say. Eventually she said, "It doesn't matter."

"I'll be the judge of that!"

She gave him a long, thoughtful look, tucked the bed-clothes more tightly around her and said with a tiny shrug of one tantalizingly bare shoulder, "I was seventeen. I thought I was in love. There's been no one since."

The cool, bare-bones summary infuriated him. She showed no contrition at all. If she'd wept, apologized, begged his forgiveness, he might have, after a judicious period, for-given her.

But this, this matter-of-fact account that explained nothing— *nothing!*—drove him wild.

He wanted to throttle her. He wanted to beat her.

He wanted to take her back to bed and make love to her until they were both insensible.

"We will talk of this in the morning," he said, and stalked from the room, slamming the door behind him.

EMM WINCED AT THE SLAMMING DOOR. SHE'D THOUGHT her lack of virginity wouldn't matter so much because their marriage had been made for purely practical reasons. And because it had all happened such a long time ago.

How wrong she'd been.

When the accusation had come, she'd been stupidly shocked. She'd been floating on a cloud of . . . bliss. Exhausted, drowsy and yet somehow . . . exhilarated. Not thinking of anything.

And then the question, harsh, accusing. For which she had no answer. No acceptable answer.

On reflection, she admitted to herself that she could have handled it better. Handled him better, instead of being stiff-necked and stubborn and refusing to apologize or beg his forgiveness.

His anger had shaken her. As if somehow it was personal, a personal betrayal.

But how could it be when they hardly knew each other?

Her emotions were all over the place. Perhaps she should have made more of an effort to tell him beforehand. But he'd shown no interest in her as a person—apart from that kiss— and the opportunity hadn't arisen.

She punched her pillow. Why should she expose herself, rip open old wounds and humiliations—and grief—open herself to the judgment of a man she barely knew? If he'd ever asked her anything about herself, ever shown the slightest interest in her life, her past, even her opinions, she would have felt obliged to tell him about Sam. But he hadn't.

She pulled the covers around her and lay staring into what remained of the fire. The glowing coals were turning to ashes of gray. The room was growing colder.

Life was so unfair. He'd obviously lain with oh, probably dozens of women, and she'd lain with one man and that only three times almost ten years ago. But she was the sinner and he was the righteously wronged.

Male pride and possessiveness.

She turned over in the bed again, unable to get comfortable, because despite her attempts to justify her actions to herself, the strongest emotion she felt was regret, because until then it had been so lovely between them. So unexpectedly sweet. Tender. She'd had no idea it could be like that . . .

Until tonight, her—admittedly limited—experience of congress between a man and woman was that it was hasty, rough and uncomfortable. But wildly exciting.

Lord Ashendon had shown her it could also be glorious . . . transcendent.

She'd felt cherished . . .

And then . . . the moment had shattered, like a delicate rainbow glass bauble crushed beneath the heel of a boot. Leaving her dazed among the shards.

She would not cry, not over this, not over anything she

could not change. Spilled milk. Story of her life. There was nothing for it but to mop it up and go on.

But how to mop this mess up?

She closed her eyes, burrowed a nest into her bedclothes as she had when she was a child and tried to sleep.

"HIS LORDSHIP SENT ME TO WAKE YOU, MISS—I MEAN, MY lady." Milly threw the curtains back, letting sunshine stream through. "Such a lovely day it is, I expect he doesn't want to waste it." She brought a tray over to Emm. "I got you sweet rolls and some hot chocolate, miss, but if you want anything else—"

"No, that will do nicely, thank you, Milly." Emm blinked at the bright sunshine. She went to sit up, then recalled she was naked. She pulled the covers around her. "What time is it?"

"After ten, but then, nobody expects you to get up early after your wedding night." Milly blushed as she picked up the silk nightgown from the floor and folded it. "It's ever such a grand house, miss—I mean, my lady." She fetched a dressing gown and handed it to Emm.

Emm slipped it on gratefully, then reached for her breakfast tray. She was famished. She poured the chocolate. "Are they treating you all right, Milly?"

"Oh, yes, m'lady. As your personal maid I'm at the top end of the servants' table. At the Duck's I was right down the other end with only the scullery maid below me." She tossed Emm a quick grin. "Of course they're all thrilled that the young master's come home after all these years, and they're beside themselves that he's married. Everyone here adores him. The previous lord, his older brother, they weren't that keen on him, but Master Cal—that's what they call him when they forget he's the earl now—he's always been their favorite, so I reckon you being his bride, you can do no wrong in their eyes."

Emm sipped her chocolate. That remained to be seen.

"Oh, and I forgot to say, the master said to tell you when you're dressed he wants to speak to you in the library."

Emm's appetite vanished. She put her breakfast tray aside.

"Draw me a bath, please, Milly." Best to beard her dragon in his den and get it over with.

"Very good, m'lady."

"WHEN SHOULD I HAVE TOLD YOU?" EMM STOOD BEFORE HIM, placed on the mat like a naughty child before the headmaster. It was petty, Cal knew, but he was feeling petty and cross. He hadn't a wink of sleep, and when he'd looked in on her this morning he'd found her sleeping the sleep of the just, looking rumpled and delectable. And infuriatingly, deceptively innocent.

It had put him in a fine temper, because of course what he wanted was to pull back the covers and take her again. And again.

But just because his body was rampant and aching with desire for her didn't mean he'd let her undermine his common sense or self-discipline. A man should be master in his own house.

A night of sleep hadn't made her the least bit more amenable or apologetic. She seemed almost indignant at his question. "When? The day you proposed? You took me so much by surprise—two minutes beforehand you'd offered me a job as a chaperone. I could hardly even believe your proposal was serious."

"If you recall, we spoke the next morning, madam."

"No, *you* did most of the speaking that day. You set out the conditions for our marriage, what you expected me to do. You never once mentioned a requirement for virginity."

"Because it was understood," he grated. Of course it was. *Bride* and *virginal* were practically interchangeable terms.

"You never asked me a single thing about myself—not about who I was, about who my family was—"

"You told me you had no family."

"And you never wondered why? Or thought to ask how I'd come to be working at Miss Mallard's, when I'd attended the seminary as a pupil?"

"I assumed—"

"Yes, you assumed." She was pacing now, back and forth.

"You assumed I'd fill the position you wanted, perform the duties you required of me, undertake the care and protection of your sisters and niece and launch them on the marriage mart—and I will. Leaving you free to pursue your 'important government duties' elsewhere."

He clenched his jaw. There was some justice in what she said, but—

"It wasn't *me* you wanted, it was a convenient wife. And that's what you got. But now you want more—you want a *perfect* wife. Well, I'm not perfect, but I *will* do right by your sisters and niece. And I will do right by you."

"I didn't mean—" He hadn't meant to insult her integrity, but was it too much for a husband to ask who'd deflowered his bride?

"After you left that day, I realized I probably should have told you then, but you'd gone to London. And then, because of your desire to have a quick wedding, by the time you returned, the invitations had gone out, the school was in a frenzy of anticipation and everything was arranged. And when I finally did see you, it was at the church. What was I to do, ask you to step into the vestry and say, '*Oh, by the way, I'm not a virgin*'?"

"No, of course not, but—" he began irritably. How did women do it? She made it sound like it was all his fault.

"Anyway, the more I thought about it, the more I decided that it wasn't relevant."

He almost choked. "Not *relevant*?"

She made an impatient gesture. "Surely the whole reason for wishing a bride to be a virgin on her wedding day is so that the groom can be assured that any child resulting from the marriage is his. Well, it's almost ten years since I had congress with a man, and I cannot possibly be pregnant." A faint blush stole across her cheeks. "Not unless last night . . ."

She lifted her chin. "But if my word is not good enough, you can refrain from . . . any further efforts to conceive until my monthly courses have passed."

Cal couldn't fault her logic. But he wasn't going to last a month, not knowing she was in the next room, all soft and lissome . . . coming alight for him at the merest touch.

"And if you conceived a child last night?"

She lifted her chin and said almost defiantly, "Then I will count myself most fortunate."

"You want a child, then?"

Her eyes went dark and dreamy. "It is my dearest wish," she said softly.

That was something, then. Cal was tempted to whisk her back upstairs and get to work on giving her one, but he had a position to maintain. And he wasn't going to let her get off too lightly. She hadn't bent an inch, damn her. She hadn't yet apologized or told him who her lover had been.

"You still haven't told me who he was." His voice was quiet, but he hoped she heard the underlying steel beneath it. He would not give up until he knew.

There was a short silence and for a moment he thought she was going to refuse to tell him. Again.

Then she sighed, all the spit and vinegar drained. She sat on the chair opposite. "Sam was a— He worked on my father's estate."

His eyes narrowed. "Your father's *estate*?"

She lifted her chin. "My father was Sir Humphrey Westwood; our home was in Berkshire."

That explained her assurance, her manners. "Was?"

"My father is dead. The estate?" She shrugged, as if to say she had no idea. And possibly didn't care.

"It was entailed?"

She shook her head. "Papa disowned me, after . . ."

He waited.

She waited a long, stubborn moment. He didn't take his eyes off her and eventually she gave a sigh, as if giving in. "I was just seventeen, naïve, innocent and wildly romantical, as girls that age often are. Sam was five-and-twenty, dark and dashing, as handsome as . . . as sin." She made a rueful gesture. "I fell madly, blindly, carelessly in love. Nothing else mattered to me, except . . . him."

"What happened?"

"Papa caught us . . . together." She swallowed. "There was a lot of shouting."

"And?" he prompted after a time.

"He offered Sam five hundred pounds to leave the country and never contact me again."

Cal's fists clenched. He wouldn't have offered him a penny—he would have horsewhipped the blackguard to within an inch of his life. Seventeen and innocent was no match for twenty-five.

"The swine took it?"

"He did." There was a long silence, then she gave a little shiver. "There has been no one since."

Cal frowned. There were gaps in her story. If her lover had been so easily bought off, why had she been disowned? And if she'd been seventeen when she was disowned. . . She was six-and-twenty now, and she'd been at the Mallard seminary for seven years. It didn't add up. A thought occurred to him. "Did he leave you with child?"

Her eyes widened with surprise. "No. There was nothing like that."

She seemed genuinely surprised by the question and showed no self-consciousness when she replied. He believed her. "Then why—"

"So, if you need assistance with the management of your estate, I can help you. I did much to assist my father before— I can, for instance, read and keep accounts. Papa had no head for figures."

"Then why were you disowned?"

"A . . . a misunderstanding." She rose and smoothed down her skirt. "So now you have the answer to your questions. I hope the knowledge of my youthful imprudence will not prove an insuperable obstacle to the smooth progression of our marriage." She gazed at him a moment with those clear sage-green eyes and said firmly, "I have not lain with any man since—except you. Nor will I."

It was a promise—and apparently as good an apology as he was ever going to get from her.

Part of him wanted to assert himself and demand some sort of gesture of contrition for not telling him about it until after they were married. But fundamental honesty forced him to recognize he hadn't exactly given her the opportunity to explain.

They were both new to this business of marriage, and they'd married not knowing much about each other. If they were both a little tense and prickly, well, that wasn't surprising.

This was what a honeymoon was for, he supposed. To get to know each other better.

That and the bedding.

He rose and rang a bell. "Thank you for your frankness, madam. I suggest we put last night behind us and go on as intended. I have work to do. This estate has been neglected for the last year and I wish to get everything organized before I leave."

"When will that be?"

"I'm not sure, not for a week at least. The girls will be arriving tomorrow."

"The girls?"

"I cannot trust them to Aunt Dottie's care; you know that."

She bit her lip. "Of course. It is after all, why you married me."

Denial trembled on the tip of his tongue, which was nonsense—it *was* why he'd married her—but he was aware it wasn't quite fair to give her a honeymoon of only two days before her chaperone duties commenced. The fact that she didn't complain, as most brides would, galled him somewhat.

"I have much to do here." He gestured to the pile of paperwork on the desk. "Later this afternoon I will be riding out to make a brief inspection of the estate."

"Oh, may I—" She broke off as a knock sounded at the door.

The housekeeper entered, and whatever his wife had been going to say remained unsaid. "You rang, sir?"

"Yes, Mrs. Moffat, Lady Ashendon would like a tour of the house." He turned to his wife and bowed slightly. "I will see you at dinner."

Emm inclined her head. "Is there any part of the house, any rooms or furniture or, or anything decorative that you are particularly attached to, my lord?"

He glanced up, frowning. "What do you mean?"

"In case I want to make a few changes. It is your home, after all, and I wouldn't wish to make any changes that would upset you."

"I haven't lived in this house since I was a boy," he said indifferently. "You have *carte blanche* to make whatever changes to the household you desire, madam."

MADAM. HE WAS PUTTING HER IN HER PLACE. *LADY ASHENDON would like a tour of the house.* He hadn't even asked her if she wanted one. She felt dismissed, like a maidservant.

But she didn't have the energy or the will to argue.

The interview with her husband had stirred up a past she'd done her best to put behind her. And the emotions that went with it.

For the first part of the tour, most of what the housekeeper told her went right over Emm's head. She kept thinking of things she'd said, and regretted. And things she wished she'd said, and hadn't.

Never mind the things she'd done and wished she hadn't.

She'd taken one look at Sam and fallen recklessly, blindly, desperately in love. And he—or so he'd claimed—felt the same about her.

Even knowing it was wrong, that their love was hopeless— or maybe because it *was* hopeless, star-crossed and impossible—she'd been determined not to have a *Romeo and Juliet* ending.

So when Sam had pushed her, begged her, tumbled her down in the hay and thrust his hands under her skirts— shocking and wildly thrilling as it was—she'd let him. Physically it had been painful and a little disappointing, but the closeness, the thrilling intimacy of his hands on her breasts and under her skirts, the half-panicked, half-shocked sensation as he'd pushed himself into her and pumped hard for a few short moments, then collapsed with a loud, satisfied groan . . .

Foolish, ignorant, dreamy young girl that she was, she'd believed it was true love.

But for Sam, it was simply an opportunity.

It was a lesson she would never forget.

Pointless to be ashamed or to apologize or make excuses at this late date. What was done was done. She was an adult now, a different person from that young girl. She could continue to wallow in the disaster of her past and endlessly punish herself for it, or she could forgive the naïve girl she'd been and accept that she was flawed and imperfect.

And learn from her mistakes.

The only reason I will ever marry is for love. Oh, the irony of that youthful impassioned statement. The opposite of what she'd actually done.

But it was better this way—a practical, unsentimental arrangement, with clear, down-to-earth expectations and no messy emotions.

She would have to be vigilant about that. The feelings her husband had engendered last night when he'd coupled with her. . . But they were not emotions. They were physical sensations, and no doubt she would get used to them and not confuse them with anything else.

The way she was with Sam, she would have done anything for him—had, in fact, let him do whatever he wanted. She hadn't actually been ready to give herself to a man, but he hadn't asked—he'd just taken. And she, lost in the dizzy, rapturous state she'd imagined was love—she'd allowed it. She would have allowed him anything.

Looking back, she could hardly imagine that girl was her. Giving herself to love, to Sam, she'd lost all sense of herself, all sense of what *she* wanted, what *she* believed in. Everything was Sam. Sam and love.

And it was all a lie.

And then, two years later, it had come back to haunt her, and she'd almost lost herself again. She *had* lost her father's respect and faith in her. And her trust in him.

When he'd heard the fresh rumors about her—when he'd been carefully *fed* those rumors, drip by cunning drip—he'd struggled against them for a while but had eventually succumbed. Because two years before he'd seen how blind, how reckless she'd been with Sam, and it had frightened him.

Knowing what she and Sam had done, and never having

come to terms with it—that Sam had been a mere groom made it even more shocking to him—her father had eventually come to believe the rumors.

That she was doing it again.

The breach with Papa was like an open wound in her heart. He'd believed in the rumors and not the word of Emm, his only daughter. He'd loved her, but he had no faith in her.

That lack of faith, that betrayal of trust, or love, had cut deep.

It was another life lesson—that trust, once shattered, could never be mended. And what was the point of life if one didn't learn from it?

She might regret Sam, she bitterly regretted how things had ended with Papa, but she couldn't, she wouldn't let her past destroy her future.

She had a new life now. And she would make of it the best she could.

Mrs. Moffat conducted a most thorough tour, giving a history of the house and family, as well as showing Emm every closet, cupboard and storeroom, and all the stores. It was the family stories that Emm was most interested in, and with a little encouragement, Mrs. Moffat opened right up, telling stories of Master Cal, who was—boy and man—very dear to her heart.

Emm got the impression of a solitary little boy, growing up under the eye of a cold, demanding father. He'd had no playfellows—his father wouldn't allow him to associate with village boys, and his brother was ten years older and away at school.

"Very stiff-rumped was old Lord Ashendon, always knowing what was due to his consequence and not accepting anything less," Mrs. Moffat confided. "But he did allow Master Cal to spend a deal of time in the stables, and the lads there were companions of a sort."

"And what of his mother?"

"Oh, she died when he was a little lad. I doubt he even remembers her."

"But his father married again . . ." Emm prompted.

Mrs. Moffat sniffed. "A beauty she was, and a good mother to her little girls, but"—she screwed up her nose—"not the sort who wanted the children of her predecessor hanging around. Especially not sons, when she'd only given her husband daughters." She clucked her tongue in disapproval. "No, little Master Cal was sent off to school—just seven he was, poor little lad—and we hardly saw anything of him after that."

"But didn't he go home for holidays?" Even as she said it, she remembered that after their mother had died, Rose and Lily had spent all their holidays with Lady Dorothea— even Christmas.

"Not much. He usually stayed at school, or stayed with friends." She turned to Emm with a smile. "Oh, but when he did come home, well, those little girls followed him around like baby ducklings. Master Cal it was that put them up their first ponies. Soul of patience he was with them." The elderly woman darted Emm a sideways glance. "Make a fine father, he will, now he's home and in his rightful place."

Emm didn't have the heart to tell Mrs. Moffat that he was leaving again, and who knew when he'd return.

I haven't lived in this house since I was a boy. And where had he lived since then? No wonder he didn't care what she did to the house. It hadn't been a home to him at all.

Emm determined then and there that she would make this place into a home—if not for her husband, who seemed to prefer life abroad, then for her and the girls. And, pray God, for any children she might have.

Mrs. Moffat continued, "And then he finished school and was off to the army, fighting that nasty Bonaparte. The fighting that boy did—well, it was a miracle he wasn't killed— mentioned in dispatches I don't know how many times. Of course we all prayed for him. Now the linen press, my lady, needs a deal of refurbishment."

The stories continued, much to Emm's fascination, and it wasn't until they were in the west wing, looking into dusty room after dusty room with furniture shrouded under holland covers, that she finally turned her full attention to the task at hand.

"Mrs. Moffat, what are these rooms? There seem to be a great many of them, all seemingly deserted." For years, by the smell of stale air and dust.

"Old Lord Ashendon's orders, m'lady. He wasn't one for entertaining, and Mr. Henry never came near the place, neither. Not even after he became Lord Ashendon. I don't remember when these room were last used."

"Well, then, we must do something about that," Emm declared. "This is going to become a family home. I want every room opened up, aired, cleaned, and the furniture inspected to see what we shall retain, what can be mended and what shall be replaced." She shuddered. "Who knows what may be lurking beneath those covers?"

"Every room?" Mrs. Moffat faltered. Emm knew what she was thinking; it was far too much work for the few servants who'd remained to run the grand old house, many of them quite elderly.

"We will hire more staff, of course. I'm sure you know some girls in the village who can be relied on to give this place a good scrub and polish. Send for them at once. I want every room shining and clean throughout.

"Yes, my lady." Mrs. Moffat's eyes gleamed with a martial light. "How many girls?"

"As many as you need—you will know that better than I—and some men to beat carpets and carry furniture about and do what needs to be done. His lordship gave me *carte blanche*, if you remember." She smiled at the housekeeper. "But we won't try to do it all at once. We will start with the rooms most likely to be used—the hall, the dining room, that little sitting room you showed me that seems likely to get some sun—and work toward the least likely. And first on the list is to prepare bedchambers for the young ladies."

The elderly housekeeper's face lit up. "Lady Rose and Lady Lily, m'lady? They're coming home at last?"

"Indeed they are, as well as Lady Georgiana, my husband's niece."

Mrs. Moffat looked doubtful. "I've never heard of any Lady Georgiana, m'lady. His niece, did you say?"

"A newly discovered addition to the family, I believe. All

three girls are arriving together tomorrow. Now, show me which bedchambers you think they will like."

Mrs. Moffat sent a message to the village to send up anyone who wanted a day's work, and in less than an hour her workforce had doubled. Under Mrs. Moffat's supervision Emm set some housemaids to scrubbing and polishing the girls' bedchambers, airing their bedding, washing the curtains and beating the rugs on the floors.

Meanwhile she gathered every able-bodied man available and set to work on the great gloomy hall. She ordered the removal of all the grisly weapons and animal heads and banished them to the attic. The portraits of grim-looking ancestors she had removed to the portrait gallery, a place she'd been told of but hadn't yet inspected.

Heavy curtains covered the windows, shutting out the daylight. Emm had them taken down to wash, and when they shredded with handling, she sent them to be burned. The room lightened considerably without them. She would commission some new ones in a lighter, less oppressive pattern.

She set two men to washing the mullioned windows, and another two rolled up the carpets—fine axminsters—and took them outside to be beaten. There wasn't enough time to wash down the walls—the family would no doubt use this room for general gathering at night—but she had the floor mopped and polished and, after a good culling of all the most uncomfortable furniture, had the rest waxed.

A few hours later, Emm stepped out into the garden for some fresh air and to see whether there were any flowers or greenery she could cut for the house. The rigid formality of the interior had been quite gloomy and oppressive. Greenery would freshen and soften it.

Hearing the sound of hoofbeats, she glanced up in time to see her husband riding out with a man who was presumably his estate manager. Her husband—could she call him Calbourne, or Cal, or would he insist on Ashendon, or even my lord?—was mounted on a powerful black gelding. He rode well, as if born to the saddle. Which he probably was.

She watched him disappear into the distance, feeling a

trifle wistful. She would have loved to ride out and see the estate.

Nonsense, she told herself. She had no reason to feel wistful. She'd been given *carte blanche* to make whatever changes she wanted. He couldn't have made it plainer. Her duty was to the girls and the house, and if she wasn't to have a honeymoon, well, it wasn't a love match, after all.

She wasn't about to complain. She was very lucky to have this beautiful old house to work on, and the prospect of the girls' company when her husband returned to Europe. She was her own mistress. She was much better off here than at Miss Mallard's.

And when Lord Ashendon was cold and dismissive, when he treated her as some kind of superior servant, well, that would serve as a good reminder. She had a foolishly tender, susceptible heart, and his coldness would remind her to reserve her love for her children. And for the girls.

She gathered an armful of greenery and returned to the house.

Chapter Fourteen

Happy the man whose wish and care a few paternal acres
bound, content to breathe his native air in his own ground.
—ALEXANDER POPE, "ODE ON SOLITUDE"

"THE WHOLE HOUSEHOLD IS EXCITED AT THE PROSPECT OF
your sisters returning," she told her husband at dinner that
evening. He'd arrived home just on dusk and hadn't apparently
noticed any change in the house. Emm was simultaneously
relieved and irritated. "According to Mrs. Moffat, it's been
several years since they were here. It surprised me, since we
aren't very far from Bath."

He shrugged. "My father probably didn't want to be bothered with them."

"Not be bothered with his own daughters?" She tried to
hide her outrage.

"He disliked children." There was no resentment in his
voice. He sounded quite matter-of-fact. Emm thought of the
boy who'd been sent away at seven and had rarely come
home again.

"They're hardly children now."

He snorted. "Possibly not, but they're still brats." He cut
himself another slice of chicken pie. She'd consulted with
Cook and Mrs. Moffat and arranged for some of his lordship's favorite dishes to be served.

"None of the servants seem to have even heard of your
niece, Georgiana," she probed.

"She only came to light after Henry's death. Turned out

he'd made a secret marriage when he was very young. A *mesalliance*, so he kept the girl hidden."

"How—how unfortunate for her." She'd been about to roundly condemn his brother, but her husband was obviously trying to be pleasant, so it wouldn't be tactful to insult his brother. Yet.

What kind of a family had she married into? Though with her history, she couldn't talk.

"It was a damned disgrace. Henry was a selfish swine." He sipped his wine, his eyes silver-dark in the candlelight, and said almost apologetically, "Georgiana is a rare handful, I'm afraid. Stubborn as a mule and utterly undisciplined."

She smiled. "She's in good company, then."

Cal shook his head. "She makes Rose and Lily look tame." He looked at his wife, seated across from him, her skin glowing softly in the candlelight. She'd had several leaves of the large table removed, and dining was now a much cozier affair.

There were flowers in the room too, and branches of greenery. He didn't remember anything like that when he was a boy. Their conversation over dinner had been pleasant, easy; she'd encouraged him to tell her about his day.

The last remnants of his anger with her faded away. She was trying to make things work.

She needed to know what she'd be dealing with, so he told her how he'd met Georgiana, first by reputation from the members of the local hunt, whom she'd apparently terrorized and thwarted for years. "They positively begged me to take her away."

She'd laughed—the first time he'd heard her laugh properly—a warm, low infectious sound.

He told her how, misliking his plans for her, Georgiana had leapt on her horse—a truly magnificent beast that ought to be far too strong for her but wasn't—and disappeared into the hills. "For several cold, bitter nights. The girl is impossible—but quite fearless."

He told her how he'd had to trick his niece into wearing a dress, and how she'd ruined one to spite him. And how he'd had to kidnap her to get her to Bath. He told her about

Finn, the great gangly smelly wolfhound, and how he'd followed the carriage until Cal was forced to let him come. "I hope you like dogs," he finished, "because she won't be separated from the animal."

"I love dogs," she assured him, laughing. She was a good listener. This dinner had been the most pleasant and relaxed evening he'd had for . . . well, he couldn't recall when he'd last enjoyed a woman's company so much. Or had such a pleasant evening in his childhood home.

He was almost sorry now that the girls were coming so soon. But of course, he had no choice. He didn't trust them an inch. And he had a job to do. Three Oxfordshire men were on his list and the sooner he checked on them, the better.

"I've sent for Georgiana's horse too. All three girls are keen horsewomen. It will be something to keep them occupied." And, with any luck, tire them out for any further mischief.

"I could—" she began.

"You'll have your hands full with housewifery, I know. As long as a groom goes with them, they'll be all right." He paused, then, feeling he had something to make up for, asked, "You don't mind, do you, that your honeymoon involves refurbishing my house, and that your peace will be invaded by three difficult young ladies?"

"Not at all," she said, and somehow the warm, laughing woman had been replaced by the cool schoolteacher. "We married for convenience, after all."

The unspoken words hung in the air between them. *His convenience.*

HE CAME TO HER ROOM THAT NIGHT, KNOCKED AND, AT her response, entered. "Are you willing?" She was sitting up in bed, reading.

She looked a little surprised but answered, "Of course," as a dutiful wife should. She put the book aside and moved over in the bed to make room for him. He hoped it wasn't only duty, but did it really matter if it was? The result would be the same.

Somehow, it mattered.

The thought of those unaccounted-for couple of years had nagged at him from time to time during the day. If her false swain had been bought off when she was seventeen, why had her father disowned her two years later? What had happened?

But now was not the time to ask. Not if he wanted to lie with her tonight—and he did. He hadn't planned to—he'd decided to punish her, ignore her for a few days until she came to him with a proper explanation. And an apology.

But despite his pique at her lack of virginity, and his exasperation at her refusal to show any proper contrition, his body had hummed with lust and anticipation all day. He hadn't been able to get the scent of her skin and hair out of his mind. He'd eaten an apple at ten, a sandwich at noon, but the taste of her still lingered. And her skin, glowing gently by firelight, those breasts, those long, slender legs that wrapped so hungrily around him . . .

So he'd decided to forgive her.

Besides, he owed it to his ancestors to get an heir.

Now, the mere act of opening the connecting door, the sight of her sitting in bed, reading—perfectly decent and covered to the neck in a voluminous thick flannel nightgown—had him hard and ready.

Rain started to fall outside, spattering hard against the windows. The air in the room was chilly. He moved to the fireplace and added a few logs to the fire. The dry wood caught quickly, lightening the room and perfuming it with the clean, smoky scent of yew.

Cal straightened, staring into the flames a moment. He was on fire for her. He didn't understand it, hadn't been quite so . . . so consumed by lust since he was a green and randy youth.

He returned to the bed, leaving the candles burning—no need for discretion on behalf of virginal shyness now—and removed his dressing gown.

She took her time, examining him with frank appreciation. Or so he hoped. Her gaze moved across him like a touch, warming him despite the chill of the night air. He was erect already, but when her wide gray-green eyes studied him so thoughtfully, he couldn't help but say, "Everything as it should be?"

She blinked, then blushed. "Sorry, was I staring? It is just that you are the first naked man I have ever seen." And it was in the nature of a gift, he decided, that he was first in something.

"You approve?" *Vanity, thy name is man.* It shouldn't matter whether she approved or not; they were married.

"Oh, very much so." Her voice was soft, a little husky. He felt himself harden further.

"Would you care to return the favor?"

It took her a moment to understand his meaning. Her blush deepened and she nodded but made no move. He reached beneath the bedclothes and found the hem of her modest cream flannel nightgown. He glanced at her again, a query in his eyes, and she nodded.

Slowly he drew it up, over the long, lovely legs, past the dark thatch of curls at their junction, easing it under her bottom, and up to reveal the smooth curve of her belly. Her breasts emerged briefly, small and exquisite, the nipples high and pink, and he hesitated. She pulled the nightgown over her head and held it clutched against her chest, hiding behind it.

He drew the garment gently from her tight grip. "Not quite the confection of silk and nonsense you wore last night." He tossed it aside and turned back to find her swathed to the chin in bedclothes. Modesty or shyness?

"I did not think you would come to me tonight," she said in a low voice.

Not come to her? The truth was, he couldn't stay away. He looked at the way she was huddled in the bedclothes. "You sure you don't mind?"

She shook her head. It was the light making her shy, he decided. She'd probably never shown herself to anyone. They'd been naked together last night, but it had been dark and shadowy.

He drew the covers back, exposing her nakedness. She made a move, as if to cover herself with her hands, then with a sigh, dropped them.

He looked his fill in the soft candlelight. Her cheeks, chest and breasts turned rosy under his heated gaze. She swallowed and did not meet his eyes. Her nipples lifted.

Cold, or aroused? She wasn't comfortable being looked at.

"You're beautiful." She was too, so beautiful his mouth dried.

Her mouth made a small movement, a moue or a grimace, as if she didn't believe him and was too polite to say so.

Or maybe she was just cold and getting fed up with being stared at. He slid into the bed beside her and drew her into his arms.

He'd planned to take her with no nonsense, hard and fast and immensely satisfying—for him—and show her who was master in this marriage. But she came to him with a sigh of acceptance, wrapping her arms around his neck and bringing her mouth so sweetly up to his, he found he couldn't do it, couldn't bring himself to take her hard and fast and have it over within minutes.

He took his time, lavishing her with tender care, nibbling gently, slipping his tongue between her soft cherry-dark lips, caressing lightly at first, but sweeping deeper, tasting tea and tooth powder and musky dark honey. And woman. This woman.

His wife.

Her taste heated his blood like the finest brandy.

He kissed her, deeply, passionately, his tongue echoing the rhythm his body already rocked with. A low hum deep within her throat was his reward.

He caressed her with hands and mouth, caressing the warm soft skin, the smooth, firm female flesh. He cupped the slight, silky breasts, his thumbs caressing the hard little pink nubbins, up-thrust and aching for his attention.

She trembled beneath his touch, caressing him in return, blindly, frenziedly, as if she did not quite know what she wanted. Or could not think.

He covered first one breast, then the other with his mouth, teasing, nibbling and sucking. She arched beneath him, making soft little noises that might have been protest, except that her fingers were tangled in his hair, holding him fast.

He stroked the smooth shallow curve of her stomach, feeling the quivers starting deep within her. His fingers slid into the thatch of dark curls at the base of her stomach and parted her. She was hot and slick and slippery, more than ready for him, but he wanted more. He sought and found the small sensitive pearl between the hot sleek folds, stroking it until she was writhing and trembling helplessly beneath him.

And then he slid down her body and put his mouth there, where his fingers had been, tasting heat and honey and salt-dark woman. His woman. She stiffened, uttering a small exclamation, but before she could make any objection, he sucked deeply and she arched beneath him on a high quivering moan.

His pulse thundered; his body, craving release, vibrated with the effort of control. Deep spasms rocked her: blind, oblivious, out of control.

He lifted himself and entered her in one long smooth thrust. The ancient, animal rhythm possessed him and he moved deep within her, thrusting fast and hard in glorious abandon until his climax took him, and he lay gasping and spent.

She came back to herself slowly and turned her face toward him. He lay on his side, watching her.

A damp curl straggled across her face. He reached out and smoothed it back with one finger. "All right?"

"Yes. More than all right." She sighed and gave a small, sensual shiver. "I never knew . . . it could be . . . like that."

"You never . . . ?"

She shook her head, blushing. "Only with you."

It was another small gift. He was the first there too. He tried not to let his satisfaction show.

He hadn't planned to spend the night in her bed—he never usually slept with a woman after congress—but somehow he couldn't make himself move. He drew her against him, curving his body around her. "Get some sleep now. Another busy day tomorrow."

She slipped into sleep almost immediately. He lay there holding her, listening to the rain and the wind outside, and wondered how he'd come to this. The marriage was supposed to be for purely practical purposes.

He'd never considered there would be . . . *feelings* involved.

His friends had all fallen in love at some time or other—

usually with some impossible or unsuitable female. Drowning in the throes of love, they'd turned into hopeless, muddled wrecks of men, unable to think of anything except their beloved inamorata.

Cal had watched with bemusement—and a touch of disdain. Rutherford men didn't fall in love. Cal certainly never had, even though he'd had several mistresses and conducted the odd few affairs over the years. None of the women he'd slept with had ever touched his heart. And at the age of eight-and-twenty he was obviously immune to it.

His friends' love affairs had never lasted long. Eventually they returned to their senses—usually because the woman had moved on to drive some other unfortunate fellow insane—and went on with their lives, sadder but wiser men. And when they married, they married sensibly.

As he had.

Lust, that was all this was. He'd made a convenient marriage and it was *very* convenient that he lusted after his wife. But he didn't want any emotional tangles. As soon as he'd tracked down his assassin, he'd be leaving England again, for who knew how long. He liked his job and he needed to keep his mind clear for it.

And in the meantime, he'd do his best to give her the child she wanted.

He made love to her again during the night, and again at dawn, having woken hard and aching and unable to resist the temptation of her lying next to him, all soft and enticing.

She woke as he slowly entered her, and she welcomed him with sleepy sensuality. He took her slow and leisurely, and it was just as intense.

He woke an hour later. The candles had long since guttered; the fire lay in ashes. His wife slept curled against him, one cheek pressed against his shoulder, her breathing even and steady. He wanted to take her again, but that would be too much. He slipped out of bed and felt her stir behind him.

"Where—?"

"I'm going for a ride."

She sat up and made as if to get up. "I'll come with—"

"No, I have work to do. Go back to sleep."

* * *

THE DOOR SHUT FIRMLY BEHIND HIM AND EMM BATTLED with mixed emotions. Why couldn't she just ask if she could go riding with him? She wasn't usually so hesitant. It was seven years since she'd ridden, and she would have loved to accompany him as he reacquainted himself with his estate and his tenants.

But perhaps it was something he felt she had no part in. He was the earl and this was his home; she was the newcomer. He'd made it quite clear what he wanted of her—house refurbishing in preparation for the girls' arrival while he dealt with estate matters. Take responsibility for his sisters and niece and free him to get on with his work. Whatever that work was.

Companionship wasn't any part of their bargain.

She lay in bed, listening to the noisy chatter of birds outside the window. It had seemed like an offer she couldn't refuse—security, position, riches and best of all, a family.

And now, after barely two days of marriage, she wanted more. She wanted to ride with him, to talk to him, get to know him better.

To make a friend of him.

Perhaps even make a real marriage of their convenient bargain.

Was she dreaming again, making castles in the air? Or simply greedy?

Or was it simply the aftereffects of lying with him, giving her body to him? There was a reason they called it "making love." It created the illusion of love, and she knew enough now to be wary of ascribing emotions to the purely physical sensations he engendered in her.

Mostly, she thought, her desire to know him better was rooted in simple compassion for the neglected and lonely little boy of the housekeeper's stories, the child who'd been sent off to school at the age of seven and had never, it seemed, been welcomed back. Was there still some remnant of that small boy in the brusque, decisive, self-contained man she'd married? She suspected there was.

There was kindness in him, even though he tried so hard to hide it. It was probably why he found it so hard to manage his difficult sisters—he couldn't bring himself to be harsh with them.

And there was kindness, just now, in his telling her to go back to sleep. Because he'd woken her several times in the night to make love to her.

She hadn't minded being woken at all. The whole physical side of marriage had taken her utterly by surprise. She hadn't expected to find such . . . such pleasure in it.

Pleasure being a wholly inadequate word. Two nights she'd been married. Two nights he'd . . . amazed her. Shocked her a little too, but taken her to . . . ecstasy.

She stretched, her body tingling with lazy sensual awareness as remembrance washed over her in slow, pleasurable waves.

Perhaps she was just being impatient. She had a whole new, privileged life before her. There would be plenty of time to go riding.

She had duties to perform, a homecoming to prepare. The girls would be here this afternoon. She was determined to make this big old mausoleum into a place of welcome. A home.

CAL HADN'T INTENDED TO RIDE OUT SO SOON IN SEARCH of the next man on his list, but this one lived close, just a few hours away. He didn't like the thought of someone who might turn out to be the Scorpion living on his doorstep, not with Emmaline and the girls so close. Best he check and be sure.

He'd dealt with the most pressing of the estate needs. The manager was a good man, and though Henry had caused problems by ignoring all the manager's correspondence, a year's neglect was not so much to repair. When Cal returned to Europe he could leave the place with a clear conscience.

He reached a crossroads, consulted the sign and turned left. After this fellow, there were only two brothers living locally, though some distance away—a good day's ride there and back. The rest of his portion of the list lived in more distant places and would involve overnight stays.

He came to the village and was at first treated with some slight suspicion—clearly gentlemen didn't often venture there in search of ordinary folks. But on production of a silver coin, he was soon directed to a shabby little cottage on the outskirts of the village. It backed onto the forest.

The man's wife answered the door—pregnant, if he wasn't mistaken—and her immediate reaction alerted his suspicions. She blanched at the sight of him and clung to the door with white-knuckled hands, peering past him to see if anyone had come with him. When he asked after Saul Whitmore, she pretended not to know who he meant. But she was a poor liar.

All Cal's instincts prickled to life. It might have been better to have brought someone with him, but Cal was armed with two loaded pistols and a knife in his boot. He could see at a glance that the mean little one-room cottage concealed nobody, so he decided to investigate further afield. The woman followed him, wringing her hands and saying variously, "Melord, there ain't nobody called Saul Whitmore livin' around here. He left long ago, he did. He ain't here, I promise you."

Cal ignored her. He was heading toward a tumbledown outbuilding when he caught a glimpse of movement from the corner of his eye. A man emerged from the forest, carrying a load of wood. Two dead hares dangled from his waist.

"Run, Saul, run!" the woman screamed. She jumped on Cal, nearly knocking him over. He staggered and tried to shake her off, but she clung fiercely to his arm, dragging him down with her weight, determined to hold him back. Cal could have knocked her out in an instant, but he'd never hit a woman in his life, let alone a pregnant one.

The man dropped his load of wood and took to his heels. Observing the manner of his retreat, Cal instantly stopped struggling.

The man ran with a pronounced, ungainly limp. He disappeared into the trees.

"What's the matter with his foot?" Cal asked the woman,

who still clung to him with all her might. Unless the injury to the fellow's foot was recent, he couldn't possibly be the assassin whom Cal had last seen escaping fleet-footed and nimble over Portuguese rooftops.

She took a moment to understand his question.

"Oh, for heaven's sake, let go of me, woman," he told her irritably. "I'm not going to chase after your husband. He probably knows that forest like the back of his hand. Just tell me, what's wrong with his foot?"

She eyed him suspiciously, then loosened her frenetic grip slightly. "Got 'is foot shot off in the war," she said eventually. "Makes it hard for 'im to get work, 'specially in winter."

"Then he's not the man I'm looking for," Cal told her.

"He's not?" Cal felt the tension drain out of her. "You're not after 'im for . . . for . . ." She broke off, biting her lip. "It's just a couple of hares."

And suddenly Cal realized what he'd seen: a crippled former soldier, carrying illegally gathered wood and poached game—providing winter warmth and food for himself and his pregnant wife.

Hanging offenses in some places. Transportation to the other side of the world at the very least.

No wonder she was so frightened.

"I have no interest in you or your husband," he told her gently. "It was another man I was looking for. This was a mistake."

She gave him a troubled look and slowly released his sleeve. "You won't say nothing about . . . ?"

"I saw nothing untoward at all," he assured her. "And I apologize for any distress I caused you and your husband." He pressed a couple of gold sovereigns—all he had on him—into the woman's shaking hand, mounted his horse and rode off.

Damn, for a moment there he'd thought he had the bastard.

Chapter Fifteen

Uncertainty and expectation are the joys of life.
Security is an insipid thing.
—WILLIAM CONGREVE, *LOVE FOR LOVE*

DUSK WAS FALLING AS THE CARRIAGE BRINGING THE GIRLS to Ashendon turned into the driveway. At the same time, Emm saw her husband riding across the park from the opposite direction. He rode slumped in the saddle, as if weary and dispirited.

Emm hung back as he dismounted and waited for the girls to alight, greeting each one with a nod and words Emm couldn't quite catch. She wanted to give them a little private time together; they were family, after all. She was the stranger here.

It was not for her to welcome Rose and Lily to the home in which they'd been born.

But they could have been strangers for all the warmth they showed. Of the girls, only Lily made any attempt at a warmer greeting, reaching up to plant a shy kiss on her brother's cheek. He seemed not to know quite how to respond, bending toward her slightly so she was able to reach his jaw.

Watching their caution with each other, their awkwardness, Emm felt a rueful pang. Somehow, she was going to make these disparate, wary people into a family. She was determined on it.

She hurried down the front steps to greet them. "You made good time, then, Rose, Lily, Georgiana. Did you have a pleasant journey? The weather was in your favor, though it's getting quite chilly now." She hugged each of the girls—even Georgiana, whom she barely knew, and who responded awkwardly, allowing the embrace rather than welcoming it.

"And who is this fine fellow?" She went to pat the dog, but he was more interested in sniffing out his new territory and leaving liquid calling cards on every nearby tree. She exclaimed over his size and noble carriage and heard her husband snort behind her.

She turned to him and was on the verge of holding out her hand to him when she decided to take the bull by the horns and begin as she meant to go on. She stood on tiptoes and planted a light kiss on his cheek. "I hope your day was productive, Lord Ashendon."

He frowned and opened his mouth to say something, then stopped.

Emm didn't wait for any further reaction. If he disliked the familiarity in front of the girls, he would no doubt tell her later. She turned to the girls. "But what am I doing letting you stand around in the cold. Come inside. You're just in time for dinner. We won't bother changing for dinner tonight—just freshen yourselves up—I've just ordered hot water sent up to your bedchambers. It should be there in a few minutes."

They entered the house in a group, the girls chattering about the journey, responding to the questions she threw at them. Emm turned toward the stairs, but Rose's gaze fell to the great hall. With a small exclamation, she walked forward and entered the room.

"What have you done to this place?" Rose stood in the center of the hall, her brow wrinkled, gazing around her. "It's almost unrecognizable."

Her words gave Emm a guilty pang. She hadn't even considered the girls' feelings when she'd had the great hall stripped of the items she found repugnant. She'd briefly considered her husband, but he hadn't seemed to care what she did—but for the girls this place had truly been their home, apart from the years they spent at school.

She'd done her best to make it less like an armament museum and more like a family gathering place. A roaring fire burned in the enormous fireplace, and she'd had comfortable chairs gathered around in groups, instead of the hard chairs that had been placed formally around the perimeter. She'd covered the stone flags with warm and colorful rugs, and some embroidered screens that had been found in the attic helped protect the inhabitants from drafts.

"Yes, it's all . . . lighter, and emptier, but somehow cozier," Lily agreed. She pointed and gave a little laugh. "All the heads and antlers are gone."

"Heads?" Georgiana looked around. "Antlers?"

Rose nodded. "Deer heads, antelopes, a nasty-looking boar, all kinds of heads—and swords and pikes and things—the bloodthirsty trophies of our ancestors. Most of Papa's beloved prizes have gone." She turned to Emm with wide eyes. "What *have* you done, Miss Westwood?"

"Lady Ashendon," Lily corrected her.

"Oh, heavens, no—call me Emm or Emmaline," Emm said, "now that we're sisters-in-law. You too, of course, Georgiana."

"George," the girl muttered, "I only answer to George."

Emm turned back to Rose. "I'm sorry if the removal of your father's things distresses you, Rose, but your brother gave me *carte blanche* to—"

"Oh, it doesn't distress me at all," Rose interrupted, her eyes dancing. "It was ghastly before—George, you can't imagine—with dead eyes staring down at you from every corner. So gloomy and depressing."

"People who cut off the heads of animals and nail them to a wall are nothing but savages!" George declared.

Lily hugged Emm enthusiastically. "It's wonderful, Miss—I mean Emm. So much friendlier. All the Hollow Knights and the Dismal Ancestors—that's what Rose and I called them—have gone. You didn't throw the Ancestors out, though, did you? Because George might want to see her family. There's a painting of Cal as a boy that looks just like her. Or is that in the gallery?"

"I wouldn't mind seeing a picture of my father too," George muttered diffidently. "Not that I care, but . . . I've never seen him."

Emm smiled, relieved and delighted with their reaction.

"All the ancestral portraits are safe and will be hung with the others in the portrait gallery," she assured them. "I haven't yet had time to have a proper look at them myself." And now that Lily had mentioned it, she wanted to see that portrait of her husband as a boy.

A sudden silence fell as her husband entered the great hall. He surveyed the room silently. Emm waited breathlessly for his reaction.

"I see you've begun," he said, then gave a brusque nod and headed upstairs, leaving Emm not knowing what to think. What did he mean by "begun"? Begun to take over the house? Begun to ruin his home? Begun to interfere? There was no way of knowing.

She turned to the girls, who were regarding her with slight consternation. "Men are hopeless about interior arrangements," she said lightly. "Either they don't notice or they hate any kind of change. Now, let me show you to your bedchambers."

The girls didn't move. "Is he planning to dump us here?" Rose asked bluntly.

Emm gave her a surprised look. "Dump you? What do you mean?"

"He said, back in Bath, that we could go to London, make our come-out in the spring. We thought when the carriage came, that we were going to London. But here we are. So he's planning to immure us in the country, isn't he, so we can't make any scandals?"

"No, of course not," Emm told her, though in truth she had only the sketchiest idea of her husband's plans. "The only reason he married me was so that you could all make your come-outs next season—"

"The *only* reason?" Lily interrupted, her face a picture of dismay. "But I thought—"

"No, not the only reason, of course." Emm hastily covered her blunder with a smile. Lily obviously wanted to believe she'd married for love, and Emm was not going to disillusion her. "I didn't mean it like that. We married for all the usual reasons, of course—but your brother did make it very clear that he wanted me to assist with your come-outs, which of course I am more than delighted to do. As for your being immured in the countryside, there is no such plan. Besides, scandals can happen as easily in the country as in the town, believe me. Now, upstairs to wash before dinner." She linked her arm through George's. "Rose and Lily have their old bedchambers, though I've made a few changes, now that they're grown up, but let me show you your room, George."

The girl hesitated. "Can Finn come too?"

"Of course, he's part of the family too."

Rose didn't move. "You promise we're not going to be stuck here?"

"I promise," Emm said.

HE CAME TO EMM'S BED AGAIN THAT NIGHT AND MADE love to her with the same focused intensity, bringing her to the edge of climax again and again, before driving into her, hard and fast, powerful and passionate, until with a loud groan, he took them both over the crest of ecstasy.

Normally Emm drifted straight off to sleep, but tonight she lay sated, dreamy, but wakeful. Her husband slept beside her, his big body curled around her possessively.

He was an enigma, this man she'd married. During the day he seemed so distant and unapproachable, every inch the brusque stranger she'd married, but at night . . . oh, at night, he took her to a state she'd never dreamed was possible.

She'd come to crave his attentions, the embrace of his strong hard body, the feeling of total possession, of utter abandonment.

Only a few days before she couldn't imagine what it would be like to sleep with a relative stranger, to reveal her nakedness to him, to have him handle and invade her body.

Now she couldn't imagine life without it, without him, this odd, spiky, difficult-to-know man. She needed time, time to get to know him better, time for him to know her, not just her body. Time to make a real marriage of this arrangement.

But he would be returning to his position abroad in a few weeks.

She woke not long after dawn, feeling him slide out of bed. She blinked sleepily as he wrapped his dressing gown around him. "Going riding again?" Bars of sunlight came through the gaps in the curtains.

"Yes, go back to sleep. I won't be home until very late."

"Take the girls with you."

"I can't. I'm not going for a recreational ride. This is business."

She sat up, drawing the bedclothes around her against the morning chill. "Take them anyway. This is their home. I'm sure they'd like to renew their acquaintance with—and in George's case, meet—the people of the estate."

"It's not that kind of business."

"You can't put it off, not even for just a day?"

"I'd prefer not to. The girls—Rose and Lily at least— know the estate well. They can show Georgiana around. Make sure they take a groom with them."

His indifference irritated her. "That's not the point. Do you realize those girls think you've brought them here to keep them out of trouble?"

He blinked. "I have."

"Yes, but they think you plan to dump them in the country."

"I do. Until it's time for them to go to London. I thought you understood—"

"They thought the carriage was going to take them to London. You did say they would go to London."

"Yes, but not yet."

"They weren't to know that. They thought you lied to them, tricked them into coming here."

His brows snapped together. "Lied?"

She shrugged. "From all I can gather, none of the girls has had much reason to rely on the men in their lives."

His frown deepened.

"They think you don't *care* about them." She softened her voice. "*I* know you care, of course, but how do you think it will look to them if, on their very first day here, you abandon them?"

He shook his head, as if that made no sense. "I'm not abandoning them. You're here."

She threw a pillow at him in frustration. "Yes, but I'm not their *brother*. Or their *uncle*! Rose and Lily have not been home for *years*. They were sent away to school and practically forgotten. In all the time they attended Miss Mallard's, the *only* person who showed the slightest interest in them was dear Lady Dorothea. Your father never wrote or visited, your brother never wrote or visited and you—yes, I know you were abroad, but you still never wrote." She was pleased to see him flinch.

"As for George, from all I can gather the poor child has been *raised* as a stranger in her own family! Neither acknowledged nor cared for. I know you were ignorant of her existence and cannot be blamed for that, but it's no wonder the poor girl is stiff and wary, hauled away—practically kidnapped!—from all she knew and expected to fit in as part of a family!"

He'd caught the pillow. He put it aside and eyed her cautiously. "I'm doing my best. It's difficult."

She made a scornful sound.

He scowled. "Why are you so cross with me?"

"Because you're *oblivious* of those girls' needs. Don't you want to be part of a family? No—don't bother answering—it's patently obvious you don't have the first idea. Go on, then, go off on your wretched estate business. I'll do what I can to make the girls feel welcome. It's what you hired me for, after all."

"I didn't hire you, I *married* you," he growled.

She snorted.

Her attitude annoyed him. "And it's not estate business, it's . . . government business."

She rolled her eyes. "Of course, the same mysterious but important 'government business' that conveniently arises whenever you want to avoid other family duties."

He stiffened. "It *is* important and it's not in the *least* convenient. And the reason I won't take the girls with me is because there is a possibility of danger."

"Danger?" She raised her brows, not caring that her expression was entirely skeptical.

Cal compressed his lips. It was obvious she didn't believe him. He hesitated, about to leave, then changed his mind.

He was married now; she had a right to know. He returned and sat down on the end of the bed, forcing his mind off the awareness that beneath the bundle of bedclothes, she was all warm and soft and naked. And delicious.

"I'm in pursuit of an assassin."

"An assassin?" She sat up straighter, hugging the blankets around her. "Tell me more."

He told her about his job, how it had changed since Waterloo, and the Army of Occupation, how it had become more. . . subtle.

"You mean you're a spy?"

"No." He hated that term. "But the world is changing, and in the wake of Napoleon, Europe is being remade; countries and principalities are merging, being annexed or absorbed, new alliances are being made, and it is in our government's interest to make sure that we are not—shall we say, disadvantaged in the balance of power."

She nodded. "It's made the teaching of the globes very difficult too—the changing borders and disappearing countries. I could hardly keep up."

Cal opened his mouth to point out it was not quite the same thing but decided discretion was the better part of husbandly valor.

He told her about the Scorpion then, and how the pursuit had become personal when his friend Bentley had been shot. "I wish you could have known him. He was a scraggly, awkward, odd-looking boy, all ears and elbows and Adam's apple, but he had an unquenchable spirit—nothing defeated him, even though he was a walking target to the bullies of the school, such an odd-bod he was." He gave a rueful half laugh. "He never did learn to box worth sixpence, though he tried, Lord how he tried."

He was silent a moment. "But a fine, fine brain—I've seen men twice his age stunned at his clever reasoning and brilliant ideas. And then . . ." His voice broke and for a moment he had to fight for control.

She slipped her hand into his and squeezed, and the calmness with which she waited and the warmth of her quiet presence steadied him until he could go on without disgracing himself.

He explained how he'd half-recognized the assassin and come back to England on nothing more solid than conjecture, and how he and a couple of others had been working though the list of men who'd been dismissed from the Rifle Brigade. "We're lucky it's a relatively short list—the Rifle Brigade is one of the few regiments that has remained at almost full strength—those sharpshooters are too valuable to lose."

"So you're what—looking for someone who left the regiment but who has been absent from their home at odd periods?"

He nodded, pleased with her quick understanding. "Exactly. And today I'm going to check on the last two in my area—Bert and Joe Gimble—two brothers. So I can't take the girls with me. Besides, it's a long ride, and I won't be returning until well after dark."

"I see." She was silent a moment, resting her chin on her knees. "I don't suppose I can argue that the girls' needs are greater than the capture of a notorious assassin," she said eventually. "Go on, then. I'll do my best to make them feel welcome and wanted."

Cal rose from the bed. "I appreciate it." He headed toward the connecting door, when she called after him, "Lord—um—Ashendon."

He turned. "We are not in public, madam. You may use my Christian name."

She raised her brows humorously. "And yet I am 'madam'?"

He inclined his head in rueful acknowledgment. "What should I call you, then? Emmaline?"

"Yes, or Emm. And what do I call you?"

"Cal or Calbourne, suit yourself. The girls call me Cal. Ashendon if you prefer—it's what Aunt Agatha calls me now." He turned to leave again.

"Cal," she called.

"What is it now?"

"If it's dangerous for the girls, it must be even more dangerous for you. You're not going alone, are you?"

He shrugged. "I work best alone."

"Then I hope you're well armed."

"I am." Cal closed the door behind him and rang for hot water. Somehow, telling his wife about Bentley had lifted a weight off his chest. She was very easy to talk to, a good and sympathetic listener.

When she wasn't arguing with him.

As he shaved and dressed, he considered what she'd said about the girls. Did they really think he didn't care about them? He'd damned well turned his life upside down for their sake.

He supposed they didn't realize that.

EMM ROSE AND RANG FOR HOT WATER. "I'LL WEAR MY RIDING habit, Milly," she told her maid when she arrived. "And wake the girls up, will you? We're going riding this morning."

Her old habit was faded and a bit shabby—she hadn't worn it for seven years—and she'd had Milly move the buttons, as she'd filled out in the bosom and hips since then, but Emm was looking forward to riding again. She would get Rose and Lily to show her and George the estate. With any luck they would not even notice their brother's absence.

She'd given some thought to keeping the girls occupied and happy while they were here. As she'd told their brother some weeks ago, Lily and Rose were bright but bored, and when young women were bored, they got up to mischief.

Vigorous exercise was one way of keeping them out of trouble.

Milly came back shortly afterward with the news that the girls were already up and dressed, that the master had summoned them for a ride before breakfast.

So he'd changed his mind about the urgency of his mission. Perhaps he'd listened to her after all. Encouraged by the news, Emm hurried downstairs and let herself out the back door. As she headed around the back of the house toward the stables, she heard voices raised in argument.

"I won't! And you can't make me. It's stupid!" The unmistakable tones of George.

"You will, my girl, or you won't ride at all." Her husband's voice. She hurried toward the stables.

"It's a perfectly ridiculous way to ride! How can I control Sultan perched up on that silly contraption? A rider—a good rider needs only his knees to control their horse, but this way—"

"It is how ladies ride."

"Well, not me! And you can't tell me how to ride my own horse—Sultan belongs to me!"

"I can always send the horse and his stableboy back to where they came from." A silky-voiced threat.

Emm picked up the pace and half skidded around the corner to see her husband standing in the middle of the stable yard, glaring in frustration at his niece. Rose and Lily, mounted on sidesaddles, watched in wary silence, as did the hound, Finn. Both girls were dressed in riding habits that Emm noticed were almost as out of date as hers. The curriculum at Miss Mallard's Seminary did not include equestrienne skills, so Emm guessed it had been nearly as long for the girls as for her.

George, on the other hand, was dressed in masculine breeches and boots. She wore a scowl that matched her uncle's so exactly that Emm was hard put not to laugh.

He stood holding the reins of his own horse and a black stallion that Emm hadn't seen before—apparently the horse George had raised herself. The stallion bore a sidesaddle.

"Good morning, everyone," Emm said blithely. "You're quite right, George, a sidesaddle is a ridiculous affair—if it were not, then men would use them too—but I'm afraid your uncle is also right. If you wish to ride when we go to London, you will have to ride sidesaddle. To ride astride would brand you as a hoyden of the worst kind."

George looked mutinous. Emm was sure the girl was about to declare that she didn't care, so she added lightly, "And that would make things very unpleasant for Rose and Lily, as well as for you."

Black brows drew together. George cast a doubtful glance at the other two girls. "Why should it make things difficult for them?"

"Because we are a family now, and what one family member does affects the reputation of the others." She let that sink in a moment, and added, "If one girl is held to be badly brought up, people will assume the other girls are just as wild and ungovernable." She let that sink in, and not only to George.

Emm produced an apple core and offered it to Sultan. His lips were velvety soft as he nuzzled the fruit from her palm. "You accepted necessity when you trained this beautiful creature, George. It's the same thing."

George looked puzzled. "What necessity?

"You raised Sultan, didn't you? Trained him from a foal?"

George nodded. Emm continued, "You could have left him to grow up wild and free, unbroken and untamed. But you wanted him to be able to go anywhere, to be respected and admired by all who saw him, so you broke him to bit and bridle and taught him his company manners."

She saw from George's expression that she understood.

"Your life has changed, George," she said softly. "You can continue to fight against bridle and bit, or you can learn to accept a different kind of freedom and find joy in your new life. It's up to you."

There was a short silence, broken only by Sultan snuffling and wuffling down Emm's front in search of another apple.

"I really do understand how you feel, though," Emm continued in a sympathetic tone. "Before I was sent away to school I always rode astride and wore breeches all the time. It's far more comfortable and practical, I agree."

"You did?" George exclaimed.

"Didn't your parents mind?" Lily asked curiously.

"My mother died when I was an infant, and my father— well, let's just say he found it easiest to treat me as a boy. I'd probably still be wearing breeches and careering around the country astride had not the good ladies of church and county descended on my father in a pack when I was thirteen and informed him I was becoming a complete hoyden, and would, if left to continue my pathway, become quite unmarriageable. They convinced him to send me away to school to learn to be a lady." She smiled at Rose and Lily. "Miss Mallard's."

She said to George, "Your uncle told me you are an excellent horsewoman." The girl blinked and gave her uncle a surprised glance. Emm continued, "It won't take you long to master the sidesaddle, teach your beautiful Sultan how to go on with it, and show him off to the world. But there are a few tricks to it. May I?" She gestured toward George's horse.

George hesitated, then nodded.

Emm checked the fit of the saddle. Perfect. "The worst aspect is that you need a mounting block or another person to help you mount. Quite irritating if you want to be independent." She turned to her husband. "Boost me up?"

He hesitated, his expression unreadable. "Just to demonstrate the seat," he said reluctantly. "We don't yet know how the horse will react to the sidesaddle."

"Of course," Emm said with a sweet smile. He passed the reins of his horse to a stableboy, cupped his hands to make a cradle for her boot and tossed her lightly into the saddle.

Sultan, unused to the weight and balance of rider and sidesaddle, fidgeted and stamped restlessly. "You seat yourself like this, George. It's actually much more balanced and comfortable than it looks. In riding, as in life, everything is balance." Emm gathered the reins, hooked her right knee around the lower pommel and slid her other boot into the stirrup, and by the time Sultan decided he didn't like the strange saddle or the strange rider, she was ready for him.

The horse reared up a little, snorting and plunging.

"Right, that's it. Off, now!" Cal came forward, obviously intending to grab the bridle and force the head down. George and the stableboy did the same, but already disturbed, and with people coming from two directions, the horse danced nervously away, shying and tossing his head.

"Stay back, I can manage," Emm called. "It's just temper, isn't it, you beautiful boy? Come on, then, let's see how you can move." And she urged the horse out of the stable yard and headed briskly down the drive. Sultan seemed a little unsure at first, champing restlessly at the bit and tossing his head in annoyance, but Emm had him firmly under control, and as she urged him faster, his gait lengthened first into a smooth canter, then a hard gallop. It was utterly exhilarating.

The thunder of hooves behind her warned her that her husband was in hot pursuit. She glanced back to see Rose and Lily following at some distance. Cal drew level with her and reached out for her bridle.

"Don't you dare!" she cried, raising her whip at him in a teasing threat. "I'm having a glorious time. Race you to the gate!" And she urged Sultan faster.

They were neck and neck when they reached the gate. "What the devil do you think—" he began.

Emm wheeled her mount around. "Race you back!"

As they neared the stable yard, she reined in her horse and entered the yard at a demure trot. She leaned forward and patted the horse's neck. "He's an absolute beauty, George," she said as George and the new stableboy came running toward them. "You did a marvelous job training him. He's taken to the sidesaddle remarkably well."

"Lord, but you can ride, Emm," George gasped. "You beat him—Cal, I mean—even with that silly saddle. I didn't think anyone could ride like that on one of those things."

Emm laughed. "I had a head start. But I'm certain once you and Sultan are used to the sidesaddle, you'll beat everyone to flinders. He moves like a dream." She lifted her leg over the lower pommel and slid lightly to the ground.

Only to find her arm seized in a hard grip. "A word with you, *madam*." Her husband tossed his reins to the stableboy and marched her into the stables. Rose slipped off her own horse and came forward, looking concerned. "Stay out of it, Rose," he growled. Emm nodded to reassure the girl and sent a quick smile to Lily and George, who were watching wide-eyed.

He was in a fine old temper but Emm wasn't the least bit worried. She was, however, interested to know why.

"You, out!" he snapped to a pair of gawking grooms. "Everyone outside until I say so." The grooms fled.

He pushed her into a stall, shut the door and glared at her, his eyes sparking flinty gray. Another magnificent beast with a temper.

Chapter Sixteen

If this be not love, it is madness, and then it is pardonable.
—WILLIAM CONGREVE, *THE OLD BACHELOR*

"Now, *MADAM*, WHAT DO YOU HAVE TO SAY FOR YOURSELF?"

She was breathless, her heart racing, and not just because of the ride. It was the way he was looking at her, so darkly furious. He'd never looked at her that way before. Not in daylight. He wasn't the cool and controlled Lord Ashendon now.

Somehow, that look thrilled her.

She gave him a bright smile. "Wasn't that utterly exhilarating? I haven't ridden for years. That horse of George's is wonderf—"

"How *dare* you ride off like that on an untrained horse!"

He really was rather rattled, she saw, and decided to push him a little further. "Oh, pooh, he took to it like a lamb!"

His jaw tightened and he took a step forward. "You weren't to know that! It was a damned foolhardy act—"

"Nonsense. I've been riding since I could walk. I can tell when a horse is merely nervous and uncertain and when he's—"

"You could have been thrown!"

"But I wasn't," she said calmly. "I don't know why you're making such a fuss."

He gave her a goaded look. "You vowed to obey me," he grated. He took another step forward. He was close enough for her to smell him now, the clean scent of linen, shaving soap and a faint tang of fresh horse sweat. And man, angry aroused man.

"Oh, you're just cross because I beat you in the race," she said provocatively.

'It's nothing to do with that—it's— Dammit, woman!" He wrapped one powerful arm around her, hauled her against him and kissed her, long and hard.

It was a conflagration of anger and arousal, compelling and possessive. Heat and frustrated anger radiated from his body. His arm enclosed her waist like a steel band as his other hand wrapped around her throat, cupping her chin, tilting her mouth to accept the demand of his kiss.

He moved forward, taking her with him, trapping her between his hot, hard body and the cold stone of the stable wall, not breaking the kiss for an instant. Plundering. Demanding. His taste, the urgency of him flooded her senses, his heat seeping into her body, setting her aflame. She felt the heavy thrust of his arousal against her belly.

Her knees weakened. A hard masculine limb thrust between her thighs, anchoring her.

She'd braced her hands behind her, against the cold rough wall, but as he deepened the kiss, scalding her with inflamed passion, she slipped them up his body, twining them around his neck, sliding her fingers through the damp tangle of his hair, gripping the thick locks fiercely as she returned kiss for kiss.

Never—*never!*—had she dreamed kissing could be like this.

Cal wasn't sure what brought him to his senses—a sound, a thought, a cold dash of sanity—but whatever it was, it was enough to let himself wrench his mouth from his wife's, release her and step back. His breath was ragged, as if he'd run a mile.

For a long moment they stared at each other. She was panting too, her mouth damp and red from where he'd ravaged it.

Good God, what had he been about to do? He'd been on the verge of taking her—here, in the stables!—up against a rough stone wall!—with the girls and the stableboys outside. Madness.

"Emm? Cal? Is everything all right?" a hesitant voice called. It was his little sister.

"Stay outside, Lily," he said hastily. He was still aroused.

"It's perfectly all right, Lily," his wife called, sounding satisfyingly breathless. "Your brother and I are, um, having a discussion."

Remembering that he'd been furious with her—and still was—for risking herself on an untried horse, he groped for something conclusive to say. "Let that be a lesson to you, madam."

Her eyes widened and then, incredibly, she laughed. "A *lesson*? I see I shall have to annoy you more often in future, then." The light in her eyes was soft, not challenging, inviting him to share the moment.

His lips twitched in response. "I wasn't annoyed," he began. "I was— Oh, to hell with it. Just don't be so reckless in future. You gave me a hell of a fright."

"I'm sorry. It was—oh, it was so very good to be on horseback and out in the fresh air again, I couldn't resist. There really was no danger—he's a beautiful animal and very well trained. But I'm sorry I worried you." She slipped her arm through his. "Shall we return to the girls? Lily sounded quite worried."

He was fit to be seen again, so he opened the stall door and led her back outside to where the others were waiting. "You're a magnificent horsewoman. I had no idea. Why did you not tell me you rode?"

She shrugged. "You never asked, and besides, you'd made it clear you wanted me to get on with the house refurbishment."

He felt a pang of compunction. He really should have taken the trouble to learn more about her. "I borrowed horses from a neighbor for Rose and Lily and had Georgiana's horse and his groom brought from her former home." He'd thought it might make her feel more at home.

His wife glanced up at him. "So there isn't a mount for me? Not even a mule or a donkey?"

He shook his head. "But I'll send for one at once."

"Which? A mule or a donkey?" She was teasing him again, he saw, and felt something loosen in his chest.

"The mount you deserve," he told her in a severe tone.

She laughed again, and there was a sense of companionship in her attitude, as though they'd crossed some threshold. He didn't know what, but it pleased him.

"Are you still going after your assassin today?" she asked quietly.

"No, I'll go tomorrow. I've been chasing the swine for two years; another day won't make much difference."

They emerged into the morning sunshine, where the three girls waited apprehensively. Their gaze immediately shot to his wife, examining her for signs of violence, he supposed.

Emmaline clung to his arm and said gaily, "We've discussed the matter and Cal is going to find something for me to ride, so we can all ride out together."

"A donkey," Cal growled.

"A *donkey*?" Rose began, a belligerent expression on her face. "But she—"

"It's a joke, Rose," Emmaline assured her with a laugh. "Your brother didn't know I could ride, so he only borrowed horses for you and Lily, for while we're here. And of course he sent for George's beautiful Sultan, because he knew George would be fretting about him—and I must say, George, he is a beautiful creature. I quite envy you."

Rose turned a surprised look on Cal. "You arranged horses especially for us?"

He shrugged. "I knew you'd want to ride, and this place hasn't been occupied since Father died. Henry sold off all the horses."

"And you brought Jem here, as well as Sultan," George said. "Thank you, Cal." It was the first openly friendly thing the girl had said to him.

"We'll drop in on Sir Alfred Chisholm—he's the neighbor I borrowed the horses from—and see if he can spare a mount for Emmaline." He turned a stern look on his niece. "He's the Master of the Hunt, and if you bother him in any way, shape or form, George, your horse is going straight back to Alderton. *And* that enormous hound of yours!"

To his surprise his niece grinned at the threat. "You called me George," she said triumphantly.

"Slip of the tongue," he said gruffly. "Now, since you're dressed in those wretched breeches, you can ride up behind me, Emmaline can take Sultan and we'll all ride over to Sir Alfred's together and presume on his generosity one more time."

CAL'S HORSE'S HOOVES CRUNCHED ON THE FROZEN GRASS, leaving a trail of round green hoofprints. The bare branches of the trees were rimed with frost, a landscape of silver and white with darkly etched silhouettes and shadows of gray and lilac. He crested the hill and turned to look back at the house. The weak winter sun was just beginning to touch the tips of the chimneys.

He'd left well before dawn this morning, taking extra care not to wake his wife, telling himself it was to get this task done in good time, but knowing he'd taken the coward's exit.

The events of the day before had disturbed him. First his loss of control in the stables. He never lost control.

And then . . . He didn't know quite why he'd found the day he'd spent with his wife and the girls so disturbing. They'd ridden over to Sir Alfred's and borrowed another horse for Emm, and of course, Lady Chisholm had insisted they come in for a bite of breakfast first, and it was quite late by then and they were all hungry, and besides, it would have been rude to refuse.

Sir Alfred's eyes had bulged at the sight of Georgiana in her disgraceful breeches. He'd turned bright red, made several loud harrumphing noises and for the rest of the visit had carefully pretended the girl was not there. He'd waxed eloquent in praise of Sultan, wanting to know his breeding and paces, and was noticeably disconcerted when Cal referred him to Georgiana, the invisible girl who'd owned, raised and trained him.

Lady Chisholm, much more tactful, had simply assumed Georgiana had had an accident with her habit, and had produced an old riding habit of her daughter's for her to wear. To Cal's surprise, after a silent exchange of glances with

Emmaline, Georgiana accepted the gift politely and donned the skirt over her breeches without fuss or argument.

Cal had to assume his wife's influence was at work in producing this unaccustomed docility in his niece, though how she'd achieved it was a mystery. All he knew was that if he'd tried to get the girl into a riding skirt she'd have resisted furiously.

After breakfast, they'd spent the rest of the morning and early afternoon riding around the estate—Georgiana learning the way of riding sidesaddle, Emmaline and the girls showing her how. Of course she managed perfectly—the girl was a natural—but it was an occasion of much laughter and spirited debate, though somehow all in fun.

And of course, as the places they visited jogged memories in himself and his half sisters, various stories and tales had emerged. It became, as well as a pleasant ride, an afternoon of recollections, family stories and laughing disputes about the truth of various events.

His wife was at the heart of it, of course, asking questions, prompting the stories and encouraging them all to share memories and impressions of times past. She even got George to open up a little.

Listening to his niece's stories, Cal was forced to admit that when she wasn't spitting and snarling in defiance of his edicts, Georgiana could be quite charming. She told a number of amusing tales—several at her own expense. But reading between the lines, he could see she'd led a lonely and often difficult life, and he cursed again the selfishness of Henry, who had deprived her of all that her birth entitled her. He would make it up to the girl, he vowed silently.

Or Emmaline would, in his name.

Cal also found himself recounting tales of events and boyish adventures he'd almost completely forgotten about. He'd shown them his favorite fishing spot, a tree in which he'd tried to make a secret hideout—the remnants of it were still visible—and even a place where hawks nested, and he told them he'd always wanted to try training a hawk but had never been allowed. He'd never told that to anyone.

Emmaline hadn't said a word about herself, except once,

when Lily had asked her whether she'd liked school. She'd pulled a face and laughed, saying, "Not at all. I was thoroughly miserable for ages. I was most unladylike and was forever in trouble. And I missed the horses and my dog desperately. But I got used to it." And then changed the subject.

Cal wanted to know more. He'd gone over her story— well, the few grudging shreds of it she'd shared with him— over and over in his mind, and it still didn't add up. If she'd hated school as a pupil, why had she then returned to become a teacher there? And why had she been disinherited by her father? But he didn't want to question her in front of the girls, and so the moment passed.

Emmaline got him and his sisters talking about things they never would normally have discussed—things about his father, his memories of his mother, of the girls' mother, of their grandparents, and Aunt Dottie and Aunt Agatha.

She'd even somehow coaxed him to talk a bit about the war—something he never did, not to civilians. Not the worst stuff, of course, but several stories and anecdotes that in retrospect turned out to be somewhat amusing.

It was, as Emmaline had said when they returned home, tired, hungry and happy, a wonderful family day.

Why that should make Cal feel unaccountably restless and uncomfortable, he didn't know. But it did.

He wasn't used to being in a family, being part of a family, doing family things. He felt . . . he felt like Gulliver being slowly trapped by a multitude of tiny strings, none of them strong enough in itself to entrap a man, but together . . .

A story, a smile, a pair of long, graceful legs, sparkling gray-green eyes, a mouth as ripe as berries . . .

He needed to get back to work, to focus on the task at hand. He couldn't afford to be distracted.

That night after dinner, while the girls were distracted with a clever puzzle, he'd spoken to Emm in private and raised the subject of Georgiana's about-face, the transformation from recalcitrant brat into demure young lady. "How did you do that? Made her do what you wanted without any fuss and bother? Rose too. I ask them to do something and it's the worst thing in the world and I'm an evil bully. You ask them and they're as sweet as honey."

She smiled. "Young girls, especially bright and spirited young girls, need to be handled delicately."

"Delicately?" He made a rude noise. "There's nothing delicate about those girls. Perhaps Lily."

"Delicate in the sense of how you would handle a spirited filly. With praise and reward. Not force."

"In the army, discipline was all about force and leadership. And trust."

She nodded. "Trust is vital here too, but it goes both ways. The girls are coming to trust you, but they need to know you trust them too. Show them what you expect, trust them to do the right thing, give them responsibility and some freedom—"

"Freedom?" He shuddered. "I hate to think what they'll get up to!"

She laughed. "And praise, lots of praise. The girls, for all their apparent confidence, are full of doubt, particularly self-doubt."

"Even Rose?"

She nodded. "Even Rose."

He frowned. He didn't want the girls to be full of self-doubt. He wanted them confident and strong. "Trust, and responsibility, you say?"

"And praise. For everything they do right, or every attempt they make to do the right thing—praise them. You'll see."

He looked doubtful, so she added, "They admire and look up to you, you know."

He snorted. "They do not."

She laughed. "They do. They just don't show it to your face. But have patience. You did well today—and so did they."

It gave him something to think of.

And then, later that night when he'd entered her bedchamber and found her lolling sleepily in her bath, soaking out the stiffness of her long ride . . .

The bath had been placed in front of the fire. The flames made her glow, her skin gleaming with water and bath oils.

She was stiff and sore from her long unaccustomed ride.

He should have left her to soak, left her to sleep in peace. By herself.

If he'd touched her at all, it should have been to rub her briskly with horse liniment—that would have soothed her aches.

But he hadn't. He hadn't been able to resist the sight of her, all creamy and pink and damp. She'd welcomed him with a sleepy smile, and that was all it took. He'd scooped her out of the bath and made love to her, once in front of the fire, and then again in bed.

He *never* lost control. Now, it escaped him on the smallest of excuses.

Cal eased his horse into a canter, and the house fell away from sight. This business of being married, of being part of a family, of handling wild and unruly hoydens *delicately* . . .

He was much more comfortable hunting assassins.

THE TWO SAGGING COTTAGES WERE JOINED BY ONE WALL. Both dwellings seemed deserted. Cal knocked on each door, then peered in the windows. The rooms were sparsely furnished, but there were signs of recent occupation.

"Told you you was too late," the ancient who'd directed him to these cottages called out in a creaky voice. "Cleared out, they have. Gorn to America."

Cal swore. The old man had told him, while puffing on an evil-smelling pipe, and with the encouragement of the occasional coin, all he needed to know to be sure that he'd found his man at last.

The Gimble brothers were as like as two peas in a pod, and close. They'd even married two sisters. They'd left the Rifle Brigade when the war was over and returned to their village, but times were tough, and they'd decided to migrate to America. Bert had gone ahead, while Joe had taken some jobs abroad to earn the money for fares for the wives and children, and to give them a good start in a new country.

Cal was sure he knew what those jobs had been.

"When did Joe and the women and children leave?" Cal asked. It couldn't have been long. There was the end of a loaf of bread on the table. It was not yet moldy, nor eaten by mice. The old man contemplated his pipe and waited until Cal produced another coin.

"Left yesterday morn, in a rush. Dunno why—they bin talking about going to America for a couple o' years. Bert, 'e went first, going ahead, like, to make things ready for their wives and the little 'uns. Got a farm 'e as, all ready for 'em. Wrote 'em a letter to say so and all."

"When was this?"

"The letter from America?" He puffed a cloud of reeking smoke as he considered it. "Couple a' months back, I reckon. Don't exactly remember, but it was afore Christmas. Lots of excitement when it come, see."

Cal jerked his head at the cottages. "Looks to me like they left in a hurry."

The old man nodded. "Joe come back sudden like day afore yesterday—well, he comes and goes, does Joe, never know where he be—but this time he come back from Lunnon and whatever he told them got 'em all stirred up and by the next mornin' they was all packed up and gorn." He grinned knowingly and sucked on his pipe. "Told ye, I did—they've gorn."

Cal swore under his breath. Obviously Joe had been tipped off by someone that people had been investigating the activities of former Riflemen. "Where did they go? Which direction?"

The old man gestured with his reeking pipe. "Lunnon."

"London?" Cal queried sharply. "You're sure it was London, not Liverpool or Bristol?" Ships bound for America most often left from Bristol or Liverpool.

The old man shook his head. "No, it was Lunnon for sure. Heard Joe say he was owed money there and would collect before they left."

"Thank you." Cal tossed the old fellow a last coin, mounted his horse and headed for home. Dammit! If he hadn't spent the day before with the girls and his wife . . .

Chapter Seventeen

All the world's a stage,
And all the men and women merely players.
They have their exits and their entrances;
And one man in his time plays many parts…
—WILLIAM SHAKESPEARE, *AS YOU LIKE IT*

"I'M LEAVING FOR LONDON FIRST THING IN THE MORNING," Cal told Emm over a late supper. He'd told her how he'd just missed the man he was sure was the Scorpion. "He would have left while we were riding aimlessly around the estate."

"It wasn't aimless in the least," she said calmly. "It was exactly what you and the girls needed. And I was glad to get to know the estate a little. Besides, if the fellow you're chasing left at first light yesterday morning, you still would have missed him, albeit by a few hours instead of a whole day. Still, I'm sure you'll catch him." She rose and moved to the door. "I'll tell the girls to be packed and ready to leave after breakfast, then."

He frowned. "The girls? No, I'm not taking the girls." He hadn't planned to take anyone. Not even his wife.

She turned back, one eyebrow raised. "You can't possibly leave them here."

"Why not? This is their home."

She gave him a pointed look. "Don't imagine one day of riding and brotherly pleasantness will rid them of the suspicion that you mean to dump them in the country—particularly if you then do dump them here while you go swanning off to London."

"I'm not *swanning* anywhere. I'm pursuing a criminal."

"Yes, in London," she said serenely. "And we will come

too. We'll need to order a great many clothes if all three girls are to make their come-out this spring, you know. Men never have the least idea how much preparation is involved. Oh, the girls will be so excited. I must tell them before they retire for the night."

"Madam," he began.

She paused, her brow crinkling. "Do you think the antiquated old coach in the stables will be up to the journey, or should we hire a second carriage? We'll need at least two carriages for all of us, including Milly, my maid, and the dog, of course."

"Madam, I'm not taking the carriage anywhere! It's far too slow for my purposes. I'm riding, which is why—"

She gave him a dazzling smile. "Oh, good, that will work nicely, then. It'll be a squeeze, especially with the dog, but we'll manage. And you can ride ahead and inform the staff at Ashendon House to expect us. Excellent."

"I wasn't planning to go anywhere near Ashendon House," he informed her. "I'm in pursuit of *an assassin*."

"Send a message to the staff when you get there, then. It won't take but a moment," she said blithely.

"I have a job to do in London—a dangerous job," he reiterated in a firm voice. "I don't have time to be looking after"—he was going to say "a wife" but decided on discretion at the last minute—"my sisters and niece." He didn't want any of them there. He wanted to keep his mind clear for his pursuit.

"Of course not," she agreed. "That's what you married me for." And she sailed through the door, leaving him glowering and slightly baffled.

It *was* what he'd married her for. It was just that when she said it like that, it sounded . . . wrong.

LONDON WAS DAMP, THE SKY OVERLAID WITH A DIRTY yellowish gloom. Cal headed straight for Gil Radcliffe's office in Whitehall. "I think I've found the Scorpion, only he just slipped through my fingers." He explained his reasoning, and at the end, Radcliffe nodded briskly.

"Sounds like our man, all right. You don't know where in London he was headed?"

"No, just that it was London and that he was owed money here. But he took two women—his wife and sister-in-law—they're sisters—and three children with him." He shook his head. "I know—needle in a haystack."

Radcliffe frowned thoughtfully for a moment, scribbled a note then called for his clerk. "Run over to the Rifle Brigade headquarters and see what information they have on these two. Most urgent status." The man took the note and hurried off.

The writing of the note jogged Cal's memory. "Is there some paper I can use for a note? I need to inform the staff at Ashendon House that my wife and sisters and niece are to arrive shortly. God knows what state the house is in—my late brother seemed to have neglected everything."

Radcliffe's brows rose. "You seem to have acquired a few more dependents since we last met. My felicitations on your marriage. But the niece?"

"Henry's daughter by a secret earlier marriage, the selfish swine. Eighteen years old, and the family knew nothing about her."

"Oh, that will please your aunt Agatha," Radcliffe said dryly.

Cal raised an ironic brow. "Does anything ever please Aunt Agatha?"

"When last I saw her she was none too pleased about your, er, rather swift marriage. Was doing her best to ferret out what I knew about your wife's family. Of course, I told her nothing."

Cal frowned. "Do you know anything?"

Radcliffe spread his fingers and looked mysterious. Typical. Secrecy was Radcliffe's middle name. He was like a bank vault; he only opened up when it suited him.

"Well, if you happen to run into Aunt Agatha again, don't tell her I'm in town. With any luck, I'll be back in Europe by the time she discovers I've been in London."

"You're still planning to return to your former occupation?"

"Of course. Why not?" he added, seeing Radcliffe's expression. "Isn't that what we agreed in the first place? You gave me four weeks' leave."

"Yes, but with the title and estate, and now this marriage, I assumed . . ."

Cal shook his head. "The estate affairs are all in order, and my wife is happy to launch the girls, so nothing much needs to change."

Radcliffe gave him a long look. That glint of amusement returned. "You just got married, have taken custody of three spirited young ladies—all heiresses, I assume—and you don't expect your life to change?"

"Why should it? My wife handles them brilliantly. I didn't marry a silly young chit, you know; I married a good woman with brains, character and common sense."

Radcliffe chuckled softly. "All the more reason your life will never be the same again. No, don't bother to argue. Time will tell. As for sending a note, it will take at least two hours to unearth the information we require from the Rifle Brigade, which leaves you plenty of time to drop by Ashendon House yourself and make what arrangements need to be done. I'll see you back here at six."

HAVING NOTHING ELSE TO DO, CAL RODE OVER TO MAYFAIR and rang the bell at Ashendon House. Were any servants in residence at all? If not, he'd have to put Emmaline and the girls in a suite at the Pulteney while domestic arrangements were made.

To his surprise, the door was opened by a butler, a man he'd never seen before. The two men stared blankly at each other.

The butler was young, as butlers went—about forty. He bowed slightly. "I'm afraid the family is out of town at present, sir."

"No, we're not," Cal told him. "I'm Ashendon. This is my house. And you are?"

"Burton, my lord, I'm terribly sorry, I—"

Cal waved his apologies aside. "Who hired you?"

"Mr. Phipps, your man of affairs, my lord."

Cal handed the man his hat and coat. He should have known it. Phipps trod a fine line between being ultra-efficient and interfering. "I came to warn you to expect my wife, Lady Ashendon, and my wards, Lady Rose, Lady Lily and Lady Georgiana."

The butler's eyes widened slightly, but he said smoothly, "When do you anticipate they will arrive, my lord?"

Cal glanced at the hall clock. "Sometime this evening, I expect. Midmorning tomorrow at the latest."

"Very good, my lord. The staff will be in readiness."

"There is a staff, is there?"

"Yes, my lord, all new, like myself, but I fancy we are working well together. Shall I fetch them for an introduction?"

Cal waved off that suggestion. "No need. My wife will do all that. The running of the house is in her hands."

Burton inclined his head. "Do you require anything at present, my lord?"

"No. I just dropped in to let you know to expect the ladies. I'll be going back out shortly."

"What shall I tell Lady Salter, my lord?"

Cal blinked. "Aunt Agatha? Why, nothing, of course." He frowned at the man's expression. "What's she got to do with anything?"

"It was Lady Salter who instructed Mr. Phipps to hire the staff for the house and prepare for your arrival. She didn't know the date, of course, but she's been checking up on us, and giving orders."

Cal swore under his breath. Giving orders would be right. Nothing Aunt Agatha liked better.

"Is there a problem, my lord?"

"No, just—just don't tell Lady Salter anything."

Burton gave him a pained look. "She visits daily, my lord."

"*Daily?* Good God!" Cal gave a hunted glance behind him. "Has she been here today?"

"This morning, my lord," the butler said in a soothing voice. "She normally comes each morning around eleven."

Cal made a note to be out of the house every morning around eleven. "I'm going out again now—I'm not sure when

I'll be back. Is there a key?" Burton fetched him a key. Cal pocketed it and left.

"Robert and Joseph Gimble have no relatives listed, except for their wives," Radcliffe said when Cal returned to Whitehall. He didn't look unhappy, though.

"And the good news?" Cal asked.

Radcliffe tapped the file in front of him and allowed himself a small grin. "One of the wives listed a next of kin—"

"The two wives are sisters."

"Exactly. And they have an aunt who lives in—wait for it—Whitechapel. She's married to a weaver."

"You think that's where he'll be?" Cal felt a surge of excitement. Whitechapel was just a short distance from Whitehall.

Radcliffe nodded. "They have small children, don't forget, so they can't stay just anywhere. I've sent men to the aunt's house."

Cal's jaw dropped. "But I—" He broke off.

"Wanted to be in at the kill? Understandable, but we can't risk losing him. There's a rabbit warren of lanes and alleys around the aunt's house. I've sent a dozen armed men. Don't worry, you'll get the credit for his capture."

"I don't care about that," Cal said impatiently. "I just wanted to lay hands on the bastard myself."

Radcliffe gave him a cool look. 'Revenge for Bentley, yes. But you know as well as anyone that the work we do is a team effort, and no one man matters, as long as the outcome is the one we want."

Cal glanced at the clock. "When did they leave?"

"An hour ago. They'll be in position by now. We should hear one way or the other sometime in the next hour or so." He produced a bottle and two glasses from a drawer in his desk. "Brandy?"

Cal nodded. If he had to wait and do nothing, he might as well have a drink.

An hour crawled past.

Radcliffe had busied himself with paperwork. Cal did his

best to tamp down on his impatience. He tried to read a newspaper but couldn't concentrate. After all this time, a hunt across the Continent and England, to have to wait tamely in an office while other men captured that swine . . .

When the clock softly chimed the passing of the second hour, Cal stood up. "We should have heard something by now. I'm going to Whitechapel." Radcliffe opened his mouth to forbid it, but Cal held up his hand. "Don't worry, I'll stay well back and out of your men's hair. I know better than to interfere in an operation, but I want to be there when he's taken into custody—to see him and be certain he's the man I saw. And if something goes wrong, I might be able to help."

Radcliffe frowned.

"It's dark. I'll be invisible in the background. You know I can do it."

After a moment Radcliffe nodded. "Very well, but stay well back."

IT STARTED TO DRIZZLE AROUND TEN. CAL, PROPPED UP against a cold and grimy brick wall in the shadows of a dim and noisome alleyway, pulled his coat collar up and wished he'd had a little more of that brandy. The rain sputtered to a halt just after midnight.

Radcliffe's men had reported that the little house in Whitechapel had contained three women, a huddle of small children and only one man—the weaver. Joe Gimble—the Scorpion—was nowhere to be found. The women tried to pretend they knew nothing about his whereabouts—had never heard of him, in fact—but they weren't very skilled liars. And were obviously frightened.

Two of Radcliffe's men had remained inside the house, waiting for Gimble's return. The rest of the men melted into the shadows, posted at every approach to the house, watching and waiting. Cal lurked in a dark alleyway, his every sense primed for the appearance of the man he'd pursued for so long.

The alleyway reeked, the odors of the filth and rubbish of the streets intensified by the rain.

Despite the rain and cold and the late hour, the streets were far from empty: a rag and bone man pushing his cart, a pieman, workers, prostitutes, beggars, drunks and thieves—the usual rabble of the poorer streets of London.

Cal scanned every face. He'd donned enough disguises to look beyond the obvious—even the women. But the only face he recognized was that of the drunk he'd interviewed weeks before, the skeletal wreck of a man whose hands shook so badly he could barely hold the gin bottle he now hugged to his chest. A new gin bottle.

The man glanced at him, stared, reeling and befuddled, as if he recognized Cal from somewhere but couldn't place him, then staggered on. He was in even worse shape than he'd been when Cal saw him last. He stumbled into a narrow alley that Cal knew from previous investigation was a dead end, and collapsed in a heap.

As the hours passed Cal became increasingly certain that Gimble wasn't going to return. Someone must have warned him.

Radcliffe joined him around four A.M. and told him to go home. "There's no point in you hanging around all night. Go home. My men will stay on for as long as it takes. If there's a development I'll let you know."

Cal was cold, wet, tired and dispirited. The investigation was out of his hands and only stubbornness was keeping him here. "All right, but keep an eye on that drunk." He indicated the huddled shape collapsed in a corner of the alley. "He's not Gimble, but he's a former Rifleman and I don't trust coincidences."

It was almost five in the morning when Cal entered Ashendon House again. The gaslights in the entrance burned low. He shrugged off his wet coat and hung it on a hook in the cloakroom, then made his way upstairs. Then paused.

Which room was his bedchamber? The half-dozen or so times he'd stayed at Ashendon House in the past, he'd had a small bedchamber on the third floor. Now . . .

Deciding that the new servants would probably have put

him in his father's old room, he made his way there. He opened the door and glanced in. The room was unoccupied but a lamp had been lit, a fire was burning in the grate and the bed had been turned down.

He began to undress, pulling off his neckcloth, unbuttoning his waistcoat and pulling his shirttails free. Looking around for somewhere to put his damp clothes, he saw a partly open door. His dressing room?

He went in and saw that it connected to another bedroom. Emmaline's? Quietly he entered and, in the dying firelight, stood gazing down at his sleeping wife. Her dark hair was spread over the pillow. She was sleeping on her back, one hand curled to her breast, one hand flung across the empty half of the bed, palm up, fingers slightly curled.

She looked young and peaceful, and utterly enticing.

A lock of hair lay straggled across her cheek. He bent and smoothed it back. Still fast asleep, she made a breathy little sound and snuggled into his hand. He stood there a long minute, cupping her soft cheek in his palm, hoping she would waken, but unwilling to disturb her.

She must be exhausted. She'd just made a long trip squashed in a carriage filled with noisy young women and a gangly great dog with a flatulent habit.

He could just slip into her bed—to sleep, not for any other reason. He wouldn't have to wake her.

He pulled his shirt over his head, intending to slide in beside her, then stopped, wrinkling his nose. Not only was he damp to the skin, but his clothes, and possibly his skin and hair, had been imbued with the stench of the street. He looked down at his sleeping wife and sighed.

He couldn't bring that to her bed.

He turned away and stripped in the dressing room, leaving his clothes piled on the floor, then slid between the cold sheets of the master bed.

He lay there, waiting to get warm, his body aching for Emmaline. How long had he been married? A week? And already he missed sleeping with her?

It wasn't a good sign.

* * *

A SLIVER OF COOL GRAY LIGHT PIERCED A GAP IN THE DRAWN curtains. Daylight. Cal yawned and stretched lazily, peering through sleep-filled eyes at the ormolu clock on the overmantel. And blinked and looked again. After ten? He never slept that late.

He rose and rang for hot water, and while he was waiting, he tiptoed through the dressing room and glanced in. His wife's bed was empty, neatly made up as if she'd never been there.

A man who claimed to be his new valet arrived with the hot water. Another of Phipps's appointments. Did the man not realize Cal was leaving in a few weeks?

Cal shaved himself, waving away the valet's services, completed his ablutions and dressed in the clothes the fellow insisted on laying out for him. Cal shrugged himself into his coat, glanced down at it and frowned. Emmaline must have packed all his clothes and brought them up to London for him. Used to traveling light, he'd shoved a few things in a saddlebag and ridden out.

Another convenience of a wife. He felt mildly guilty.

He went downstairs, intending to have a quick breakfast and head off to Whitehall to see what had happened overnight.

He was halfway down the stairs when a voice accosted him. "There you are, Ashendon." A thin, immensely elegant elderly lady stood in the middle of the hallway, watching him critically through a lorgnette. Aunt Agatha, the elder of his two aunts.

Her hair was iron gray, with two dramatic wings of silver swept up from her temples. Like Aunt Dottie, she'd aged, though in quite a different fashion; the two sisters had always been chalk and cheese. She wore a smart black-and-white outfit that nobody would imagine was for mourning. "Lolling abed till all hours, were you? I cannot abide slugabeds."

Cal hoped his sigh was not audible. "Good morning, Aunt Agatha."

She sniffed and held out her gloved hand to him. "That remains to be seen. Where is this wife of yours? I wish to meet her."

Cal looked around, hoping to see Emmaline somewhere about. Burton the butler cleared his throat. "Yes, Burton?"

"Lady Ashendon and the young ladies went out earlier, my lord. Shopping, I believe."

Aunt Agatha made an exasperated sound. "No doubt she'll purchase all the wrong things. Nobodies from the country invariably do. Now explain to me, Ashendon, if you please, the reason for this disgracefully hasty marriage to a complete and utter nobody! Did you give *any* consideration to what you owe your name? Obviously not!"

"I beg your pardon?" said Cal, outraged by this description of his wife.

"Apology accepted," Aunt Agatha said regally, "but you still haven't explained yourself."

"My wife," he began stiffly, "is not a nobody. She is—"

"Oh, pish tosh, of course she is. Nobody has ever heard of her, and those that have know nothing good of her. A *governess*, Ashendon! Could you find anyone *less* distinguished? A washerwoman, perhaps, or a milkmaid? Milkmaids have good skin, or so I've heard—does she have good skin, at least?"

Cal leashed his temper. "My wife is well educated, well born and—"

"Well born? Nonsense! According to my sources she is a nobody, a spinster long past her prime with neither background nor looks to recommend her."

"Rubbish!" snapped Cal. "She is the daughter of a baronet—"

"Exactly—not even a member of the nobility!"

"She is *perfect* for my needs. I wrote to you and asked for your help with the girls, remember? And you washed your hands of them and me. Told me to solve my own problems. And I did. Marrying Emmaline was the best thing I could have done."

"Nonsense. If you'd asked me to find you a suitable wife, I would have found one—someone with birth, breeding, background and looks. A wife you could be proud of. And you would have been married decently, in front of everyone, all the ton, not in some hasty, scrambled marriage in the wilds of—"

"In Bath Abbey, by the Bishop of Bath and Wells."

"I know that," she said irritably. "I wrote to the bishop, if you recall, and arranged for him to conduct the ceremony. Otherwise you would no doubt have married in a wayside chapel or—heaven forbid—a civil ceremony in a dusty office somewhere."

"Emmaline has done wonders with the girls already."

"Well, of course she has—she's a governess. That's her job! But you don't marry women like that, you *hire* them."

Cal clenched his jaw. He'd rather have all his teeth pulled than admit to Aunt Agatha that in fact he had tried to hire Emmaline at first. If she ever got hold of that, he'd never hear the end of it.

"I am very satisfied with my marriage—more than satisfied."

She snorted. "You have to say that. Rutherford men never admit to an error of judgment—or any other kind, for that matter. Pigheaded. Your father and brother were just the same."

Cal's fingers curled into fists. Why nobody had yet strangled his aunt was beyond him. "Delightful as it is to chat with you, Aunt Agatha, I'm afraid I have an urgent appointment and must leave you now."

Burton instantly glided out of nowhere with Cal's coat and hat. He must have been listening; he probably couldn't help but hear. Not that it would have made the slightest difference if he'd remained by Cal's side the whole time. To Aunt Agatha, servants' ears existed for one reason only—to take orders. Otherwise they were deaf, dumb and blind to their betters' conversations.

"That's right, rush off, don't even offer me tea. No manners at all, this generation," Aunt Agatha declared.

Cal, stupefied by the statement, opened his mouth, closed it, bowed over her hand and made his escape.

* * *

CAL MADE STRAIGHT FOR WHITEHALL, BUT WHEN HE GOT to Gil Radcliffe's office he found it empty. Mr. Radcliffe, he was informed, had just this minute left for Whitechapel.

Cal headed immediately for Whitechapel. He arrived at the same time as Radcliffe. He glanced at his surroundings but could see nothing much different from the previous night. "What's going on?"

"There's no point in maintaining this vigil," Radcliffe told him. "Gimble obviously knows we're here. We'll have to flush him out by other means."

"How?"

"I'm going to take the women and children into custody. I'll put the word out that they will only be released if Joe Gimble comes forward."

Cal frowned. That didn't seem right to him at all. "You'd lock up innocent women and children? But they've done nothing to deserve that."

Radcliffe shrugged. "You don't know what they know, whether they were in on the Scorpion's activities or not. But it doesn't matter. Seems to me everything Gimble and his brother have done has been to get the women and children to a better place, to give them a better life. If I've read him aright, he won't abandon them now."

"What if he does? How long will you keep them imprisoned?"

Radcliffe gave him a hard look. "For as long as it takes."

He beckoned to one of his men, who came over. Radcliffe issued a series of terse instructions; the man nodded and signaled to the rest of the men to come out of concealment. A short briefing, and then they approached the house in a tight semicircle, some with pistols at the ready. They banged on the front door, shouting, "Open up in the name of His Majesty."

People stopped to watch, speculating as to what was going on.

"Do they have to brandish those damned pistols?" Cal

asked. "They're women and children, for God's sake. You'll terrify them."

"I want them terrified and for people to see it," Radcliffe responded coolly. "Gimble needs to know we're serious." He glanced at Cal. "They won't be hurt, if that's what you're worrying about. This is theater, not war. The more people see this, the more pressure Gimble will be under to rescue them."

Theater or not, Cal didn't like the use of women and children. But that was why Radcliffe had the job he had. He had to be ruthless. He operated on the demands of the larger picture, where individuals didn't matter, as long as the greater good was achieved.

Cal, after half a lifetime at war, had decided that individuals mattered. It was why he'd never make a general.

He watched as the women were led from the house, red-faced and weeping. One of the women was visibly pregnant. Three children followed, a young boy of about eight or nine leading them. He was thin as a lath, with short, ragged hair from which his ears stuck out woefully. He held the hand of a little boy about four years old and carried a toddler, a little girl. The two small ones were sobbing, but the boy was silent and grim-faced. His eyes burned dark and intense, stark against his pale young face.

Cal ached for the lad.

Radcliffe's men led them into a waiting high-barred cart. Ignoring the shouts from the gathering crowd, they loaded the women and children into it—the boy handing his siblings up himself, refusing the aid of the soldiers.

"It looks like a damned tumbril," Cal muttered. The women clutched at the bars; the little ones cried out piteously. The crowd was turning ugly and started pushing at the barrier of Radcliffe's men.

"Theater," Radcliffe reminded him. "If they look as though they're going to their execution, all the better." His head man glanced at Radcliffe, who gave a crisp nod. The cart rumbled off. The women wailed, the children screamed, the crowd shouted.

Cal turned away from the sight in disgust. It was not at

all how he'd envisaged the conclusion of his hunt for the assassin. As he turned, he met the accusing gaze of the drunk former sharpshooter across the other side of the road.

A night in the cold rain seemed to have sobered him up a little. He gave Cal a filthy look, then spat in his direction. Then he lifted his gin bottle, drank deeply and staggered away.

Cal felt like doing the same.

Chapter Eighteen

A woman would run through fire and water
for such a kind heart.
—WILLIAM SHAKESPEARE, *THE MERRY
WIVES OF WINDSOR*

EMM AND THE GIRLS ARRIVED HOME AROUND NOON. THEY'D
spent a delightful few hours exploring the London shops and
had decided to go back to Ashendon House, have a quick
luncheon and then visit the Tower of London. It was their first
time in the great city—even Emm had never been there
before—and they were determined to see all the famous sights.

The Tower was first on the list. Rose wanted to see the
grim place where so many famous people had met their
doom—she liked grisly stories—while Lily and Emm were
keen to see the Crown Jewels. George, once she'd heard
about the Royal Menagerie, was eager to see the exotic animals.

"You have a visitor, my lady," the butler, Burton, murmured as he opened the door for them.

"Really? Who is it?" Emm couldn't imagine who it could
be. She didn't think she knew anyone in London and, more
to the point, nobody knew she was here.

"Lady Salter, Lord Ashendon's aunt. She's waiting in the
green sitting room."

"Oh, what a lovely surprise." Emm handed him her hat
and glanced in the mirror to tidy her hair and check that she
was presentable.

"I gather you've never met Lady Salter, my lady," Burton
murmured.

"No, not yet." Emm turned to the girls. "Rose, Lily, your aunt Agatha has come to call. Isn't that delightful? George, come and meet your first London relative." She led them to the green sitting room.

An elegant elderly lady looked up as they entered. She'd been perusing a magazine. She set it aside, raised her lorgnette and directed it at Emm. She said not a word.

Emm came forward, saying warmly, "Lady Salter, I'm sorry to keep you waiting; I didn't know you intended to call. I am Emmaline, Lady Ashendon." The title still felt odd on her lips.

Lady Salter made no attempt to rise. She glanced at Emm and pursed her thin lips. "So I gather." She looked at the girls, clustered reluctantly in the doorway. "Well, come in, gels, don't stand there loitering. Let me look at you."

The girls shuffled forward. The old lady scrutinized them carefully through her lorgnette. "Don't any of you gels know to curtsey when greeting your elders and betters?"

She watched critically as they hastily curtseyed, and snorted when they were finished. "You, gel at the end, where did you learn to curtsey? You're about as graceful as a bear."

George lifted her chin. "Thank you," she said. "I like bears."

The old lady stiffened. "Cheek! I suppose you're Henry's bastard."

George clenched her fists. Emm placed a soothing hand on George's shoulder and said, "This is Lady Georgiana Rutherford, your nephew Henry's perfectly legitimate daughter. Tragically lost to the family for some years, but we're thrilled to have her here, where she belongs—with us—aren't we, girls?"

Lady Salter's lip curled. "Speaking for *my* family, are you, gel? And you a bride of how many days?"

"Almost a week," said Emm composedly. She had this old woman's measure now but was determined not to come to cuffs at their first meeting.

"Why are you and the gels not in mourning? Henry's not been dead much more than a month."

"My father's will forbade it," George told her.

"Pfft! *Henry?* Forbidding the wearing of mourning? I don't believe it. That boy never gave a moment's thought to anyone else in his life."

"Be that as it may, my husband, as head of the family, has ordered that his brother's wishes be respected," Emm said.

There was a long silence, then Lady Salter said, "Well, if that's true, it's the first sensible thing that boy's done since his return to England." She jabbed her lorgnette in the direction of the girls. "From what I've heard, those gels need to be married off as quickly as possible."

"No," Emm said pleasantly.

The old lady's eyes sparked flint. "What do you mean, *no?*"

"There's no rush. The girls will take as long as they wish. I won't allow anyone to put pressure on them concerning marriage."

"You won't *allow*—?"

"That's correct, I won't." Emm gave her a steely smile to underline her message. "Now, may I offer you some refreshment, Lady Salter? Tea? Something to eat? The girls and I were planning to have luncheon shortly. We'd love you to join us."

Lady Salter sniffed and glanced at the girls. She pointed her lorgnette at Lily. "That one could do without her luncheon. Put her on a reducing diet—potatoes boiled in vinegar was what did it for Byron. Give her nothing but potatoes in vinegar for a month; then she might look—"

Emm put her arm around Lily. "Nonsense," she said briskly. "Lily is a beautiful girl and we love her just exactly the way she is. I would no more think of putting her on a reducing diet than"—she smiled sweetly—"trying to fatten you up, after your long illness."

"What illness? I've never been ill a day in my life."

"Oh?" said Emm with false sympathy. "I thought you must have been ill. So many recovering invalids are excessively thin and crabby and bad-tempered. I'm so glad it's not illness that has caused it."

The old lady's flinty gray eyes narrowed, her thin bosom swelled and Emm decided to get the girls out of the way before the explosion came. As it was, both Rose and George looked to be on the verge of saying something rude to their aunt, and Lily was on the verge of tears—real ones.

"Girls, run along now and get changed for our outing this afternoon. Rose, will you ask Cook to hold luncheon for another half hour? George, that dog of yours will be needing a quick walk, don't you think? Lily dear"—she groped for something to ask the girl to do that would make her feel good about herself—"would you run up to my room and select a scarf for me to wear this afternoon. The wind is getting brisker, and you have such exquisite taste, I can rely on you to choose the perfect one. Say good-bye to Lady Salter—she's not staying for luncheon."

The girls dropped a hasty curtsey and fled. Emm resumed her seat and smiled at Lady Salter. "They're lovely girls, aren't they?"

The old lady sniffed. "Rose is a beauty—she'll do well enough. Lily needs to reduce, no matter what you say. And as for the other one"—she rolled her eyes—"no breeding at all. What was Henry thinking?"

"George is an original. I think she'll take the ton by storm."

"You do, do you?" Lady Salter said acidly. "Know a lot about the ton, do you? Whom, precisely, do you know in London?"

"Since I have no idea who is in London at present, I cannot say."

"Who are your people?"

Emm gestured to the house around her. "They are here."

"I meant your family."

"They are here."

Lady Salter's lips thinned. "Don't be obtuse, gel, I meant your father and mother."

"My father was Sir Humphrey Westwood; my mother was Alice Carsgood."

The old lady leaned forward. "Of the Hampshire Carsgoods?"

She was, in fact, but Emm couldn't resist saying, "Of the nowhere-in-particular Carsgoods—it was a love match, you see."

Lady Salter snorted. "Love! Tawdry middle-class sentiment."

"But *soooo* romantic." Emm produced a gusty sentimental sigh and fluttered her eyelashes.

"Pshaw! Blood is what counts in marriage. Blood, breeding and land."

"Really? How interesting. It's important when breeding pigs too," Emm said brightly. She rose from her seat. "Are you sure you can't stay for luncheon, Lady Salter?"

The old lady glowered at her, and for a moment Emm could see the resemblance both to Cal and to George. "Send for my carriage, gel."

Emm inclined her head. "With the greatest of pleasure."

CAL, FEELING SOURED AND DEPRESSED BY THE MORNING'S events, needed a distraction, and as he wandered past Covent Garden, he decided an evening at the theater was just the thing. Among the various entertainments listed on the playbill was *As You Like It*, which he felt would please Emmaline, who, as a former teacher on her first visit to a London theater, might want something Shakespearean, but since it was also comedy, it should suit him and the girls.

He sent a message to Ashendon House to let them know he'd be home for an early dinner before escorting them to the theater.

He then decided to visit Tattersalls and came away quite pleased with himself. He'd conducted several very satisfactory transactions and had also run into two old friends who, learning he was here with his new bride, invited him and Emmaline to a party and a musical evening in the following week.

The commencement of the season was still several months away, but a few small parties would ease his wife into the London social scene gradually and by the time the season started, she'd be much better prepared to make her way in London society.

"I MET YOUR AUNT TODAY," EMM SAID OVER DINNER. "LADY Salter."

Cal almost choked on his soup. "Damn—I mean blast. I meant to warn you."

Her brows rose. "Did you know she would visit, then?"

"No, but she was waiting when I came downstairs this morning. According to Burton she's been coming every day around eleven."

She nodded. "To check up on the domestic arrangements before we arrived, yes, Burton told me after she left. It was very kind of her."

"Kind?" Cal gave her a cautious look. "You *liked* her, then?"

"Oh, yes, I'm sure we're going to become fast friends. George dear, could I trouble you for the salt, please?"

"Fast friends?" Cal repeated, stunned. Aunt Agatha's few friends were a small collection of well-born but down-trodden ladies whom she ruled with a rod of iron. Unfortunately some of those ladies were very influential in society.

"Yes, indeed," his wife said enthusiastically. "We had a thoroughly delightful exchange. I enjoyed myself immensely."

Cal could hardly believe his ears. "You're sure it was Aunt Agatha you met, not some other lady? Skinny, elegant, dressed in black and white, tongue like an asp?"

"That's her. She was utterly charming. We simply adored her, didn't we, girls?"

It was at that point that Cal realized his sisters and Georgiana were smothering giggles. And that his wife was teasing him.

"Ah, I see. Well, sorry I didn't warn you beforehand."

Emmaline laughed. "I quite enjoyed myself, as a matter of fact."

"You should have been there, Cal," Rose interjected. "Emm gave Aunt Agatha as good as she got, but so perfectly politely there was no way the old horror could take offense. I mean, she knew Emm was saying cutting things back, but they were, on the surface of things, polite, so she had nothing to get hold of. It was brilliant, Emm."

"You shouldn't call your aunt an old horror," Emm said. "Whatever you think of her, outwardly at least, we will all show her the utmost respect."

"She *is* an old horror," Cal said.

Emm shrugged. "You can't choose your relatives."

"She's also my godmother," Cal said.

"And mine," Lily said gloomily. "I've always hoped she'd turn out to be some kind of fairy godmother, but all she could say to me was that I was fat and should be forced to eat nothing but potatoes boiled in vinegar."

"What?" Cal exclaimed. "That's disgusting—and wrong! You are not in the least—"

"Oh, don't worry, Emm had the perfect response," Rose said warmly.

"Yes, thank you, Emm," Lily said. "I was ready to sink until you spoke up."

"Don't you dare let her get the better of you, Lily," Georgiana said fiercely. "She's not a fairy godmother, she's a feral one."

There was a short silence, then they all burst out laughing.

"Stop maligning your relatives and eat up, you disrespectful females," Cal said a few minutes later. "We don't want to be late for the theater."

Who knew that Aunt Agatha would turn out to be the very thing he needed? It should have occurred to him sooner: In the face of a common enemy a disparate group would usually unite. Good old Aunt Agatha.

"HAS SOMETHING HAPPENED TO DISTURB YOU?" EMMALINE asked Cal that night as they were undressing for bed. "You've been very quiet all evening."

"What do you mean?" He'd done his best to be cheerful and entertaining. He'd thought he'd done quite a good job.

"We've had a lovely night—I think you can tell from the conversation in the carriage coming home from the theater how very much the girls and I enjoyed ourselves. It was so thoughtful and kind of you to take us. But you haven't said a word to me about how it went with your assassin this morning."

"Oh. That." He shook his head. He didn't want to talk

about it. He didn't want the ugliness of the morning spilling over into his marriage. "It doesn't matter. Come to bed."

He made love to her then, using all the skills at his disposal, seeking forgetfulness, oblivion, finding comfort in the warmth of her acceptance, in the sweet response of her body.

But after they'd climaxed and lay spent, exhausted and satisfied, sleep didn't come—not to Cal, and not to Emmaline; he could tell by her breathing. She lay wrapped around him, their legs intertwined, her cheek resting on his chest, her palm pressed against his heart, one finger caressing him softly. They often fell asleep in that position, but not tonight.

In the hearth the coals glowed and hissed, sending out a soft, dim light. The silence stretched between them.

She murmured, "It sometimes helps to talk, you know. And I really would like to know what happened."

"You don't."

She raised her head and looked at him, her eyes dark and troubled. "Was it really so bad?"

He sighed. "No, I suppose not. It's just . . ." He didn't know why he felt so . . . He didn't even have a word for how he felt. He supposed it wouldn't hurt to tell her. Nobody was injured, after all. Nobody killed.

So he told her about the decision to imprison the women and children as hostages for the assassin. Told her about the tumbril cart and the weeping women and children. And about the young boy carrying a burden too great for his scrawny young shoulders, stiff with pride—and shame.

"But they will be released, won't they? They won't be hurt."

"No, they won't be hurt." Not physically. He tried to think of words to explain how he felt. The trouble was he didn't *know* how he felt. He was a turmoil of contradictory thoughts and feelings.

"Their father did murder your friend and many others."

"I know and I despise him for it, but . . . it's not as simple as it seemed before. When I was hunting him, it was just him and me—clear-cut, straightforward. As it had been during the war—you didn't think about it—there was the enemy shooting at you, so you shot back. Now . . ."

It was different now, but he couldn't explain how. Cal lay quiet for a while, trying to gather his thoughts. The fire was dying. He got out of bed and added coal, poking savagely at the embers until he had a bright blaze going.

He slid back into bed, gathered her against him and tried to give words to the jumble of feelings inside him.

"A man's wife and children should not be punished for what he has done. It's bad enough during a war, when innocents get caught up, their homes looted and destroyed, their crops ruined, robbed of their livestock, their women despoiled and their children—" He broke off as images came to mind that he'd tried for years to forget. He closed his eyes, breathing deeply.

She hugged him, stroking his skin, pressing herself against him, not seeking anything, not trying to comfort him with empty clichés, not saying anything. She simply listened.

The soft warmth of her body, the grave, sympathetic attention she gave to his words was more comforting than any words could be.

Savagery and destruction and the ruination of the lives of innocents were inevitable in wartime. It had sickened him at the time, but he'd become resigned to its inevitability.

But the war was long over. This was England in peacetime. *Theater, not war.*

"But it wasn't theater today for those women and their children," he said. "They were terrified, distressed, taken away like criminals with the whole world watching. The memory of that—the *shame* of it—will stay with them the rest of their lives. Perhaps not the little ones, but the women. And that boy . . ." He would never forget the burning shame in that boy's eyes and the youthful dignity with which he bore it.

He remembered thinking when he'd first returned to England how green and pleasant and peaceful his country was. But it wasn't the England he thought it was, not anymore, not since he'd embarked on the search for the assassin.

He'd seen a different side of his country then. Oh, there

was wealth and abundance and beauty—for some—vast estates and glittering mansions. But behind all that, beneath the prosperity and the glamor, there was poverty and desperation and despair.

"Cal?" she said softly. He looked down at her. "Don't blame yourself. You did what you could. It's not your fault. And now it's time to sleep." She drew him down and kissed him.

They made love again, slowly, tenderly, without words.

It was a kind of healing.

Emmaline fell asleep almost at once. Cal lay spooned around her, breathing in the scent of her skin and hair, and thought about their conversation. He'd told her more about his life and shared more of his private thoughts with her than he had with anyone else in his life. And he'd only known her a few weeks.

He'd never talked about this kind of thing with any of his male friends. Men turned such concerns into a joke, or didn't mention them at all, shoved the doubts and fears and questions—and feelings—down deep as far as they could go. Pretending they didn't exist. Or didn't matter.

Women were different. No, that wasn't right; he'd never talked to any other woman like this. Maybe it was wives who were different. That wasn't right, either. He thought of the females who'd pursued him since he arrived in England. He couldn't imagine talking like this, sharing such thoughts, with any of them.

It was Emmaline who was different.

He pulled her closer, closed his eyes and slept.

"I THOUGHT YOU SAID YOU'D HIRED A FEW HACKS FOR US to go riding this morning," Rose said, staring as a couple of grooms led five horses up to the front door of Ashendon House. "They don't look like hacks to me."

"And look! That's my Sultan—and Jem's with him!" George exclaimed, and ran down to greet them.

Cal shrugged, trying to hide a grin. "Well, we couldn't borrow Sir Alfred's horses from this distance, and I couldn't let Georgiana outshine us, could I?"

Rose turned to him breathlessly. "Do you mean to say these horses are for us?"

He nodded. "The gray one is for Emmaline, and you and Lily can decide between you which of the other two you want." The two girls immediately began to confer in low voices.

Emm looked down the road at the approaching horses and gasped. "The gray—you mean that beautiful Arab mare is for me? Cal! But when—?"

"Yesterday. I called in at Tattersalls after I bought the theater tickets, saw the mare, took one look at her and thought— well, that you would need a horse. And the girls too, of course," he added hastily, but they weren't listening.

Emm struggled for words. He'd seen this beautiful creature and thought of her.

"Do you like her? She's spirited, but I tried her out and her paces are lovely. She's fast too. She might give Sultan a run for his money." At a signal from her husband, the groom leading her brought her up at a trot, and oh, the high-stepping elegance of her gait.

Emm was breathless with admiration. And emotion. "She's graceful as well as beautiful. She moves like she's floating." The mare was silvery white, with soft clouds of light gray dappling, large dark expressive eyes, and a silky dark mane and tail, held high and carried proudly like a banner.

"I never did give you a wedding present," he said gruffly. "Go on and see how you like her."

"Come with me." Emm grabbed his hand and they hurried down to meet her new mare. She was exquisite—dainty, aristocratic and strong. Emm had a quartered apple in her pocket. She proffered a piece on her palm.

Her mare tossed her head and eyed Emm and the apple coquettishly from liquid, dark, long-lashed eyes, then stretched out her neck and sniffed, her velvety black lips whuffling delicately against Emm's skin. She downed it in two crunches, then came back for more, nudging Emm's arm suggestively. Emm laughed with delight.

"Well, will she do?"

"Will she do? She's a darling." Emm threw her arms around her husband and kissed him warmly. "Thank you, Cal. I've never had such a wonderful present in all my life."

He looked a little self-conscious. The whole street could see her kissing him, and it was not *done* to do such things in public—but Emm didn't care. She was torn between being thrilled and being moved, and kissing him was better than bursting into tears in public.

She was so touched that he'd done such a generous and thoughtful thing for her and the girls, especially after his miserable, shameful morning.

Rose had chosen the black gelding, and Lily chose the pretty bay mare. "Come on, girls," Emm called gaily. "Let's try out their paces. Cal, your services, please." She put out her booted foot. He cupped his hands and tossed her into the saddle, and they rode off in a cavalcade with Kirk, the new Scottish groom her husband had hired for the girls, coming up in the rear.

Emm did her best to appear carefree, but this, coming after the thoughts and feelings he'd shared with her last night . . . On the outside he was a hard, stern soldier, but beneath that disguise—and she was starting to think it was indeed a disguise—he was a sensitive, thoughtful and deeply honorable man.

He'd ached for that family—the family of his enemy. And for that little boy.

And then, having no power to change their situation, he'd turned his mind to how he could make his own little family happy, taking them to the theater and buying them horses. Saying not a word about his own deep unhappiness and frustration.

And despite his anger, he'd made love to her—twice— with unbelievable tenderness.

They reached the park, and the girls raced off joyfully on their new mounts, the silent dark man who'd made this possible quite forgotten. He kept a protective eye on them, but as soon as he saw Kirk, the new groom, following them, he turned to see how Emm was getting along with her beautiful new mare. The quiet concern, the protectiveness in his expression . . . It was this in him she wasn't proof against.

It wasn't the gifts, the quiet kindnesses or the bone-melting pleasure he gave her in bed; it was nothing she could put a finger on or explain away . . . But the barriers she'd erected around her closely barred heart were slowly unraveling.

Chapter Nineteen

To look almost pretty is an acquisition of higher delight to
a girl who has been looking plain for the first fifteen years
of her life than a beauty from her cradle can ever receive.
—JANE AUSTEN, *NORTHANGER ABBEY*

LADY SALTER WAS WAITING FOR THEM WHEN EMM AND THE
girls returned home. "Like a crocodile at the river," George
muttered.

"Be nice, George," Emm said, her look taking in all the
girls. She supposed such a glorious morning had to be paid
for in some fashion.

Cal had gone with the grooms to check on the horses'
accommodation. The stables, except for Hawkins the coachman and Jem the stableboy from George's old home, were
also newly staffed and he wanted to ensure all was to his
liking there. He'd be back shortly expecting breakfast and
a little more laughter and nonsense.

They were becoming a family.

And this elegant, bone-thin old woman looking down
her nose at them was part of it. But Emm would not allow
her to destroy the fragile happiness they'd achieved so far.

She mentally girded her loins and entered the sitting room
with a warm greeting. "Aunt Agatha—how delightful to see
you this morning. Have we kept you waiting again? I hope
not for long this time. You really must let us know when you
plan to visit."

"So we can be out," muttered Rose *sotto voce*.

"You don't mind if I call you Aunt Agatha, do you?"

Emm hurried on. "My husband told me I should, now we are related by marriage."

"You've been out riding!" the old lady said accusingly. She pulled out her lorgnette and raked Emm and the girls with it. "Those habits are atrocious! Yours, Emmaline, is positively shabby, that one"—she pointed the lorgnette at Rose—"is dowdy and out of date. That one"—she pointed to Lily—"is just as dowdy *and* too tight. And as for that one"—she fixed her beady gaze on George—"I cannot believe that habit was made for you at all."

"It wasn't," George said cheerfully. "It used to belong to Lady Chisholm's daughter, but she grew out of it, so Lady Chisholm gave it to me."

"A Rutherford—wearing castoffs from the village squire!" Lady Salter closed her eyes in horror and shuddered delicately.

After a moment she opened her eyes and fixed Emm with a gimlet gaze. "You must never be seen in public in those, those *garments*, again—none of you! You will order new habits at once."

"We intended to do so this afternoon. Now that we have horses of our own." Emm sent a swift smile to the girls, reminding her of Cal's wonderful surprise. They grinned back.

Lady Salter pulled out a visiting card, turned it over, scribbled something on the back of it and handed it to Emm.

Emm glanced at it. "Madame Vestée?"

"My habit maker. She will provide you with all that you need—and everything of the first stare."

"Thank you, but my patronage in that area will go to George Meredith and son," Emm said. "He made all my habits when I was a girl, and my mother's before me." Meredith's might not be "of the first stare," but it was an old and highly respected firm, and their habits were beautiful.

"Loyal, are you?" the old lady said mockingly.

Emm gave her a direct look. "In all matters."

There was a short silence. She sniffed. "So you refuse my advice?"

"In this case, yes. But thank you for thinking of us."

Lady Salter gave her a narrow look. She took the card back, crossed Madame Vestée's name off and wrote something else down. "That," she said with aweful majesty, "is the name of my mantua maker, Hortense"—she pronounced it '*Ortense*—"the foremost dressmaker in London. Show her my card when you order your gowns and she will give you special treatment. Of course it is ridiculously late to be ordering your gowns for the season—and bringing three girls out at once!" No one was left in doubt of her disapproval of that scheme. "But she will wish to oblige me and will do her best to fit you in."

"Thank you so much. It's very kind of you." Emm took the card and tucked it in her reticule.

"And do it soon," the old lady ordered. "The dresses you and the girls wore the other day were quite provincial."

Emm stiffened. She loved those dresses, the first new, fashionable dresses she'd had in years. And the girls always looked lovely. She lifted her chin and said proudly, "They were made by Madame Floria, in Bath."

Lady Salter was unimpressed. "As I said, provincial. Go to Salon Hortense. Give those other dresses to your maid. Or burn them."

Burn her lovely wedding dress? Over her dead body. Emm gritted her teeth and tried to think of something polite to say. "Thank you for your advice and your recommendation, Aunt Agatha. The girls and I will certainly consider Salon Hortense."

The old lady's fine-plucked brows rose. *"Consider?"* Her voice was brittle ice.

"Yes, indeed we will consider her."

The thin breast swelled. "You do understand that I am held to be one of the best-dressed ladies in London."

"I can see that for myself," Emm said pleasantly. She could see that Lady Salter didn't think much of a compliment from a country nobody with, apparently, no dress sense. "But tastes differ, after all, and the girls are young and are bound to have ideas of their own."

"Young people should have no opinions," Lady Salter declared magisterially. "They should be guided by their elders."

"Do you think so? I like hearing young people's thoughts

and ideas—they're often less rigid and hidebound than their elders, I find. As for finding the girls a suitable dressmaker, what suits an older lady—fashionable as she might be—is not necessarily flattering to a young one."

Lady Salter had no difficulty detecting the barb in that one. She glared at Emm. "You should be grateful if Salon Hortense even gives you an appointment."

"As I said, thank you for the recommendation. We will definitely consider her." For all Emm knew, Hortense might be the perfect choice for her and the girls, but Emm was not going to be bullied.

All three girls were being launched at the same time; all were rich and titled. They'd make a splash on the London scene if Emm were any judge. Rose was a beauty. Dressmakers would be falling over themselves to outfit her for the season. George was tall, slender and very pretty and would wear any dress with grace—as long as she was prevented from wearing her breeches under it, a habit Emm had not yet broken her of.

Lily was not so simple. She was very pretty, but she needed the kind of dressmaker who would appreciate her curves and make the most of them, not try to drown them in frills and flounces, as she'd seen happen to some girls. Dressed properly, Lily could shine, and Emm was determined to find her a dressmaker who would appreciate her potential and make the most of it.

She very much doubted Hortense would be that person.

There was a short tense silence in the sitting room. With gratitude Emm heard male voices outside in the hall. Cal must be back. Thank goodness. He could deal with his aunt. She'd had enough. And the girls were looking restless as the scent of breakfast wafted in. They'd been very good.

Emm rose to her feet and said brightly, "We were about to go in for breakfast, Aunt Agatha. And judging by that delicious toast and bacon smell, it must be ready. Would you care to join us?"

"Thank you, no. I have broken my fast already."

"Probably wasps on toast," George muttered.

Emm pretended not to have heard. "Then you will not

wish to stay any longer." She rose. "Delightful as always to see you, Aunt Agatha."

OVER BREAKFAST THE GIRLS RELATED THE CONVERSATION TO Cal, with much laughter and joking. "At least she acknowledged George's legitimacy this time," Emm said.

George laughed. "Yes, today I was a Rutherford, though not one who met with her approval."

He frowned. "What do you mean?"

"She called me 'Henry's bastard' the first time I met her." George reached for another piece of toast and spread it lavishly with marmalade.

Cal turned to Emm. "You didn't tell me that!" To George, he said, "She *knew* you were entirely legitimate. I informed her weeks ago, long before we came to London."

George shrugged. "I've been called a bastard before."

"Not in my house," Cal growled, clenching his fist. "And never again."

Emm could see from his expression that he was quietly furious.

He leaned across the table and took his niece's hand. "My late brother did you a grave injustice, Georgiana. The way he treated you—and your mother—was disgraceful. Shameful. You should have been known to us—to the family— since your birth, if not before. You should not have had to struggle to support yourself—and others—should not have been so alone—" He broke off, his voice a little ragged, and took a mouthful of coffee. Recovering his composure, Emm thought.

"In short, George, this family owes you a massive apology, and I will do everything in my power to make it up to you."

She glanced at George, who was regarding Cal gravely, her gray eyes, so like his, shining with liquid emotion. "Thank you, Cal," she said huskily.

Emm was glad now that she'd mentioned it, glad Cal had taken the opportunity to say what he felt—show what he felt—to George. She didn't think he'd truly explained to the

girl before. He tended to do things quietly and not draw
attention to them.

Now, hearing him like this, nobody could doubt his sincerity. It was clear to them all that his fine sense of honor
had been flayed by his brother's neglect of his daughter.

"Once probate is finalized, I've instructed my lawyer to
arrange the same settlement for you that my father made for
my sisters. A sum of money that will be yours—to be kept
in trust until you marry or turn five-and-twenty."

"You mean if I don't marry, I will still have money."

He nodded. "You will never go hungry again."

The other two girls looked at George in surprise. "Hungry?"

She saw their shocked expressions and laughed. "Don't
look so horrified, aunts-of-mine. It's not as bad as he makes
out. I'm pretty good at shooting rabbits and catching fish,
so we never did go really hungry."

George didn't realize it, but her casual admission had
only underlined the desperation of her former situation.

"I thought you hated hunting," Lily said.

"I hate hunting for sport—fifty men and a hundred hounds
chasing one little fox. It's beastly. Hunting for food is different. It's natural."

"Well, you'll never need to do that again." Cal's face was
grim. "And in the meantime, I'll have a word with Aunt
Agatha."

"She only said it that once," Emm reminded him. "I don't
think she'll do it again." She looked meaningfully at Rose
and George. "Unless she's provoked, of course."

Cal nodded. He addressed himself to the girls, but Emm
knew he was including her as well when he said, "I know
Aunt Agatha can be outrageous and unbearably rude at
times, but I'd be grateful if you at least *tried* not to antago-
nize her. She is one of the leaders of the ton, you know, and
has enormous influence. Like it or not, with all of us knowing hardly anyone in London, we're going to need her help."

The girls exchanged glances but said nothing more.

After breakfast was over and the girls had gone upstairs
to change, Cal said to Emm, "I'm sorry Aunt Agatha is
being so difficult. I'd hoped she would help you launch the

girls. For some reason I can't quite understand, she's a very popular member of the ton."

"I'll try to be good," Emm said. "But if she rips into Lily again—she goes on about her being fat, and honestly, Cal, if you'd seen the poor girl's face. And she's not fat."

"I know. Rose has Aunt Agatha's naturally slender build, as does George, but Lily is built like Aunt Dottie and has her affectionate nature as well." He gave her his arm, and they climbed the stairs together.

"It seems so wrong that your aunt Agatha married three times and yet sweet-natured Dottie never married at all," she mused.

"I know. According to my father, Dottie had a tremendously successful season and had more than a dozen extremely eligible offers."

"Really? Then why do you think she didn't marry?"

"No idea. I gather she didn't much like London, because my grandfather had to rail and storm to get her to do a second and a third season. Which she did, and had even more eligible offers. A duke, a marquis, all sorts of quite brilliant matches were offered her—she was quite a beauty, you know—but she turned them all down and couldn't wait to get back to Ashendon."

"And later she moved to Bath?"

He nodded. "And has lived there happily on her own ever since. I know, it seems odd, because she's not the least bit shy or antisocial, but then Aunt Dottie has always been an original."

They reached the landing and heard a gust of laughter coming from the girls' rooms. Cal said ruefully, "I fear Rose might have inherited Aunt Agatha's pithy way with words too."

Emm laughed. "She's quick witted, and very sharp, I agree, but she's fundamentally a kind girl and, at the moment at least, lacks your aunt's arrogance."

SHORTLY AFTERWARD CAL LEFT FOR WHITEHALL TO CHECK on developments. Emm and the girls went shopping, piling into the carriage with Hawkins driving. Lady Salter's criticism of her clothing notwithstanding, Emm urgently needed evening dresses for the events to which she and Cal had been invited.

They visited Salon Hortense first. No sense being prejudiced against the woman because of her number one client.

The salon was austerely elegant, furnished in many shades of gray with gold highlights. There was a deep silver-gray carpet, a large gilt-edged looking glass, some spindly black-and-gilt chairs, a small black marble-topped table with gilt legs, and not much more. Gray silk and velvet curtains were draped across the back of the room.

Several elegant, aristocratic-looking middle-aged ladies loitered, chatting quietly, presumably waiting for someone. They slid Emm and the girls curious, sidelong glances but otherwise pretended not to notice.

A thin assistant dressed in black and white approached them. Emm gave her Lady Salter's card and asked to speak to Hortense. The woman murmured that she would inquire.

Ten minutes later a brisk, bony Frenchwoman dressed all in black appeared from between the draped curtains. She was holding Lady Salter's card.

"You wish to speak to me, my lady?"

Emm introduced herself and indicated the girls, who were gathered at the window looking out into the street. She explained that their aunt, Lady Salter, had recommended they visit Hortense with a view to ordering some gowns for the forthcoming season.

Hortense's deeply plucked brows practically disappeared. "*This* season? I don't know such a thing can be done. Hortense, she is the foremost mantua maker in London, you understand. All the ladies come to her, because they know she is the best. The order book is full." She glanced at the girls, just as Rose turned around.

The dressmaker's eyes widened. Her gaze fixed greedily on Rose. "*Almost* full, I meant. On the other hand, Hortense might be able to fit you in. If the young ladies would approach?"

Emm gestured them forward. Hortense gushed over Rose's beauty, lavishly praising her bearing, her coloring, her complexion. The narrow black eyes gleamed at the sight of George. "Hortense can see the resemblance to Lady Salter in this one—a dark beauty, the perfect foil for your golden beauty."

Then she turned to Lily, pursed her lips, then gave a very Gallic shrug. "And I am sure we can do something with this little one. Hortense is up to any challenge."

Lily, whose eyes had been shining with excitement, seemed to droop a little.

"Thank you, madame," Emm said briskly. "We'll let you know. Girls?" And she swept them out of the shop, leaving Hortense with her mouth most unfashionably agape.

"But I thought—" Lily began.

"We should visit a number of dressmakers, don't you agree?" Emm said. "And then choose the ones we like best."

Rose slipped her arm through Emm's and squeezed. "I didn't like skinny old All-Tense at all. Besides, I cannot bear people who refer to themselves in the third person."

Lily's brow furrowed worriedly. "But do we know any other dressmakers in London?"

Emm stared at her blankly a moment. Not a single one. Then she recalled the box her beautiful wedding nightgown had come in. "The House of Chance."

Rose looked as though she didn't quite believe her. "The House of *Chance*?"

"Yes," Emm said triumphantly. "Do you and Lily remember Sally Destry from school?"

Rose laughed. "How could we forget? She became one of Miss Mallard's famous 'five countesses.' Not counting you, of course, Emm."

"I remember Sally," Lily said. "She was nice."

"She certainly was," Emm said. "And Sally, who is now the Countess of Maldon, patronizes the House of Chance. And that's good enough for me. She always had excellent taste and I have no doubt she's become quite dashing and fashionable."

They climbed into the carriage. "The House of Chance, Hawkins, please," Emm said. "It's off Piccadilly, I think." She hoped.

"What famous five countesses?" George asked, and Lily

and Rose explained. Emm was amused to hear that they also finished with "and a partridge in a pear tree."

Emm leaned back against the leather upholstery and prayed that the House of Chance wasn't one of those places that specialized in naughty nightwear.

In a few short minutes the carriage pulled up in front of an elegant shop with a large picture window. It looked very discreet, with green velvet curtains draped behind the window, a simple white-and-gold painted daisy on the glass and *Chance* lettered in elegant gold script.

Taking a deep breath, Emm pushed open the door. Inside it was light and airy, with creamy walls and a soft green carpet. There were several large gold-edged looking glasses, and though it wasn't dissimilar to Salon Hortense, it felt much less oppressive.

A young woman came out to greet them. Emm explained that she'd come on the recommendation of the Countess of Maldon, and wondered whether the House of Chance made evening gowns.

The woman assured her they made day dresses, ball gowns, nightgowns and everything in between, except for gowns for a young lady's Royal Presentation. "You'll want to talk to Miss Chance. She does all the designing. I'll fetch her. Would you like some tea?"

Relieved, Emm agreed that tea would be most welcome, and she and the girls sat down to wait.

In two minutes a small, smartly dressed young woman limped out. "Lady Maldon sent you, did she? That's good of her. How do you do? I'm Daisy Chance, the proprietor— welcome to my shop. Polly will be back in a minute with some tea. So, ladies, how can I help you?"

To Emm's surprise the woman had a more than a hint of a Cockney accent. Emm decided she liked it. It was a refreshing change from all those false French ones.

She explained what they wanted. Miss Chance looked at each of the girls in turn. She gave Rose a long thoughtful look. "You're a few years older than the usual young miss— I reckon something a little different, for you. What's your style, Lady Rose? Sweetly pretty or bold?"

"Bold," all four of them answered at once, and Miss Chance laughed. The young woman had returned with a tea tray and Miss Chance said, "Polly, love, fetch out the night sky fabric and the ice blue. And the lavender. This young lady wants to stand out from the crowd a little." Polly hurried off and Miss Chance pulled out a pad and made a few sketches.

Emm, a little surprised but rather charmed by the odd little woman's warmth and brisk informality, poured the tea.

Polly came back with an armful of fabrics and a couple of half-finished dresses.

The girls gathered around and examined the fabrics and dresses excitedly. Rose was unable to hide her pleasure.

"That one she calls night sky is gorgeous, Emm," she whispered. It was a soft, dark azure blue gauze, with tiny sprinkles of glitter dotted through it. Rose draped it against herself. "What do you think?"

It was perfect.

The same thing happened with George. Miss Chance seemed to know instinctively the kind of thing that George would like and seemed quite understanding of George's awkwardness—it was the first time she'd ever shopped for dresses. But at least she wasn't sullen and uncooperative about it. The presence and excitement of her youthful aunts had made a difference to her attitude.

Like Hortense, Miss Chance thought George and Rose would contrast and complement each other beautifully, but Emm was most impressed that she didn't turn a hair when George announced she preferred breeches. She told George not to worry, she'd make her some nice long drawers that would feel just as comfortable as breeches but wouldn't spoil the line of her dresses.

Now came the real test—Lily.

Emm could feel them all tense up as the woman turned to Lily and examined her the way she had done Rose and George. "Oh, I'm going to have fun with you, Lady Lily," she said with a grin. "You're just luscious, you are. Like a ripe peach. Oh, the men are going to be panting after you when I've finished with you. I hope that's what you want."

Lily blushed rosily and nodded. "Yes, please."

"What sort of thing do you plan for her?" Emm asked, pleased with the woman's kind words but not yet convinced it wasn't empty flattery.

"As I said, Lady Lily has the sort of luscious figure that a lot of men go wild for," Miss Chance said. "All those curves, I'm going to frame them, not show 'em off vulgarly, but hint at what's there. Polly," she called, "bring out the dress we're making for Mrs. Huntley-Briggs." She made a quick sketch on her pad. "Yours wouldn't be exactly like this one, but it'll give you an idea." In a few lines, she sketched a lavishly curved woman.

Polly brought out the dress, and Emm could immediately see that it was the sort of thing that would suit Lily perfectly. She looked at Lily. Her eyes were shining.

"Well, girls?" Emm said. "What do you think? Shall we order some dresses from Miss Chance?"

They nodded eagerly, and Miss Chance sent them behind the green curtains with Polly to have their measurements taken. "Now you, Lady Ashendon, would you be wanting anything?"

They discussed Emm's needs, and Miss Chance said it would be tight, but she could get an evening dress to Emm in the next two days, and another two days later. "But there won't be time for fittings, mind, with such a rush job."

"Aren't you all booked up for the season?" Emm asked, suddenly worried that Miss Chance's easy acceptance of new customers might indicate a lack of business.

"Lord, yes, the orders are pilin' up, but we can cope. I got a waitin' list of skilled seamstresses wantin' to work for me. When fresh orders come in, and my regular girls can't manage, I hire more." She grinned wryly. "I'm the slow cog in this machine, keepin' up with the designing. But I love it, and I'm goin' to enjoy dressin' your girls. Somethin' special they are, all three of them. Now"—she became businesslike again—"let's talk about these two dresses for you, Lady Ashendon. I'm thinking green gauze over silver tissue—does that sound like something you'd like?"

It was, and when they finally left the House of Chance their order had grown enormously. The girls were thrilled with everything they'd seen—even George. They all liked Daisy Chance, who, they'd discovered, was actually married with the sweetest little girl who was in the back room with her nursemaid.

And when Miss Chance was measuring Emm up, she'd told her how much she loved the wedding nightgown that Lady Maldon had sent her.

"Oh, that was you—in Bath, wasn't it?" The little woman grinned. "She said she wanted something special for a favorite teacher who was gettin' married. Glad you liked it."

Now, with the carriage headed home, Emm sat back, a little dazed at all they'd ordered from Miss Chance. She hoped she hadn't made a terrible mistake.

Chapter Twenty

They come together like the Coroner's Inquest, to sit
upon the murdered reputations of the week.
—WILLIAM CONGREVE, *THE WAY OF THE WORLD*

THERE WAS NO NEWS AT WHITEHALL. JOE GIMBLE HAD
made no attempt to communicate with anyone, made no
attempt to come forward. A discreet round-the-clock watch
was being conducted at the aunt's house. He hadn't been
sighted there, either.

The women and children were still in custody.

Frustrated, Cal found himself an hour later staring across
the road at the house in Whitechapel where Joe Gimble's
aunt by marriage lived.

He waited for an hour, saw nothing suspicious, saw the
drunken former sharpshooter, whose bottle of gin was now
gone. Again the man saw him and spat. He was a pathetic
sight. Cal turned away.

He didn't know why he'd gone to Whitechapel in the first
place. There was obviously nothing he could do. He couldn't
exactly magic Joe Gimble out of thin air.

In any case, according to Gil Radcliffe, Joe Gimble and
the Scorpion were no longer Cal's business.

He was wasting his time to no purpose. Cal decided to
visit Aunt Agatha and beard the dragon in her den. Until
they'd arrived in London, Cal hadn't realized Emmaline
had never even visited the capital. She would need help
launching the girls.

* * *

"YOU BRING ME A BADLY DRESSED NOBODY OF NO PARTICULAR beauty—and no wealth!—a gel who has no aristocratic connections—no connections at all as far as I can see!—and you expect me to launch her and your two pert half sisters as well as Henry's impossible tomboy—all in this coming season?"

"No, I expect you to help Emm launch the girls—you are their aunt, after all. I hope you will also help my wife find her way in the ton—you know you could if you tried. There's no one better connected or more fashionable," he finished, laying it on with a trowel.

She considered his words, pouting a little. "The girls are one thing—of course I will do all I can to assist Rutherfords born. That goes without saying. But this woman you have married—"

"Lady Ashendon," he interrupted in a hard voice. He was pleased to hear her refer to George as a "Rutherford born," but he'd had enough of her complaints against Emmaline.

His aunt gave him a baleful look. "I will admit she has a certain raw potential for elegance, *if* she would take advice from one who knows. But she won't! She's stubborn, willful and headstrong—"

"Tautology."

She held up her lorgnette and withered him through it. "I beg your pardon?"

"Apology accepted, Aunt Agatha," he said smoothly, ignoring her swelling indignation. "A tautology is when all the words mean the same thing—stubborn, willful, headstrong—two of those words are redundant. There's no need to list all of them."

"You, sirrah, are being frivolous!"

"Aunt Agatha, there is no use continuing to rail at me for my choice of wife. What's done is done—and I am well content."

She sniffed.

He decided to try a different approach. "Are you saying it is beyond you to assist her in launching the girls?"

There was a short, pithy silence.

"I'm sorry, it was thoughtless of me. I'd forgotten how much you'd aged since I left England. Things must be getting more difficult for you and—"

She cut him off. "Nothing is beyond me," she said with lofty hauteur.

"Excellent. Then I'll leave you to get on with it. Thank you, Aunt Agatha." He kissed her hand and made a hasty exit.

To Emm's great relief, the dress arrived from the House of Chance in plenty of time and proved her fears to be groundless. It was stunning, and it fitted perfectly.

In the two days previous, she and the girls had embarked on an orgy of shopping. Gloves, scarves, shawls, shoes, boots, dancing slippers, habits, hats—the list was endless. And the season hadn't even begun.

But tonight was to be Emm's first appearance in London society, and she was understandably a little nervous.

She stood in front of the long cheval looking glass and gazed at her reflection.

"Oh, my, m'lady, you look lovely," Milly murmured behind her. "I never seen such a beautiful gown."

Emm hadn't either; she had certainly never worn one. The gown was made of silver tissue that shimmered through the green gauze overdress like a wintry lake gleaming through the mist. The neckline was scooped low but was modest enough not to make her feel uncomfortable.

She felt beautiful, elegant and yet deeply feminine. She pirouetted slowly in front of the mirror. Milly had dressed her hair, piling it high at the crown and letting soft ringlets fall at the sides.

A whistle at the door made her jump. Her husband stood there, immaculate and dazzlingly handsome in formal dress. His eyes devoured her. "Lady Ashendon, you are a sight to behold. That dress . . ." He whistled again.

Emm smoothed the fabric with nervous hands. "Will it do, do you think?"

"More than do. It's going to make me the envy of every

man there." Then he frowned and stroked his chin thoughtfully. "There's just one thing missing."

"What?" She whirled around and examined her reflection in the looking glass. "I can't see anything miss— Oh." She broke off as, from behind, he slipped a delicate gold chain around her neck. A dainty pendant hung just above the shadow between her breasts. It glittered. One large emerald surrounded by a host of tiny diamonds.

"Oh, Cal, it's beautiful."

"This?" He was trying to sound offhand, but she knew he was pleased with her reaction. "This is just a small thing—a part of the Ashendon emerald ensemble. It's part of the entail and is handed down from countess to countess." He placed a heavy box on her dressing table. "The full set is in there, for grand occasions: a proper necklace, several pairs of earrings and a bracelet. Also a tiara, but you won't want that for an affair like this. This is a small party, so you just want something pretty and tasteful. But you might want to wear some earrings."

She selected a pair of emerald teardrop earrings and fastened them in her ears. Emeralds. She'd never worn anything so grand in her life. Pearls were all she'd owned before, and she'd left hers behind when she'd left home.

Her husband's eyes met hers in the mirror. "Would a kiss be permitted, Lady Ashendon, or is it hands off until tonight?" The slate-gray eyes burned with promise.

She stood on tiptoe and kissed him. "Later," she whispered.

IT WAS ALL GOING BEAUTIFULLY, EMM THOUGHT. IF THIS was a "small informal party"—there was quite a crowd, and even a musical ensemble—she would hate to imagine what a big formal one was.

She'd been introduced to a host of people, all of whom had been very kind. There had been dancing, which she hadn't expected. Her hostess, Lady Peplowe, explained that the young people had begged for it, and confided that she thought it a good idea for girls about to make their come-out to acquire a little town bronze before the season started by attending informal parties like this.

"And where are your young ladies, Lady Ashendon? I understood you were launching three this season. Three! You have my sympathy. I've fired off two girls—both now married, I'm glad to say—and the third and last, Penelope there"—she indicated a robust-looking redheaded girl dancing with a laughing young dandy—"will make her come-out this spring. After which I will no doubt hie me to my chaise longue and go into a decline."

Emm laughed. "I didn't realize the girls had been invited." She glanced around the room. "It's a lovely party. I'm sure they would have loved to come."

"Men!" Lady Peplowe shook her head. "I told my husband I should have followed up his casual invitation with a proper written one, but he assured me it was all in hand and that I fuss too much. What a pity. I thought your three might like to team up with my lone chick. It's more fun for girls if they have friends."

Emm knew very well that Lady Peplowe's "lone chick" had no need to have friends found for her; she obviously knew most of the young people at the party. Her hostess's kind consideration was for Emm's girls, who knew practically no one. She thanked her warmly and they made plans to meet for tea the following afternoon.

Emm lowered her voice. "Lady Peplowe, who is that lady in the yellow gown—the tall one with the dashing turban?" Emm had caught the young woman staring at her a number of times, but as far as she knew, she'd never seen her before in her life.

Lady Peplowe squinted across the room. "Oh, that's the Carmichael girl—married that fellow Jeremy Oates last season. Do you know her? Would you like an introduction?"

Emm shook her head. "No, thank you. I was just curious." The name rang no bells at all. It was very odd.

Just then a gentleman came to ask Emm for the next dance, and for the next half hour she was well occupied. After the dance finished, Emm thanked her partner and, feeling rather warm, wandered out onto the balcony. There were plenty of people there, so she felt quite comfortable.

"You're Emmaline Westwood, aren't you?"

She turned. It was the woman in yellow.

"I was, but I'm married now and am Lady Ashendon."

"Yes, I'd heard that." The woman tilted her head, watching Emm with an odd little smile. "Incredible."

"Have we met before?" Emm asked, puzzled by the woman's behavior.

She shook her head with a little laugh. "Oh, no, but you were pointed out to me once when I was a girl and visiting my cousin."

"What is your cousin's name?"

"She's married now, you wouldn't recognize it." Her smile was sly as she added, "But she used to live in Bucklebury."

Bucklebury. A sour taste flooded Emm's mouth.

"My cousin knew all the best gossip. Some quite shocking scandals happened in the sleepy little village of Bucklebury. You'd be amazed." Her smile was now openly malicious. "Or perhaps you wouldn't. So nice to chat, Lady Ashendon."

Emm didn't say a word. From being overly warm a few minutes before, she was suddenly chilled to the bone.

Bucklebury was her home village.

She breathed in the chill night air, taking deep, slow breaths until she'd regained a semblance of composure, then returned to the party.

She felt it the minute she stepped back into the light, the attention of a small knot of young women, heads together, whispering. They turned to look at Emm, their expressions avid, almost gleeful, then they returned to their whispering.

It was starting again.

"ARE YOU FEELING UNWELL?" CAL ASKED WHEN HE SAW her. "You're very pale. Do you want to leave?"

Emm nodded. She was feeling sick, but not the way he thought. Gossip had ruined her life once, and now it was back. She'd thought she'd been able to put it behind her, move on. She'd been wrong.

She was going to have to tell him. Tonight, before someone else did.

"Take me home, please, Cal."

In minutes they'd made their farewells to their host and hostess and were in the carriage heading home. Cal looked worried, his eyes dark and full of questions, but Emm didn't want to talk, not here, not in the carriage. She closed her eyes and leaned against him, finding refuge in his strength and warmth and the dear, familiar smell of him.

She loved him. She'd resisted it from the first but hadn't been able to help herself. She'd fallen, head over heels, and it was as unlike her first experience of "love" as anything could be. She knew now the difference between infatuation and love.

But of course, she couldn't tell him. They'd made a marriage of convenience—he'd made it perfectly clear what his expectations were, and they didn't include love. So it was not for her to burden or embarrass him with unwanted emotion.

Besides, if she told him now, and then he heard what people were saying, he'd probably think she was saying it out of desperation. That she was lying to save herself.

They arrived home and he walked her up the stairs. "Is there anything I can do? I don't like to see you so pale. Shall I fetch your maid?"

"No. Just give me a few moments and then come in. We need to talk."

"Talk?"

She felt another pang of guilt, remembering the unspoken promise of lovemaking after the party. Lovemaking was the last thing on her mind.

"I'll just take this coat off." He left her in her bedroom and went through to the dressing room. Emm stripped off her jewelry and the lovely dress, pulled out her hairpins and pulled a brush quickly through her hair, then slipped on her thickest, warmest, most unseductive flannel nightgown, wrapped her lovely cashmere wedding shawl around her—

for comfort as much as warmth—climbed onto the bed and waited.

"So, what's this about?" he said when he returned wrapped in his favorite dressing gown. "I take it you're not actually sick."

"No. Sit down." She indicated the end of the bed. "It's going to take a while."

He sat, closer than she'd intended.

"You asked me once why my father disowned me."

He waited, his eyes somber.

"It's hard to explain; I didn't even understand how it happened myself, until long afterward, when it was all too late anyway." She took a deep breath. "But somehow, suddenly, everyone in Bucklebury—that's the village closest to our—to Papa's house—was talking about me behind my back, saying—" She swallowed, unable to force the hateful words out.

"Saying?"

"Saying that I was, that I—that I'd been fornicating with stableboys and grooms." She looked at him, anguished. "This was more than two years after Sam had left the country, you understand—not that I'd ever . . ." She shook her head. "They weren't talking about Sam. Papa had kept that very quiet. But somehow, it came out, two years later, only . . . vilely twisted and horribly exaggerated. They said—" She broke off, her voice shaking. Her whole body was shaking.

She forced it out. "They said I'd been acting the whore for anyone in breeches, all over the parish, preferring farmhands to the attentions of gentlemen."

He made a small sound. She didn't look at him. She couldn't, not until she'd told him everything. "It wasn't true, I promise you—but everyone seemed to believe it, everyone was talking about it. Someone told Papa—well, half the village seemed to have told Papa, including the vicar. But in particular our neighbor, Papa's friend, Mr. Irwin, passed on all the dreadful stories—but they weren't true, none of them."

Tears were rolling down her cheeks, "None of it was true, Cal, I *promise* you. I never did *any* of those things they were—"

"Hush." He reached forward and placed his finger over her lips. "I don't need you or anyone else to tell me those rumors were a pack of filthy lies."

She blinked at him through her tears. "Really? You believe me?"

"I think I know you a little by now." His voice was gruff.

Her mouth wobbled. "Do you?" Papa didn't seem to, even after a lifetime.

He nodded. "I know you give yourself with reckless generosity—and I'm not talking about that swine who seduced you when you were seventeen, I'm talking about agreeing to marry a man you'd met a bare handful of times—none of them particularly auspicious."

His voice deepened. "You married me, you took on my wild girls, became their guide, their friend and their defender. You took me on and showed me how to be a brother and an uncle. And a husband."

Her face crumpled. The tears were flowing faster now.

"You're reckless, you're loyal and you're true. I couldn't have found a better wife if I'd searched for a decade. Even if those vile rumors were true—and don't look at me like that, I *know* they're not—but even if they were, it would make no difference to me."

He cupped her face in his hands and wiped away the tears with his thumbs. "*Marry in haste*, Aunt Agatha said to me, but marrying you is the best thing I've ever done in my life."

"Oh, Cal . . ." Tears flooded her again, and he drew her into his arms and started kissing them away.

"Don't worry about the rumors. We'll fix everything."

"How?"

"I don't know yet, but we will. We'll face them down together, my dear. Don't worry." There was a little pause and then he said in quite a different tone, "Now, since you're not feeling ill, how do I get to you through this amazingly thick and voluminous nightgown?"

She gave a tremulous laugh and showed him.

He was such a gift, this dear, kind, trusting, honorable man. Emm ached to tell him how much she loved him, but it wasn't part of their arrangement, and though he'd made it clear he was pleased with their marriage, and with her, he'd never said anything to make her think he felt anything deeper toward her.

It was gratitude he was talking about. And satisfaction with his choice of wife. She would hate to spoil everything by spouting words he could never return.

She showed him instead.

THE NEXT MORNING, DESPITE THEIR LATE NIGHT, THEY ROSE early, as usual, to go riding. At that hour the few other people in the park were those who were also actually riding their horses, instead of walking them in order to be seen and admired, as people did during the fashionable afternoon hours.

It was fast becoming their family habit, as long as it wasn't pouring with rain. As soon as they reached the park and had a good gallop in the morning mist, the three girls rode off, their groom, Kirk, a phlegmatic middle-aged Scotsman, following behind to keep an eye on them, while Emm and Cal walked their horses and talked.

"You said you didn't understand how the gossip happened until long afterward," Cal said, showing that it was on his mind as much as hers. "So what did happen?"

"I think it all came from Mr. Irwin, Papa's friend and our neighbor."

"Why do you think that?"

"He wanted to marry me. He was younger than Papa, not quite forty, but of course to me at the time that seemed quite old. He'd asked me before, and I'd refused every time."

Cal gave her a sharp glance. "He asked more than once?"

"Oh, yes." She gave a humorless laugh. "Easily a dozen times. But I wasn't interested. He didn't love me. I don't even think he liked me, really. He just pretended he did, flattering me and protesting undying love until it became quite irritating."

"You're sure he didn't love you?"

She shook her head. "No, though at the time I took him at his word and tried to be kind but firm. Afterward I realized he wanted my inheritance. I was Papa's only child, you see, and the estate is not entailed, so I was something of an heiress."

"So what changed? Why would he think spreading vile and untrue gossip about you would entice you to marry him?"

"I suspect he was desperate for money. As for why he spread the rumors, I think his plan was to force me into marriage to save my reputation. It's what he urged Papa and me to do when the scandal broke, nobly offering to save me, saying that I would be able to hold my head up in church again once we were married and under his protection."

Cal swore under his breath.

"I refused, of course—but I expected Papa to, to . . ."

"To believe you?"

She nodded, close to tears again. "But he didn't. Because of Sam, you see. Nobody else knew about Sam, but I think Papa must have told Mr. Irwin at some stage, and that's what gave him the idea. And so Papa had a precedent for believing in my bad behavior."

They walked on a little. "It was when he asked the vicar about it, and the vicar confirmed he too had heard the rumors— I think that's what tipped the balance. In the end Papa gave me an ultimatum—marry Mr. Irwin or leave his house."

"So you left."

She nodded. "I don't think Papa expected that of me at all, but I don't take kindly to being bullied and I certainly wasn't going to be bullied into marrying a man I disliked because of something I didn't do."

"And so your father disowned you."

She nodded. "And then he died, and it was too late to mend things with him. It's the thing I most regret, not being able to explain, to have him understand that I did nothing wrong, not since Sam." Tears clustered on her eyelashes. She blinked them away.

"Is this Irwin fellow still around?" Cal asked in a voice that boded nothing good for the man.

"No, he married a rich widow from Manchester and went to live in the north. Strangely, he was the one who told me Papa had died and left me nothing. He was visiting Bath on his honeymoon with his new wife, and we bumped into each other in the street by accident. He had no idea I was living there, of course."

She pondered the memory for a moment. "I think it pleased him to tell me that. He was quite vindictive in the manner of telling me, as if it served me right for not marrying him." She shuddered. "A vile man."

"A complete villain," Cal said quietly. "He tried to destroy your life."

She lifted her head and said resolutely, "But he didn't succeed then, and I won't let it ruin my life again." She saw Rose waving in the distance. "Come on, race you to where the girls are." And she took off on her lovely Arab mare.

THE GOSSIP WAS SPREADING. WHEN, LATER THAT DAY, EMM and the girls met Lady Peplowe and her daughter Penelope for tea and ices at Gunters—George had never eaten an ice before—Lady Peplowe drew her aside, saying, "I don't know if you've heard, my dear, but there is a nasty tale circulating about you." She gave Emm a clear look and added, "I don't believe a word of it, of course. Anyone who has met you can see that—but it's quite nasty and I thought I should warn you."

For a moment Emm was so surprised and touched she couldn't say a thing.

Lady Peplowe laid a gloved hand on Emm's arm. "I'm sorry, I've shocked you. Perhaps I shouldn't have—"

"No, you did exactly right." Emm smiled at the older woman. "Very few people would have had the courage to tell me to my face, and I'm very grateful—more than grateful, in fact. Especially for your belief in me. You could not know the gossip was untrue."

"Of course I could, don't be silly."

It seemed she had found a friend. Emm blinked away incipient tears. She was becoming a veritable watering pot. She straightened her spine and set herself to explain. "They were lies, deliberately spread to discredit me and force me into— Oh, it is a long story."

Lady Peplowe glanced at the table where, despite the cold

weather, the four girls were spooning up ice cream and nattering nonstop. "They're happily occupied and we can be quite private. Now, my dear, tell me what happened and let us see what we can do to scotch these vicious rumors."

THE FOLLOWING DAY CAL, EMM AND THE GIRLS RETURNED home after their morning ride to find Aunt Agatha waiting for them. "I wish to speak to you in private," she told Emm.

Cal sent the girls on their way with a jerk of his head, took Emm's hand and sat with her on the chaise longue. "What is it, Aunt Agatha?"

She gave Emm a narrow look. "Are you sure you want Ashendon here?"

"Quite sure," Emm answered. "I have no secrets from my husband." *Not anymore*, she thought guiltily.

Aunt Agatha's brows rose. "Very well, then. There is a disgraceful tale circulating, that you had a lover—multiple lovers, in fact—before you married my nephew. Is it true?"

"It is partly true. I had a lover. Just one, long before I met Cal."

"Outrageous! I knew you were unworthy of my nephew, but never did I imagine you were *that* kind of female."

"I'm not!" Emm snapped. She'd had enough. She might regret Sam, might have been imprudent and reckless giving herself to him, but she would not go on being punished for it the rest of her life. Her husband had accepted it, and that was good enough for her.

She went on the attack. "Did you never fall in love, Lady Salter? Never take a lover?"

To her amazement the old lady flushed. "None of your business, Miss Impertinence!"

Emm twirled her wedding ring. "*Mrs.* Impertinence."

"*Lady* Impertinence," Cal interjected with a wink at Emm. Something settled inside her. She was not alone. He was here, supporting her against all comers.

"Just as your past is your business and nobody else's, Lady Salter, so is mine."

"Except when it's your husband's. And his family's. And

the whole wide world's. Besides, I went to my wedding a virgin."

"To your first wedding, perhaps," her nephew reminded her. "In any case, Emmaline told me about her lover before the wedding, so what does it matter?"

If it hadn't already done so, Emm's heart would have melted at the gallant lie.

"So you admit it brazenly, do you, gel? Showing no remorse, no shame, no guilt?"

Emm shrugged. "What's done is done. Spilt milk." Of course she regretted it, but she wasn't going to bare her soul to this horrid old tartar.

"The rumors say multiple lovers, grooms, stableboys and farm boys, that you lay down in the fields and rutted whoever wanted you, like a bitch on heat."

"Filthy slanderous—" Cal exploded. Emm gripped his hand tightly and he calmed.

"It's not true," she said coolly. "It was all a vicious campaign to force me into a marriage I didn't want. All the stories came from him." And for the third time in two days, Emm found herself explaining, only this time to a stiffly judgmental and hostile listener.

When she'd finished, Lady Salter said nothing for a long time. "Most edifying," she said at last. "The truth of the matter is neither here nor there—it is the damage it can do now that matters. You've been invited to the Braxtons' party the day after tomorrow, have you not?"

Cal confirmed it with a nod.

"You will not attend it. Send your apologies. Take your wife back to Oxfordshire, Ashendon; keep her and the girls there until the season is about to start, give it all time to blow over. Another, newer scandal will have taken its place by then."

"No," Emm said. "I'm going to the party. I won't run away and hide. I will face down these cowardly spreaders of old muck. I know from whom the story started this time—"

"Who?" Lady Salter demanded

"A Mrs. Oates, née Carmichael, who had it from her cousin who lived in Bucklebury, the village I came from. I met her the other night. She's a nasty, spiteful piece of work, and I will not be bullied into leaving. I have nothing to be ashamed of."

The old lady made a scornful noise. "Confronting the mischief makers would only give people more reason to believe there was truth to the tales. No smoke without fire."

Emm gave an angry shrug. "They will believe it anyway, and if I retreat, it will certainly confirm their suspicions."

Lady Salter lifted her lorgnette and gave Emm a long, steady look. Emm lifted her chin and stared back, refusing to be cowed.

"Well, then." Lady Salter folded her lorgnette with a snap and glared at Emm. "If that's going to be your attitude."

"It is."

The old lady gave a brisk nod. "Excellent. Couldn't be better. Keep that up. I'll do my part and we'll see what we can do. Storm in a teacup. Stupid Oates woman got the wrong end of the stick. Family solidarity. Ashendon, your arm."

Emm blinked in shock as her husband helped his aunt rise. Had Lady Salter just said she would support Emm?

At the door, the old woman paused and turned back. She pointed her cane at Emm. "Never apologize, never back down. Show one shred of shame or fear and the vultures will be on you in an instant. Ashendon, my carriage."

As the carriage steps were let down, Aunt Agatha turned to Cal. "She might be a nobody, but at least she has a spine."

Chapter Twenty-one

But having done whate'er she could devise
And emptied all her Magazine of lies
The time approached...
—JOHN DRYDEN, *IPHIS AND IANTHE*

"CAL, WOULD YOU FRANK SOME LETTERS FOR ME?"

"Letters, Rose?"

She gave a careless shrug. "Just writing to a few old school friends, exchanging news, that sort of thing. But if you don't want to frank them for me—" She held a slender sheaf of letters, half a dozen or more.

"No, it's all right, I'll take them." There was something about the way Rose had asked—the almost ostentatiously casual nature of the request that raised his suspicions. Was she up to something? Had the weeks of good behavior come to an end?

He took the letters into his office and checked them. They seemed harmless enough: all addressed to females, and most of them in London—Mayfair, actually, so there was no need to put them through the postal service, let alone frank them, which strictly speaking was for government business. "I'll send them off with a footman," he told Rose, who was hovering in the doorway.

"So they'll arrive today? Good. Thanks, Cal." She hurried off.

He blinked. Regular exercise, shopping and a social life seemed to have wrought a miracle in his sisters. *Long may it last.*

Speaking of government business, it was time he checked

on the status of the assassin affair. He handed the letters to
Burton on the way out, who promised to have them delivered
immediately, and headed for Whitehall.

Joe Gimble and his family were not Cal's only concerns
this time. He wanted to ask Radcliffe's help in dealing with
these vile rumors that were causing his wife sleepless nights.
The Braxtons' party was the following night. Radcliffe knew
everyone. He was discreet and could keep confidence.

"No news of Gimble," Radcliffe said the moment Cal
arrived. He was deep in paperwork. "One thing you might
be interested in, though—your drunken sharpshooter friend
is dead."

"Dead? How?"

"No suspicious circumstances. Fell down drunk in a gutter the other night. It's a toss-up whether he froze to death
or drowned in a puddle. The state he was in, the fellow wasn't
long for this world anyway."

Cal agreed.

Radcliffe looked up from his papers. "Something else
you wanted?"

"Yes, but it's personal."

"Ah, those rumors about your wife, yes. Nasty stuff."

"Bloody hell, that spread fast."

Gil looked complacent. "Everything comes to my ears.
Now, what can I do to help?"

FOUR BOXES FROM THE HOUSE OF CHANCE HAD BEEN
delivered, Burton informed the Rutherford ladies when they
returned from their morning ride. The boxes were upstairs
in the relevant bedchambers. Each box was clearly labeled
with the name of the recipient.

With squeals of excitement the girls raced upstairs, breakfast forgotten.

Emm gave Cal a rueful look. "We won't be able to stop
them going to the Braxtons' party now."

At her party, Lady Peplowe had spoken to her friend
Mrs. Braxton, who'd immediately sent a written invitation

that included the three girls in Emm and Cal's invitation. At that stage the nasty rumors about Emm hadn't surfaced.

Naturally the girls were excited to be invited to their first London party, but Emm had demurred, privately hoping Miss Chance wouldn't get the girls' gowns finished in time. She knew there would be some kind of scene at the Braxtons', had been metaphorically girding her loins for it, and she didn't want the girls to witness it, especially not for their first society party.

"We're going to have to tell them," Cal said.

"I know. But let's let them enjoy their dresses first." She wasn't in a hurry to see hers—she was dreading the night too much—so she and Cal went into the breakfast parlor and shared a quiet, companionable meal.

"Ahem." Burton stood at the door and cleared his throat portentously. His face was its usual bland self, but his eyes were dancing. "May I present Lady Rose Rutherford."

Rose, a vision in long white gloves and a gown of soft dusky blue, glided in, her head held high as if she were about to meet royalty. Or as if she were royalty. The dress was perfect for a young lady who was not an ingenue but who was nevertheless making her first appearance in society. It was simple yet sophisticated and floated around her body like dark flame.

"Oh, Rose, that's—" Emm began, but Rose raised her hand, as if to say *stop*, her expression stern. Clearly they were to admire in silence. Rose looked at the butler and inclined her head graciously.

"A duchess in the making," Cal murmured in Emm's ear. He was rewarded with a ducal frown.

"Lady George Rutherford," intoned Burton from the doorway.

George paced in like a lithe young leopard, not exactly the glide that Rose had achieved, but with a charm all of its own. She looked splendid in a gown of rose-tinged bronze, the gown cut to emphasize her high bosom, upright bearing and slender legginess.

"By George, she's a stunner too," Cal murmured, and Emm chuckled softly at his inadvertent pun.

"Hush!" Rose hissed, and turned to the door.

"And finally, I would like to present Lady Lily Rutherford," Burton said.

Emm took one look at Lily, framed in the doorway, and clapped her hand over her mouth. "Oh, my, Cal, will you just look at Lily." She blinked away tears as Lily, proud and straight as a young duchess, glowing like a candle lit from within, glided into the room. Her dress was the softest, palest shade of peach, cut simply yet cunningly to frame her unique beauty. She looked, as Miss Chance had promised, round and feminine and utterly delicious.

"Oh, lord, my baby sister! I'm going to be beating them off with sticks," Cal groaned.

Lily heard him, blushed and gave a happy little twirl. "Don't we all look pretty, Emm? I think I love Miss Chance."

Emm nodded. She did too.

"So we can go to the party after all?" Rose said. "Now that the dresses have arrived."

Emm sighed. "Yes, but run upstairs and change into a day gown first. There's something I need to explain to you— warn you about actually, seeing as you're going to the party."

"You mean about those horrible stories people have been spreading about you?" Rose said.

Emm's jaw dropped. "You knew?"

All three girls nodded. Rose said, "Penny Peplowe told us the other day. Everybody knows."

'That's why we were so desperate to come," Lily added.

Cal said, "I thought all the subtle nagging was because you wanted to go to the party."

"We do, of course," George said. "At least Rose and Lily do, though I don't think I'm going to like parties much. But you don't imagine we'd let Emm face those bitches alone, do you?"

Emm had a large lump in her throat. The dear, sweet, loyal girls.

"But you're not allowed to punch that Oates woman, George, remember—you promised," Rose said severely.

"Or slap her," Lily added, "no matter how much she deserves it."

"All right, but I still don't see why," George grumbled.

"Because we are a family now, and what one family member does affects the reputation of the others," Lily said, echoing something that Emm had said an age ago. "If you punch that horrid woman it will reflect badly on Emm."

Emm's mouth trembled. She pressed her lips together, striving for composure, unable to speak, deeply moved by their unquestioning support. And their faith in her.

Seeing her dilemma, Cal slid an arm around her. "That's what happens when you're a family. We're all going to be there tonight, even Aunt Agatha."

"Aunt Agatha?' the girls chorused.

He nodded. "Facing down the hounds of hell."

George corrected him. "Not the hounds, the bitches."

THERE WAS A SUDDEN HUSH IN THE BRAXTON BALLROOM when Emm and Cal entered, followed by the three girls. Their names hadn't been announced—it was just an informal party—but the hush, followed by a buzz of conversation, showed that people knew, that either they had or hadn't expected Emm to show up, and that now they were speculating as to what might happen.

Cal led them to a line of seats opposite the entrance. Emm had told him she wanted to be there if and when Mrs. Oates arrived. She intended to have words with the woman.

He seated them and then went to fetch champagne for her and the girls. Emm smoothed her skirt. Miss Chance had sent her a dress in pale jonquil silk. It was beautiful, but Emm was wound up tight as a spring and couldn't enjoy it as she wanted.

She sat up suddenly, spying a familiar face. "Look, isn't that Sally Destry? Lady Maldon, I mean." Sally was looking very different from the sensitive young schoolgirl Emm remembered, very dashing and fashionable and confident-looking. "I hope she hasn't heard what's been said about me. I must have a word, oh, but then I might miss the guests arriving." She hovered indecisively. It wasn't like her.

"And there's Susie Morton from school as well," Lily commented. "She married some viscount, I forget his name."

"Viscount Burford," Rose said. "And see who she's with tonight? Julia Hampton."

"Goodness me, what a lot of former Mallard girls there are here tonight," Emm exclaimed, noticing several more. "I had no idea they were all in London, and what a coincidence that they're all at the same party. Of all the nights. Oh, I almost wish we hadn't come."

"An amazing coincidence," Cal said. He recognized some of those names from certain letters recently delivered.

Rose smiled at him. "Isn't it just?"

Emm stiffened. "There she is, Mrs. Oates." She handed Cal her glass. "Right. I want this over and done with. I'll just— Oh!"

For as Mrs. Oates entered the room on her husband's arm, a group of dashing and elegant young women, led by the former Sally Destry, linked arms with her and bore her gaily off to an adjoining anteroom. She went with them, flushed and laughing. Emm counted five former Mallard girls.

Emm sat back down with a thump. "They must be friends of hers. How very disappointing. I'll have to wait until she comes out. I don't want to involve anyone else." Cal handed her the champagne glass. She emptied it in one gulp.

"There's your aunt, Cal."

Aunt Agatha entered, dressed magnificently in silver and deep claret. She gave Emm and Cal a gruff nod and started to move toward a group of her cronies. Then she noticed her three nieces and stopped in midstep. The elegantly plucked brows drew together, she pulled out her lorgnette and gave each one of them a long, unnerving scrutiny. Her forehead furrowed a moment, then she turned away.

All three girls heaved a sigh of relief. "I thought for a minute she was going to come over and yell at us for not getting our gowns from All-Tense," Rose said.

"Yes, and if she'd told me I looked fat in this I would have had to kill her," Lily said.

Rose laughed. "Silly, You don't look fat. Haven't you noticed the admiring glances you've been getting?"

Cal had. He was torn between wanting to protect his wife from the vicious rumors and wanting to lock his sisters and niece in a tower. Or at least throwing a blanket over them to stop all those fellows from staring. Lily's dress was perfectly modest and covered her quite adequately. And yet . . .

He gritted his teeth. Rose's and George's dresses were no better.

Cal speared an icy glare at a pair of dandified young fellows who looked as though they were nerving themselves to come over and meet the girls. The boys blanched, straightened their cravats and strolled away, trying to look unconcerned.

One of them glanced back. Cal bared his teeth and the lad recoiled, bumping into a dowager, who gave him a blistering rebuke. Served him right.

It was just a taste of things to come, Cal thought gloomily. The season was going to be hell.

"They're out." Emm jumped to her feet. The dashing young women emerged from the anteroom with Mrs. Oates. "Now."

But just as they released her, Lady Peplowe, Mrs. Braxton and some of their friends took Mrs. Oates's arm and led her back in.

"What's going on?" Emm gave Cal a puzzled glance. Cal shrugged, snagged another glass of champagne from a passing waiter and gave it to his wife.

"You don't think they're—? No." She sipped thoughtfully. "I don't suppose—?" And shook her head.

Cal didn't know what was going on, but he was pretty sure the nasty young woman was getting an earful from Lady Peplowe and her friends. As for the fashionable young women who'd carried her away so gaily the first time, whatever they'd said to her hadn't been anything gay or frivolous. She'd emerged from the anteroom looking quite shaken.

From the corner of his eye, Cal noticed Radcliffe was here. Even as he watched, Radcliffe casually drew Jeremy Oates into their group. Oates, a pushy fellow at the best of times, looked very flattered to be included in such company. So he might. The group included several of the most important and influential men in London and the city.

As he watched they drifted quietly out onto the balcony.

Interesting. He would love to hear what they said, but his place was with his wife.

Ten minutes later Mrs. Oates emerged from the anteroom looking rattled and sulky. She glanced around the room, looking for her husband, he supposed.

"Finally!" Emm set down her glass for the third time. It was very wearing, waiting, nerving herself for the confrontation, and then having to put it off again. Knowing all the while that people were watching, though pretending not to.

She would be glad to get it over with.

But what was this? Lady Peplowe and Mrs. Braxton were escorting Mrs. Oates toward her. The crowd in the middle of the floor parted like the Red Sea.

Emm rose a little shakily to her feet. What was going on? It wasn't what she'd planned at all, not a public confrontation like this. She wanted the privacy of the anteroom.

Nerves fluttered in her stomach. She straightened her shoulders. *Get it over now and be done with it.* She took several deep breaths—not too many or she'd feel dizzy.

An expectant hush filled the room. People edged closer, the better to hear and see.

"Lady Ashendon," Lady Peplowe said. Her voice was clear and well modulated. It also carried. "This misguided young woman repeated a number of false and nasty stories about you last week at my party. She's admitted it here tonight."

"And at my party, she wishes to apologize," Mrs. Braxton said. "Don't you, Mrs. Oates?"

Mrs. Oates looked trapped and furious and anything but remorseful. She wrenched herself out of the two society matrons' grip and tried to escape. She moved to the left. A steely line of grim-visaged dowagers stepped forward, blocking her escape. Aunt Agatha and her cronies.

She turned to the right. Five former Mallard girls linked arms and blocked her way with ferocious gaiety.

Behind Emm, Rose and Lily chanted softly, "*Three duchesses, two marchionesses, five countesses, six viscountesses . . .*" And George joined in, "And a dowager with a lorgnette."

Emm blinked rapidly. She would not cry, she would not.

Mrs. Oates looked around the room, looking for support. She found none. "Oh, what's the fuss about? It was just a bit of harmless fun. Everyone gossips, after all."

Nobody said a word.

"All right, then," she said pettishly. "I'm very sorry I gossiped about you, Lady Ashendon. My cousin knew it wasn't true, by the way. Most people did. Stuck up and strait-laced, that's what we called you." She turned to Mrs. Braxton. "There, will that do? Can I go now?"

It was a travesty of an apology.

Emm itched to slap the nasty creature silly. Her fingers had curled into fists with the effort of not doing so. But she occupied the moral high ground. Dignity and grace in victory was what she must strive for now. It was what she'd taught the girls. *We are a family now, and what one family member does affects the reputation of the others.*

Lady Peplowe and Mrs. Braxton were waiting. As was the entire room.

The apology was blatantly insincere, but indirectly it had cleared Emm's name. *Stuck up and straitlaced, that's what we called you.* Nobody could mistake the petty adolescent jealousy in that.

Emm stared at Mrs. Oates with her coldest teacherly withering look. After a moment, the woman reddened a little and dropped her gaze.

It would have to do. Emm gave Lady Peplowe and Mrs. Braxton a stiff nod. They released Mrs. Oates, who flounced away and seized her husband's arm. "Jeremy, these women are—"

"Shut up, Fanny. You're an embarrassment. We're leaving."

Everyone watched as her husband led her from the room, his face beet red and furious. She looked sulky and petulant. "This party was a dead bore anyway," she said loudly as they exited.

"I left something in the cloakroom," Rose said suddenly, and hurried toward the exit.

A moment later Emm—and everyone in the ballroom— heard Rose say, "Mrs. Oates, a moment please." Then came the sound of a loud stinging slap followed by a howl of pain and outrage.

Nobody moved or spoke. An instant later Rose entered the ballroom, head high, looking like the cat that ate the cream. She crossed the ballroom, a young Boadicea, dressed in flames of dusky blue.

There was a spatter of applause, quickly hushed, and everyone immediately started talking. And trying to suppress smiles.

Rose rejoined her family.

"*You* said I wasn't allowed to punch her," George said indignantly. "You made me *promise*."

"I didn't punch her," Rose said with dignity. "I slapped her." And then she grinned like a mischievous urchin. "A good hard one it was too. Did you hear the bitch yell?"

Emm, caught between laughter and tears, just shook her head.

Aunt Agatha arrived. "You handled that well, Emmaline." She turned to Rose. "But you—"

Rose raised her chin defiantly. "You have something to say to me, Aunt Agatha?"

Her aunt sniffed. "You, young lady, have possibilities. And that's all I'm going to say."

"That's a relief," George murmured.

"I might be old, but I'm not deaf, Georgiana."

"Lily?" She turned the lorgnette on Lily's dress. They all tensed. "Pretty dress. It suits you."

Leaving them all breathless with shock, Aunt Agatha stumped regally away.

Suddenly it was as if a weight had been lifted off the entire party. The musicians struck up a lively country dance, and in moments the floor was full of laughing, twirling men and women dancing as if they had not a care in the world.

Emm, relieved and a little dazed at the way events had turned out, sat for a moment watching her girls dancing, her dear, dear girls. All eight of them—Rose, George, Lily and the girls from Miss Mallard's, who'd rallied around to support Emm in her hour of need. She would talk to them later, thank them and catch up with their news.

She sipped champagne and smiled to herself. *Three duchesses, two marchionesses, five countesses, six viscountesses . . .* She looked across to where Aunt Agatha was laying down the law to some hapless minion. *And a dowager with a lorgnette.* She smiled at Lady Peplowe and Mrs. Braxton. And some friends she didn't know she had.

She felt the warmth of a large hand on her shoulder. And throughout it all, standing quietly in the background, her rock, her love, her husband. He bent over her. "Do you want to dance?"

She shook her head. "Later. You go on and circulate. I just want to sit for a while."

She tried not to be disappointed when he took her advice and moved away.

Chapter Twenty-two

**Take hope from the heart of man and you
make him a beast of prey.**
—OUIDA (MARIE LOUISE DE LA RAMÉE)

CAL FOUND RADCLIFFE AND THANKED HIM FOR COMING.
"What did you and your friends say to that harpy's husband?"

Radcliffe smiled. "Oates and his foolish wife are dedicated social climbers, and Oates has been angling for a knighthood. But he's also a businessman to the core. When we pointed out to him that his wife's so-called harmless gossip could endanger his business prospects as well as the knighthood—well, I'd be surprised if we heard much from her in future. He's quite ruthless in business. At home . . . ?" He shrugged.

"Thank you."

Radcliffe waved his thanks away. "Not sure it was necessary. The ladies carried it, I think. Those young women, Lady Maldon, Lady Burford, Hampton's girl and the rest, make up a set she's long been trying to become part of—the dashing younger set, future leaders of the ton. They took her aside and threatened to ostracize her."

"How could you possibly know that?"

Radcliffe smiled, sphinxlike, which was all the answer Cal knew he'd get.

"You put on a good show there, family and friends rallying around, public show of support for your wife. Well done. Surprised your father-in-law didn't show, though."

Cal frowned. "My father-in-law? If you mean my wife's father, he's dead."

Radcliffe gave him a sharp look. "Sir Humphrey? Dead? I didn't know that. When did he die?"

Cal looked at him oddly. "Years ago."

"Ah, I thought you meant he'd died in the last week or so—but now I come to think of it, if that were the case your wife wouldn't be dancing at parties, would she? He's not dead."

Cal glanced over to where his wife was now dancing with some fellow. He lowered his voice. "Are you saying my wife's father—Sir Humphrey Westwood, of Bucklebury in Berkshire—is alive?"

Radcliffe nodded. "Became something of a recluse in the last seven or eight years, I believe, but otherwise, as far as I know he's hale and hearty."

Cal's brain was spinning. "Would you mind not mentioning that to my wife? Or anyone else. Just until I can confirm it."

Radcliffe gave an indifferent shrug. "You know me. I'm a vault."

"Thank you. I'll call on you tomorrow."

"What for? I can tell you now there's no news of the assassin fellow. I'm beginning to think we were mistaken about him. I think he's fled the country."

"No, it's not about him," Cal said. "I'm coming in to formally resign my commission. You were right. I'm needed here."

CAL AND HIS FAMILY RODE OUT THE MORNING AFTER THE Braxton party, a little later than usual, not only because of the party, but because his wife had been in a strange mood—emotional, exhilarated and several times on the verge of tears. And very, very affectionate.

They'd made love three times during the night, and each time, she'd made love to him, taking the lead, lavishing on him every skill he'd taught her, and a few she was making up as she went along. They were so attuned to each other's bodies now, the experience was deeper, more intense. And after the triumph of last night, more joyous.

Cal would have been happy to spend the morning in bed. But she rose bright and happy and eager for her morning ride.

He'd offered her a different kind of ride and she'd laughed, a joyous peal of delight, and reminded him the girls would be waiting. In this mood she was irresistible, and Cal had crawled out of bed. And was now glad he had.

It was a glorious morning—crisp, but clear—and to see his wife and sisters and niece laughing and chattering as they picked over the evening's events made him feel . . . well, he couldn't name the feeling, but it filled his chest.

He hadn't yet told Emmaline of the decision he'd made a few days before, the decision to resign his commission and take up his life here. He'd never really considered the future before. By necessity, he'd lived more or less from day to day. Now . . .

He looked at his wife on her spirited little gray mare. He had a future now. And a purpose.

They raced at first, and George won. She was a sight to behold on horseback. His sisters were good, but she . . . She'd mastered the sidesaddle and was now teaching Sultan to jump with it, starting with fallen tree trunks. And whenever she jumped, he caught a glimpse of breeches beneath her smart London habit.

The girls cantered off, their groom following, and, as had become part of their morning routine, Cal and Emm walked their horses quietly and talked.

"I didn't expect to be supported," she told him. "Not like that. I knew you'd support me." She reached out to him and they held hands for a minute before the horses parted them. "I've been so alone for so long. Surrounded by people, yet essentially on my own, and facing a lifetime alone—and I thought I was content with that, honestly I was. But last night, when people—the girls, the Mallard girls especially, most of whom I thought had forgotten me the moment they left school, and Aunt Agatha, and, oh, everyone—came forward to support me . . . I was un, un*womanned* by their generosity, Cal."

He nodded. It had renewed his belief in basic human goodness.

"Cal," she said abruptly, in quite a different voice. "What is that man doing?" She pointed. "There's a man crouched in that tree and he's got a—"

Several things happened at once. Just as the man in the tree swung a rifle up in an action that curdled Cal's blood, George, screaming like a banshee, galloped up to the tree and flung something. There was a loud bang, and the man overbalanced. Flailing wildly, he twisted to grab a branch, dropped his rifle and fell to the ground with a loud thud. He didn't move.

Cal swung around to his wife. "Emm, are you all right?"

She was pale but nodded shakily. "Fine. You?"

Cal breathed again. "He missed, thank God. Stay here, I'll see to it." He galloped toward the tree, shouting, "George, stay away!" to his niece who was about to dismount.

"He's alive, I think," she said. "But he doesn't seem to be able to move."

Cal flung himself off his horse and bent over the man. His eyes were open, but he was breathing with difficulty. From the angle at which he lay, Cal thought he might have broken his spine.

"Joe Gimble?"

The man tried to nod, couldn't and grunted. It confirmed Cal's suspicions. This man was dying. "Keep everyone away, George," he said quietly, and turned back to Gimble.

"You're the Scorpion."

There was a short silence, then the man rasped, "Dying, ain't I?" A bubble of blood came from his mouth.

"Yes." There was no point pretending otherwise. Soldiers were realists.

"Wanted you . . . my last kill . . . Bastard," Gimble gasped. "Lock up . . . wife . . . children . . ."

"Not me," Cal said. "I had no part of that."

"Jerry . . . told me . . . you . . ."

Jerry was the name of the drunk who'd died. It all fitted.

"It wasn't me. But don't worry. Your wife and sister-in-law and children—they'll be released. They will be all right, my word on it."

The man swore. "Going to . . . 'merica . . . brother . . ."

"I know about your brother Bert in America. I'll make sure they get there."

Gimble struggled for breath. There was blood in his mouth. His eyes were desperate. "Promise?"

"I promise."

Gimble looked at him. "Money in pocket. Give . . . wife?"

Call felt in the man's pocket and found a thick roll of notes. He held it so Gimble could see it. "I'll make sure this goes to your wife and no one else. My word of honor."

Again Gimble tried to nod and couldn't. He was fading fast. "Tell her . . . love . . ." Blood bubbled from his mouth as the man who'd been the Scorpion breathed his last breath.

There was a long silence, broken only by the breeze in the bushes and the far-distant sound of the city waking up.

"Is he dead?"

Cal looked around. It was Emm. She sounded shaken. The girls waited a short distance away, watching with somber eyes. Emm's horse took a few steps closer.

He straightened. "Don't come any closer, Emm, it's not a pretty sight. I'll wait here with the body while you and the girls go for help."

Her horse took two more steps toward him. "The thing is," Emm said in an odd voice. She was as pale as parchment. "He didn't miss after all. I love you, Cal." And she toppled off her horse in a dead faint.

Cal leapt to catch her. He lowered her to the ground and, frantic, ripped open her jacket. The shirt beneath was soaked with blood.

CAL RIPPED OPEN EMM'S BLOUSE. SOMEBODY SCREAMED. Her whole chest and shoulder was covered in blood. He found the source of blood—a shoulder wound—and breathed again. It was serious, but not necessarily fatal, not if she got good, swift medical attention.

And if no infection came afterward. Infection was usually the killer, not the wound itself.

He yanked off his coat and waistcoat and ripped off his neckcloth and shirt. He bared her shoulder, folded his shirt into a thick pad and tied it on with his neckcloth.

He looked around. The groom, Kirk, stood holding the reins of Cal's and his own horse. Cal waved him closer. "I'm going to take Lady Ashendon up with me."

"Wouldn't a carriage—" Rose began.

"No time." Cal mounted his horse. "Lift her up to me, Kirk. Gently." He held out his arms.

Kirk bent and carefully scooped Emm up, then placed her in Cal's arms. She was as pale as paper. Cal's heart thudded painfully in his chest. She wasn't dead, and she wasn't going to be, not if he had any say in the matter. Not until next century. Or longer.

"Rose, George, you two ride ahead and let Burton know what's happened. Tell him to fetch a doctor—one who understands bullet wounds."

The girls galloped off.

"Lily, I want you to walk your horse beside me and help me. If she needs anything, if my horse stumbles . . . my hands are full."

"I'll do whatever is needed, Cal, don't worry."

"And, Kirk—"

"I'll stay with this fellow's body, m'lord," Kirk said. "Off ye go."

Lily took his horse's reins and led them toward the park exit. A part of Cal wished they could ride *ventre a terre* and get to a doctor as soon as possible, but of course they had to walk so as not to jolt Emm's wound any more than necessary. He cradled her against his bare chest. Her stillness, her pallor frightened him.

He told himself she would recover. A shoulder wound wasn't so bad. He'd had two himself.

But this was *Emm*. His wife. The convenient wife he was now sure he couldn't live without. Or wouldn't want to.

I love you, Cal. The first time she'd ever said it.

Why? Because she thought she was dying?

Joe Gimble had asked Cal to tell his wife he loved her. Was that what people said when they thought they were dying?

He gazed down at the face of his pale, frighteningly still wife. Maybe it took death, or the threat of death, to jolt people into the realization that they loved.

Because in that moment when he'd ripped open her coat and saw her awash in her own blood, it had struck him like a thunderbolt: that he loved her, loved this dear, precious woman with every part of his body and soul.

And that he'd never told her.

He bent and put his mouth to her ear. "I love you, Emm," he said. "Do you hear me? I love you. You're going to be all right—and I love you."

Lily looked over and said gently, "She knows you do, Cal."

"How?" he said, anguished. "How could she know? I've never told her, Lil, never once." He hadn't even realized he did—let alone how much—until now.

His little sister smiled. "We know you love Emm, Cal. And if we do, she must. And when she wakes up, you can tell her."

Oh, God, he hoped so.

"Did I happen to mention that I love you?"

Emm, propped up against her pillows in bed, smiled. "Only about a dozen times. And that was just this morning. I think it was more like fifty yesterday."

Cal bent and kissed her gently. "Just so you remember."

It was three days since she'd been wounded. There was no sign of fever or infection; she was making a good recovery. The doctor who'd attended her was physician and surgeon both—a rare combination—and had attended troops in the war. He'd extracted the bullet skillfully and had given Emm laudanum for the pain and some powders for the fever that usually followed bullet wounds.

He'd also given the nod to Cal's sisters' suggestions of willow bark tea, reputed to be good for counteracting fever.

Apparently they'd picked up a smattering of sickroom remedies from conversations in the Pump Room.

"Would you mind if I left you now? I have some business to attend to."

She nodded sleepily. "I'm ridiculously tired. I think I'll have a nap." She grimaced. "Another one."

CAL WENT FIRST TO WHITEHALL.

"So, you meant it about resigning your commission," Radcliffe said.

"I did." Cal handed him the signed papers.

"Because you have a family to care for now. How's your wife, by the way?"

"Recovering well, thank you."

Cal blamed himself for her injury. If he hadn't come hunting for the assassin in the first place . . . He'd never have met and married her.

He just wished she and the girls hadn't been there when Gimble shot at him.

But if they hadn't, Cal would probably be dead.

"Have the Gimble family been released?"

Radcliffe nodded. "A few hours ago."

"Not yesterday? Or the day Gimble was killed?"

Radcliffe shrugged. "There were things to follow up. The funeral to arrange."

"I'll pay for it."

Radcliffe looked up in surprise. "The funeral?"

Cal nodded. "They don't have much. They'll need every penny they have to get to America." He hadn't told Radcliffe about the money Gimble had on him. Radcliffe would want to confiscate it. "I'm going to pay their fares to America too."

"Good lord. What's gotten into you? Founding an assassin's benevolent society?"

"Just balancing the score. The wife and children weren't responsible for what he did."

Radcliffe gave him a shrewd look. "You're not feeling guilty, are you? Because guilt is pointless for the likes of us."

Cal didn't agree. "I think the 'likes of us' haven't been doing as good a job as we should. That's partly why I've resigned my commission. Europe is one thing, but there are things to be done in England, a future to be forged."

"Very laudable."

Cal didn't bother trying to explain the deep disillusion he'd felt, seeing what had become of England's former soldiers. For so long he'd hated Gimble, hated him with a righteous passion, but as his enemy lay dying, Cal saw that he was just a man like any other, who loved his wife and children and worried about their future.

A murderer, but not wholly evil. And perhaps it wasn't entirely Gimble's fault.

This country had taken men like Bert and Joe Gimble— and the others Cal had met—taught them to shoot and to kill, and then, when the war was over, tossed them back to their former lives—into a country in dire economic turmoil— without care whether they starved or not.

Could he really blame Gimble for using the only skill he had to try to earn enough money to give his family a fresh start in a young country?

But Radcliffe would never see it like that.

"They'll be at the aunt's house, then?"

Radcliffe nodded, occupied with his paperwork again. Cal saw himself out.

THE GIMBLE FAMILY RECEIVED CAL'S VISIT WITH SUSPICION, if not outright hostility. He couldn't blame them.

The woman who answered the door wouldn't open it more than a crack until he said, "I was with Joe when he died—I didn't kill him. He fell from a tree and broke his neck—but I was there, and before he died he gave me a message for his wife and children. Would that be you?"

Grudgingly she opened the door and gestured for him to come in. Her eyes were red with weeping. The three children gathered around her, the little ones clutching her skirt. The young boy stood stiffly apart, his eyes full of grief and anger.

"I'm sorry for your loss," he said to Joe's widow, though in all honesty he couldn't be sorry Joe Gimble was dead. "Joe died quickly and in no pain." He didn't know if the latter was true, but he was comforting the living.

"I have made arrangements to pay for Joe's funeral. He won't be going in a pauper's grave."

"Why?" Mrs. Gimble said bitterly. "Feeling guilty?"

"Not guilty, but partly responsible. What was between Joe and me was nothing to do with his family, and I'm sorry you were imprisoned. I had no part of that."

She eyed him skeptically a moment, then gave a reluctant nod. "You said Joe had a message for us."

Cal pulled out the roll of notes, to which he'd added tickets for a passage to America for two women and three children. Not steerage, either. "He gave me this to give to you."

She stared at the roll of money, likely more than she'd seen in her life. She gave him a disbelieving look. Cal nodded, and she reached out a trembling hand and took the money, clutching it to her chest as if frightened he'd snatch it back.

"Tickets to America are in there, for you, your sister and the children."

She nodded, her mouth working.

"Joe's last words were to tell you he loved you."

Her face crumpled, her eyes flooded with tears. She gave a loud sob and fled the room.

Cal looked down at the boy. "I watched you, the day they took you all away to prison. The way a person behaves in a crisis is very revealing of character."

The boy watched him from narrowed, suspicious eyes.

"You took care of the little ones, and you helped your mother and aunt."

"Gotta," the boy muttered. "I gotta be the man of the family when Da's away." His face struggled as he remembered his father was never coming back.

"Your father said he was very proud of you." The boy turned away abruptly, his hands over his eyes.

"You're a son any man would be proud of," Cal said, and quietly let himself out.

*   *   *

HE TOLD EMM ABOUT IT THAT NIGHT. SHE LAY SNUGGLED against his chest.

She wept a few tears when he told her about Mrs. Gimble and the money. And about what he'd said to the young boy. "You're a good man, Calbourne Rutherford. No wonder I love you so much." They kissed then, but softly, because her shoulder was still painful and he didn't want to jar her.

He ached to be able to make love to her again, this time in the full knowledge that he loved her, and that she loved him. The glow in her eyes told him she felt the same.

"So you're not going back to Europe?"

"No. I've resigned my commission."

"What are you going to do?"

"Become the Earl of Ashendon."

"You already are the Earl of Ashendon."

He shook his head. "In name only, I'm afraid. There's a lot more work to be done. Speaking of which, I have to go out of town for a few days. I hope you don't mind."

"No, of course not, I'm stuck in this bed until Dr. Duncan says I can get up."

Bed rest? For a shoulder injury? When Cal was shot in the shoulder he'd been back at work the minute the fever had passed. But probably women were more delicate than men.

"Where are you going?"

He rose from the bed and stirred up the coals in the fire. It didn't need tending, but he couldn't lie to her face. "To the country. Just some estate business. I hope to be back in a few days."

THE VILLAGE OF BUCKLEBURY WAS QUIET AND PRETTY. AT the local inn Cal asked directions to the home of Sir Humphrey Westwood and was soon bowling up the driveway of Westwood House—a rather grander place than Emm had led him to believe.

He presented his card at the door. The elderly butler took

it with a sorrowful air. "Sir Humphrey rarely receives visitors these days, my lord."

"I think he'll want to see me," Cal said. "I'm his son-in-law."

The butler's eyes widened, then his face lit up. "You have news of Miss Emm?"

"She's Lady Ashendon now," Cal said proudly.

The butler's hopeful gaze shifted to the traveling carriage. "She's not—"

"No, but I'm hoping to bring Sir Humphrey to her. In London."

The butler's eyes filled with tears. "He hasn't been off the estate since he came home nearly seven years ago, after combing the country for weeks, looking for signs of her. Brokenhearted, he was, to come home alone."

Cal's sympathy was limited. The man should have had more faith in his daughter in the first place. But he wasn't here to rake over old coals but to heal old wounds. "Take me to Sir Humphrey."

Chapter Twenty-three

The voice of conscience is so delicate that it is easy to stifle
it; but it is also so clear that it is impossible to mistake it.
—MADAME DE STAËL, *GERMANY*

EMM WAS UPSTAIRS GETTING DRESSED WHEN CAL ARRIVED
home four days later. Burton told him the doctor had just
left. He'd given her permission to be out of bed and moving
around again.

When she saw him she ran toward him, flung her arms
around him and then winced. "Forgot my stupid shoulder.
Kiss me, Cal darling. I know it's only been a few days but
you wouldn't believe how much I've missed you."

He proceeded to demonstrate that he had, in fact, missed
her much more. She drew him toward the bed, saying, "The
doctor said it's all right."

Cal abruptly recalled himself. He drew back. "Not yet.
I forgot to tell you, you have a visitor downstairs who's very
eager to see you."

She sighed. "People have been very kind; you have no
idea how many callers and flowers and succession-house
fruits I've received. I didn't even know I knew so many
people. In fact, I don't. I think it's mostly because shortly
after I weathered a horrid scandal, I was shot by a notorious
assassin and thus I have become something of a celebrity.
It's all a bit overwhelming. Let us hope people soon find
something else to fuss over."

She paused and said mischievously, "Do I really want to
see this visitor? I could still be confined to bed, you know."

It was tempting, but this couldn't wait. Besides, when he finally took his wife to bed, he wouldn't want to leave it for a week. He offered his arm. "You do want to see him, and he very much wants to see you. Come, my lady, I'll escort you downstairs."

"Oh, very well, if I must." She took his arm.

She was still holding Cal's arm when he signaled for Logan to open the sitting room door, and Cal was glad of it, because when she saw the stiff, pale-faced gentleman who rose nervously to greet her, she stumbled and almost fainted again.

"Papa?" she whispered. "Papa, is it really you? But I thought— Oh, Papa!" And she ran across the room and flung herself weeping into her father's arms.

An evening followed then of tears, apologies, explanations and forgiveness. Sir Humphrey was so obviously grieved at the breach with his daughter, blamed himself so savagely by being taken in, was so remorseful at not having more faith in his daughter, and so very apologetic, that even Cal forgave him.

Emm, of course, had forgiven him long ago.

Just one thing now puzzled her. "Papa, when you were searching for me, why did you never think to look for me in Bath? Did it never occur to you I would seek refuge with Miss Mallard?"

He shook his head. "Why would it? You *hated* that place. You wrote me long letters every week begging, pleading, *imploring* me to rescue you from that dreadful place and bring you home—and don't shake your head at me, Emm. I still have every one of your letters, a large stack." He indicated how large with his hands. "Yes, of course I kept them. I've read them over and over, since you left. They were all I had left of you."

His voice broke and, when he had mastered himself, he added almost to himself, "You hated that place."

"Yes, when I was first sent there I did," she agreed gently. "But I was thirteen then. And after a while I got used to it."

"I didn't know. You never said, not in any of your letters."

"I suppose I didn't." She gave him a tremulous smile. "But we've found each other now."

He took her hands in his. "Yes, we've found each other now."

When the girls came home from their outing, they were amazed to discover they had a new relative. Dinner lasted a long time, with reminiscences—happier ones now—and plans for the future.

When Emm escorted her father up to the best guest bedroom—for of course her dear papa was not allowed to stay in some horrid hotel or club when his home was here, with his family—he was a man who looked ten years younger than the man Cal had first met a bare handful of days before.

And Emm? Emm just glowed with happiness.

A FEW WEEKS LATER, CAL RECEIVED A NOTE FROM GIL Radcliffe.

Dear Ashendon,

Took the liberty of inquiring into the situation of that Irwin fellow. It might gratify you to know his situation is far from happy. The widow he married is a harridan of the first degree, a grim-faced harpy with the disposition of a peevish rat. She was, and is, immensely rich, but the fool didn't make any further inquiries before he married her. He got nothing—it was all tied up in trusts. She holds the purse strings, he has to ask her for every penny and she keeps him on a very tight rein.

I'm told he's about as miserable as a man can be. She's as healthy as a cow, and no doubt he would dream of killing her, except that she's made it known far and wide that he gets nothing in her will.

I don't know what Irwin was like when your wife knew him, but these days he's a miserable whipped dog of a man.

Of course if you still wish to track him down and give him the thrashing he deserves, you could, but I hardly think it's necessary. It might actually gain him some sympathy.

Revenge might be a dish best eaten cold, but sometimes it's just not practical.

Yours etc., Radcliffe.

Epilogue

Thou art my life, my love, my heart,
The very eyes of me:
And hast command of every part
To live and die for thee.
—ROBERT HERRICK, *TO ANTHEA WHO MAY*
COMMAND HIM ANYTHING

Three months later

IT WAS THE NIGHT BEFORE THE GRAND BALL TO LAUNCH
the three Rutherford girls. For weeks the household had
been a frenzy of preparation. Cal lay in bed with Emm.

"I should have just auctioned off those dratted girls," he
grumbled. "There's been more planning and fuss over this
one ball than there was for an entire campaign against Boney.
It's completely exhausted you."

She laughed. "No, you've exhausted me." She stretched
languorously.

They'd made love, dozed off, woken and made love again.
And now they were in that postcoital state of quiet bliss.

"It's all working out, isn't it, Cal?"

"Couldn't be better. Even Aunt Agatha approves of you
now."

She gave him a shocked look. "Who, *me*? The badly
dressed nobody who dared to marry into the Rutherford
family?"

"You might be a nobody," he informed her loftily, "but
at least you have a spine." He'd told her about that one, of
course.

She laughed. "I'm glad she approves of my spine."

"I approve of it too," he said, demonstrating.

After a while she said, "I didn't mean that. I meant our marriage. Are you happy with how it's all going?"

He wrapped his arms around her. "Do you even need to ask?"

"Not really. It's just—everything changed so quickly and I know it's not what you wanted when you asked me to marry you, so sometimes I wonder. I mean I'm happy, and you seem happy enough, but—"

"Well, now you come to ask me, I have to admit that things haven't turned out the way I wanted them at all. Not at all," he said severely. "You were supposed to be a convenient wife. I married you for one reason and one reason only."

"To look after the girls, I know. And I did. I do."

"You did. You do," he acknowledged grudgingly. "But what of all the other things you did that were not part of the bargain?"

"You mean all the trouble I caused you?"

"Exactly. You turned my big gloomy house into a home!" He fixed her with an indignant look. "What's more, you filled it with laughter. And flowers!"

"I'm sorry," she said humbly.

"So you should be. And then you turned a lonely man and three unhappy girls into a family. Turned my life upside-down, you did, without so much as a by-your-leave."

She clapped her hands to her cheeks in dismay. "Oh, dear, did you want a by-your-leave, Lord Ashendon?"

"Lady Impudence! I didn't know what I wanted." He kissed her. "But you gave it to me anyway. "

He kissed her again. "You gave me a purpose in life, a home, a family and most of all you gave me yourself, my strong, loving, loyal, beautiful—"

"Not beautiful."

"Don't argue—I said beautiful and I meant beautiful. Now where was I? Oh, yes—I thought I was one of the coldhearted Rutherford men—immune to love. But you, my beautiful, precious one, are the love of my life." He cupped her face in his hands. "I love you, Emmaline Margaret Westwood Rutherford, with all my heart, with all my body and all my soul. And. I. Thee. Worship." He punctuated each word with a kiss.

"Oh, Cal," she said tremulously.

After a long, loving interlude, when they lay quietly in the aftermath, Emm said quietly, "There's something else you should know."

"What?"

"Remember how I've been getting tired a lot lately? And how I've been weeping at the drop of a hat?" She took his hand, placed it on her stomach and said mistily, "I'm afraid I'm going to turn your life upside-down again."

ABOUT THE AUTHOR

Anne Gracie is the award-winning author of the Chance Sisters Romances, which include *The Summer Bride*, *The Spring Bride*, *The Winter Bride* and *The Autumn Bride*. She spent her childhood and youth on the move. The gypsy life taught her that humor and love are universal languages and that favorite books can take you home, wherever you are. Anne started her first novel while backpacking solo around the world, writing by hand in notebooks. Since then, her books have been translated into more than sixteen languages, and include Japanese manga editions. As well as writing, Anne promotes adult literacy, flings balls for her dog, enjoys her tangled garden and keeps bees. Visit her online at annegracie.com.

NATIONAL BESTSELLING AUTHOR
ANNE GRACIE

Find more books by Anne Gracie
by visiting prh.com/nextread

"With her signature superbly nuanced characters,
subtle sense of wit and richly emotional writing, Gracie
puts her distinctive stamp on a classic Regency plot."
—*Chicago Tribune*

"I never miss an Anne Gracie book."
—Julia Quinn, *New York Times* bestselling author

annegracie.com

 AnneGracieAuthor
 AnneGracie